WORTH
FIGHTING
FOR

ALSO BY KIRSTY MOSELEY

Fighting to Be Free

WORTH
FIGHTING
FOR

KIRSTY MOSELEY

FOREVER

New York Boston

Copyright © 2016 by Kirsty Moseley
Cover design by Elizabeth Turner. Cover images from Shutterstock.
Cover copyright © 2016 by Hachette Book Group, Inc.

Forever
Hachette Book Group
1290 Avenue of the Americas
New York, NY 10104
forever-romance.com
twitter.com/foreverromance

First Edition: December 2016
Forever is an imprint of Grand Central Publishing.
The Forever name and logo are trademarks of Hachette Book Group, Inc.

The Hachette Speakers Bureau provides a wide range of authors for speaking events. To find out more, go to www.hachettespeakersbureau.com or call (866) 376-6591.

Library of Congress Cataloging-in-Publication Data
Names: Moseley, Kirsty, author.
Title: Worth fighting for / Kirsty Moseley.
Description: First edition. | New York : Forever, 2016.
Identifiers: LCCN 2016033607 | ISBN 9781455595037 (softcover) | ISBN
    9781478940548 (audio download) | ISBN 9781455595044 (e-book)
Subjects: | BISAC: FICTION / Coming of Age. | FICTION / Romance /
    Contemporary. | FICTION / Contemporary Women. | GSAFD: Romantic
suspense
    fiction. | Love stories.
Classification: LCC PR6113.O86 W67 2016 | DDC 823/.92--dc23 LC record
available at https://lccn.loc.gov/2016033607

ISBNs: 978-1-4555-9503-7 (paperback), 978-1-4555-9504-4 (ebook)

Printed in the United States of America

LSC-C

10 9 8 7 6 5 4 3 2 1

To Terrie Arasin.
Without you this book simply wouldn't exist.

ACKNOWLEDGMENTS

The first thank-you goes to Lorella Belli, my amazing agent. You floor me with your dedication. x

To the fabulous team at Forever: the cover designers, editors, proofreaders, formatters, and everyone else who works so hard to make this book what it is, thank you!

To Leah, thanks for joining me on this roller-coaster journey and for encouraging me to push myself and make Jamie and Ellie's story the best it could be. x

To my girls Kerry Duke and Chloe Meyer, thank you for your endless support and incredible cheerleader-like encouragement when I so desperately needed it. Love you girls.

To my family, you guys are amazing and I'm lucky to have you all.

To you, dear reader, first I must apologize for the raging cliffhanger in *Fighting to Be Free*...oops...my bad. #SorryNotSorry. Second, thank you for taking this journey with me. I really hope you enjoy the conclusion of Jamie and Ellie's story as much as I enjoyed writing it.

As always, a massive shout-out to all the fabulous, hard-working, and dedicated bloggers across the world who give up hours of their time, all for the love of books. I can't say thanks enough. You guys are my rock stars. x

And last but certainly not least, to Terrie Arasin, my "superstar" PA. You came along at a time when I was drowning in social media and barely had time left in the day to actually write. I don't know what I'd do without you (and your hot Texas accent that brightens my messenger!). I'd most certainly still be a disorganized mess who bumbles her way through, trying fruitlessly to manage everything on my own. As I said in the dedication, simply put, without you this book wouldn't exist. Love ya, darlin' (said in my best imitation of a Texas accent). Doughnuts on me. xx

WORTH
FIGHTING
FOR

PROLOGUE

'TIS BETTER TO have loved and lost than never to have loved at all." Alfred, Lord Tennyson, said that in some poem in the 1800s. In my opinion, Alfred, Lord Tennyson, was full of shit.

Maybe Lord Tennyson had never truly loved someone; maybe he'd never cared for someone else more than he cared for himself, because if he had, if he'd loved someone so deeply he'd been willing to die for them, how could he have written such a horseshit line? I'm merely speculating, of course. I'm no academic, so I know nothing about the guy other than that one quote. So how then, you may ask, does my opinion so vehemently disagree with his?

Because I was in love once.

Only once.

And I lost her.

And I would give any fucking thing in the world to have never loved her at all. No, it most definitely is *not* better to have loved and lost.

Fuck love. And fuck Lord Tennyson.

CHAPTER 1

JAMIE

HIS FIST CONNECTED with the side of my jaw. Hard. Pain instantly exploded, stretching across my face and neck. My head whipped to the side, my eyes seeming to rattle in their sockets at the sheer force of the blow. He obviously wanted this over with quickly.

I took a step backward, my hand going to my chin, touching the site of the blow as a slow, lazy smile stretched across my face. A low chuckle escaped my lips as I wiped my mouth, ignoring the blood that smeared across the back of my hand.

"That was good. More," I encouraged him, beckoning him closer. I didn't bother to put my hands up to defend myself; that would defeat the purpose of me coming here tonight.

The guy looked around, clearly disturbed by my apparent lack of interest or pain. Around us in the large abandoned warehouse, the venue for tonight's fight club, the crowd was screaming and cheering—some of them yelling at me to get my act together and crush this guy, some of them encouraging him to knock me the fuck out. They wanted this over quickly—but I wanted to string it out as long as possible. The pain was a welcome distraction from the turbulence churning inside me. I was just happy to be thinking of something else, anything other than...her.

"Come on, dude, you gotta have more than that," I taunted, spitting a mouthful of tangy blood at the floor. I held my arms out wide at my sides, granting him clear access. "Give me your best shot."

His eyes narrowed and his lip curled into a sneer as he stepped forward, quickly throwing a punch at my stomach. Air rushed out of my lungs as I bent forward, struggling to draw breath. His knee slammed into my face. I fell backward, hitting the cold concrete with a harsh thud that seemed to echo through my bones.

The eruption from the crowd was almost deafening as they screamed at me. I closed my eyes and laid my head back, chuckling quietly to myself. The copious amount of alcohol I'd consumed tonight before the fights began was still sloshing around my system, making me disoriented and detached, even from the pain that I was sure to feel in the morning once the effects wore off.

"Kid, what the hell are you doing? I knew I shouldn't have let you talk me into this! I'm stopping the fight!"

With colossal effort, I opened my eyes and turned my heavy head to see Jensen standing on the side of the makeshift fighting arena. He shook his head, his expression a mixture of horror, worry, and disbelief. His eyes narrowed, his jaw set tight. As owner and organizer of the illegal club, he'd stand to lose a lot of money if I lost this fight. Jensen clearly didn't like me toying with him and putting his not-so-hard-earned cash at risk like this.

"Don't you dare. I got this. Just calm down and feel inside your pants for some balls. You seem to have lost them," I joked.

Even I could hear the drunken slur to my words. Awkwardly rolling to my side, I eased my arms under me and slowly pushed myself up to my unsteady feet.

From the corner of my eye, I saw Jensen pulling out his cell phone, speaking into it quickly, his eyes still locked on me. "Are you almost here? This is getting out of hand. Okay, well, hurry the fuck up!"

I frowned. "Oh yeah, go on, tell on me, call someone down here to babysit me," I huffed. "Dirty fucking snitch," I added, laughing moronically again.

Because I wasn't paying attention, or simply because he was a coward who liked to attack from behind, the guy I was fighting slammed into my back, lifting me clean off my feet, and we both flew forward. The crowd, not wanting to be crushed or covered in blood, parted, so we smashed into the side of the truck parked at the edge of the fight ring. The ragged breath of my opponent came out thick and fast as he threw punch after punch into my lower back and side.

As pain radiated across every part of my body, I knew that I'd made the right choice coming here tonight. This was definitely my idea of a good distraction.

He grabbed my shoulder, jerking me backward, and then I was on the ground again, breathing heavily.

"Kid!" Of course Jensen would have called Ray. He was one of my best friends and Jensen's cousin. I resisted the urge to roll my eyes.

Ray shoved through the crowd, dropping to all fours at the side of the ring. I turned to look at him, seeing the concern in his brown eyes.

"What's up, buddy?" I muttered, trying to grin, but I was sure what I accomplished was more of a grimace.

"What the fuck are you doing? Jensen says you've been

drinking! What the hell is this?" he ground out, shaking his head. I noticed with some satisfaction that he hadn't broken the fight circle or attempted to touch me—that would be against the rules and would result in the match being forfeited.

Before I could answer, my opponent grabbed two fistfuls of my shirt and hauled me to my feet. I flinched, preparing for another blow, welcoming it like an old friend. As his fist connected with my cheekbone, I heard Ray speak, his voice firm and full of fury.

"Jensen, stop this damn fight or I will!"

"Okay, okay," Jensen replied quickly.

Anger boiled inside me. If they stopped the fight, I'd lose. "No!" I roared, shaking my head firmly, turning to look at them each in turn. "No," I growled angrily. Kid Cole didn't lose, not ever.

I knew what I had to do. Losing wasn't acceptable. I'd had my fun, I'd achieved what I set out to do—I'd had a reprieve from my thoughts for a while—but now it was time to take back control and end this.

I reached out, gripping the guy's hand that was holding me in place. His eyes widened fractionally, his body stiffening because he clearly thought I was out of it and that he was about to apply the last blow that would secure his win and name him tonight's victor. He was oh so wrong.

"Looks like I have to stop dicking around now. Sorry." As soon as I finished speaking, I slammed my head into his face with such force that I heard his nose break even over the roar of the crowd. And that was it, as simple as that, no more dancing around and letting him beat the shit out of me for my own pleasure. His unconscious form sank to the floor instantly, his body limp.

I staggered a few steps, blinking to clear my blurry vision, ignoring the pounding in my head. My mouth was dry; my tongue felt furry. I desperately needed another drink because the effects of the alcohol were beginning to wear off.

Ray and Jensen both rushed forward. Jensen reached me first, gripping my arm and shoving it into the air. "Tonight's overall winner...Kid Cole!" Only half the crowd cheered; the other half balled up their betting slips, tossing them down distastefully, or cussed under their breath. Either they were new and didn't know never to bet against me, or they'd been taken in by the fact that I'd put away enough hard liquor to kill a small horse. Looks can be deceiving.

I smiled lopsidedly, leaning on Ray heavily as he wrapped his arm around my waist and guided me off to the side, toward the waiting plastic chair. I plopped down into it, my body so numb and uncoordinated I almost fell instantly off the other side.

Ray knelt down in front of me, holding out a bottle of water that he seemed to have magically procured from somewhere. "Drink this. Shit, you look rough," he said, sliding his eyes over me and wincing.

I reached out, pushing the bottle away and grinning as I pointed at my leather jacket, which hung over the back of another chair. "Pass me my jacket?"

He obliged, his eyes concerned.

Without a word, I reached into the inside pocket, my hand closing around the object of my desire: a smooth, small glass bottle. Pulling it out, I heard Ray groan when he saw the half-empty bottle of whiskey.

"Kid, seriously?"

I winked at him, unscrewing the cap with fingers that were bruised and covered in scratches and blood. Taking an enormous gulp, I relished the burn down my throat. "Want some?" I offered, my voice slurred and unintelligible.

He didn't answer, just took the bottle from my hand and screwed the top back on, setting it on the floor. "What's all this about, Kid? Seriously, I got a call from Jensen, who said you turned up here drunk off your ass and insisted on being entered into the fights tonight. You look like shit. That guy almost beat you!"

I scoffed distastefully at that. I'd been in control the entire time. "He can't beat me."

"It looked to me like he was killing you! One more punch and you'd have been out of there."

I shook my head adamantly. "He only did what I allowed him to do. What I wanted him to do."

"You wanted him to fuck you up, then, did you? You wanted this...this...mess?" He waved a hand in the general direction of my face as an example of said mess.

I shrugged, looking away from his inquiring eyes. Ray seemed to have this remarkable ability to read me and know what I was thinking a lot of the time—I hated it.

He sighed, setting a hand on my shoulder, squeezing gently. "What's this about, Kid? When I saw you earlier today, you were fine, and then you go get hammered and come here wanting to fight. I don't get it." His tone was encouraging, soft, caring.

"I just needed to think of something else. I needed a distraction. I didn't mean to come here, I just thought a couple of drinks would help, but it turned into three, then four, and..." I glanced down at the half-empty bottle, not admitting that it was my second bottle tonight. I swallowed and shook my head. "The drinking didn't help, I kept going back to it, and then the fighting seemed like a good idea. I thought maybe someone would beat it out of me and give me something else to think about. Even that didn't work, though. It's still there." I hit the heel of my hand roughly against my forehead a couple of times, trying to knock the thoughts out, forget them.

"Kid, you're not making sense."

My chest ached, and not from the beating I'd just sustained. This was a deep-rooted ache that had started three hours ago, when I'd stumbled across something on the news. I couldn't say the words, so I reached into my jacket pocket, pulling out the pages I'd printed from the CNN website earlier, before I'd gone on my destructive drinking rampage.

I held them out to him and closed my eyes, wishing I could unread the words.

Ray took the papers, unfolding them, and started to read the article aloud. My heart seemed to constrict further with every syllable, my grief intensifying.

"A hit-and-run accident on I-95 this afternoon leaves one dead and another fighting for life. Police said the driver, Michael Pearce, aged forty-five, died instantly when a dark blue Ford pickup truck careened into his lane, forcing Pearce's car into the highway divider at high speed. The pickup failed to stop and then fled the scene.

"Michael Pearce was killed instantly. His wife, Ruth, forty-four, is in critical condition and was rushed to the hospital by emergency personnel.

"Police are appealing to any witnesses or anyone with information regarding the pickup or its driver to come forward."

Ray turned his attention back to me. "Michael and Ruth Pearce, who are they?"

I huffed out a deep breath. "They're Ellie's parents."

He recoiled, understanding instantly flickering across his face. "Oh, shit." Silence rang out for a full minute before he spoke again. "I guess...I guess that means she'll be coming back, huh?"

My eyes dropped to the floor, my body sagging into the chair. Ellie was going to be crushed by this news. She was a total daddy's girl, and the loss of her father would hit her hard, let alone the fact that she now faced losing her mother, too. All I wanted to do was hold her, but I hadn't seen or spoken to her for over three years, not since I made the phone call that shattered both our hearts.

"I guess it does."

CHAPTER 2

ELLIE

BORED. SO BORED that I'd spent the last five minutes ruthlessly picking off my hideously grown-out gel nail polish. Laura, my nail technician, wouldn't be very impressed with my peeled and chipped manicure when I turned up next week, but I couldn't help it. Standing around doing nothing wasn't something I was good at. It was either pick at my nails or pick at the snacks that sat in cardboard boxes behind me. Something had to take my mind off the fact that the balls of my feet were burning because I'd been standing so long. At least the night was almost over, though, just another couple of hours to go.

I sighed and looked around for something to do, settling on wiping the already-clean chunky mahogany bar one more time.

For a Friday night, the pub was pretty dead. At this time, the King's Arms would usually be full. The quaint, typically English pub with its dark wood, chintz wallpaper, and red patterned carpet would be packed with locals who had just finished up work for the week. But tonight there was a grand total of nineteen customers in the bar. And everyone's glass was full, hence my boredom. I was already well ahead of schedule: The dishwasher had been emptied and refilled, the glasses had been polished and stacked in the little racks at my knees, and the toilets were already checked and cleaned. Once the last customers left, all that would be left to do was cleaning up after them and locking up. There wasn't much I could keep busy with.

Walking up to Toby, my manager, I cleared my throat. "Sorry to interrupt," I said, smiling apologetically at the two regulars he was speaking with.

Chuck, the elder of the two customers, grinned, causing crinkles to form at the corners of his eyes. "No worries, we don't mind being interrupted by a pretty young thing." He winked at me as he tugged on the unkempt grayish-white beard that he'd grown for the winter months and would soon be shaving off now that spring was on its way. He grew one every winter to keep his face warm, he'd told me when I remarked on it. Chuck was one of my favorite customers. He was kind and cheerful; he reminded me a little of my paternal grandfather before he'd passed away.

Toby laughed. "Stop flirtin' with my staff, I've told ya before. What ya like, 'ey?" he scolded Chuck, rolling his light green eyes playfully. Toby was a born-and-bred south Londoner—a cockney, if you preferred the term. His accent, like everyone else's around here, was a little hard for me to understand at first; a cockney's seeming inability to pronounce their *h*'s or finish a lot of words was confusing to say the least. But after almost two years in London, I was now practically immune to it. In fact, I actually quite liked it. Well, apart from the fact that half of the rhyming slang still went over my head.

Chuck held his wrinkled hands up in defense. "Not my fault you 'ired the prettiest American barmaid in town, is it?"

I scoffed at that. "I'm the *only* American barmaid in town." This earned a laugh from everyone and so I turned to Toby.

"Seeing as it's not busy tonight, you want me to do a stock take or something? I'm bored out of my mind." Doing inventory would keep me busy for an hour at least.

He shrugged, still grinning, and swept a hand through his light brown hair, pushing it off his forehead. "Yeah, that'd be good. I gotta put in an order with the brewery tomorrow, so that'd save me doin' it in the mornin'. Thanks."

"No problem," I replied, already turning on my heel and heading toward the back hallway to grab the stock-take sheets.

On the way through to the cellar, I noticed that next week's schedule had been pinned on the bulletin board. Stopping to check my hours and day off, I frowned when I saw my name down next to the day shift on Saturday. I'd specifically told Toby I couldn't work that day. As if on cue, Toby stepped through the curtain and reached into the box of crisps, pulling out a pack of cheese and onion.

"Toby, why am I down to work next Saturday? I can't work that day, I have plans," I stated, pointing at my name in the box.

He frowned and walked up behind me, looking over my shoulder. "Change your plans."

"I can't." I turned to face him, setting my hands on my hips. "You'll have to change it and get someone else in instead."

Raising one eyebrow, Toby turned the corners of his mouth up into a playful smile, and his eyes twinkled with mischievousness. "I'll get someone else in to cover if you have sex with me tonight."

I gasped, my frown deepening. "That's sexual harassment!"

He shrugged, grinning as he turned on his heel. "Report me, then."

"Maybe I will!" I called, smiling at his retreating form before turning back to the schedule sheet. Pulling out my pen, I crossed out my name and wrote his instead before heading down to the cellar to complete the stock take.

When I heard the last order bell chime just before eleven, I scribbled down the final few numbers on my sheet, noting how many packets of salted peanuts we had, and then headed upstairs again.

The bar was almost deserted; only six people remained. Toby had already collected most of the glasses, setting them on the bar to be washed. "That's time, ladies and gentlemen. Drink up. Don't you 'ave 'omes to go to?" he joked, stacking stools on top of tables so the carpet could be vacuumed in the morning.

A few of the patrons groaned and asked for a lock-in, but the tired circles around Toby's eyes were evident for all to see, so they didn't push it too far.

As the last couple left the bar, Toby locked the heavy doors behind them and turned back to me. "Get the stock take finished?"

I nodded. "Yep. All done."

He yawned, stretching his arms above his head as he walked back around the side of the bar. "Thanks."

I pulled open the dishwasher, setting a couple of glasses inside. As I reached for another couple, hands took hold of my hips. I jumped, startled, as Toby pressed against me, his warm body covering the length of my back. "So, do we have a deal about Saturday, or do you want to work?" he whispered, his hot breath fanning across my cheek and down my neck. His hold on my hips tightened as he pressed harder against me, the crotch of his jeans rubbing against the slightly exposed skin where my top had ridden up a little.

I gulped, and my skin broke out in goose bumps. "Seriously, this is sexual harassment to the highest degree," I replied as my muscles tightened all over.

"Uh-huh," he mumbled, his lips already on my neck. "Leave the cleaning, I'll do it in the morning."

Resigned, I turned to face him. His light green eyes were intense with desire as they roamed my face. "I guess I *do* need the day off," I mumbled, letting my gaze drop to his mouth as his tongue slowly swept across his bottom lip.

He stepped back, holding out his hand to me as a grin split his face. Setting the last glass on the bar, I slipped my hand into his, allowing him to pull me through the curtain, along the hallway, and up the stairs that led to the residential quarters. As I walked, I kicked off one shoe and then the other, letting them rest where they dropped, watching as he did the same.

When we made it to the top of the stairs, his restraint vanished and his passion surfaced in full force.

He pulled me to him, wrapping his arms around me tightly as his lips crashed onto mine. His hands were everywhere as we stumbled backward toward the bedroom, his mouth barely leaving mine for more than a second at a time. My shirt was removed in a flash as his fingers worked deftly on the button of my jeans. When the backs of my knees hit the side of the bed, we tumbled down onto it, a tangle of limbs and heated breaths. I giggled as he landed on top of me, almost crushing me before he righted himself and covered my body with his.

He grinned and pulled back slightly as I tugged his T-shirt off over his head. His eyes burned with want and need as he slowly eased my jeans down, his fingers tickling the skin on my outer thighs. "What you doing Saturday, anyway?" he whispered, leaning down and planting soft kisses at the base of my throat, his five-o'clock shadow scratching at my skin in a delicious way.

I tipped my head back, my hands running up his naked back and digging into his shoulders as my body thrummed with pleasure. "Going to a wedding show with your mother," I answered breathily.

He laughed and pulled back, his lopsided grin causing one to slip onto my own face. "Seriously? Why do you keep letting her drag you to these things?" he asked, rolling his eyes.

I shrugged, wriggling underneath the weight of his body. "She's so excited about the wedding. I keep telling her that we're having a long engagement, but…you know what she's like. I think she's hoping that I'll see a dress or a cake or a balloon arrangement that will blow me away and make me want to finally set a date."

His face turned serious for a second. "You know what would make her leave you alone, don't you?"

"Us breaking up?" I suggested, giggling as he dug one finger into my ribs in reprimand.

"Or we could just set a date…"

I sighed deeply, my sexy mood beginning to deflate. "Can we not talk about this now? I thought we were getting our freak on…" To really ram the point home, I raked my nails gently down his back before firmly gripping his ass and pulling him down tighter onto me.

Men are too easy. Mention sex, offer sex, even slightly hint about sex and they are putty in your hands. My fiancé was no different.

Unfortunately for me, the whole sex distraction was over before I even had a chance to get going. It wasn't that Toby was an inconsiderate lover—he could actually be great when he took the time; unfortunately for me, tonight he was tired, which meant no foreplay, no sweet words or time to get the home fires burning before the climax. Nope, he went straight to the endgame, and soon he was spent and slumped down on top of me, breathing heavily. Of course, I'd sensed he was close, so I'd done what most women do during sex: I'd faked a bit to spare his ego. Only a little bit, though—it wasn't like I didn't enjoy the intimacy with him, I just didn't get the full "happy ending" this time around.

When he planted a kiss on my cheek and rolled off me with a satiated grin on his face, I chuckled.

"Well, that was definitely worth giving you the day off," he mumbled, his eyes already half closing as he pulled me closer to him, his tired arm lazily slung across my belly. "And just ignore my mother. I'll speak to her again."

I snuggled into him, nestling my head into the crook of his neck. "Okay, thank you."

"Anything for you," he replied. His breathing started to even out and deepen, readying for sleep.

"Don't get too comfortable, I need to go clean up," I said, wriggling out of his embrace. He groaned but let me go. I smiled down at him, bending to plant a small kiss on the tip of his nose.

He grinned, his eyes still closed. "Hurry up and go to the bathroom before you drip everywhere. No one likes to sleep on a wet patch."

"Toby!" I cried, chuckling. "That's not the most romantic thing I've ever heard after sex."

He shrugged unashamedly. "Oh, come on, real romance is never actually how it's portrayed in those dirty novels you read," he teased, winking at me.

"Evidently," I replied sarcastically, rolling my eyes.

"Nope, those books just like to mislead women and portray an unrealistic version of what relationships are like. It's an impossible comparison we men have to deal with every day. Sadly, we can't live up to it." He shook his head in mock sorrow. "In real life, an intimate relationship is when the man farts and then 'olds his girlfriend under the covers while screaming, 'Dutch oven!' They never write about that."

I gasped, picking up my pillow and swinging it at his face. "If you ever do that to me again, I swear to God…"

Despite the unpleasant memories that surfaced at his words, I burst out laughing. This was a talent that Toby had—the ability to make me laugh. It was that ability that had drawn me to him in the first place. We'd met two years ago, and he'd offered me some part-time bar work while I was seeing London. He was the first person to truly make me laugh and forget, even if it was only for a moment or two, the pain that was crushing me from the inside out. We'd started out as friends, but however unplanned, our connection had grown into something more. Over time, he'd healed me, made me open up and trust again. He'd quite literally laughed his way into my heart. We'd been together for a year and a half now, and engaged for six months.

Our relationship was straightforward, uncomplicated, and based on mutual respect. He didn't necessarily set my world on fire with one scorching look or one of his smiles, but he loved me, and I loved him. He was a good man. Dependable, trustworthy, and safe—everything I craved so badly. Toby would never break what was left of my heart, that I was sure of. Quite simply, I adored him for how he'd healed me and made me see the lighter side of life again. For me, that was everything.

He reached out and snagged my wrists, tugging me gently toward him as he raised his head, planting a soft kiss on my still-laughing lips. "Go clean up if you're going," he said, releasing my wrists. "Oh, and tie your 'air up, will ya? If we're gonna spoon, I don't wanna be coughing up fur balls all day tomorrow." He winked at me as I eased out of bed. I threw a smile over my shoulder, picking up his discarded T-shirt and slipping it over my head. My smile was a genuine one as I padded barefoot out of the room and down the hall to the bathroom.

After cleaning up, removing my makeup, and brushing my teeth, I slipped out of the bathroom. Before heading back into our bedroom, I made a quick detour into the room next door, easing the door open as quietly as possible. I crept over to the bunk beds, going up on tiptoes to look in the top bunk, and smiled.

Empty. Just as I'd suspected it would be.

I bent to peer into the bottom bunk. Curled up in the single bed, Toby's two boys from his previous marriage slept peacefully, the book they had been reading propped open on the bed, the flashlight they had been reading by still illuminated, although the beam was now dim. I smiled and picked up the flashlight—or *torch*, as they liked to call it here in England— switching it off and making a mental note to buy new batteries for the next time they came to stay. Christian and Sam were still in that "cute" stage; at seven and five respectively, they still found reading a book by flashlight to be an adventure. They were great kids.

I planted a soft kiss on each of their foreheads, easing the covers up over them and deciding to leave Christian where he was rather than attempt to move him into the top bunk without waking him. Their soft breathing made me smile as I crept out of the room and closed the door behind me, heading into my own bedroom.

"Kids are sound asleep. Chris is in the bottom bunk again. They're—" I stopped talking abruptly when I noticed Toby, flat on his back, one arm folded under his head as he snored lightly.

I rolled my eyes and smiled. *So much for spooning...*

Snagging a hair tie from the dressing table, I scraped my hair back into a low ponytail before flicking off the light and walking across the room in pitch-blackness, hands out, feeling for the edge of the bed. Climbing in, I scooted up close to Toby and snuggled against him, laying my arm across his chest. In his sleep, he rolled to his side, his heavy arm wrapping around me and holding me against him securely. I smiled contentedly against his chest and fell asleep almost instantly.

What felt like mere minutes later, I was rudely dragged from my slumber by the shrill sound of a phone ringing off to the left. I groaned and rolled over, trying to force my stinging eyes open, blinking as I tried to focus on the numbers of the alarm clock.

Toby sat up. "Fuck's sake! It's four in the morning, who the bloody 'ell is that?" he grumbled, reaching to pick up the landline phone, which continued its earsplitting assault. "What?" he barked into the phone. I moaned and closed my eyes as he flicked on the bedside lamp. "Oh, sorry. No, she's right 'ere. Is everything okay? Oh, shit. Yeah, I'll just get 'er, 'old on." His hand touched my shoulder, shaking me gently, but the distinct change in his tone had already jolted me wide awake. His tone had me fearing the worst and knowing somehow that whatever this phone call was about, it wasn't good news. "Ellie, it's your grandmother, she says there's been an accident."

CHAPTER 3

THERE'S BEEN AN ACCIDENT.

Accident. The word turned over and over in my head as I reached for the phone. I drew in a ragged breath, my heart squeezing in my chest. My stomach clenched and my mouth was instantly dry as I pressed the phone to my ear, my hand wrapped around it so tightly that my knuckles ached.

Please. Please don't be bad.

But I already knew my mental begging was futile. You don't call people up at four a.m. just to tell someone you stubbed your toe or broke your arm. This was bad; I somehow felt it deep down in my gut.

I looked over at Toby for reassurance, but instead his expression made it worse. The sympathetic eyes and firm set to his mouth made my heart race in my chest. I opened my mouth to speak, but nothing came out. Toby placed his hand on my knee, squeezing gently. I cleared my throat awkwardly and then tried again.

"Hello?" My voice was almost a whisper.

The caller sniffed. "Ellie, oh darling." Even though it was

husky and filled with emotion, I recognized her voice instantly—
my paternal grandmother, Nana Betty.

My eyes prickled already. "Nana, what's happened, is everything okay?"

"No, it's...oh, Ellie, I don't even know how to say this."

I swallowed around the lump in my throat, my lungs beginning to ache from holding my breath, trying to steel myself
against whatever she was going to say. My imagination was running wild, my panic setting in, wondering what type of accident
had happened, who had been injured, how bad it was.

"Nana, please. What?!" I begged, desperation leaking into my
voice.

"There was a car accident. Your parents..."

I gasped in a quick breath. "Oh my God, are they okay?" My
free hand balled into a fist that I pressed against my chest, as if
trying to slow my hammering heart. I could feel Toby staring
at me, attempting to work out what was going on, his grip still
firm on my knee.

"Your mom, she's badly injured, Ellie. She has a fractured
skull and internal bleeding, and something called a hematoma.
They've taken her into surgery to try to repair some of the
damage."

I groaned, the sound filled with pain. I swallowed, my eyes
falling closed. "Surgery?" The word felt like acid on my tongue,
burning my throat on the way out. "She'll be okay, though,
right?" I clenched my jaw, waiting for her reassuring words,
words that would calm the storm of emotion building inside me
at an alarming rate. Panic was taking over, my hands beginning
to shake.

"We won't know more until she's out. They're doing everything they can for her, but she's very badly off right now." Nana's
answer didn't offer the reassurance I was hoping for.

"I...I..." My brain didn't seem to be working. My heart hurt. The pain in my chest was overwhelming. My mom was in surgery; she was fighting for her life with a fractured skull. My lip trembled as my eyes prickled with tears. I couldn't lose her. I simply couldn't. "Nana, is she going to—?" I stopped abruptly, unable to say the last word. It was too final; I couldn't bear it. My voice didn't even sound like mine, the words barely intelligible, but she somehow understood what I was asking.

"I just don't know, honey." No sugar coating it, just brutal honesty that felt like a kick to the gut.

I wished with every bone in my body that I were there at the hospital, waiting for her to come out of surgery. My dad and sister would need me; we should all be together supporting each other. The fact that I wasn't there for them made an extraordinary amount of guilt mingle with the grief inside me.

"How are Dad and Kels coping?" I croaked.

"Kelsey is fine. She was at my house at the time, she was planning on staying with me for the weekend. Your parents had just dropped her off and were heading home when..." She stopped and cleared her croaky throat, sniffing loudly. "She's here with me at the hospital now, I've just slipped out to call you."

I nodded, more than a little relieved that Kelsey hadn't been in the car at the time, too. "Okay. Where's Dad, why didn't he call me himself?"

My words were met with nothing but silence. It stretched on and on to the point of being uncomfortable. Impending horror built in my stomach, but I was unsure why.

"Nana?"

"Oh, Ellie. I'm so sorry to tell you this...Your dad, he didn't make it." As she said the words, her voice cracked, and so did my heart, splintering off, shattering like glass into a thousand pieces. "He's gone."

Gone.

When I'd heard the news about my mom, I'd thought that was the worst that could happen. I wasn't even close.

Gone.

The word was like physical pain, like a knife to the gut, twisting, tightening, slowly killing me. My lungs constricted, making it difficult to draw breath. My father, the first love of my life, the man I looked up to, the man who was my role model for all men—he'd died. Everything in me ached, my insides clenched, my heart thundered in my ears.

Dad. Gone.

An involuntary, guttural grunt left my lips. I blinked, my vision becoming a little blurry as tears slid silently down my cheeks. My bottom lip trembled as I struggled to find something to say. But what was there to say? My mom was fighting for her life, and the man who'd raised me, given me everything, encouraged me to be the woman I was, the one I ran to for help, my rock...*gone*. There were simply no words to cover that.

I pictured my dad's smile, the cheeky glint in his brown eyes, the conspiratorial wink he would throw me when we were ganging up on my mother. I remembered the hugs, how his large arms would wrap around me, dwarfing me and making me feel so small. Memories, all of them good, hit me at once: Christmases, birthdays, pancakes, his terrible jokes, his love for white chocolate, his laugh...

It was too much. I couldn't bear it.

"Ellie?" Toby said, scooting closer to me, his hand rubbing gently at my leg. "Sweetheart, what is it?" To my ears, he sounded a million miles away, his voice slightly muffled.

I shook my head, unsuccessfully trying to clear the fog that was settling over me.

Gone.

I was losing it. I could feel things slipping away, fading out. The grief was consuming me, dragging me under, drowning me.

The phone slipped from my sweaty hand, thudding to the floor. My eyes followed it, not making sense of it, not comprehending anything that was going on around me. Memories, grief, guilt, horror, sadness—all swirled dizzyingly inside my head, tangling together, not making any sense. My vision swam as tears continued their torrential flow, running down my cheeks and neck, wetting the collar of Toby's T-shirt I was wearing.

And then Toby was kneeling in front of me, wrapping his arms around me, pulling me tightly against him as I sobbed, my heart broken.

"My dad, he's..." I pressed my face into his neck, crying harder. "And my mom, she's in surgery, and I'm not there. I'm not there!" I wailed, losing the final part of my control.

"I'm sorry, I'm so sorry," Toby whispered, pulling back, his eyes narrowed with sympathy, his face contorted in grief too, grieving right along with me for the people he'd never even met.

"I gotta go," I whimpered, bringing my arms up between us, pushing him away from me. "I have to be there. There's so much to do. I have to get a flight and pack, I have to...I have..." I stood, but my legs were so weak I stumbled and Toby's arms wrapped around me again, holding me steady.

His eyes, alight with concern, met mine. "You 'ave to breathe, Ellie. Shh, just breathe and calm down, sweetheart." He dipped his head, planting a kiss on my forehead. "Just breathe."

My eyes dropped closed as I sagged against him weakly, letting him hold me until I gained control over myself again.

CHAPTER 4

JAMIE

THE GIRL'S RED hair fanned out around her face as she looked over her shoulder at me. When those distinctive grayish-blue eyes met mine, there was such an intensity there that it almost made me lose my breath. Her lips curled into a playful smile, and an unconscious smile tugged at my lips, too. The subtle freckles on her cheeks danced as she laughed quietly, stepping closer to me.

"Kid." Her voice was like music to my ears, so beautiful it made my heart ache. "Kid?" she repeated, placing a slender hand on my shoulder, squeezing gently.

A slow frown replaced my smile as her choice of word sank in. She never called me that.

The pressure on my shoulder intensified, even shaking me a little, which cut through the fog, and it suddenly hit me that I was dreaming. She wasn't here. Squeezing my eyes shut tightly, I tried to hold on to the dream, to hold on to her, but it was no use. The dream was slowly fading, slipping away, and disappearing in a fog of confusion. Sounds from around me were starting to register now: the chink of glass, paper being crumpled up, and a steady thrum of music somewhere off in the distance.

I groaned loudly, shrugging off the hand that roused me. My cheek rubbed against something hard and unforgiving. That was when I registered the ache in my head that intensified with each tiny movement.

"Oh, he lives," a sarcastic voice stated from behind me. Without needing to look, I already knew it was Dodger, one of my closest friends and my lieutenant.

I frowned, slowly raising my head, lazily blinking my stinging eyes. I lifted a hand and swatted away a Post-it note that was stuck to my cheek, wincing as I moved because every single one of my muscles was stiff.

"Fuck off, Dodge," I grunted.

The pungent smell of alcohol was unmistakable. My office slowly came into focus, and I groaned again at the sight before me. It looked like a frat house after a weekend-long party that had gotten out of hand.

Moving caused an unpleasant lump of vomit to rise in my throat. I choked it back down, turning to look at Dodger, squinting because that seemed to marginally dull my self-induced headache. He didn't look amused as he bent and picked up a half-empty bottle of the good brandy I kept in stock for important clients. Frowning disapprovingly, he screwed the bottle top back on and headed toward the cabinet where I usually kept it.

"This place looks like it's been ransacked," he muttered. "And you look like death," he added, scowling down at the cluttered sideboard before picking the trash can up from the floor and sweeping five or six empty beer bottles into it. The clink and clatter of the bottles caused a searing pain to lance through my head. I pressed the heels of my hands to my temples and closed my eyes, willing myself not to hurl.

I feel like death. "Thanks."

"What the hell is that?" Dodger's tone was clipped as he motioned with the neck of one of the bottles toward the desk that I'd made my impromptu bed for the night.

I glanced down, seeing a suspicious white powder dusted over my desk. My tongue felt too big for my mouth as I licked my furry-feeling teeth, wincing at the putrid taste of stale, morning-after alcohol. I shook my head to clear it. Was that a drug-induced fogginess that clung to my vision? Maybe. I couldn't tell.

I frowned, thinking back to last night. Then it hit me. I'd been fighting. I'd gotten wasted here, then went to the fight club, and Ray'd had to come get me and take me home. But I hadn't been able to sleep, so I'd taken a cab back here instead, hoping to find more booze. Judging by the bottles littered around, I'd definitely found it.

Dodger sighed deeply and shook his head, silently picking up another bottle, tossing it carelessly into the now-full trash can. Clumsily, I reached out toward the white granules, catching a few on the pad of my finger and popping them into my mouth. The taste caused another retch, but I managed, with extraordinary effort, to hold it back again.

"Salt," I muttered. "I must have been drinking tequila." I was more than a little relieved to learn that it wasn't cocaine. I pushed my rolling chair back and stretched my legs in front of me. My whole body ached.

The tension seemed to leave Dodger's shoulders at my words. "Good, because the police are coming here today. You know this, Kid."

I nodded. I did know they were coming, courtesy of the detective I'd had on my payroll for the last year and a half. Not that I needed a heads-up for this visit. The club was one of my few *legal* businesses. They would find nothing here to cause suspicion or tie me to any of my other, less legitimate business ventures, but the notice was appreciated.

It hadn't always been like this. *I* hadn't always been like this. There had been a time when I'd tried my hardest so that I would never end up as what I was now—a dirty, despicable, drug-dealing, car-stealing scumbag who cared about nothing other than where the next opportunity would take him. Back then, when I was Jamie Cole, a person trying to make something of himself, I would never have gotten so blind drunk that I smashed up my office and fell asleep not knowing if it was salt or drugs that speckled my table. Back then, I had hope; now, not so much.

I was almost out of this life once. Three years ago, I was a mere few hours from casting off my past and flying into the sunset with the girl of my dreams. But one night had changed all of that. One night had ripped my world apart. Oh, how different my life could have been.

The night before my girlfriend, Ellie, and I were due to give up everything and tour the world together, I had one last job to do for my old boss, Brett Reyes. Just one last job and then I was out for good. It sounded so simple. It wasn't. Things took a turn for the worse just hours before I was due to pick Ellie up and go to the airport. Police raided the meeting place, resulting in a shootout, and every fucker from Brett's organization and the rival Lazlo organization we were there to meet was either killed or arrested.

Somewhat unfortunately for me, I'd been arrested rather than killed. In a lot of ways, it would have been better if I hadn't made it; at least then I wouldn't have had to call Ellie and crush her dreams. My death would have spared me the gut-wrenching agony of having to lie to her and break her heart so she wouldn't know that her boyfriend was being sent back to jail like the scumbag he really was. Ellie deserved better than to be a convict's girlfriend, visiting once every couple of weeks, carrying that stigma around with her while she waited for me to be released. So I'd done what I felt was right. I'd set her free.

Losing the only thing you care about can change a person irrevocably.

Thanks to my lawyer, Arthur Barrington, instead of spending the remainder of my youth behind bars, I served just under a year and a half.

I was astounded to get out and discover that Brett Reyes, having no children of his own, had named me his sole beneficiary, making me director and CEO of three companies that amounted to a multimillion-dollar enterprise. The club that I was currently fighting my hangover in the back room of, the security company I'd headed before being sent down, and his shipping and haulage company were all left to me, as per his wishes.

I could have gone straight and run those companies to the best of my ability, really made something of myself. But after giving up Ellie, I had nothing left to be "good" for. So when one of Brett's old contacts approached me about an opportunity, I grasped it with both hands and never looked back. I was much better at being bad, and it was what everyone expected of me anyway, so why not embrace the darkness? So, for the last year and a half, since my release from prison, I'd immersed myself in the life I once fought so hard to get out of, and I excelled in it. "Go big or go home"—that was my motto now. And I definitely went big.

"What time is it?" I grunted, pushing myself to my feet, gripping the arms of my chair when the world slanted to the left. I'd definitely overdone the booze last night.

Dodger glanced down at his watch. "Just after ten."

I blinked a couple of times and nodded, trying to right my head. The tip I'd received said that the police would be making an appearance during lunchtime. Meaning I had a couple of hours to fix my office and make it look like a whirlwind hadn't blown through it last night while I was drunk.

Dodger put down the trash can and turned to face me, his eyes showing his concern. "Ray told me about Ellie's parents. You want to talk about it?"

I frowned and shook my head sharply. "No."

He recoiled slightly but nodded anyway. "If you change your mind, you know I'm here for you."

I didn't bother to reply. I hadn't wanted to talk about it before, so why would I start now? I reached for my phone, picking it up from my desk and brushing off the salt that dusted the screen.

Opening it up, I saw four missed calls and one new voice message, all from Ed. Jabbing at the voice mail button, I rubbed my forehead, waiting for the message to start.

"Kid, I have that info that you asked for. Call me back."

I frowned. Information I asked for? My brain whirled, trying to piece it together. I couldn't remember asking him for anything—unless I'd done it last night while intoxicated. Ed was my go-to guy for the jobs I didn't have time to do myself. It made sense that I'd ask him to do something, but what it was I had no clue.

As Dodger walked out of my office, carrying a full trash can, I dialed Ed's number, hearing him answer on the second ring. "Kid, hey, you got my message, finally."

"Yeah, what's going on? What info are you talking about?"

"You called me late last night, asked me to find out about that girl, the one with the dead parents. You don't remember?"

I groaned. So in my intoxicated state I'd called him and asked him to stalk Ellie. Perfect. "Yeah, I remember," I lied.

"Right. You wanted to know if she was coming back. Well, I asked a guy we have in London to keep his eye on her. She left for the airport there early this morning. He watched her check in for a nine a.m. flight to New York. According to the flight number he gave me, she's due to land at JFK in a couple of hours."

My chest tightened. I'd expected her return stateside, but not so soon. I'd barely had a chance to prepare myself for it.

"What time will she land?" I croaked.

"Twelve twenty-five."

I nodded, my headache growing. "Okay, thanks."

"Kid, one more thing," he said, just as I was about to disconnect the call. "She checked in by herself. Her fiancé went to the airport with her, but she got on the flight alone."

Alone? She was fucking alone? Toby had let her fly, grieving and emotional, alone? Motherfucker! My teeth gritted, anger churning in my stomach. I hung up on Ed and shook my head, trying to clear some of the murderous thoughts. How could he let her make the trip by herself? She'd just lost her father, her mother was in critical condition—he should have been by her side the whole time, wiping away her tears, supporting her. What a fucking cocksucker!

I'd never exactly been fond of Toby Wallis—he had my girl, after all—but I'd respected the guy because he loved her; he'd made her smile again, gave her everything she needed. That much I'd found out easily enough when I got out of prison. The undercover surveillance in the form of Ray's sister-in-law had stopped once the girls parted ways when Ellie decided not to return home with Natalie after a year of traveling together, but I'd put other measures in place after that. A private detective, hired to check in on her and report back to me periodically.

By the time I'd left prison, the private detective had provided evidence that Ellie was happy, that she'd recently moved on, that this Toby Steal-Yo-Girl Wallis was actually good for her. Background checks on him revealed he was a decent guy with no criminal record, a thirty-three-year old divorcé with two kids, and a hard worker. Toby was the sole reason I hadn't booked the first available flight and gone to her, confessing everything and begging for her to forgive me. But now the fucking prick was letting her fly alone? Maybe he wasn't as decent as I first thought.

* * *

Two hours later, I stood in JFK's international arrivals terminal. I hadn't been able to help myself. Dodger could deal with the police raid on his own. I wasn't sure what my plan was. All I wanted was to see her, hold her, and drive her safely to wherever she wanted to go—probably the hospital, as that's where the rest of her family would most likely be.

I stood to the side, away from the crowd, leaning against the wall of a Starbucks, watching, waiting, my hands twitching with both excitement and sheer terror.

Ellie's plane had arrived safely, so right now she was probably making her way through customs or baggage claim.

When a collective jostling and fidgeting of the waiting relatives and loved ones started, I straightened, holding my breath, and looked eagerly in the direction they were all smiling in. Small groups of people wandered out, pushing their luggage carts, grinning, waving, squealing excitedly as they spotted their friends and families.

I waited, my heart in my throat, and then there she was.

The air rushed out of my lungs in one big gust at the sight of her dragging her suitcase behind her.

Ellie didn't smile; in fact, her lips were pressed firmly in a straight line as she looked around, stopping off to one side to tap away on her cell phone. Her copper-colored hair fell around her face in messy, untamed tangles. It was shorter than it had been the last time I saw her, now cut just above the shoulders. My eyes dragged over her while a familiar ache, a longing settled over me. She'd put on a little weight since I last saw her, her hips and legs a little thicker, her cheeks slightly fuller, her tummy no longer flat as it had been when she was a cheerleader, but the changes suited her perfectly. She looked as beautiful as the day I met her and still took my breath away.

When she looked up and scanned the room, searching for something or someone, I noticed the dark circles under her eyes and pain filled my chest. She looked exhausted, both physically and emotionally.

Everything in me wanted to stride over there, close the gap between us, and wrap her in my arms. I needed to comfort her, to kiss her hair, to stroke her back and tell her everything was going to be okay, that I was here for her and that I'd never leave her again. But my legs just weren't moving. I stood stock-still, hidden from view by the gathering people, wondering what she would do if she saw me. Would it make it worse or better? If I strode over to her, covered in bruises, reeking of last night's alcohol, with my opponent's blood dried and spattered on my sneakers, what would she do? I'd come here to see her, to help her, but now that I was here, I somehow knew that I would make it worse for her if I revealed myself. She was already dealing with so much that being confronted by the guy who broke her heart probably wouldn't help.

While I was still wrestling with what to do, a blur of blonde breezed through the crowd. Ellie's eyes twitched; her lips parted, then pulled into a small, sad smile, and the blonde girl crashed into her at practically full speed.

I sighed, my hope for any kind of reconciliation fading as Stacey stroked Ellie's hair, just as I had wanted to do, and comforted her with an embrace. I'd never been jealous of a girl until now.

I turned, scowling down at the floor, and slinked out of the airport, heading back to my car before I could be seen.

CHAPTER 5

ELLIE

THE BAGGAGE CLAIM area of JFK airport was a hive of activity. People buzzed around me, pushing their carts, talking to each other about where was the optimal place to stand so they could make a quick grab for their luggage. They chatted excitedly about their vacation plans, where they were supposed to meet their transfer buses; they laughed, smiled, carried on as normal. I was numb to it all, wondering silently how these people didn't know I was screaming inside, breaking, grieving so badly that it felt like a hole had been punched directly through my chest. Surely it was etched as clearly on my face as it was on my heart?

I moved slowly through the crowds, checking my phone every few seconds. I'd turned off airplane mode as soon as I was off the plane, but it was taking a while to find a network to connect to—too used to being on UK networks for the last couple of years. It was still searching for a signal when I stopped next to the designated conveyor belt for my flight.

After a minute or so, the quintessentially British family who had sat behind me on the eight-hour flight squeezed into the gap next to me. Their little girl, who was probably no older than six, was whining about how she was tired, how she was bored, asking and asking how much longer it was going to be before they could start their holiday. Her voice, getting louder and louder by the second, was making my head throb.

On the plane she'd been excitable, babbling about what she wanted to do and see first in New York, speculating about their hotel, how warm their pool would be. She'd sat nicely for hours on end, watching in-flight movies, laughing at whatever she was engrossed in. Now, though, it seemed her patience had worn thin, and she wanted out of the airport immediately.

I glanced down at her, not really seeing her. I hadn't been able to focus on much since the phone call fourteen hours ago, the one that ripped my life apart and threw me into a spiral of grief, loss, and guilt. I was on autopilot, going through the motions: show passport, collect ticket, sit on plane, get off, show passport, collect baggage—I was still on that part.

"Sorry, she's a little overexcited. And she didn't manage to get any sleep on the plane, so it's been a long day."

I dragged my gaze up from the little girl, who was now being distracted by her mother with a packet of candy, and met her dad's eyes as he smiled at me apologetically. Graham, his name was; I knew this from the plane.

I couldn't quite summon a smile but tried anyway. "It's fine, don't apologize." My voice came out as a mumble as I watched the little girl reach out and take her dad's hand. My chest squeezed at the small gesture, the bond between father and daughter. Something I would never have again. I wrenched my gaze away from them—this perfectly cute little family of three, the girl and her dad—as memories of trips, plane rides, hand holding surfaced in my mind. Seeing it hurt, and I wanted to turn to him and tell him not to let her take it for granted, to treasure every second because you never know when it could be taken away from you.

I didn't, though. I held my tongue, instead busying myself by jabbing at the screen of my phone, willing it to connect so I could see if there was any news from my grandmother. Before I'd boarded the plane in London, my mother's condition had been stable. She had come out of surgery with no complications and had been admitted to recovery. Then I had to turn my phone to airplane mode, so I hadn't heard anything else. A lot could have happened in those eight extremely long hours. I just prayed she was still there, still fighting, because I wasn't sure how I would cope if I lost them both.

Just as luggage started to appear on the conveyor belt, the mockingjay whistle from *The Hunger Games* sounded from my phone, alerting me of a new message. It had finally connected to a network. A couple of texts came at once, and I held my breath as I unlocked my screen, punching in my passcode to awaken it.

Two messages: one from my best friend, Stacey, the other from Toby. I sighed, more than a little relieved that there was no message from my nana. No news was good news, wasn't that how the saying went? No message meant that my mother was still with us, recovering from her operation. At least, I hoped that's what it meant.

I opened Stacey's message first: I'm on my way! Late as usual. Stuck in traffic. Be there in a few xxx

I smiled, remembering my least favorite trait of hers—her inability to ever be on time for anything. In a weird way, I'd even missed that about her. I'd called her before I boarded, asking if she could pick me up from the airport. I knew I'd need to see a friendly face after hours of being on my own during the flight. Stacey had agreed at once, as I'd known she would. I could barely wait to see her; it had been way too long.

I didn't bother to reply; she was driving and would be here soon anyway. I opened the message from Toby: I love you. Text me when you land and call when you can xx

A lump formed in my throat at his short but sweet message. Toby had been amazing since I heard the news. He'd stepped in and taken control, soothing me, settling me, and even making me a cup of tea for the shock a Brit's answer to everything. He'd called my nana back, getting the full story of what had happened because I still couldn't bring myself to say it out loud. Then he'd booked the first available flight out to New York, and he'd even packed my clothes for me. I wasn't sure what I would have done without him.

Unfortunately, though, he hadn't been able to come with me. At least, not straightaway. He had his kids staying over, and their mother was on holiday so he couldn't send them back early. Plus, he had the pub to run, and that would take a couple of days to get covered even if he hadn't had the kids over. He'd tried to persuade me to wait a few days before leaving so that I wouldn't have to make the trip alone, but I hadn't been able to wait. I needed to get there. I needed to see my sister, hold her, cry with her, and tell her everything was going to be fine.

As I read his message again, a wave of loneliness hit me, causing my stomach to clench and my skin to goose-bump even though it wasn't particularly cold in the terminal. Taking a deep breath, I wrapped my arms around my torso, hugging myself tightly as I watched the cases pass me slowly, none of them mine.

When mine finally came around, I struggled to lift it, the weight and movement of it catching me off guard, and Graham, the dad from the family next to me, had to grab it for me and hoist it off the belt and onto the floor.

"Thank you," I mumbled, still fighting my loneliness.

The little girl's mother frowned, her eyes narrowing in concern as she reached out and placed a hand on my elbow. "You okay, honey? You look a little pale. You feelin' all right?"

I tried to smile but my mouth just wasn't cooperating. Instead, I gave a small nod. "I'm fine. Just tired," I lied. "Have a nice vacation." Without another word, I turned and followed the crowd of people who already had their cases, heading through the NOTHING TO DECLARE exit and finally stepping out into the arrivals lounge.

After a quick glance around at the people milling there, holding name cards or flowers, at the one lady with her WELCOME HOME banner, I noted that Stacey wasn't among the crowd, so I stepped to the side, leaning against the wall as I sent a quick reply to Toby, telling him I'd arrived safely and would call him later.

I tried to keep my eyes down, focused on the floor, not wanting to see the hugs and kisses that were sure to accompany the squeals of delight when people met up with their relatives and loved ones. But I lost the battle and looked around, watching as they walked into each other's arms, smiled, laughed, embraced. A stab of jealousy hit me when I saw a guy in a full dress suit walk out of the exit and straight into the waiting arms of the lady with the homemade WELCOME HOME banner. The family that had sat behind me walked out too, the little girl happier now as she perched upon the luggage while her dad wheeled the cart along. I ground my teeth, glancing around again, silently hoping Stacey had appeared in the last few moments. I didn't want to stand here alone anymore. As if my hopes had been answered, she darted through the door, her lithe, athletic body dodging around people as she mumbled "Excuse me" to them.

Some of the tension seemed to leave me at the beautiful sight of her, and for the first time since I woke at four a.m. to the sound of the ringing phone, I felt a small smile tug at the corners of my mouth. I stepped forward, dragging my case behind me, and Stacey crashed into me, the force of it almost knocking us both off our feet. Air left my lungs in a rush as her arms wrapped around me, her fingers digging into my back as she clutched me to her tightly. When warmth enveloped me, I felt the emotional wall I'd constructed around myself on the plane begin to splinter and crack. I closed my eyes, fighting to regain my composure and not break down. I couldn't afford to lose control of myself again; there was no Toby here to look after me this time. I *had* to be strong. I was the one who needed to do the looking after; I was going to be the one who had to reassure and be a tower of strength for my thirteen-year-old sister. She deserved for me to be there and be strong for her; I couldn't turn up a watery, blubbering mess of hysteria.

I pulled back, looking into Stacey's red-rimmed eyes. "Hi," I croaked.

"Hi," she squeaked, pulling me into another bone-crushingly tight hug. "Oh, Ellie, I'm so sorry. I don't know what I can do, but if there's anything, *anything...*"

She didn't need to finish the sentence, I knew what she was saying. I nodded, biting my cheek just hard enough that the pain from it kept my mind focused. No one paid us any mind as they walked around us, oblivious to the pain we were sharing.

She pulled back again, sniffing and plucking a Kleenex from her pocket, proceeding to wipe her eyes with it. I let my gaze wander over her; she looked the same as I'd left her three years ago—tall, slim, and effortlessly beautiful, even with the messy topknot and the bloodshot eyes.

Her smile, warm and comforting, somehow made it seem a little bit easier to breathe. "Come on, let's get you home."

I shook my head in rejection. "I want to go straight to the hospital."

Her arm looped through the crook of my free one as she guided me along toward the exit. "It's between visiting hours, they won't let you in. Your nana said to bring you home first and you can go to the hospital later."

"Oh." I tugged my jacket tighter around my body, shielding myself against the chill in the air as I blindly let her lead me along, stopping to pay for her parking ticket, before guiding me to her car—a brand-new Mercedes S-Class, the coupe version. My eyes widened in surprise as she pressed a button and raised the trunk.

I picked up my luggage, forcing it into the small trunk, thanking my lucky stars that I'd only packed a medium case and not tried to bring all my things in a large one; there was no way anything bigger would have fit.

"This is a nice car," I mused as we slid into our seats. "Did you come into some money while I was away?" I joked, shifting in my plush leather seat and reaching to turn on the heat because March weather here was slightly colder than what I was used to in London.

"It's not mine. It belongs to my boss, Owen," she answered, starting the car with the push of a button.

"And your boss doesn't mind you borrowing his car?" I asked, wanting to keep the conversation going so there wasn't any silence. When the silence started, my brain whirled, and my grief intensified and became too painful.

She shrugged, smiling over at me before pulling out of the

space and heading toward the exit. "Owen likes to make me happy, because he knows if I'm happy, then I keep him happy. If you know what I mean..." She trailed off suggestively, leaving the meaning hanging in the air.

Understanding washed over me. "You're sleeping with your boss?" I asked, a little shocked she hadn't told me this tidbit of information before. I knew Stacey was personal assistant to some rich businessman who made a fortune from real estate developments, but in all the times we'd spoken, she'd never once mentioned the fact that she was seeing the guy outside of work.

She pursed her lips, glancing at me from the corner of her eye. "When it suits me to, yes."

The drive from the airport to my house seemed to take forever. Stacey talked practically the whole way without much encouragement or participation needed from me—for that I was grateful, because my exhausted brain wasn't up to much socializing.

As we pulled into my street, drove up the road that I had learned to ride my bike on, passed trees that I had climbed and doors I had knocked on at Halloween, my heart became heavier. When the familiar white house came into view, my heart seemed to skip a beat. My eyes took in everything: the polished windows, the immaculately cut grass, the spring flowers just beginning to peek through the freshly overturned earth in the borders, the perfectly edged lawn, all of it so familiar it was like the last three years hadn't happened.

I popped my seat belt and climbed out of the car still in a daze, my body just going through the motions while my brain was still playing catch-up. Stacey was quicker than me, already having lifted my case from the trunk and standing by the curb, waiting for me with a sad smile on her face. I smiled back, or tried to, and her arm wrapped around my shoulders, giving me a small comforting squeeze as we walked up the stone path toward the blue front door.

At the door, we stopped, and I reached out, my hand on the cold knob, unsure if I was strong enough to go in. Inside, people were grieving, just like me, people hurting, and I was supposed to be able to be strong enough to hold them all together. What if I couldn't cut it? What if I broke down and made things worse? What if I—

But I didn't have enough time to complete my worried thoughts, because the door swung inward, and there stood my nana in one of her floral dresses, an apron tied around her waist. She had aged quite visibly since the last time I saw her, the wrinkles around her eyes and mouth more prominent, her hair thinner, her cheeks hollowed, her small frame now looking frail instead of sturdy. The dark circles under her eyes betrayed how tired she was. Her thin lips twitched into a smile, her eyes shining and pooling with tears as she opened her arms to me.

Without hesitation I stepped into her embrace, wrapping my arms around her, noticing how much weight she'd lost. I could feel the bones of her back and ribs pressed against me. The three years had changed her so much, and I suddenly realized how old she had gotten.

"Oh, Ellie, I'm so glad you're here," she said, pulling back and holding me at arm's length, her eyes shining as she cupped my cheek softly with her cool hand.

I gulped, willing my voice to work. "It's great to see you. I've missed you so much."

Her smile grew, but in her eyes, I could see the sadness swelling. She looked stressed, worn, close to the breaking point. I could see the desperation and sadness in her eyes as she stroked the side of my face, just looking at me softly. Finally, as the silence stretched out and neither of us knew what to say, she blinked a couple of times and stepped back, pulling the door open wider. "Well, don't just stand there all day, we're letting all the heat out." Nana smiled weakly over my shoulder. "Hello, Stacey dear."

As the door swung open, a wave of nostalgia hit me at seeing the hallway and all of our possessions there: the umbrella stand, the oil painting my dad had purchased for my mom when I was young, the side table with the old-fashioned dial telephone on it that didn't actually work but was there just for show because my mom had thought it pretty. Seeing it all was like a stab to the gut as memories intensified my heartache.

I took a deep breath and stepped over the threshold, instantly noticing how quiet the house was. It was never quiet like this unless it was empty. There was always a TV or radio on, always Kelsey singing or dancing around, my mom's foreign language tapes playing lightly in the background while she repeated the words she couldn't quite pronounce. The house was always warm, bright, and full of noise. Now, though, it felt cold and devoid of life, even though there were people inside.

I gulped, my eyes moving around slowly, stopping on the shoe rack that was off to one side. My heart stuttered as I saw a pair of large shiny black men's shoes neatly stacked there. My dad's shoes. My body suddenly felt cold, so I wrapped my arms around myself, dragging my eyes away from the shoes and back to my nana's face.

"How's Mom?" I asked, my throat scratchy.

Nana's eyes dropped to the floor as she unconsciously wiped her hands on her apron. "She's still in recovery. They sent us home a couple of hours ago and promised to call if there was a change."

I nodded slowly, not knowing what else to say. I couldn't bring myself to mention my dad—not yet, maybe not ever. "Are you okay? You look tired."

She shook her head as if to clear it, a forced smile gracing her lips but not reaching her eyes. "I'm fine, honey. Don't worry about me. I was just making some lunch. Are you hungry, have you eaten?"

Food. My nana's answer to everything. The Brits had their tea, and my nana liked to feed people until they were fit to burst. "I'm not hungry," I answered automatically. I *should* have been hungry; I hadn't eaten all day. Being on UK time, it was now dinnertime and I'd skipped three meals already, but my body was too tightly strung to feel anything as mundane as hunger. Food was way down on the list of priorities.

"You sure? How about I make you a plate anyway?" she cajoled, already heading to the kitchen, where I could smell the unmistakable scent of five-bean chili, Nana's specialty.

"I ate on the plane, Nana," I lied, wanting this conversation to be over already. She stopped, turning back to me, her disappointment evident in her slouched shoulders. I knew she was just trying to keep busy, keep herself distracted, but I wouldn't even be able to force down a single bite. "Where's Kels?" I asked, looking over her head and into the empty living room.

Nana's body seemed to tighten. "She's up in her bedroom. She wasn't hungry, either."

I could sympathize with her there. "How's she holding up?"

Nana didn't answer, but she didn't need to; her teary eyes said it all. Kelsey wasn't holding up very well at all.

I gulped, glancing toward the stairs, steeling myself to go up and see my little sister, offer some words of comfort that I was hoping were going to magically come to me because right now I had nothing. There were simply no words that were ever going to make this better. "I'll, um, go see her, tell her I'm here and see if she wants to come downstairs."

Stacey cleared her throat. "I'm going to go, let you get settled." She smiled awkwardly. "If you need anything, then call me, all right? I can take you to the hospital later if you want," she offered, stepping forward and wrapping her long, slender arms around me, pulling me tight against her body.

"Thanks," I muttered, hugging her back tightly, clinging to her, not really wanting her to leave. She pulled back and smiled sadly before turning and walking out the front door.

Silence filled the hallway again. Deafening, awful, mind-whirling silence.

Nana sniffed loudly, raising her chin and pulling back her shoulders. "I'm going to fix you a plate. I know you said you're not hungry, but you might want it when you come down."

I forced a smile and nodded, knowing she just needed to do something, to feel like she was looking after us. "Okay, thank you." I shrugged out of my jacket, hanging it on the rack before glancing back up the stairs, wondering if I had the energy to make it up the thirteen steps. My body now felt heavy, uncoordinated, and weak. All I wanted to do was curl into a ball and cry, but instead I took a deep breath and forced my legs to work, taking the steps one at a time.

I stopped outside Kelsey's bedroom door, listening for any sounds of life from inside, but there was nothing. I raised my hand and knocked—no answer.

"Kelsey?" I knocked again, still to no response. Frowning, I reached down and gripped the handle, turning it and cracking the door open, peeking inside. Kelsey was lying on her bed, staring at the ceiling, a pair of red Beats headphones covering her ears and an iPhone resting on her belly.

My eyes widened as I looked at her. She was so tall, her body so much longer in her bed than when I'd left. Her brown hair, the exact shade of our father's, cascaded over her shoulders and halfway down her arm. Her body was perfectly proportioned, her breasts already prominent and easily the same size as mine even though she was only thirteen. The skin on her face had a few teenage pimples that she'd covered with concealer that was one shade too light for her, making them stand out more than if she'd left them alone.

I swallowed awkwardly around the lump that had rapidly formed in my throat. I'd missed so much of her growing up. This young lady in front of me was nothing like the little girl I'd said good-bye to. I wasn't sure what I had been expecting to see; it actually shocked me that this wasn't the ten-year-old who followed me around and sang One Direction songs way too loudly, the girl who jumped on my bed and applied my lipstick and deodorant when I wasn't looking.

"Kelsey?" I said, pushing the door open wider and peering in.

She started, her head whipping to face me as her hand shot up to the phone, catching it as it fell off her tummy and onto the bed.

I smiled weakly, not knowing where to start. "Hey. Sorry, I didn't mean to scare you."

She didn't smile back; her lips pressed into a thin hard line as she reached up and pulled the headphones from her ears, letting them rest around her neck. Her eyes wandered over me as she sat up, swinging her legs over the side of the bed. "You're here, then." There was something off about her voice, a hard edge that made my spine straighten.

"Yeah, Stacey just dropped me off." I bit my lip, willing the words to come to me, some words of wisdom that would somehow take her pain away.

"Nice of you to bother," she huffed, standing up and ripping her headphones from her neck, carelessly dropping them and her phone onto the bed.

I recoiled at her tone, unsure why she sounded so angry. I wasn't expecting anger, hadn't prepared for it one bit. "I came as soon as I could," I replied, my eyebrows pinching together in confusion.

She made a scoffing noise in the back of her throat and crossed her arms over her chest, raising one eyebrow in challenge. "You came as soon as you could? Not good enough."

"Kelsey, what?" I mumbled, frowning, unmoving, my whole body frozen against the doorframe by her steely glare. "I got the first available flight. I've just come up to see if you're okay."

Her top lip turned up into a sneer, a look I had never seen on my loving, sweet little sister before. "You came to see if I was okay? Of course I'm not fucking okay!" Her f-bomb shocked me, and I blinked rapidly, taking in her words. She shook her head forcefully. "It's just too little too late, Ellie. You should have been here—you should have been here for Mom, for me, for Dad. You should have been here when the police officer brought the news, you should have been here for the hour-long drive in the police car to the hospital from Nana's, you should have been here when they took Mom into surgery. You should have been here when Nana had to go in and formally identify Dad's body. You should have been here when she broke down crying and then passed out from the pressure of it all. We needed you, and you weren't here! Instead, you were off swanning around in another country without a care in the world while my world was falling apart!" she all but screamed.

The lump in my throat seemed to swell, emotion bubbling up inside me, her hurtful words cutting and full of acid. The guilt at not being here like she said, it was crushing. "It's not like that," I croaked, my eyes filling with tears.

She raised her chin, her eyes hard as she walked the six or seven steps over to me. "You should have been here, but you weren't. If you think turning up after so long is going to make everything okay, then you're dead wrong." She grasped the door, swinging it forward forcefully and slamming it in my face.

CHAPTER 6

FOR A COUPLE of seconds I just stood there, my mouth agape, staring at the white painted grains in the wood that was less than two inches from my face, my mind not really responding to what had just happened.

What had *just happened?*

I recoiled, my heart aching, my lungs too tight to draw in anything other than a short, sharp breath. I gulped. The force of her words, the anger, the acid and purposeful hurtfulness to them. She'd meant every word.

A tear escaped, trickling down my cheek as I blinked a couple of times, the guilt and grief overwhelming. My knees weakened and I reached out, placing one hand on the wall for support as I thought of my poor nana having to identify her son's body, of her frail body not being able to cope with the pressure, of Kelsey being alone, her father dead, her mother in surgery, her nana blacking out at the hospital. It was all too much, too much sadness, too much to take in at once.

I leaned forward and placed my forehead against the cold wood of Kelsey's door, closing my eyes, taking deep breaths to try to calm my raging inner storm of emotions. All I wanted to do was stagger to my bedroom, fall face-first onto my bed, and cry into my pillow. Her words hit me hard, and I suddenly realized she was right. Me simply turning up here wasn't enough; I needed to make up for it, starting right now. Crying on my bed was not an option.

I sucked in a deep breath and pulled back, reaching up to dry my tearstained face with the back of my hand before turning for the stairs, deciding to leave Kelsey to calm down for a little while. I'd try again in a little while and see if she was ready to talk. Maybe she just needed a bit of space.

As I reached the bottom of the stairs, I followed the sound of dishes clinking and the delicious scent of chili wafting out of the kitchen. Nana was standing by the stove, stirring an enormous pot with a wooden spoon. I stood silently. Watching her cook was something I had always enjoyed; she was a whiz in the kitchen. When I was younger and would stay over at her house, she would let me help her make dinner; we'd bake cakes and cookies almost every visit.

"How'd it go?"

I jumped, startled by her words. I had been purposefully quiet when I entered and hadn't realized she'd known I was here. She smiled sadly over her shoulder as she picked up a bowl and scooped a ladleful of chili into it.

I didn't have the words to answer. I shrugged, walking forward and fingering the soft leather of a dining chair, noting it was new. In fact, the whole kitchen looked different. It had been painted a pale green; the porcelain on display was now green instead of the yellow set that had once been there.

"She's..." I gulped, swallowing the hurt. "...Angry with me for not being here when it happened."

Nana let out a long breath and nodded slowly, shuffling over to the table and setting down the bowl and a plate of crusty bread rolls. "Come sit down, you must be exhausted after all that traveling."

I sat obediently, my hands folded in my lap, my eyes firmly on the table.

"Kelsey's just upset. Everyone deals with grief differently. She's young and doesn't know how to take it all in. Sometimes anger is easier to deal with than sadness." She sat down opposite me and I looked up into her soft, sorrowful eyes. "She doesn't mean it, being angry is just her way of coping, and it appears you're getting the brunt of it. Unfortunately, sometimes we hurt the ones we love the most. She'll come around."

I nodded, taking in her words, hoping they were true. Nana's eyes were tight, watching me, her gaze flicking down to the spoon I hadn't touched. Resigned, I picked it up, seeing some of the tension leave her shoulders as I scooped some chili from the bowl and put it in my mouth, chewing slowly. It tasted just as delicious as it smelled, but I still wasn't hungry in the slightest. For my nana and her peace of mind, I forced myself to keep going, though, knowing that in some strange way, it made her feel better.

The silence was almost too much to bear as I ate, so I decided to broach the subject of the accident. She had been vague on the phone, just told me it was a car crash, no details. Now, with only the clink of spoon against bowl to cut the silence, the details seemed important.

"Nana, the car accident," I started, my voice cracking slightly— talking about it made it even more real, somehow—"was there anyone else hurt?" I'd been so wrapped up in my own grief that I hadn't even considered the fact that there could be other people injured or dead.

Her eyebrows knitted together as she picked at a loose thread on her apron. "No one else was hurt. They're not sure how it all happened. There was only one witness, who was driving a fair bit behind, so they didn't see much. They said that a blue Ford pickup truck had sped past them, driving erratically. They said it collided with the side of your father's car, which caused him to lose control and hit the central barrier. The other car sped off, and they haven't been able to find the driver."

I recoiled at her words. *The other driver didn't stop?* What kind of person was involved in an accident and didn't stop? "Do the police think they were drunk or something?" The words *driving erratically* stuck in my mind.

She sighed deeply and gave a small shrug of her shoulders. "They just don't know. They've checked the traffic cams, but haven't managed to get a picture of the driver, so at this point, they're not sure what really happened."

I ground my teeth, anger flaring in my stomach at this unknown driver.

She reached out and placed her soft hand over mine, squeezing gently. "They'll find the person responsible and bring them to justice, don't you worry about that." Her voice was set, firm, confident, and more than a little angry. "Trust that the police will do their jobs. We have other things to worry about."

I nodded, a lump now firmly lodged in my throat. I put down my spoon and pushed the bowl away from me gently, knowing I couldn't force down another bite. Nana stood silently, picking up my bowl and walking over to the garbage disposal to scrape my barely touched food away. Her shoulders sagged, her movements slow.

"Why don't you have a little nap or something?" I suggested, standing and walking over to her. "I can clean this up, you look exhausted." I put my arm around her and gave her an encouraging squeeze.

She sighed, not looking at me, and nodded. "I think I will." She turned and planted a soft kiss on my cheek. "Wake me if there's any news. Visiting starts again at three, but I think I'll skip the afternoon visit and just go tonight instead. Unless you want me to come with you?"

I smiled and shook my head. "I'll be fine. I'll go this afternoon, and then we can all go up again tonight."

She nodded in agreement, and I watched her walk out of the kitchen before glancing at the clock. Just before two. Just over an hour to wait before I could go see my mother. I sighed and dug in my pocket for my cell phone, heading over to the Wi-Fi router to get the password so I could connect to it. Once I'd connected, I dropped down into the kitchen chair and called Toby. He'd be climbing the walls waiting for news, but I knew he wouldn't call me in case I was at the hospital or something.

It took a few seconds to connect, but he answered on the second ring. "Hey, sweetheart. You okay?"

I closed my eyes, pressing the phone harder against my ear. In the background, I could hear the beep of the cash register, the clink of glasses, the murmured chatter of patrons. He was working. "Hi. Is now a good time?" I asked.

"It's always a good time where you're concerned." His voice was warm, loving. "Just 'old on one sec." The line became even more muffled, as if he had covered the mouthpiece. "Trev, look after things for a bit, 'lright? It's Ellie." Then he was back to talking to me. "Sorry, sweetheart. 'Ow's everyone coping? 'Ow's your mum?"

Nana looks like she's a minute from collapsing and Kelsey hates me.

"They're doing okay," I lied. "I haven't been to see my mom yet. I have to wait for visiting hours, but Nana said she's still in a coma."

"Aww, I'm so sorry, Ellie. I wish I was there, I've been so worried 'bout ya."

"Don't worry about me, I'm all right," I muttered, opening my eyes and looking down at the table, tracing the grains of wood with my fingernail.

"It's my job to worry, ain't it?" His voice was deliberately light, playful.

"I suppose," I admitted. "Are the boys okay?" They had still been asleep this morning when Toby and I left for the airport. I hadn't even had a chance to say good-bye to them before Toby's mother had come over to watch them so Toby could accompany me in the taxi.

"They're fine. They both send their love. Christian made you a drawing. 'E said I 'ave to bring it with me when I fly out to you."

My heart squeezed at the gesture. They really were sweet kids. "Tell them I said hi."

We chatted for another ten minutes, mundane conversation, nothing heavy. Mostly about the flight, Stacey, the pub, his kids, and Nana's chili. At the end of the call, he told me he loved me and apologized again for not being here with me, and made me promise to call again tonight, screw the time difference. He told me he'd arranged cover at the pub and had booked his flight for Wednesday—four days' time—once the kids were returned to their mother. When I disconnected the call, I felt a little better. Talking to someone who wasn't so closely involved and hearing the regular pub sounds in the background was a welcome distraction to the blackness that was inside me, consuming me by the second.

After quickly washing the dishes, I walked into the living room to see Nana asleep, sitting up in the armchair. I watched her rhythmic breathing for a few seconds, wondering what would have happened if she hadn't been here, if Kelsey had been on her own with no support. This woman was a rock, and I would be eternally grateful for her stepping in and taking care of my sister in my absence. I walked forward, picking up the throw from the sofa and laying it over her carefully. She didn't stir.

Not wanting to sit down, I wandered slowly around the house, touching things I hadn't seen for years, my eyes lingering on family photos that adorned the walls. When my gaze landed on the key rack that was mounted on the wall by the front door, I saw my old, battered Volkswagen Beetle key ring dangling there. I frowned, heading over to it and picking it up, memories of my beat-up little car swirling to the front of my mind.

I had no idea my parents had kept her.

Tightening my fist around the keys, I headed to the garage through the internal door and there she sat. My beloved green bug.

The fluffy green dice that Stacey had bought me when I passed my driving test still hung from the rearview mirror. I smiled and shook my head, finding the right key and pushing it into the lock eagerly.

As the door opened, a waft of polish and leather hit my nose. Slipping inside, I noticed that the inside was spotlessly clean, sparkling even. Someone, most likely my father, had kept the car clean for the last three years—probably in the hope that one day I'd come home and want to drive her. Pain stabbed at my heart as I touched the soft, ripped leather of my seat. Swinging the door closed, I leaned forward and rested my forehead against the steering wheel. The loss of my father was something I would surely never recover from. Everything inside me hurt—my heart squeezed painfully with each beat as I closed my eyes and saw his smiling face, his twinkling eyes, heard his laugh.

A strangled sob left my throat.

I dragged in a couple of ragged breaths, opening my eyes and staring at the ceiling of the car, forcing my mind away from my

father in a bid to keep the tears at bay. Needing something else
to do before I fell into the grief abyss, I shoved the key into the
ignition and turned it, pushing my foot down on the gas pedal,
pumping it like I used to. The engine ticked over, but didn't
catch. On the second try I pumped the gas faster and...bingo!
There was a little life left in the old girl yet! I smiled, leaving the
engine running as I reveled in the loud roar.

When it was finally time to start thinking about going to the
hospital, I sent a quick text to Stacey, saying that we didn't need
a ride, that my car was still in working order, and that I'd actually quite like to drive myself. She replied quickly and asked me
to message later and let her know if there was any change.

Leaving the car running, not wanting to risk turning it off
in case it didn't start up again, I headed back into the house
and crept through the lounge and up the stairs toward Kelsey's
room. I knocked softly, taking a couple of deep breaths outside
her door, bracing myself for another confrontation and more of
her anger-fueled grief.

"What?" she called from inside.

I gripped the handle, twisting it and opening the door a little,
poking my head in. She was back on the bed, this time with
her laptop open in front of her. Her shoulders stiffened and her
eyebrows knitted together in a frown when she saw it was me.
"Hey." I cleared my throat. "I'm going to the hospital. Nana is
sleeping downstairs and said she was going to hold off and come
tonight instead. Do you want to go with me?"

Indecision flickered across her features, and finally she shook
her head. "I'll go later too."

My stomach twisted in a knot. A very small part of me had
been hoping she wouldn't want to come because I didn't want
to bear the brunt of her anger and resentment, but a bigger
part of me was devastated because it meant that I had to face

going there alone. I needed my sister, I needed someone to share this with, and she was being so hostile to me. In her mind, though, I guess it was perfectly reasonable to feel resentment. I hadn't been here when she needed me, after all. I fought to keep my expression neutral and not show her how much she was hurting me.

"Okay." The word came out more like a squeak than anything else. "I'll call if there's any change." I closed the door quickly, not wanting to hang around where I clearly wasn't wanted, and headed down the stairs, grabbing my jacket and purse as I slipped into the garage again and opened the roller door.

As I pulled out of the garage, I gripped the wheel tightly. I'd almost forgotten what it was like to drive. I hadn't been behind the wheel for the last three years, and driving my little bug had always been hard going at the best of times when I had to fight to change gears and haul the wheel heavily to go around corners.

When I finally pulled into the hospital parking lot, I was actually a little relieved. After spending almost two years being ferried around in cars and cabs in England, it was a bit weird to be on the right side of the road and not the left. Funny how quickly you get used to things.

As I left the safety of my car and made the short walk to the entrance of the hospital, I tried to prepare myself for what I was about to see, but in all honesty, I wasn't sure what I was about to be confronted with. I dared not even try to imagine.

Inside, the hospital was busier than I thought it would be. I had to line up at the reception desk, waiting behind other loved ones, to ask where I needed to go. After being directed to the ICU department, I walked slowly, ignoring people around me and counting my footfalls as I made my way up the long corridor to my mother's ward. When I finally got to the right place, I squirted some sanitizer on my hands, as directed by the laminated sign just above the dispenser, and pushed open the hefty wooden door.

As I stepped inside, the smell of the place changed. In the hallway, you could have been anywhere, but this ward had a distinct medicinal smell that was so strong it made my nose wrinkle. I stopped in my tracks, my feet firmly planted, unsure if I could stay here. The scent was overpowering, the clean lines, the white walls, the thick wooden doors with patient names written on a whiteboard attached to each door—it was all too much to handle. I didn't want to go in. I didn't want to see my mom's name there; I wasn't sure I was strong enough.

Now I understood why Nana and Kelsey had both opted to skip this afternoon visit. I wouldn't have wanted to come back here again so soon after leaving, either. Just as I was mentally chastising myself for coming alone, a nurse walked past. When she caught sight of me she stopped and smiled warmly.

"Can I help you?" she asked, tilting her head to the side and regarding me with sympathetic eyes.

I opened my mouth and closed it again. Words failed me. "Um..." I tried again. "I'm here to visit my mother, Ruth Pearce." As I said her name, there was another twist in my gut.

"Oh, you must be Ellie," the nurse replied, her smile widening. "Your grandmother told me you were flying in today. England, right?"

I nodded blankly, my mind slightly numb.

"Come on in, I'll show you where your mom is. There's been no change since this morning. The doctor is monitoring her. All her pressures are good, her heart is steady. She's still in a coma, but given the nature of her injuries that was not unexpected. She's hooked up to the ventilator at the moment, so don't let the machinery scare you." She gripped my elbow, leading me inside the ward, forcing me to walk with gentle persuasion as her soft voice reassured me. She stopped outside the third door on the right and released her grip on my arm. "She's in here. You want me to come in with you?" she offered, nodding to the door.

There, on the whiteboard, printed in neat script, was my mother's name.

It felt like a weight had been laid on my chest, pressing, squeezing. It was finally sinking in, all the things I was struggling to contain inside: My father had died, and my mother was inside this room fighting for her life. I could lose them both. And then what? What would happen then, to Kelsey, to me, to Nana?

"Are you okay, dear?"

I blinked a couple of times, realizing she was waiting for a response, and turned to look at her, willing my voice to work this time. "I'm fine. I'd like to go in alone." That was a lie. I would actually like to turn and run, run so fast that my head spun and I left this horrible waking nightmare far behind me.

"Okay, give me a shout if you need anything or have any questions. I'll let the doctor know you're here, I know he wanted to speak to you." She threw me one last sympathetic smile and then turned and hurried off into the nurses' office.

I turned my attention back to the door, reaching out tentatively and pushing it open. I held my breath the whole time.

As the door swung open, I caught my first glimpse of her. She was lying on the bed in the center of the room. She looked incredibly small, so still and lifeless. Seeing her there, so fragile and helpless, the pain in my chest somehow, *impossibly*, doubled.

My hand shot to my mouth as a little whimper left my lips. She looked childlike lying there, peaceful even. Tubes and wires protruded from her mouth, attached to the ventilator that was keeping her alive. Clear liquid pumped into her veins via an IV in her hand. I stepped into the room, letting the door swing closed behind me as I raked my eyes over her. Bruises and cuts marred her usually perfect creamy skin. Her hair was tangled instead of being perfectly and meticulously straightened; there was even some dirt under her fingernails. My body hitched with a sob. If my mother could see herself right now, she would hate it. I made a mental note to bring a hairbrush and some cleaning wipes when I came next time. When she woke, she would be horrified if there was dirt under her nails.

Then it hit me, the absurdity of my thought: *If* my mother woke, she wouldn't care about a little grime or dirt because she'd then learn that my dad had left us. I held my breath, my eyes fixed on her as I approached the bed.

The heart rate monitor beeping steadily and the slow rhythm of her chest rising and falling softly with the forced intake from the ventilator were the only indications that she was alive. If not for them, I would have sworn she'd already left, followed my father, and the two of them were watching me as I stood vigil over a lifeless body.

I reached out and traced her cheek with the back of one finger as my grief consumed me. "Oh, Mom," I croaked. "I'm so sorry I wasn't here. I'm so sorry."

This was the first time I had seen my mother in three years, and these were the circumstances—where was the justice in that? Sure, we'd called each other, chatted on FaceTime, and used Skype a few times, but this was the first time I'd physically touched my mother since I left for Rome over three years ago. Toby and I had been planning on seeing them soon; they were going to fly over with Kelsey during the school holidays and spend the week with us, but now . . .

I choked back a sob and reached out, taking her hand softly. "I'm so sorry."

I don't know how long I stood there for, lost in my grief, but it must have been a while because when the door opened and a middle-aged man in a white coat walked in with that sympathetic smile that they must all practice in the mirror, my neck ached from standing and looking down at my mother for so long.

"Ellison? I'm Doctor Pacer. Is now a good time for us to chat? There are a few things I need to talk to you about," he said.

I nodded, stepping back, licking my dry lips. "Yeah, and it's Ellie."

He nodded once in acknowledgment and motioned toward the two chairs next to my mother's bed. "Shall we sit?"

Sit? Is this more bad news? What more is there that can go wrong?

"Um, okay." I plopped into one chair, my eyes trained on him as he clasped his hands in his lap and sat forward, looking at me intently.

"There are certain arrangements that need to be made. I didn't bring this up with your grandmother because I wasn't sure how she would cope after her fainting episode earlier. I'm not sure how she'd cope under the pressure, she already seems a little...delicate," he said, seeming to be choosing his words carefully.

Delicate, that was a good word for her right now. I nodded, actually grateful that he hadn't piled any more pressure onto my frail grandmother. "What sort of arrangements?"

His lips pressed into a thin line before he spoke. "Funeral arrangements for your father. His body is currently down in the morgue. We've done everything that we need to do and the police have given permission for his body to be released to a funeral home so you can start planning for what you'd like to happen."

Funeral arrangements. Ouch.

"Oh," I mumbled.

"If you want, I can have someone help you with the arrangements, or if you don't wish to deal with it, then I can speak with your grandmother next time she comes in. I know it's a lot for someone to deal with; losing a parent is never easy, and under these circumstances"—he shot a quick look at my mother in the bed—"it makes it even harder."

I shook my head quickly, my mind made up and set. "Don't talk to my nana. I'll deal with it, I'll arrange it all. I don't want her doing more than she has to."

CHAPTER 7

JAMIE

THREE DAYS ELLIE had been back stateside, three fucking days. The longest three days of my life, they felt like.

Since seeing that article, all I could think about was her. She'd taken over everything, consumed my every thought. And now she was back here, so tantalizingly close, and I'd been wrestling with the decision of whether I should go and see her, offer my condolences, ask if there was anything I could do to help. I'd almost caved a few times, but had managed to maintain my resolve. I wanted what was best for her—I always had—and I was almost positive that what was best for her wasn't me. But there was still that selfish need, that incredible desire to be near her, touch her face, run my fingers through her hair, pull her body against mine, and hold her so tightly we'd never be apart again. It was one thing staying away from her while she was halfway around the world, but quite another making myself stay away from her now that she was just ten miles down the road.

I groaned and gripped the small knife in my hand tightly, looking up at the dartboard mounted on the wall. I needed a drink. I needed to get so shitfaced drunk that I couldn't even stand; maybe then my chest would loosen and I'd be able to breathe properly. For the hundredth time in three days, I thought about how much easier my life would have been if I'd never even met that playful little redhead. She came into my life with an unexpected bang that turned my world into something I'd dared not even hope for. If I hadn't met her, if she hadn't made me fall in love with her so deeply that it devoured me, then I wouldn't feel this *emptiness* inside me.

My heartache had gone beyond pain now, beyond loneliness, beyond grief; now it was just emptiness, which, in my opinion, was fucking worse. I could barely stand it.

I needed a distraction, an escape, something to take my mind off her. Seeing as it was barely eleven a.m. I couldn't exactly drink myself into oblivion like I craved, so it would have to be something else. Closing my eyes, I thought of some of the more menial jobs that needed doing—there were a few emails that required my attention from the legitimate businesses I ran, I needed to sort out hiring two more security guards for a new contract we'd just signed, I had a couple of people I needed to call back—but I wasn't inclined to do any of these things.

My hands itched to do something more exciting, to find some thrills. Maybe to steal some rich prick's pride and joy and crush it into a cube at the junkyard, just for kicks. There was all sorts of depraved shit I enjoyed lately. I was constantly pushing myself, wanting—no, *wanting* wasn't the right word, *needing* was more fitting—needing bigger and better.

"Go big or go home." My mantra.

But daytime limited what distractions could be had.

Fighting was out. I was still recovering from the beating I'd received on Friday night, the yellowing bruises on my face evident. There were no gun or drug deliveries scheduled until the weekend. Stealing cars was one of my favorite pastimes—one of the only things that made me feel alive in this unfeeling, boring, pointless existence—but that was ruled out, too. I liked taking risks, but stealing cars in the daylight was for the brainless, uncouth, low-class thief who mainly just wanted the car radio or a little joyride.

So, all in all, I was pretty much useless today.

As if he knew I was falling down the black hole of boredom, Ray shouted my name from downstairs in the workshop. The sound of metal clanging against metal drifted through the floor. I blinked, thankful for the reprieve from my negative thoughts, and drew back my arm, throwing the knife, letting it fly across the room, and watching it find its target in the double-six slot on the dartboard, grouped nicely with the two others I'd thrown moments before my mind wandered to redheaded places. An acquaintance I'd met in prison had liked knives; he'd told me that to master a knife you first had to understand it, respect it. I wasn't sure I'd quite become a master at throwing knives, but I was a pretty skilled shot now.

I pushed myself up from the black leather chair and headed out of the office that had once belonged to Brett. Downstairs was the workshop where I'd spent so many hours of my life, hiding from the beatings that going home would bring, earning money so I could save for plans that never came into effect. As I reached the bottom step, the smell of stale sweat and grease hit me. I smiled a half smile. This workshop was my favorite place in the world.

Ray was over to one side, perched on a stool working on some sort of circuit board, his array of tools spread all over the workbench. The radio thumped behind him while he sang along to some Kanye West shit.

Ray had been with me from the beginning. As soon as I had been released from prison, he'd sought me out, taking me into his home with his wife and daughter, trying to convince me to go onto the straight and narrow, something he had been doing for the year and a half while I was doing hard time. When it became obvious to him and everyone else that my mind was set, he quit his mechanic job and helped me take back the territory and business that Brett had built before he died. Ed and Enzo had also come on board, and I'd headhunted Dodger, convincing him to come work with me, too. Together, we'd streamlined the business, dropping the things I had never liked doing while under Brett's charge—the robberies, the neighborhood protection racket, and the moneylending. We kept the bread-and-butter jobs, the real moneymakers—drugs, munitions, and of course, the cars. We certainly weren't the massive enterprise that Brett had run, fingers in all the pies, but we were a formidable force within our three areas.

Go big or go home.

We went big.

Other local gangs and organizations despised us for it because we took all the best deals, leaving the scraps for them to fight over. I delighted in it. What else had I ever had to be proud of in my life?

"What's up, buddy?" I called to Ray's back.

"Hey, Kid." He turned to me and smiled warmly, wiping his hands on a rag. "Thought that was your car outside. Here, I got you something."

"Oh yeah, what?"

He pointed to a little white box on the workbench, so I picked it up and lifted the lid. Inside was a small metal object that made my heart leap in my chest. "Is this what I think it is?" I gasped, eyeing him hopefully.

He nodded, his smile smug as he folded his arms over his chest. "It certainly is. I called in a favor. Had it overnighted from China for you."

I pumped my fist, excitement bubbling in my stomach. Now I had something to keep me occupied for a couple of hours. "You're the best. Thanks, man." I grinned, walking over and slapping him on the back.

He raised one eyebrow. "You might not thank me when you find out how much it cost."

I waved a dismissive hand. Money wasn't an issue for me at all. "I owe you big time. Buy you a drink later?" I offered. He nodded in response as I walked over to my pride and joy, parked in the corner. Grinning, I gripped the blue tarp that covered it and pulled it off, revealing my 2004 Subaru Impreza WRX, the limited Petter Solberg edition. A proud, dreamy sigh left my lips. She was a beautiful thing—when she worked, that was. Of all the cars I owned or had driven, this was one of my favorites.

She really was a piece of art, in my opinion—ice-blue paint job, 316 horsepower, zero to sixty in 4.5 seconds, limited edition too because they'd only made five hundred of them. I'd had her shipped in from Japan earlier in the year when I'd accidentally fallen into my new hobby—street racing.

I hadn't driven her in two weeks, though; during my last race she'd snapped a clutch cable and had been unusable since.

"I got you new spark plugs too, I know you said she was a little sluggish so that should help," Ray said, walking up behind me with another box.

I grinned over my shoulder. "Thanks, bud," I said, digging in my pocket for my keys and unlocking the car.

"Want me to help you fix her up?"

I shook my head quickly. "Nah, I got it. Thanks." Grinning, I popped the hood. A long, slow exhale of breath escaped my body as I looked at her beautiful engine. I could feel some of the tension leaving my shoulders, my mind now fully occupied on something other than a grieving Ellie.

Maybe I could race tonight. That would certainly make me feel better. I dug in my pocket for my cell phone, shooting a message to Rodriguez, one of the organizers of the races that I entered, asking if there was anything planned for tonight. There hadn't been any whisperings of one on the streets, though, so chances were there wasn't a race planned. *Shame.*

I'd make sure she was in perfect working order, just in case.

★ ★ ★

It took almost all afternoon to fix up the car and have her purring like a kitten. She was ready, raring to go, a thing of beauty. After I'd finished working on her, I'd hoisted myself up on the bench, and Ray and I were having a celebratory beer. I was halfway through the bottle when Ed walked in, his face stern and his mouth set in a tight line.

"Kid, I've been calling you. Why are you not answering?" he asked, frowning at the beer in my hand as if it were the sole reason I hadn't responded to him.

I shrugged, glancing down at my cell phone on the bench next to me, seeing three missed calls from him. "Ah, sorry, I must have accidentally put it on silent when I took it out of my pocket." I picked it up now, also seeing a text from Rodriguez confirming there was no race tonight, but he said to make sure I checked my messages again in the next couple of days. Meaning a race was on the horizon once they found the perfect venue.

Ed sighed, running a perfectly manicured hand through his slicked-back brown hair. I frowned, taking another sip of my beer, looking him over. He seemed more stressed than usual; his double-breasted suit jacket was even unbuttoned—something I rarely saw. Ed prided himself on image. He liked to wear expensive suits and a $30,000 watch to show everyone he had money and status. In all honesty, he was a douche who worked for me, someone who aspired to be number one but never would be. He was an ass-licking, smarmy prick who thought too much of himself. When he'd worked for Brett, he'd had more say in what went on—he'd been Brett's voice a lot of the time, his number two in command. Under me, though, he ranked distinctly lower, but he still hadn't given up his penchant for expensive suits.

"So what's up, then?" I asked, cocking my head to the side, waiting for his reply.

His eyebrows knitted together, and his lips pursed in distaste as he spat two words. "The Salazars."

At the name, I frowned, too. The Salazars were my biggest opposition in town. The two Salazar brothers, Alberto and Mateo, had arrived about nine months ago from Mexico, bringing some cheap-as-shit drugs with them, and had set up camp on my turf. At first they'd wanted a partnership, wanted us to start selling their drugs—some cocaine shit cut with God only knows what—and when I'd not so politely told them to take a hike, we'd become rivals. They were the lowest of the low, in my opinion. They didn't care that their drugs were laced with rat poison or levamisole, a drug used to deworm animals that I'd heard literally rotted people's skin off. They weren't like us; they had no morals and didn't care how many people they hurt or killed with their impure product. We'd had many a battle with them over territories and where they were "allowed" to sell their second-rate drugs. We had an agreement.

"What have those greasy punks done now?" I growled, tightening my hand around the bottle.

"They sent some of their little skank girls into one of our clubs last night, peddling their shit. One guy had an epileptic fit in the middle of the dance floor, and now the police are sniffing around to try to find where he got it from. I've been fielding questions all day; really could have done with you answering your cell!" he replied, his tone clipped and accusing.

"Motherfuckers! Why are they sending pushers into our clubs?" I snapped, shaking my head angrily. "Call Alberto, tell him I want to meet with him. Tonight," I ordered, pulling my arm back and then launching my bottle across the workshop in anger, hearing it smash against the wall and spray glass everywhere.

I'm going to kill that son of a bitch!

CHAPTER 8

ELLIE

EACH HOUR OF the three days I'd been home felt like a pain-filled eternity, yet at the same time there had barely been enough time for me to do all that was required.

Since that first visit to the hospital when the doctor had suggested I take control of the situation and make arrangements for my father's funeral, I hadn't stopped. I hadn't realized how much planning and organizing was involved or how much time each task would take. Simple things, or things you would assume were simple, such as picking out flowers, took hours. Other things, like designing the order-of-service programs—and even finding a reputable place to have them printed—took even longer. I'd spent almost every spare moment sorting through photographs of my father, picking out his favorite music, and choosing readings that would be good for the service. It was painful, heart-wrenching work that seemed never-ending. Each photograph or meaningful piece of music was like a vise tightening around my heart. I'd barely managed to hold myself together; I was hanging by a thread at the moment, on the edge just waiting to tumble back over the grief cliff. I knew it would happen eventually; at some point I'd start to cry again, and when that happened, I wasn't sure I would ever stop. Luckily, though, I was doing a good job of holding my emotions at bay— so far, anyway.

Today had been close, though. Today's task was pushing me extremely close to that breaking point.

I looked down at my mother's beautifully penned address book and ran my finger down the page, stopping at the last entry. Julie and Peter Watkins. I bypassed their address, finding their number and punching it into the phone. As it rang on the other end, I rubbed at my forehead, willing the headache that I'd had from sleep deprivation for the last two days to subside.

"Hello?" a woman's chipper voice answered.

I closed my eyes and prepared myself for another painful conversation; this was the forty-second call I'd made today, working my way through my mother's address book starting with the letter A and ending with the last couple named—the Watkinses.

"Hi, is this Julie Watkins?"

"It is."

"Hi, Julie. My name's Ellie Pearce. You probably won't remember me, I think I was about fifteen or sixteen the last time I saw you," I said, massaging my forehead a little harder. I knew my parents kept in touch with the Watkinses, but the last time I saw them was at their son's christening about five years ago. They were friends of my parents from their college days.

"Ellie! Of course, I remember you," she replied, her voice warm and cheerful. "How are you?"

I opened my eyes and looked down at her name in the address book, knowing I was about to obliterate that cheerful tone in her voice. I frowned. "I'm calling to tell you some bad news." I swallowed awkwardly; no matter how many times I'd said this exact same thing today, it hadn't gotten any easier. "My parents were involved in a car accident this weekend. My father has passed away, and my mother is currently in critical condition in the hospital."

There was a sharp intake of breath on the other end of the line, a few moments of silence, and then came the words, ones I had heard so many times today that they were now meaningless to me. I knew they were uttered with good intent, but they were just words now in varying phrases but all meaning the same thing.

"Oh, Ellie. I'm so sorry!" she cried.

I'm so sorry, sorry for your loss, I'm sorry this happened. Sorry. Sorry. Sorry. Everyone apologized like it was their fault.

"Thank you," I muttered. "I know you and your husband knew both of my parents from years back, so I just wanted to let you know a couple of details about my dad's funeral in case you wanted to attend. It's Friday at three p.m., at the crematorium on Everglade Drive. There's a wake after at our house."

"Of course, thank you for telling us. We'll both be there," Julie answered, her voice quivering as she spoke. "How is your mother? You said she was in the hospital?"

I nodded slowly. Throughout all of these calls, I'd tried to remain detached, not to think about what I was saying or people's reactions to the news. It was so much easier for me to remain numb, to pretend I was talking about something else, someone else's family, some person who meant nothing to me at all. It was the only way I could get through it. If I let myself feel the words, I never would have gotten through these calls and would probably still be a blubbering mess after the first one.

"She sustained a blow to the head during the crash, which resulted in a brain bleed. She's currently in a coma. We're waiting to see what happens at the moment." My words were matter-of-fact, no emotion involved.

The hematoma, or brain bleed, I'd since learned, was the

worst thing that happened to my mom. The broken bones, internal bleeding, and other injuries were now under control, but the hematoma was causing severe pressure on her brain. When I was alone with the doctor that first day, I'd begged him to be honest with me, and I'd heard something I hadn't wanted to hear. They simply weren't sure if she would wake up, and they'd told me to go ahead and arrange the funeral and not wait. My mother's condition wasn't good; at this point, it was a wait-and-see game. There was also a significant chance there would be permanent brain damage, but they wouldn't know the extent until she woke... *if* she woke at all.

"Oh, goodness. Poor Ruth!" Julie squeaked, now sniffing. "Will she be okay?"

I chewed the inside of my cheek, testing the soft skin between my teeth. "We don't know. We hope so."

"Oh, Ellie. I'm so sorry."

There it was again: *sorry*. "Thank you. I'd better go, I have other people to call. I'll see you Friday afternoon, if you can make it," I said.

Then came more of the overused phrases that had been said to me today: "I'm thinking of you and Kelsey. If you need anything, then let me know. I'll pray for your mother."

I wasn't a religious person—none of my family were—but I appreciated the gesture. At times like these, people did what they felt best and whatever brought them comfort. Let her pray if that was her thing; it surely couldn't hurt.

I didn't answer, just disconnected the phone and leaned back in the chair, letting out a long, slow breath. It was done. It had taken me—I looked at the clock, almost four p.m.—over three hours to make all the calls. I set the phone down on my father's large oak desk and unclenched my hand a couple of times, trying to ease my stiff fingers.

I looked up, letting my eyes slowly drag over my father's private room. He'd worked from here in the evenings sometimes, maybe even the odd weekend. My gaze settled on the faded, ripped fabric of the armchair next to the window. My mom had badgered him every time she entered about throwing the chair out because it was an eyesore, but it was my dad's favorite so he'd fought tooth and nail to keep it.

I stood and walked over to it, running my fingers over the velvety material. I smiled weakly as memories came to me of this chair. My dad would allow me in here sometimes when he was working. I'd sit on the chair under the window and do my homework, read a book or magazine, or do some coloring. Sometimes I'd pretend to read but I'd secretly be watching him, sitting behind his desk tapping away at his laptop or speaking on the phone to some important client. Sometimes when he'd look up and catch me watching, he'd make a stupid face, going cross-eyed, tongue sticking out the side of his mouth, before continuing his call as if nothing had happened. I'd spend hours in here just watching him work, escaping as he did, for a bit of quiet to read. Sometimes he'd lift me onto his lap in this chair and we'd read a book together. My father and I had discovered the wonders of Harry Potter together in this chair.

I smiled to myself, fingering the hole in the arm of the chair. It was the silly little things that seemed so unimportant at the time that could end up meaning the most after, the things that came at you all at once and reminded you that you took so much for granted when you thought your world was unbreakable.

I stood there for another couple of minutes, then left the room, closing the door behind me. As I walked into the living room, seeing Kelsey and Nana sitting there, Kelsey turned toward me. Her eyes narrowed, a little line forming between her eyebrows as she stood and left the room without another word. I clenched my jaw at the action. It had been the same for the last couple of days—she'd leave the room every time I entered, opting to spend most of her time holed up in her bedroom, making her scorn clear every time her accusing eyes landed on me. I had no idea how to make her feel better or what I could say to mend our damaged relationship. Maybe she'd never forgive me for not being here when it happened.

I turned and watched her walk up the hallway and up the stairs toward her bedroom. My heart felt heavy. I needed her, could she not see that? Could she not see that I was hurting too and that I needed a hug from my sister? Did she not see that my world fell apart at the same time hers did? I wasn't sure how long I could pretend to be unaffected by her indifference. After sitting alone in that room for the last three hours repeating that my father was dead over and over, I just needed someone to hold me, and that someone clearly wasn't going to be Kelsey, no matter how much I stared at her back and willed it to happen.

"Are you okay, darling?"

I sniffed and turned back, seeing Nana sitting on the sofa, her knitting on her lap, her kind and caring eyes watching me with evident sympathy. "I'm fine, Nana," I lied. "It's all done, I called everyone I found in the address book, plus a few I found in Dad's Rolodex."

Nana nodded, her eyes on me. "That's good. You should have let me do some."

"It's all done now." I shrugged one shoulder, leaning on the doorframe and picking at a loose thread on the sleeve of my sweater so I didn't have to look at her. She'd offered to call around too—she'd wanted to help—but I could see she was barely keeping herself together. Since I'd been home, she looked like she'd aged ten years. She wasn't coping, and at her age I wanted to protect her from as much as I could. I saw how the stress of this situation had made her arthritis flare up in her hip again; I saw the tired circles under her eyes and how her dresses hung off her shrinking frame. I saw her drift into a daydream, her knitting or the food she was cooking long forgotten, and I saw how she sometimes cried when she thought she was alone in the room.

Although I was doing my damn best to hold it together, my family was falling apart at the seams and I was powerless to stop it. The least I could do was shoulder as much of the burden as I could. My mom's parents were no help; they'd been informed about the crash, but they were both older and in fairly poor health so they weren't up to making the trip across the country. It was doubtful that they'd even make the funeral.

"I'm going to make you some tea," I murmured, slipping into the kitchen and starting to make it in a daze.

When I reentered the room, two steaming-hot mugs in hand, I saw that Nana was asleep on the sofa, her knitting still grasped in her hands. I sighed and set the teas down, carefully plucking the wool and needles from between her bony fingers and placing them into the basket at her feet. She needed sleep. I heard her at night, down here cleaning or putting things away, making food that no one ate, keeping herself busy. She was probably awake more than I was at nighttime.

Not wanting to sit and dwell on what I'd spent my day doing, I decided to go to my room and lie down. I headed upstairs, stopping to listen outside Kelsey's door for a couple of seconds, checking she wasn't upset or anything. It was quiet in there so I continued into my room.

My room was just the same as I'd left it three years ago. My possessions were still displayed on the side tables and windowsill—not collecting dust, though, because my mother would never have allowed that. My bed was still made, my carpet vacuumed. I hadn't really spent much time in here, I'd simply unpacked my case when I'd arrived and slept in here, nothing more.

I stopped in the middle of the room, looking around at it all. It felt strange being in my childhood bedroom, a nice strange, but weird nonetheless.

I headed to my desk, picking up one of the sketch pads that were stacked neatly there. I turned the pages slowly, seeing all the drawings I'd made, the clothes I'd spent hours dreaming up and giving life to on the page. I frowned, running my hand over the designs. I hadn't sketched for three years, just hadn't been inspired or had the motivation. I set the book aside, picking up the swatches of material instead, rubbing them between my thumb and finger, remembering nicer times when I'd be bursting with creativity and desperate to get my ideas down on paper. So much time had passed, I was almost a different person from the girl who used to dream of being a fashion designer.

I sighed and let my hand drop to my side as my eyes wandered over everything else and settled on the wall. I frowned at the sight before me.

It was the map that I'd stuck up there when planning my travels, the one where I'd pinned clipped-out photos of the places I wanted to visit with Jamie, but now it looked different. I stepped closer, my curiosity piqued.

And that was the thing that smashed down the emotional wall I'd built around myself.

That map—and the photos and postcards my parents had pinned onto it, the ones I'd sent them each time I'd gone to a new place. On each one there was the date I'd arrived there and the date I'd departed. A sob left my lips. They'd been following my progress; they'd mapped it all out, following me around Europe with their pins and little flags. My chin trembled, uncontrollable tears streaming down my face as my eyes darted over all the places they'd marked: Italy, Germany, Greece, Cypress, Spain, France, Ireland, Scotland, and lots more. My gaze stopped at the photo pinned on London, England—one I'd sent them six months ago. It was Toby and me, both of us grinning, me holding my left hand out to the camera to show them the nice sparkly new addition to my ring finger. A Post-it note was stuck to the bottom; there, in my mother's beautiful script, were the words *Ellie finally stops running.*

I closed my eyes, hugging myself tightly as the tears fell and my breathing turned into shallow gasps. That was when the anger built up: irrational, blazing rage burning through the hollow in my stomach. My eyes dropped open and landed on the map. I'd been off gallivanting, having a good time—"running," my mother had called it—instead of being here, spending time with them, making more memories. I'd left without a second thought that something like this could happen. I'd never dreamed that when I'd said good-bye to them on the grass outside the house, it would be the last time I would get to hug my father, and possibly my mother too if she didn't wake. I'd taken them for granted, assumed I could come back anytime and pick up where we left off. I'd been so wrong.

Without thinking, I reached out and grabbed at the photographs, the map, and the postcards, tearing them from the wall with wild abandon, not caring about the pins that flew all over the place, dotting the carpet in multicolored sprinkles, not caring about the paper cuts that tore into my fingertips as I wrenched the map down in several tattered pieces. A guttural cry left my lips as I bent and picked up the largest section of the map, tearing it in half and screwing the pieces into a ball before tossing it to the floor with the rest of the litter I'd created.

Tears fell, wetting my pink T-shirt, as I gasped for breath, kicking out at the photos, sending them fluttering away from me. When my legs gave out, I sank to the floor, put my face in my hands, and cried.

I wasn't sure how long I sat there, probably a long time. Eventually, the tears dried up and my breathing evened out. I hadn't gotten up; I'd just scooted over so I could rest my back against the wall and pulled my knees to my chest. And that was how Stacey found me. Eyes glazed, head aching, room littered with traveling souvenirs, brain fuzzy, and anger still fizzing in my stomach.

"Ellie, what happened in here?" she asked, letting herself into my room, eyeing the chaos.

I looked up and shrugged one shoulder. I had no words.

Her lips pressed together. I looked away from the sympathy in her eyes. She didn't speak, just walked over to me and slid down the wall to sit next to me, her arm coming up to lie across my shoulders. I tilted my head, resting it on her shoulder and pressing against her tighter, grateful for the hug that I so desperately needed today.

She blew out a slow breath, her hand rubbing my arm soothingly. "Your nana called earlier and asked me to come over after work. She said you were going to have a rough day and would need some cheering up."

"Oh." I'd wondered why she'd just showed up out of the blue like this.

She turned slightly and pressed her lips to the top of my head softly. "Are you okay?" she whispered into my hair.

I shrugged again, not even sure if I was all right or not. "Not really," I admitted, pulling away and swiping at my sore eyes. "I guess it all just got on top of me. I saw the map and my mom, she'd…" I frowned at a photo of Natalie and me picking grapes in France that peeked out from under a torn section of map. "I don't know. I just got angry, I guess."

"At what?" Stacey pressed.

"At myself for leaving. I should have been here. I never should have gone in the first place, or I should have come home two years ago when Natalie left. I should never have stayed in London."

Stacey was quiet for a few seconds; then she reached out and snagged a photo of me standing in front of the Eiffel Tower, smiling at it before showing it to me. "When your mom got this picture, she drove all the way into town and came to the café I was working at just to show it to me. She gushed about how proud she was of you for living your dream and seeing all these beautiful sights. She stood at the counter while I served and bragged to everyone in line about how her smart, gorgeous daughter was taking time off and traveling. She was so proud of you, Ellie. She never said it when you were living here, goodness knows that, but she just gushed about you while you were gone."

I scowled down at my hands, seeing the paper cuts for the first time as Stacey's words sank in.

"Ellie, you needed to go, it was the best thing for you. You needed time away to heal yourself, to find yourself again after"—she ground her teeth angrily—"him."

Him. Jamie. The beautiful, wounded boy who tricked me into falling in love with him only to shatter me completely. I swallowed around the lump that formed in my throat at the mere thought of him. Three years on and thinking about him still hurt, opened up old wounds, left my heart bleeding.

I knew she was right. The trip had been a necessity. I'd *had* to leave; I was broken and lost, damaged so badly that at times I wasn't sure I would ever put myself back together again. But time away had helped, Natalie had helped, traveling to different places that didn't remind me of him helped, Toby had helped.

"I should have made time to see them or talk to them more. Came back to visit. Brought Toby to meet them. I should have done things differently," I croaked.

"Hindsight is a spiteful bitch," Stacey replied softly.

"Ain't that the truth," I mumbled.

Stacey cocked her head to the side and smiled at me sadly, reaching out and taking one of my hands in hers. "You'll drive yourself crazy, thinking like this." She rubbed a small circle on the back of my hand. "You need a break. You're under so much stress, got so much going on that you just need a break. I have an idea." Her eyes brightened as she straightened her shoulders. "We're going out tonight. Dinner, just the two of us, and maybe a drink or two after. You need to loosen up or you're going to have some sort of mental breakdown." She looked around at my messy room and her eyebrows rose. "Well, more like *another* breakdown," she corrected.

I shook my head. "Nah, I just don't feel like it."

One of her perfectly plucked eyebrows rose. "You're going. No arguments. You haven't had a proper American cheeseburger for three years. I'm taking you out, that's the end of it."

I laughed humorlessly, knowing there was no arguing with this girl—she always got her way and she knew it. Besides, I actually could do with thinking about something else, even if it was only for an hour or two. I sighed, resigned. "Okay, fine. You had me at cheeseburger."

"Atta girl." She grinned. "Oh, but how about you have a shower first? No offense, Ellie, but…you stink." She playfully waved a manicured hand under her nose.

"Cheeky git!" I laughed.

"'Cheeky git'? Aww, you've picked up cute little British cuss words!" she gushed.

I grinned and rolled my eyes as I pushed myself to my feet. I dipped my head and sniffed in the direction of my armpit. I hadn't showered since London, simply hadn't made the time or felt like it. Four days and one long-ass plane ride. She was right, I smelled pretty ripe. "Eww, I'll go shower," I muttered, wrinkling my nose in distaste.

CHAPTER 9

JAMIE

THE FLOOR AND walls in my second-most-used office quivered in time with the thumping bass of the music being played downstairs. Red's, the newest acquisition in my club line, had benefited from a full sound system upgrade as well as an aesthetic makeover in the last couple of months. I thought a refurb would bring in classier frat boys who spent more on their booze, and it meant I could up the door price. But with the music making my whiskey vibrate with impact tremors similar to those in the movie *Jurassic Park*, I was thinking I'd made a huge fucking mistake. I couldn't concentrate, which meant I'd have to redo all this shit tomorrow. This place wasn't just used as a means of income—as far as my income went, it was way down the list of high earners—but the eight clubs and bars I owned across the city did serve a purpose: laundering some of the money from my less-than-legal ventures. I just had to get a little creative with the paperwork and let my extremely overpaid accountant take care of the rest.

As one song seamlessly morphed into another, I groaned and closed my eyes, reaching up and massaging my temples in small circles. Tomorrow I'd put in orders to have the office sound-proofed.

A knock at the door interrupted my internal grumblings. "What?" I barked, leaning forward and picking up my drink.

Dodger stuck his head around the door. "Alberto Salazar is here. His car just pulled up outside."

"Okay. Have Ed show him up here, will ya?" I replied.

A frown lined his forehead. "Looks like he brought Mateo with him." He practically spat the name, his loathing glaringly apparent.

"Oh, great." I snorted, raising the glass to my lips and throwing the amber liquid into my mouth, swallowing the whole thing in one gulp and reveling in the burn, warming all the way down to my stomach. I'd requested a meeting with the elder Salazar brother, not his sociopath sibling. Mateo was a loose cannon with a reputation for being both reckless and ruthless. He had a crazed look in his eye most of the time, like he was envisioning twenty different ways to kill you. I'd heard rumors about him, a lot of fucked-up rumors, not the least of which was about his penchant for little girls who had a couple of years to go before becoming legal. Mateo Salazar was the one person in this world I would love to shoot right between the eyes. I would happily do time for it too, because assholes like him shouldn't be allowed to walk the streets, but taking him out would start a turf war that I simply couldn't get my crew involved in.

I met Dodger's eyes and could see the concern there. He was worried about this, and probably rightly so. The last time I'd been in close quarters with Mateo, the little prick had tried to kill me—pointed a gun at me and everything. Being in a crowded place would definitely be safer on this occasion. "Tell you what, seeing as that junkie bastard came too, let's have the meeting downstairs," I suggested thoughtfully.

Dodger visibly relaxed at my suggestion, his shoulders losing some of the tension. "Good thinking."

I stood and picked up my favorite automatic switchblade, pushing it into the pocket of my dress pants before walking over to Dodger. I wasn't one for carrying guns—I had guys I paid for that particular task—but there was no way I was going to be near Mateo and not have at least something on me. "Come on then, buddy. Let's go remind the little pricks who runs this town." I gripped his shoulder, squeezing a couple of times in a supportive gesture. Dodger really hated this side of the business; he was into the cars, but he'd tried to convince me several times over to leave the other stuff alone and let the other organizations pick up the slack. But it wasn't in me to do half-assed jobs.

As we walked down the stairs, the music grew louder. Once in the club I looked around, taking in all the crowds of people. Carl, one of the security guys who stood at the bottom of my office stairwell and stopped people from going upstairs, dipped his head in greeting. "Boss."

I stepped closer to him, motioning with my chin toward a table over on the other side of the club, barely visible through the hordes of people around me who were all having a good time and spending their hard-earned cash. The table was at the opposite end of the club from the DJ and the five-foot speakers that were mounted on the stage. It was currently occupied by six women sharing a bottle of the cheap house white.

"Carl, get that table empty for me, will ya? Give them a couple of bottles of champagne for their trouble," I instructed. There were other tables free, but that one would be the best option—quieter, off to the side, but still within the thick of the club so Mateo would keep himself in check.

"Sure thing."

"There'll be some other security up in here in a bit. I have a meeting, so you just hang back and keep your eye on the crowds as usual. All right?" I instructed. Carl was just security, hired because of his massive stature, someone to prevent trouble in the clubs.

I watched him walk over to the table, flashing his best smile as he declared that the ladies needed to vacate the table because Mr. Cole himself needed it. I didn't hang around any longer, but wove my way through the throng of people, skirting the edge of the dance floor, saying hello to anyone I recognized, politely refusing a couple of drink offers from regular customers who I should know by name, but didn't.

"Want me to sit in on the meeting?" Ed offered, coming to my side when I finally made it to the coatroom.

I shook my head. "Dodger and I can handle it."

I didn't miss the disappointed twitch to his eye or how his jaw clenched. Ed hated that I didn't let him get too involved in the organization; I was pretty sure he resented me for taking over Brett's crew and bumping him way down the ranks. He was old enough to be my father, after all. It probably irked him to no end to have a boss almost half his age telling him what to do and demoting him. Too fucking bad.

His mouth opened, probably to protest and tell me again how useful he could be and that he'd like to be more involved in things, but that was when the door opened and the Salazar brothers, along with three of their crew, sauntered in.

Alberto entered first—tall, lean, and confident—striding toward me with his hand outstretched. I raised one eyebrow and looked down at his hand incredulously, then back up to his face, not bothering to reciprocate the polite gesture. He'd been selling on my turf; I hadn't summoned him for polite gestures. After a couple of seconds, he obviously came to that conclusion too and dropped his hand to his side.

"Kid Cole, nice to see you again," he greeted me, his native Mexican accent thick in his words.

I didn't answer, just looked past him at his brother. Mateo didn't stand as tall as Alberto or have his build, but there was something about him, maybe the way he carried himself, that put me at unease. I had always been skilled at reading people, and my gut told me that Mateo would rather kill me than look at me. There was just something off about him. If it weren't for his brother's influence he probably would have disrespected our boundary agreement a long time ago.

Mateo's brown eyes locked on mine, a hint of amusement dancing there; a black teardrop tattoo at the outer corner of his right eye was prominent against his olive skin, as was the large spider tattooed on the side of his neck. When he reached up and scratched at his jaw, I saw the thin black lines inked like tally marks on the side of his left pointer finger—his trigger finger. Rumor had it each line represented a murder he had committed. I counted two sets of five and one single line there. It seemed he'd been busy since the last time I saw him. There had been nine there a couple of months ago when he'd pointed that gun at me.

Mateo didn't speak, his lip curled slightly with disrespect as I looked him over, assessing whether I would have problems with him today. He was slightly twitchy, as usual, a by-product of his heroin addiction no doubt, but he looked like he was in control of himself.

I turned my attention back to Alberto. "Did you have to bring *that* with you?" I asked, jerking my chin at Mateo, ignoring the snarl and the string of Spanish expletives that were thrown at me from his direction.

Alberto shrugged, a smile tugging at the corners of his lips. "Can't trust him to be left alone," he joked. I snorted a laugh. At least we were both being honest. I didn't like Alberto and the way he practiced his business or peddled his cheap product, but at least he was honorable and, usually, true to his word.

"No weapons allowed in the club. If you're carrying, then you can leave them here and collect them on the way out," I stated, waving one of my security guards forward.

Mateo frowned, his hand going to the weapon under his brown leather jacket, but Alberto nodded and instantly reached inside his own jacket, pulling out a black semiautomatic and placing it in the tray the security guard carried over. His crew followed suit, putting their weapons in the tray. Mateo still hadn't made a move.

I raised one eyebrow, pulling back my shoulders, daring him to make the move his eyes were telling me he wanted to make.

Dodger stepped forward. "If you prefer, you can go play with your gun in the car while the big boys have their meeting," he suggested, his tone condescending. I grinned over at him.

A couple of seconds passed before Alberto turned to his brother, uttering something in his native tongue that I didn't understand. Mateo's jaw twitched in anger, but he removed his ivory-handled pistol and matching knife, placing them on top of the other weapons, his eyes filled with longing as he watched the guard walk off with them into the security office.

"Perfect. Follow me, then." I turned without waiting and walked back through the double doors and into the main area of the packed club, heading to the table I'd requested Carl clear.

The waitress, a slim girl with golden-tanned skin and raven-black hair, came over almost immediately, weaving through the crowd and silently setting a bottle of whiskey and four filled glasses on our table before sauntering off.

I eyed Mateo, who was eyeing the retreating waitress. "Thought you'd been picked up yesterday," I said, selecting a drink and taking a sip.

Mateo rolled his shoulders as his gaze met mine. "They didn't have enough to hold me."

I'd heard from my source inside the police that Mateo had been arrested for aggravated assault the previous day. From what I'd been told, it was an open-and-shut case with several witnesses to attest it was him who shoved a pool cue all the way through his opponent's thigh because he'd lost the frame to him.

"Oh, really? Shame." Was a fucking shame, too.

A cocky grin spread across his face. "Turns out the witnesses changed their minds about making statements."

Alberto sat forward, cupping his glass between his palms. "Look, can we get down to why you asked me to come here tonight? All this pussyfooting around is just wasting time, and I'm sure both of us have better things we could be doing."

Straight to business; I liked that. "Fine," I agreed, turning my full attention back to him. "I want you to stay the fuck out of my clubs. The next time you send pushers into my place of business and disrespect me like that I'm going to bring down a shitstorm on you so bad you won't even know what happened. You know your boundaries. We allow you to sell your shit on the city streets, within reason." I leaned forward, looking directly into his eyes so he knew I meant every word of what I was saying. "If you cross the line again, I will take everything you've built and make it fall down around you. Don't think I don't know where you cook your shit up. One phone call and I can have people there in a matter of minutes to firebomb your labs to the ground. I'd like to see how you conduct your business then."

His eye twitched while I said my piece. "Now, Kid, let's be reasonable."

I sat back in my chair, picking up my drink, watching him

over the rim of it. "Reasonable," I repeated. "So you think I'm being *unreasonable* somehow?"

He flinched slightly, his shoulders stiffening at the threat in my voice. He knew I could crush him in the blink of an eye. "Not unreasonable, no," he backtracked. "I just think you're not even considering how good a partnership between us could be."

I had to laugh at that. "What exactly do I have to gain from joining forces with a liability like you two?" I poured another drink, shaking my head in amusement.

The hordes of people near our table were getting slightly rowdier now, a couple of the guys whooping and chinking their bottles in a toast. I glanced over, and almost instantly, a flash of copper at the back of the group farthest away from me, over near the podium, caught my attention. Even in the darkened club, the color was like a beacon, calling to me, grabbing my attention and holding it.

Oh, shit. It can't be. There's no way it is. She can't be here...can she?

My glass stopped halfway to my lips as I squinted through the crowd, willing the red-haired girl to turn toward me, even just a fraction so I could get a glimpse of her face. Was it her?

Turn around. Please turn...

"Well, we have built up a fairly large following," Alberto said, dragging me back to reality.

Dodger snorted. "A following? You make yourself sound like some sort of freaking cult."

I swallowed and blinked a couple of times, forcefully dragging my eyes away from the redhead girl's back even though it took everything in me to do it. "I don't care how big your client list is. We have our own clients, high-end ones. We don't need to occupy ourselves with people who deal on the street. I've told you that before."

"Ah, but our overheads are far less than yours, I bet. We make twice as much profit per ounce as you," Alberto protested. "If you were to purchase our product and pass it on to your clients, we would both profit from it."

"That's because your product is cheap-ass shit. My clients wouldn't be my clients very long if I tried to give them levamisole-cut coke," I replied calmly. We'd had this discussion before; my answer had been the same then.

Without my permission, my eyes drifted back in the girl's direction. I watched the way her hair swished as she danced, the way her black jeans hugged her hips and the curve of her ass. I fidgeted in my seat, willing her to turn. And suddenly, as if she could tell I was staring at her, waiting with bated breath to see if this was the girl I'd fallen so deeply in love with, she and the tall blonde bombshell she was dancing with linked arms and did a little drunken twirl, giggling to themselves.

Air rushed out of my lungs as my eyes landed on the girl who had stolen my heart with one innocent blush and beautiful smile. Ellie had always captivated me, even the first time I laid eyes on her, and three years later it was no different. She was stunning, so beautiful that it made my heart sing. To me, she was perfect. Everything about her was mesmerizing, from her bright red hair to her freckled nose, right down to her Converse-loving feet. The girl was still everything right in my world.

I couldn't take my eyes from her. I watched as she clinked glasses with her friend, who I now realized was, in fact, Stacey, and they both then downed the contents. I was unable to fight the smile as Ellie instantly winced and brought her hand to her mouth, pressing the back of it to her lips for a couple of seconds and wrinkling her nose like she always did after a shot. I'd missed that. Such a small thing, but even that made my heart ache and my balls clench.

"Kid?" Alberto's voice was almost a distant memory as I watched Ellie, entranced.

Stacey glanced behind her and then turned back to Ellie, grinning and grabbing her hand, tugging her toward one of the podiums. They were just small raised stages that we sometimes had dancers in on Saturday nights, but on regular weekday nights, they were empty and girls liked to go up there for a bit of extra space to dance. Ellie was reluctant at first, shaking her head as a furious blush colored her cheeks, which I could easily make out even from the other side of the club in the dim light. I smiled. She never had liked being the center of attention. But Stacey was adamant and boosted herself up onto the four-foot podium, beckoning Ellie with a pleading expression until Ellie finally gave in and climbed up, too.

"Kid!" The voice was louder this time, so I turned, scowling at Alberto.

"What?" I snapped. Couldn't he see I was fucking busy?

He raised one bushy black eyebrow. "Is everything okay? You seem kind of distracted." His tone was clipped; clearly he was angered that I wasn't giving him my full attention.

Mateo sat forward, his eyes locked on Ellie, who was now dancing on the podium, her movements shy because people were watching. "You know that girl?"

"No," I answered immediately, my reply coming out harsher than I'd intended. "Nice ass, that's all," I lied, shrugging, willing them to believe me.

Mateo sat back in his chair, and a slow smile spread across his face, drawing attention to the white scar that ran through his bottom lip. "She has got a sweet ass," he agreed, reaching for his drink and taking a slow sip. His sharp, keen eyes locked onto mine, twinkling with what appeared to be excitement.

I gripped the edge of the table so tightly my fingers ached, trying not to react. I needed to remain in control, not show any emotions or how important Ellie was to me. I ran the city because people knew not to challenge me—they always had more to lose than I did. I didn't have anything I cared about, so there was never any leverage for people to use against me. It didn't matter to me if I lived or died, because I had nothing worth living for anyway. That loneliness made me hard, confident, overly cocky, and practically invincible. I was less afraid than people who had more to lose than I did. That couldn't change.

"Let's just get on with this, shall we? I called you here to tell you to keep your drugs far away from my clubs. I think I've made my point clear, so this meeting is over," I growled.

Alberto sighed deeply, shaking his head. "Look, Kid, I apologize if one of our pushers came into your club. I don't know who it was, but I'll find out and they'll be punished. We didn't order it, so it was probably just a rogue seller wanting to make a few bucks extra by selling in a club. Can we not let this sour the relationship we already have?"

Mateo was totally uninterested now and was tapping away on his cell phone, a wry smile on his face that I wanted to smack off for him.

"We don't have a relationship. I allow you to conduct your business. You're grateful," I answered drily. I was fighting a losing battle to keep my eyes from Ellie. My whole body was jumpy, twitching in my seat, desperate to get up and go over to her. I gripped the table tighter to keep myself in place.

"But it can be so much more. We can help you. We have the numbers and can bring so much to your organization," Alberto urged.

"So much fucking butt hurt you mean," Dodger chimed in.

"Now, don't be like that," Alberto implored.

From the corner of my eye, I saw a tall, well-built man

making his way through the crowd, heading toward Ellie. He stopped at the side of her podium. My lip curled and my hands unconsciously clenched into fists. The guy was tall, well over six foot five, so his face was level with the girls' chests as he leaned in and said something to them. Stacey laughed and shook her head; Ellie looked blatantly uncomfortable.

Around me I could hear Dodger and Alberto talking, but I couldn't focus, couldn't drag my attention from the steroid-filled brick shithouse who was still leaning in and trying to get Ellie's attention.

My body jerked when his meaty hand reached toward her, brushing against Ellie's hip. She twisted to the side, shaking her head, saying something to rebuff his advance as she shot him a nervous, please-go-away smile.

The crowd around them had parted now, giving him space, looking at him a little warily, as if he was intoxicated and needed a wide berth. He said something else to Ellie and she frowned, shaking her head again. I could almost read her lips saying "no, thank you" before she turned her back on him and continued to dance with Stacey, her shoulders stiff now, her movements awkward and uncomfortable.

The guy wasn't giving up, though; he clearly didn't like to take no for an answer. He laughed and shoved his hand into his pocket, pulling out a couple of dollar bills. I frowned, grinding my teeth, assuming he was going to offer to buy her a drink. Instead, he reached up and tapped her on the shoulder. When she turned, her tight smile polite but exasperated, he quickly reached forward and shoved the notes into the waistband of her jeans like she was some kind of stripper as he clapped exaggeratedly along to the music and jeered in encouragement.

That was when I saw red.

All rational thought flew from my head. All I could see was

his hands on her, her being disrespected, him degrading her. I sprang from my chair, sending it flying in the process, and bounded over there. Ellie was busy yanking the money from her waistband, her scowl seething, so she didn't see me approach.

Neither did he as he jeered encouragingly, laughing. "Oh, come on, sugar tits, show us how you dance real nice."

He barely finished his sentence before my fist collided with the back of his head, sending him sprawling forward onto his knees, his chest hitting the podium with a loud thunk. My hand burned from the impact, but I barely felt it as I strode forward another step, throwing my knee into his side twice, hearing the satisfying grunt of pain that left his lips. All around me was red fog; there was just me and him and my blazing anger. I wanted him to bleed, I wanted to pull my knife from my pocket and slit his throat, watching as he gurgled for breath, but some small part of me was conscious of the spectating crowd. So instead, I fisted my left hand in his hair, yanked his head back, and brought my right fist down square into his face.

His nose gushed with blood on the first strike, the skin above his cheekbone split on the second, his hands came up to weakly defend himself on the third, and his lip burst open on the fourth. Anger made my blood boil. I drew in ragged breaths as I threw my bloodied fist into his face a fifth time. His body had gone limp now, wobbling on his knees as his arms dropped to his sides and his eyes fell vacant. I untwisted my hand from his hair, and his body slid to the ground with a dull thud, blood running from his face and dripping onto the hardwood floor I'd had installed only a couple of months ago.

All around me, people had stopped moving. Shocked faces looked on, watching the scene with morbid interest. The rage was subsiding a little as I glared down at the guy's battered, un-conscious body. A shiver of unease ran up my spine as I looked past the blood on his face. I recognized him: one of the men who had come here with the Salazars. My gaze flicked to his bare forearm for confirmation, and sure enough, there was his crew ink: the snake wrapped around a dagger with the letter *S* carved into the hilt of it.

My eyes darted to the table I'd vacated. Dodger was standing, his expression wary as he looked over at me; Alberto was on his feet too, eyes wide and shocked, but Mateo—Mateo was watching the scene before him with his arms folded across his chest and a shit-eating grin plastered on his smug face.

That was when it hit me. Mateo had been on his cell phone, obviously telling this guy to come and harass Ellie to see if he could get a rise out of me. He hadn't believed me when I said I didn't know her. Mateo had orchestrated this whole thing, and I had played right into his hands.

I'd fucked up. Badly.

I turned back to Ellie, noting she was still on the podium, her body now perfectly still as she stared down at me, her face ashen, her mouth agape. She looked as though she'd seen a ghost.

"Get down. Now!" I barked.

She gulped, her eyes locked onto mine. "Jamie?" she whispered.

CHAPTER 10

ELLIE

BLOOD, FISTS FLYING, grunts of pain, shrieks from people around me as the guy who seconds before had pushed money into the waist of my jeans and called me a *puta*, which I was pretty sure was Spanish for "whore," slumped to the ground, unconscious.

Stacey's fingers bit into my arm, trying to tug me backward, closer to her, but my body was fused to the spot as my eyes took in every detail about *him*. And it definitely was him, even though I'd doubted myself for a couple of heartbeats. But no, I'd recognize that face anywhere, despite the fact that his beautiful features were still twisted with rage, like some sort of wrathful avenging angel come to save me in my hour of need.

He was breathing rapidly, staring down at the guy he'd just beaten with such contempt it practically rippled from his body. Then his head snapped up, and he turned to face me.

The second my eyes met his I forgot how to breathe.

Jamie Cole.

In that moment, everything else seemed to stop. I no longer

heard the music that had been thrumming around us; all I could see was him and those eyes, the ones I'd stared into for hours on end, the ones I knew every fleck of color in, that rich chocolate brown that drew me in and melted my heart all those years ago. My lips parted, my throat suddenly tight as I let my gaze wander quickly over him.

His hair was different from the last time I saw him; it was kind of messy, curling out around his ears and the nape of his neck as if it needed a trim. He had scruff on his jaw. Fading bruises were visible on his cheek and the side of his neck. A three-inch scar sliced just above his eyebrow—another to add to his extensive collection. My finger twitched; even after all this time, after all the hurt he'd caused me, I still wanted to reach out and touch that scar, to trace my finger across it and ask him how it happened.

But the thing that was most apparent as I looked at him was that he'd changed.

This man standing before me in his white-collared shirt and black dress pants, with his knuckles dripping someone else's blood onto the hardwood floor, wasn't the boy I once knew. Something had altered him, hardened him, ruined him.

His posture was stiff, imposing, aggressive, furious even. An unconscious man lay at his feet, beaten and broken, and I didn't see one inch of regret on Jamie's face. I'd never seen him like that. The darkness swirling in his eyes made my stomach clench.

"Get down. Now!" he growled.

I gulped, trying to swallow around the lump in my throat. "Jamie?" My voice barely worked and it came out as more of a whisper, but he heard. His jaw twitched again; he shifted his stance slightly, but his eyes never left mine.

My body was numb, my brain struggling to catch up. He was

here. I was face-to-face with the boy I'd cried myself to sleep over for months on end. Seeing him now, so unexpectedly, I had all of those feelings come crashing back at once, swallowing me up and spitting me back out again. Crushing me, throwing me right back into that sea of hurt that I'd struggled to drag myself out of.

This man in front of me was the reason I hadn't come back home. I never wanted this meeting to take place, I never wanted to look into those eyes again because then I'd have to find the strength to be without him all over again, and I wasn't sure I could do it twice.

"Get down now!" he repeated, his tone sharp and commanding.

My eyes began to sting with tears and I fought them as memories of us and our good times surrounded me like a smack in the face. I'd loved this boy unconditionally; I'd loved everything about him, even the bad parts that I didn't understand. He had me, body and soul, and he threw us away because of a stupid mistake. My heart squeezed painfully in my chest.

His posture was tense as he flicked a quick glance over his shoulder. "Ellie, get down from there, will you? Jesus fucking Christ, will you just do as I say?" he demanded, thrusting his hand toward me so he could help me down from the podium Stacey had made me climb.

But as I stared down at him, my feelings suddenly changed. My shock at seeing him suddenly morphed into intense anger. *He's just beaten a guy to a pulp even though I was handling it perfectly fine on my own, and now he has the audacity to make demands of me... after what he did to me?*

My hands clenched into fists, and I opened my mouth to say some of the witty things I'd concocted over the years, comebacks I should have said to him on the phone that day instead of begging him to give me another chance, but before I could speak, he stepped forward and grabbed me, pulling me to him effortlessly. And then I was tipping upside down, my body draped over his shoulder, my ass in the air as his arm wrapped around my thighs, holding me in place as my face bumped against the small of his back.

I squealed from the shock, blood instantly rushing to my head, and all I could see were shoes and the injured guy who lay on the floor. I gasped, feeling my face glow with embarrassed heat.

"Hey!" Stacey shouted from the podium.

The surrounding crowds of feet parted as Jamie turned, walking through them with me draped over his shoulder like a sack of potatoes, my body bumping against him with each step he took.

Anger rippled inside me with a ferocity I wasn't even aware I still possessed. "Put me the hell down, asshole!" I screamed, wriggling, kicking my legs and banging my fists against his back. "Get off me! Jamie Cole, put me the fuck down right now!" I demanded, grasping at anything I could, digging my nails into his back in a bid to get his attention.

He'd made it less than ten steps when one of my flailing legs connected with something, possibly the side of his face, and he stopped walking. I took that as my opportunity and wriggled harder, pushing against his back, futilely trying to get myself upright again so I could shimmy down.

"Take your hands off me!" I pinched the skin at his side, still bucking like a horse trying to get free.

"Ugh, fine! Fucking calm down!" He bent his knees, tugging on my legs so I shifted on his shoulder. His grip on me loosened as my feet touched the floor. I gripped his shoulders, using them for leverage as I pushed myself upright, taking a second to adjust to being back the right way up. His hands were still on my hips, holding me steady as he straightened, standing full height, looking down at me with hardened features and blazing eyes.

He's pissed right now, seriously pissed.

I pulled back my shoulders, shoving his hands off me and taking a step back to get some personal space. My head was all over the place as I absentmindedly attempted to fix my hair, which was sure to be an absolute mess after that ruckus.

I glared at him. I was pissed, too. "Seriously, what's wrong with you? You just storm over and start fighting in the middle of a club like a freaking delinquent, and then you have the audacity to touch me? You don't get to touch me, not anymore. You have no right!" My words came out harsher than I'd even intended. Years of hurt pooled into them, making them acidic and bitchy.

"Ellie," he said, his eyebrows pulling together in concentration. His lips moved, but nothing else came out as he huffed out a breath and raked a hand through his hair. The soft caress of his voice around my name made my heart stutter. I never thought I would hear this boy say my name again. Even though I didn't want it to, the sound of it set butterflies loose in my stomach.

I shook my head. He had no damn right to cause butterflies, not after breaking my heart, and my traitorous body should be with me on this one. *Bitch.* "Three years of silence, and then you just walk over and think you can pick me up and carry me around like a freaking caveman?" I pointed my finger at him, trying to even out my breathing. The anger was dissipating and I could feel my emotions swelling inside me, threatening to spill out. "You don't get to do that, Jamie. You don't get to pretend like nothing happened and swoop in like some knight in shining armor. You don't get to pretend that you didn't break my heart. You just don't." By the time I got to the last word, it was almost a whisper and my eyes were brimming with tears.

I couldn't do this anymore, I couldn't stand here in front of him and hold it together. Tears were imminent, and I refused to show him a single one. Behind him, I could see Stacey climbing down from the podium, making her way over. I turned on my heel, my eyes finding the exit, knowing she'd follow me out. I was just about to take a step when a hand closed around my wrist and I was pulled back, my body colliding with his.

I gasped, looking up into Jamie's face. His eyes were heated, his jaw set as he stepped even closer to me, his grip on my wrist steely as his other hand came up to cup the side of my face, his fingertips threading into my hair. I didn't have any time to react before his mouth covered mine.

I squeaked, my body going rigid as he pressed against me. His warmth seeped into me as his lips brushed softly against mine. The kiss was over in an instant, but he didn't pull back. His nose brushed against mine as his breath fanned down across my lips and chin. He released my wrist, his hand sliding to cover my hip instead, the move giving me the opportunity to step away if I so wished. But I didn't.

My body reacted of its own accord, my breath coming out in shallow gasps as I arched, pressing against every rock-hard inch of him. His body was so taut, firm, warm, and familiar that my heart raced in my chest. I stared at his mouth, at lips that had explored every inch of my body so lovingly, at the mouth that had whispered *I love you* while I was wrapped in his arms. A groan of longing built in my throat as I stared at that mouth.

Everything was forgotten: the pain, the heartache, the tears, the club we were in, the people watching; everything was gone in an instant, and I was lost in him.

So when his lips brushed mine for a second time, my eyes fluttered closed and I kissed him back, rejoicing in the blissful feelings a simple kiss from him could create. He groaned against my lips, his hand sliding around to my back, holding me tightly against him. A wave of longing and desperation hit me full force, so I gripped a fistful of his shirt, holding on for dear life as the kiss grew in intensity.

My legs weakened, but his strong hold around my waist kept me in place as the passion inside me spiked to levels it hadn't reached in years. It was an all-consuming, *I need to have you inside me now* passion, almost painful it was so immense. It was a passion only Jamie had ever evoked in me.

When his lips parted and his tongue gently brushed across my bottom lip and an ache of longing built in my chest, I realized I hadn't been kissed like this since Jamie. This want, this absolute need and desperation to be closer to someone, was something I'd only ever experienced with him. Toby had never made me *feel* this much, not with a kiss, not with an hour spent exploring each other's naked bodies, not ever.

And as soon as his name entered my head, everything was over.

Toby. My fiancé. The guy who had given me a job and a reason to stay in England when I was so desperate not to go home, the guy who'd fixed me, the one who made me laugh when all I could see was darkness. Sweet, adorable, dependable Toby who absolutely did not deserve this.

The passion was gone in an instant, replaced by an anger so bright it made my palms itch.

Sliding my arms up between us, I shoved Jamie away from

me, sucking in a couple of ragged breaths. Rage burned within me, heating my entire body. Without even knowing what I was doing, my hand came up and I slapped him across the face. Hard. The watching crowd gasped, their eyes wide and excited. I could see Stacey behind Jamie, her mouth open, her shock evident.

Jamie's head whipped to the side with the force of the blow, but other than that small movement he didn't react at all. Anger made my vision blurry, or maybe that was the tears that I could no longer hold at bay.

"You asshole! I'm engaged! You can't just kiss me like that anymore. You had your chance and you blew it! You blew it, Jamie," I shouted. I shook my head, dropping my eyes to the floor because I couldn't look at his wounded expression for another second. "I honestly don't know how you have the gall to even approach me, let alone kiss me after all this time," I said. "Just leave me alone. I have enough shit to deal with without you coming in to complicate things and stir up stuff that belongs in the past."

I turned and ran through the crowd, pushing my way through the gyrating people on the dance floor who were completely oblivious to any scenes that had happened at the back of the club, my eyes firmly locked on the green glowing sign with the words EMERGENCY EXIT on it. I ran away from him and, I thought, my problems. But as I burst through the fire escape door and into the dark, trash-filled alley at the side of the club, I realized that my problems were rooted deep within me and no amount of running would help.

I stopped and leaned against the cold brick wall, my fury still raging as I struggled to catch my breath. But as the fresh air dried my tears and new ones replaced them, it hit me that my anger wasn't even directed at Jamie, not really. It was directed at me. He'd just been the scapegoat because it was easier to project it than take responsibility.

I'd kissed him back. That was what I was angry about. I'd kissed him back even though I was engaged to someone else. And I'd loved every freaking second of it. I hated myself for that.

CHAPTER 11

JAMIE

I WATCHED HER back disappear into the crowd, heading toward the side door to the club. My left cheek stung. She'd given me a damn good strike, but the slight pain was nothing compared to seeing the disdain in her eyes as she looked at me. I hadn't been prepared for how much she would hate me. Seeing that look made my whole body cold.

"You had your chance, and you blew it," she'd said. And I had, I really had. I'd given up the best thing that had ever happened to me. But not for the reasons she thought. She thought I'd cheated, she thought I didn't love her, she thought I didn't want her, and of course she did; those exact words had come from my lips. But the reality of it was, nothing could be further from the truth. I had always loved and wanted her. She was my life. I had just been trying to save her from wasting her time on someone who didn't deserve her.

Right now, watching her copper hair disappear through the exit door, I wondered if I'd made a huge mistake all those years ago. Maybe I should have told her the truth, asked her to wait for me, and then once I was out, we could have built a life together if she was still willing. Maybe I'd been wrong to take the choice away from her.

I ground my teeth. I could still feel the ghost of her lips on mine, still feel the warmth of her body in my arms, her taste on my tongue. God, I'd missed her more than I'd even allowed myself to admit.

Before I even had a chance to think about it, I was on the move, heading after her.

"Hey!" Stacey cried behind me, her hand closing around my upper arm. I stopped and turned to look at her, meeting her icy stare. "Where the hell do you think you're going? You've done enough, don't you think?" she snapped, stepping in front of me, blocking my path to Ellie.

I frowned, my eyes flicking behind her as I watched the door swing closed and click into place. "I just need to talk to her."

She crossed her arms over her chest and raised one eyebrow. "You have some nerve, Jamie, you really do. She doesn't want to talk to you!"

"Look, Stacey, you can kill me with your eyes all you want, but I'm going out there to talk to her and you're going to let me, or I'm going to have one of my staff come over and restrain you," I warned.

"You really are a douchebag. I saw what you two had, how you were together. She would have done anything for you, and you just threw it all away and broke her heart. She might not want to tell you how much of an asshole you are, but I have no problem saying it. You, Jamie Cole, are a prize dick, and she's better off without you."

A small laugh escaped my lips at the words and the venom that went into them. Stacey hated me—that was glaringly apparent. But she'd never be able to hate me as much as I hated myself.

"Straight to the point, no mincing your words. I always liked that about you," I replied. I bent to look in her eyes before she could make the bitchy comeback I could see brewing. "Look, you're a good friend, and Ellie is lucky to have you, but I told you I'm going out there to talk to her whether you like it or not."

I signaled Ed, who had begun walking over to me earlier but had stopped a few feet away, and nodded toward Stacey. "Hold this one for five minutes. In five minutes you can let her go," I ordered, sidestepping as Ed instantly reached for her, wrapping his large hands around her upper arms, holding her in place as he whistled for one of the security guards to come over and help restrain her.

Ignoring Stacey's roar of protest and struggles behind me, I headed for the door, stopping next to Carl and digging into my pocket for my car keys. "Get my car and bring it to the side alley. There'll be two girls out there in a few minutes who will need a ride. I want you to drive them and make sure they get home safely. Understand?"

He nodded, so I dropped the keys into his outstretched palm and pushed on through the door and into the alley. I squinted into the darkness, letting my eyes adjust to the dimness of the night. I heard her before I saw her. She was on the other side of the alley, leaning against the wall, crying softly.

My heart sank at the sound. I hated the fact that she was sad and that I'd been the cause of it. She looked up as the door opened, her posture stiffening as she reached up to swipe at her eyes.

"I told you to leave me alone," she snapped, anger still fizzing in her tone.

"I just wanted to come and see if you were okay. I didn't want to leave things like that," I said. "We have too much history for those to be the last words between us."

She sniffed and looked down at her hands, but didn't say anything else. I'd never seen her so low. Ellie was usually such a bright spirit, soaring high, but now it was like her wings had been clipped. All I wanted to do was close the distance between us and wrap my arms around her, shield her from all the hurt, be there to support her. My whole body ached seeing her so sad.

"This is kinda awkward. I mean, what are you supposed to say to the guy who cheated on you and left you to fend for yourself in a foreign country?" she asked, her voice sarcastic as she stared at the floor.

Her words cut like a knife because none of it was true. I cleared my throat, hoping my voice would work. "Um…how about, 'Hi, how are you?'" I joked, just trying to lighten the atmosphere a little.

She laughed softly, but it was humorless, not one of her heartfelt laughs or the little giggle that I loved to death. The weight of the world was inside that laugh, and all I wanted to do was lift it off her.

I sighed and walked to her side, leaning on the wall next to her. I wished I could close the gap, take her hand, stroke the back of it, raise it to my mouth, and kiss her fingertips. I missed the closeness we used to have, even with just the simplest contact. I hadn't had that intimacy with anyone else. Since her, it just didn't appeal. It was Ellie or nothing.

"It is awkward," I admitted. "Look, I'm sorry I kissed you, all right? I was shocked to see you. I hadn't ever expected you to be in my club and I just…I don't even know…you were there, and I hadn't seen you in so long, and you looked so beautiful, and you were walking away from me, and I couldn't let you. I just…" I stopped talking, frowning down at the floor because I couldn't express myself properly. I always rambled and said the wrong thing when I was around her.

Silence hung in the air and stretched on for what seemed like forever, the only sounds the muted music creeping through the door, until finally she spoke. "Red's is your club?" she questioned, obviously choosing to ignore my "you looked so beautiful" remark.

"Yeah," I replied, waving my hand at the posters stuck on the side of the building, advertising upcoming themed or party nights. The logo of the club blazed from the top—a redheaded girl in a white crop top and red shorts, holding a tray of drinks while winking seductively. Ellie didn't say anything, and I wondered if she picked up the significance of the name or the beautiful red-haired girl I'd had drawn there. "I have a few bars across town and couple in Queens too, but this one is my favorite," I said.

She licked her lips slowly, seeming to be deep in thought. "So you're not into stealing cars anymore, then?"

"Not tonight," I answered, sidestepping the truth.

Her nose scrunched up, her lips twisted in thought. "What happened to you, Jamie? You wanted out of all this stuff. You said you wanted to go straight…or was that just a lie, too?" she asked, her eyes meeting mine.

You happened. Brett happened. Everything happened. Nothing happened.

I shrugged. "I guess I lost my reason to change."

Her forehead creased with a frown, and she studied me carefully before speaking again. "Why did you come over and batter that guy? I was handling it myself. You didn't need to jump in and go all macho like that. Now you're bound to get in trouble for it."

I shrugged, not looking away as I answered truthfully. "I was jealous."

Her mouth popped open. "You have no right to be anymore."

"I know."

"I'm engaged," she continued.

"I know."

She swallowed awkwardly. "He's a really good guy; he takes care of me. I...I love him."

I nodded slowly, trying to keep the hurt from showing. "I know that, too."

Her eyebrows knitted together at my responses. "How could you possibly know that?"

I smiled ruefully, unsure how to admit that I was basically her stalker and that I had people check in on her to make sure she was happy. Thankfully, as if someone was sending me some sort of reprieve, the side door to the club squeaked open and I turned to see Ed standing there.

"It's been five minutes, Kid," he said.

I held up one finger. "I just need another minute or two," I answered, silently telling him to keep Stacey inside for a little longer. He nodded and went inside again, closing the door behind him.

I turned my attention back to Ellie. "I never thought I would see you again. You were traveling for so long that I figured you'd never come back."

She kicked at the wall with the heel of her sneaker, a small sob hitching in her throat. "Yeah, well, I had to come back."

Sighing, I reached up and dragged a hand through my hair, wanting to keep my hands busy because they were itching to touch her. "Yeah, I heard about what happened on the news. I'm so sorry about your dad." Loss and sadness swelled inside me. "He was one of the good guys."

She raised her chin, her eyes flicking up to the sky as she blinked a couple of times, probably trying to quell her tears. "Yeah. Sucks," she croaked.

I turned my head, watching her, taking in every mesmerizing inch of her, committing her to memory. If possible, she looked even more stunning than she had three years ago.

"How's your mom?" I asked, even though I already knew. I'd made a few calls, asked around, had people everywhere. I reached out, brushing my little finger against hers, reveling in that small touch of skin on skin, wishing I could steal more of it, but she whipped her hand away quickly, hugging herself across her middle.

Ellie scowled over at me. "As if you care. You never liked her."

I recoiled from her anger. She was like a little feral cat, poised and ready to strike. "I care, Ellie," I replied firmly. No, I had never liked the woman and the feeling was mutual, but I cared because she was important to Ellie. I would always care about things that had the power to hurt someone I loved.

She stared at me for a few seconds, her hard eyes locked on mine before they softened and her lip trembled and she closed her eyes. "She's in the hospital still. There's a ventilator helping her breathe. It's bad."

"I'm sorry," I whispered.

"Everyone always says that. Like it's their fault or something. Every person I called up and told about my dad today said sorry to me, every single one. I'm kind of sick of the word," she said.

I sighed and edged closer to her, noting how she didn't move away this time and how my arm gently pressed against her side. "Is there anything I can do to help you?"

She shook her head, the movement making our bodies brush against each other where we were so close. "I've done everything and arranged the funeral. There's not much left to do."

"You've made the funeral arrangements?" I questioned, hating that she had to do that and take responsibility for something so morbid.

"Yeah."

"When is it? I'd like to come, if that's okay." Michael Pearce had meant a lot to me, had always shown me kindness and treated me like I was one of the family. He'd never thought I wasn't good enough for his daughter.

She gasped and pushed away from the wall, rounding on me, her eyes furious again. "No. It's not okay. Toby will be there and everything else is going to be hard enough already."

"Ellie, please? You won't even know I'm there, I just want to pay my respects," I pressed.

Her mouth opened and closed a couple of times, her face un-decided, but before she could answer, a car pulled up at the end of the alley, my black BMW i8. Ellie and I both looked up at it at the same time. I held up one finger to Carl, who rolled down the window and nodded to me in understanding before rolling it back up again.

"Who's that?" Ellie asked.

"My driver. I've asked him to take you and Stacey home, I just wanted to talk to you first." I sighed and walked over to the metal door, banging my fist on it a couple of times. Moments later, the door swung outward, and I nodded to Ed, who was on the other side. He turned and motioned with his hand, and then a blur of blonde head shoved past me, deliberately bumping me with her shoulder as she stormed past, her face like thunder.

"Ellie!" she cried, going straight to her side and wrapping an arm around her shoulders before turning back to me. "You're an absolute asshole; I have half a mind to call the cops and tell them you held me there against my will."

Ellie frowned, looking between the two of us. "What?"

I raised one shoulder in a half shrug. "Carl will take you two home."

Stacey made some sort of snort and looked away from me distastefully.

I reached for the two girls' coats, which Ed was holding, and turned, passing them to Ellie, who smiled gratefully, slipping on hers and passing the other to Stacey.

"Thanks," Ellie muttered, turning toward the car, pulling Stacey along with her.

"Hey, Ellie?" I called to her retreating back. She turned, her red-rimmed eyes curious. "You didn't say if it was okay for me to attend the funeral or not."

Stacey's scowl deepened, but Ellie sighed and nodded. "You can come to the service, but I don't want you back at the house. It's three p.m. Friday at Everglade Drive."

I smiled gratefully. "Thank you."

I watched them get safely into the car and drive off before I turned back to Ed, who was still standing in the doorway. "The Salazars still here?"

"Yep. Dodger is with them. Mateo wanted to wait until you got back, apparently," he replied, holding out a paper towel to me. "Your hand is bleeding."

I nodded, taking it, and dabbed at the small cut that had opened up on my knuckle as I followed him back into the club. The music drummed around me as people danced and laughed, completely over the incident that had happened a few minutes before. I walked past a guy with his arm around a girl, a big grin on his face, and a wave of envy hit me. All around me people were with friends and lovers, and I was alone, as always. A week ago—hell, just four days ago—I wouldn't have even noticed this couple, but now here I was jealous of the guy because he had his girl and I didn't.

As we wove through the crowd, I spotted Dodger standing off to the side, talking to one of our crew. When he saw me he came over, his face a mask of concern. "Hey. All right, buddy?"

I nodded and looked past him to the Salazars, who were still sipping whiskey, though the bottle was now almost half gone. Sitting with them was the guy I'd knocked unconscious; he seemed a little dazed as he held a rag to his nose to stanch the blood flow.

"Come with me," I instructed. Dodger and Ed followed me to the table, and both the Salazar brothers looked up in unison. A slow grin spread across Mateo's face, his eyes locked onto mine, his posture slumped cockily in the chair.

"Why are you still hanging around? Was there something I forgot to say?" I snapped, looking at each of them in turn. The guy with the bloodied rag flinched in his chair, shying away from me. I turned back to Alberto. "This meeting is over. Take your prick of a friend who thinks it's okay to degrade women and get the hell out of my club. I don't want to see any of your scumbag dealers in my establishments again, you hear me?" My voice was thunderous, livid. I wanted this night over; I wanted the guy who dared put his hands on Ellie out of here before I finished what I'd started.

Alberto sighed and stood, and the other two followed suit immediately. He didn't speak as he turned and walked off, signaling for his crew to leave, too. I stood still, raising my chin and watching them carefully.

Mateo stopped in front of me, a huge smirk on his face. "Looks like Kid Cole does have a weakness after all."

I saw red again. Fuck, I saw all colors. Anger so extreme I could almost taste it flowed through me, and I reached out and grabbed him with both hands, yanking him closer to me. My face was so close to his I could see his pupils dilate and feel his whiskey breath on my face. "If you even look too long in her direction, I swear to God, I will beat you into the fucking ground," I growled, tightening my grip. "Don't fucking try me. I'll kill you, but first I'll kill your brother and make you watch," I promised.

Alberto had come up behind Mateo, pulling on his shoulder, his expression concerned as he tugged his brother away from me and toward the exit. Dodger was holding me in place, obviously feeling the volatility of the situation, too. The whole time, I keep my eyes locked on Mateo's, letting him know I was serious. If he went anywhere near Ellie, I would ruin him; I would rip his fucking heart out.

CHAPTER 12

ELLIE

ELLIE, DARLING, ARE you awake?" Nana called from downstairs.

I groaned and squinted at the clock on my nightstand. Just after seven. "Yeah," I replied, propping myself up on one elbow, hoping she'd hear me even though my voice was barely above a croaky whisper. "I'll be down in a minute."

I hadn't managed to get much sleep last night; my nerves had been fried, my emotions jangled. All I'd been able to think about was Jamie and how it felt to see him again. It was painful. It brought back a lot of memories that I had buried so deep inside I didn't think they'd ever resurface, but somehow they managed it as soon as my eyes locked on his. My mind had been whirling ever since, replaying things he said, things he didn't say, the way he looked at me, the way his lips felt against mine. I'd lain awake for hours on end, thinking about what a good thing we'd had and how much it had hurt when I found out he'd cheated on me and we'd broken up. I'd never felt pain like that before. I hadn't realized one person could crush you and your spirit with just a few simple words.

Everything was still bubbling inside me, my feelings swirling around to make one big jumbled mess. I hadn't wanted to talk about it last night when Stacey had tried to get me to open up in the back of the car, but now I was wondering if that had been a mistake. Maybe talking about it instead of bottling it up would have helped.

But how would I have put my feelings into words? I didn't even know what I was feeling or why.

Before last night I'd thought I was over him. I'd thought I'd finally come out the other side of that dark, long tunnel, but maybe I wasn't mended completely. I guess I couldn't be, because there was still a part of me that was unwilling to open up entirely—even with Toby I always guarded myself a little, afraid of what might happen if I gave all of myself to someone else. I'd been there before, I'd loved Jamie unconditionally and with no exceptions. He'd scarred my heart irrevocably, so I didn't know how to fully trust another man. He'd taken so much from me, made me guarded, so frightened of being hurt again, it even managed to taint my relationship with Toby.

Another wave of anger washed over me at the thought. I couldn't remember the last time one person had made me so furious. It was almost as if everything I felt, Jamie managed to magnify somehow. This level of powerful emotion—either good or bad—seemed to be limited to him.

I blew out a big breath and squeezed my eyes shut, deciding to just forget the meeting ever took place. I had enough to deal with; I didn't need to be thinking about an ex-boyfriend who pretended to care about me but didn't. I pushed myself up to sitting, unclenching fists I hadn't even realized I had made, and looked down at crescent-shaped marks my nails had left on my palms. Jamie had taken enough from me; I wouldn't allow him another moment of my time, I decided.

Swinging my legs out of bed, I grabbed a robe and headed out, following the pleasant scent of bacon and coffee downstairs. I stopped short when I saw Kelsey seated at the kitchen table; she was already dressed and her schoolbag was propped on the chair next to hers. She hadn't been to school this week—she hadn't wanted to, so I'd called the school and explained on Monday that I wasn't sure when she would be in.

I cleared my throat, smiling softly when she looked in my direction, her fork halfway to her mouth. "Morning," I said, hoping for more than a grunt and her walking out of the room, which was what I'd been subjected to the last five days.

Her head nodded in acknowledgment, and then she turned her attention back to her breakfast and iPhone. Nana turned, smiling warmly as she picked up the coffeepot, pouring me a cup. "Morning. Hungry?" she asked.

I gave a half shrug and sat down on one of the empty chairs. "A little." I turned to Kelsey. "Are you going to school today?"

Her eyes flicked up to mine. "Better than sitting around here doing nothing," she replied, her voice clipped and tight.

I nodded, smiling at my nana when she put a steaming hot cup of coffee in front of me. "I think it's a good idea. It might help you get a little normalcy back," I said thoughtfully.

"Normalcy? What part of this is normal to you?" Kelsey snapped, scowling.

"I didn't mean normal," I backtracked, scrambling to explain my meaning. "I meant that it might help you to be around your friends, get some routine back. Being busy will help you too, that's all I meant."

"Whatever," she huffed, setting down her fork and pushing her half-eaten food away from her.

I sighed. "Kels, how long are you going to be like this with me?"

She shoved her chair back, making a loud screeching noise. Her face contorted, her nose scrunched in anger. "Until you leave and abandon me again!" She grabbed her bag and stormed out of the room, not giving me a chance to reply. I didn't even have a reply. I was stunned into silence. My brain was replaying the word *abandon* over and over. Is that what she thought? That I had abandoned her? I knew she hadn't wanted me to leave home, but I'd never thought she would hold animosity toward me for it.

I looked up at my nana for some wise words, but she just shrugged, her smile sad and sympathetic. "Keep at it, she'll come around." She placed a pancake and a couple of slices of bacon on a plate before setting it in front of me. "Eat up, you need to keep your strength up, darling."

"Thanks."

"Still okay to take me home this morning so I can grab a few things?" she asked.

"Of course."

"Thank you, Ellie. I've washed this dress three times already this week. I've tried borrowing some of your mother's clothes, but they don't really fit me. Sadly she's much more ample in the bosom department than I am," she said, pointing down at her basically flat chest. "Ruth has what I think you kids call a 'great rack.'"

I laughed, almost choking on my coffee. Hearing my eighty-year-old grandmother saying the words *great rack* was not something I'd ever imagined happening in my life.

* * *

The drive to Mount Pocono, where my grandmother lived, was pleasant, as always. When we pulled up outside the familiar wooden-slatted house, I couldn't help but smile. I had many great memories of this place. My grandparents had lived here for as long as I could remember, retiring out here to a quieter life. Sadly, about six years ago, my grandfather had passed, leaving Nana alone. We'd come out to see her as much as possible, my parents making the trip every Saturday to spend the day here with her before coming home. Kelsey and I were frequent weekend visitors too, and Nana Betty had her friends and clubs to keep her busy. She wasn't one to rest on her laurels and was president of some wine appreciation club as well as being president of the bowling club.

"Oh, it's so nice to be out of the hustle and bustle of the city." Nana sighed as she pushed the passenger door open and stepped out of the car. She took in an exaggerated deep breath. "Oh my, the smell, I've missed it."

I smiled and followed her out, leaning against the car as one of her elderly neighbor friends, Nora, came out of her house, waving at her before heading over to chat. I closed my eyes, letting the sun beat down on me, and realized that the air *was* different here, fresher, cleaner. I guess you got used to living in a city—London was the same, full of smog and fumes as you walked the streets. I'd forgotten what clean mountain air smelled like.

My parents had always had a dream that one day they'd move out here, too. My dad dreamed of a place on the edge of the lake that they could turn into a B and B. My mom would take care of the guests and cook breakfast, and he'd teach kayaking lessons from off a jetty at the back. It would have been perfect. *Would have* being the operative phrase. It couldn't happen now.

When my eyes began to sting with building tears, I forced my mind away from what could have been and turned to my nana. She was just wrapping up her hushed conversation with her neighbor; I could tell they were talking about my parents' accident, so I hung back and walked deliberately slowly up to the house. They followed me and hugged at the doorway, Nora telling Nana to call if there was anything she could do.

When Nora turned to leave, her sympathetic eyes met mine. She was a lovely lady; we'd roasted s'mores over her cast-iron fire pit in her backyard every summer. "Oh, Ellie. You've grown into a beautiful, strong woman." She walked forward and hugged me tightly, her musty perfume filling my nose. "You take care of your grandmother for me, all right?"

"I will," I replied, awkwardly pulling out of the hug and stepping back a step.

She ambled off back to her own house next door, and I stood watching a little squirrel foraging for food in the front yard while Nana unlocked the front door.

Before she stepped over the threshold, I decided to broach the subject that I'd been thinking about for the last couple of days.

"You know, Nana, you don't have to come stay at our house if you don't want to. I mean, I'm back now, so I can take care of Kels. If you wanted to stay here, you could," I offered. We hadn't spoken about it, but I knew she hated the city, and she had to have missed her own house and bed. In the beginning, she'd come to stay with us because it was closer to the hospital and it was Kelsey's home, but now that I was here, there was no reason for her to come back with me.

"Are you trying to get rid of me?" she joked, nudging my arm with hers.

"Of course not, I love having you around, and I'd miss your cooking tremendously," I replied, grinning sheepishly. "But... you know, Kelsey and I will be okay on our own if you did want to stay home."

Her eyes met mine, her expression serious. "Ellie, you know there's a good chance your mother won't wake up. You need to prepare yourself for that, just in case."

I recoiled, shocked at the abrupt turn in the conversation. "I know that."

She nodded, reaching out and setting her wrinkly hand on my cheek. "If that happens, then there'll need to be some permanent procedures put in place for Kels. She's still a minor and will require a guardian. I'm coming home with you now because after, when this is over and we know what's going to happen, I'll be there for Kelsey. It's not right for such a burden to fall on you when you have a life across the pond."

A lump formed in my throat. I reached up and placed my hand over hers on my face, smiling gratefully. "You really are the best grandmother a girl could wish for," I said. "But if the worst happens and Mom doesn't wake up, then I'll be staying here to take care of Kels. You don't need to worry about either of us, I got it, I promise." It was the easiest decision I'd ever made; it didn't warrant thinking about. I would never have expected my elderly grandmother to take on a teenager.

Birds tweeting were the only sounds around us as we stood in silence for a few heartbeats, and then her eyes brimmed with tears and I reached out and engulfed her in a hug.

"I can't believe this happened. Your parents were such good people. Why do bad things happen to good people?" she asked softly, her voice muffled by my shoulder.

"I don't know, Nana," I answered truthfully.

She pulled back and sniffed, pulling a hankie from her pocket and wiping her nose with it. "Have you spoken to your fiancé about what happens if the worst happens?"

I looked down at the floor and frowned. "I'll talk to him later." I was picking Toby up at the airport in a few hours. It was a conversation we'd avoided so far in our daily phone calls, but we couldn't put it off forever. I wasn't sure how it was going to go because he had responsibilities in England and I had responsibilities here. I feared there wouldn't be much middle ground to compromise on.

"Let's just keep praying that it doesn't happen, that your mother wakes up and everything is fine. She's a fighter, that one, we may be worrying about something that will never happen," she said, reaching out and squeezing my hand.

I nodded but her words didn't help, because deep down inside me I was already thinking that I wanted to stay here, whatever happened. I'd left my family once, wasted time I could have spent with them, and I wasn't sure I was strong enough to leave them again. The dilemma was real and the feeling intense. I wasn't sure what the future would hold for my mother, but I was pretty sure I already knew what it held for me.

★ ★ ★

I stood at the arrivals gate later that day, watching for Toby to walk through the glass doors, with a strong black coffee in my left hand and a BLT sub in my right, as per his texted request. Apparently the airplane food was less than to be desired, and he was wasting away with starvation—his words, not mine.

He was one of the first into the baggage claim area, along with a middle-aged woman he was chatting up a storm with. His face split into a grin when he saw me.

I bit my lip and looked him over—jeans and his blue Millwall FC shirt, worn Nike sneakers (or as he liked to call them, trainers), and a sweater tied loosely around his waist. He still wore a travel pillow looped around his neck and had a rucksack slung over one shoulder as he dragged his carry-on behind him. His hair was in disarray, one side flat where he'd most likely been asleep, and the dark circles under his eyes showed he was already feeling the jet lag.

He said something to the woman he was with, and she looked over at me, sending me a little wave and a smile. I waved back awkwardly, my hands full so it was more of just a coffee salute. I smiled. Toby could talk to anyone; you could put him in a room with a bunch of strangers, and in no time, he'd be talking to them all like old friends and would know their life stories.

"Hey," I said as he stopped in front of me.

He grinned, stepping closer and wrapping his arm around me, pulling me against his body as his lips found mine. I squeaked from shock against his lips, awkwardly holding my arms out straight, trying not to spill coffee down his back. When he let me go and broke the kiss, his tired eyes met mine. "You're a sight for sore eyes," he said.

"Me or the coffee?" I joked, holding the cup out to him.

"Mmmmmm," he groaned, taking it and swallowing a large gulp.

A bad smell of rancid meat or something hit me, and I wrinkled my nose in distaste. "Ugh, what is that smell?" I held my nose, breathing through my mouth.

He groaned again, this time not in appreciation of the coffee, and shook his head. "Oh, man, I smell like vom, don't I?" He dipped his head, taking a few tentative sniffs of his shirt. "Flight was rough; I puked. A lot. Managed to get most of it in those stupid paper bags, but I'm pretty sure my Millwall shirt is gonna stink like chunder forever now."

I grinned wickedly. "You poor baby."

He nodded, his lips turning down at the corners playfully. "I know, right? I told you I wasn't a good flyer. Me Gregory is killing me too, 'ad to buy a stupid ruddy pillow on the plane, cost a fortune. The things a guy 'as to do to please his fiancée, huh?" He sighed jokingly, reaching up and rubbing his neck—or his "Gregory Peck," as cockney rhyming slang translated.

"You totally took one for the team," I replied, smiling gratefully. "I'm glad you're here." That wasn't a lie. Toby always had this ability to put me at ease and brighten anybody's mood. It was part of his sparkling, jokey personality.

"I missed ya," he replied, leaning down to kiss me again.

"You, too." I looked up at him and willed there to be some spark of passion. I hadn't seen him for days, I should have wanted to rip his clothes off and lick him all over, but other than a small pitter-patter in my heart and gratitude that he was here, there was nothing. I guess it was hard to lust after a guy when he looked like death and smelled like vomit, though. Well, that was what I told myself anyway.

"Come on then, let's go home and you can shower," I suggested, waving my hand under my nose as we headed for the exit. "We'll have to drive with the windows open," I added, grinning.

He gasped, faking horror. "We can't do that, me 'air will go all poufy," he joked, winking at me. As we stepped out of the door, he stopped and looked around. "So this is what all the fuss is about, is it? The Big Apple."

I nodded. "Yep. Welcome to New York. What d'you think?"

He looked left and right, then up at the cloudy blue sky. He drew in a big breath and then coughed dramatically. "Smells just like London."

I burst out laughing. For the first time in days, I actually felt like laughing. It was definitely a talent Toby had.

CHAPTER 13

JAMIE

HOW IS IT you can be surrounded by people but feel so alone? It was almost tragic that I'd gotten so used to loneliness that I barely even registered it. But now that I'd seen Ellie again, touched her, kissed her—even if it was only for the briefest of seconds—all I wanted was more. Half my crew sat around me, listening to Dodger's plans for the weekend boost we had lined up, but I barely heard a word.

"So, we'll need two people Saturday night to drive the cars back once Kid and I have boosted them," Dodger said, looking around the room. "Volunteers? I know a few of you are off this weekend for the rager that is Shaun's wedding."

Shaun wasn't with our crew anymore. Once he got out of prison, he'd decided that he wanted to go straight. Well, actually, his girlfriend, who had popped out a kid while he was inside, "strongly encouraged" the decision. They were getting married this weekend. I'd been invited and would probably make an appearance at the ceremony but ditch early during the reception.

Dodger had agreed to this boost for the weekend, forgetting

that half of his reliable workers knew Shaun from years back and would want to go. Now, he was short on staff.

"I'm in," Chase offered. He was fairly new to my crew, young, a little hotheaded for my liking, but loyal.

Dodger nodded, scribbling his name down on his pad before looking around for the next brave warrior.

Ed sat forward. "I can do it. I wasn't planning on going to the wedding anyway." I smiled to myself at that. He hadn't been invited in the first place. "I know I don't usually get involved with boosting, but I can drive a car," he offered.

"Great," Dodger answered, nodding in appreciation, picking up his pad again. "That's settled, then. Kid and I will boost, Chase and Ed will bring the cars back, and Ray will handle things here and get the shipment ready and loaded."

I held one finger up in a *wait a second* gesture. "I need Ed for Saturday night. If I'm busy all night, I need someone on protection duty," I said, shrugging when Dodger groaned in frustration. I looked over at Ed, who was frowning in my direction, clearly pissed that he was being pulled back from a job for something that he no doubt considered a menial task. Nothing menial about it, though; To me, it was the most important job I ever trusted anyone with. "I'll pay you the same rate the boosters are getting. I just need someone there to watch and make sure the Salazars don't go near her."

For the last two days I'd had people parked outside Ellie's house around the clock, watching to make sure Mateo didn't do anything moronic like sign his death warrant. I'd taken a few shifts, usually the evening ones, but I couldn't do it all by myself. So far nothing bad had happened. In fact, other than yesterday, when she drove to her grandmother's house and did an airport run to pick up the guy I hated with a burning passion because he got to touch something I so desperately wanted to be mine, she barely left the house other than to go to the hospital or the grocery store.

I was right to be cautious, though, no matter how much these guys looked at me like I was acting crazy. Rule number one in this business: Never show anyone that you cared about anything. Never show emotion, never show vulnerability, because there were always people watching, waiting to exploit any weaknesses. There were always people like Mateo out there, wanting to gain any advantage they could get. I'd fucked up royally on Tuesday night, and now I was desperately trying to rectify the situation and ensure Ellie was safe and they weren't going to go after her to get to me. I wasn't sure they would, but I was covering all bases just in case.

Dodger sighed, but his eyes showed me he understood. He knew how I felt about Ellie and what she meant to me. He and Ray had been the only two I'd really confided in about it. "Okay, so still need one volunteer…" He looked around the room slowly.

After a tiny bit of persuasion, Enzo agreed to leave early with me. The money was too big of a draw for him while he was trying to get that dream apartment.

"That's a wrap, then. You guys can all knock off for the night, ain't nothing brewing around here that needs doing tonight," Dodger said, waving everyone else out of the room. He turned to me once we were alone. "What about you, what are you up to? Wanna go grab some food?"

"Sure, why not," I replied. In my pocket, my cell phone buzzed with a new message. I pulled it out at the same time Dodger pulled his out, both of us reading the preview message. My heart leaped in my chest. There was a race organized for tonight, starting in three hours. Dodger did a little jig on the spot and pumped his fist. I drummed on the table excitedly.

"About damn time!" The timing was perfect too, especially as I'd just managed to get my beauty of a car fixed up this week.

"I'm so gonna kick your ass tonight." Dodger grinned, slipping his cell back into his pocket. "I'll give you a little wave from the winner's podium, all right?" He winked at me and turned for the door. "Better go gas up my baby."

"So we're not doing food?" I called to his back, laughing.

★ ★ ★

The place was set, a sleepy town on the North Fork of Long Island. It was almost midnight when I followed behind Dodger's red Ford Shelby GT500 as we made our way slowly, and as inconspicuously as possible, to the designated starting area.

Excitement built in my chest and my palms itched with eagerness during the hour or so it took us to drive to the destination. This couldn't have come at a better time for me. Racing brought me an inner peace. The power of the car, the speed—all of it accumulated into one huge adrenaline rush that I reveled in. After the distractions of late, I needed something like this to take my mind off everything else so I could just live in the moment, even if it was only for a fifteen-minute race.

Dodger slowed at the end of the road and a guy with a two-way radio bent down to talk to him. I saw the glowing light of a cell phone being shown, and then he was waved forward. I crept along, my cell phone already open, showing the race invitation text I received. The guy glanced at the invite then waved me on, too.

I drove slowly, seeing the brightly colored and heavily souped-up cars lining the edge of the road and the spectators milling around, cooing over the cars and their drivers. I pulled into the available space next to Dodger and popped the hood of my car.

These things always started with spectators and other racers surveying the cars' engines, clucking over the modifications they'd had done.

I climbed out, already smelling that the air was thick with the scent of gas. Dodger met me by the side of my car, and we walked through the crowd, checking out the contenders parked along the edge of the road. I spotted a few who raced in most of these competitions and a few newbies.

I groaned at two cars that stood out from the rest because of their exaggerated paint jobs and the overly large spoilers mounted on the backs of them. Two Mitsubishi Lancer Evolutions, one custom painted orange with a lime-green lightning bolt on the side, the other lime green with an orange lightning bolt. They belonged to identical twin brothers, Regan and Harley. Most people called them the Kamikaze Twins, not because they were reckless, but because they were fearless. They were my biggest competition. Alongside Dodger and myself, one or the other of the Kamikaze Twins won almost every race they entered. Their driving was smart, slick, and effortless. The pair of them were big on the karting circuit, and I'd heard they even tore up the other big street-racing scenes in Los Angeles and Miami, too. I liked them, though, despite the fact that they were cocky little shits who caused me to lose a race on occasion. They were good guys and always offered a handshake after.

Dodger pointed at the two cars. "I'm gonna kick their asses, too," he bragged confidently.

I chuckled and we made our way over to where the group of drivers were all huddled together at the end of the row of cars. The contenders who raced here were from all walks of life; street racing wasn't limited to the bad boy or the guy from the wrong side of the tracks. One guy who frequented the scene was a top-end lawyer; another was a low-paid schoolteacher. They could be anyone on the street during the day, just someone who indulged in a fast-paced hobby in the evenings. That was one of the things I liked about it; everyone was simply here because they were passionate about cars and speed.

Someone sidled up next to me. "What's up, bro?"

I turned to see who'd spoken and came face-to-face with one of the twins, though I had no idea which one it was. To me, there was no difference between them except for the hair—both were blond and wore it about the same length, but one liked to spike it up and the other swept it to the side.

"Hey, um...Harley?" I guessed.

He shook his head and grinned. "Regan," he corrected. His brother, who had come up beside him, held his fist out for a bump, which I delivered.

"One day he'll guess right," Dodger chimed in, leaning over and knocking their fists, too.

"Probably not," I replied.

The twins shrugged in unison, their grins equal in size. "So you came, then. To be honest, we were kind of hoping your car was still toast and you wouldn't show up tonight," Regan said, his eyes twinkling with mirth. "Oh well, more prize money in the pot for when I win."

I opened my mouth to answer, but a loud throat clearing to our left halted me. A guy in a fluorescent high-vis vest with a half-smoked cigarette between his lips stood there with a black canvas bag. "Entry fee," he grunted, dropping ash down onto his protruding stomach and wiping it off absentmindedly with the back of one hand.

Each of us pulled out the five-hundred-dollar entry fee, silently dropping the money into the bag.

"Now check out the route and then get your cars into place so we can get this started," Rodriguez told the drivers. Everyone moved forward to look at the large map where a big red oddly shaped ring had been hastily sketched. A list of street names and our randomly drawn starting positions were handwritten down the side.

Dodger and I took a slow walk back to our cars, letting the crowd around them disperse as spectators made their way to the starting point.

"You ready for this?" Dodger asked as I unhooked the hood of my car and let it fall shut and click into place.

"Yeah, she's running great now. I owe Ray big time for sourcing that part for me," I replied, lovingly smoothing my hand across the paint job.

"That's not what I meant," Dodger said, folding his arms across his chest. "You've been a little distracted lately. I just want to make sure your head is in the game tonight. You can't race if you're thinking about other things, that's how accidents happen and people die."

This was about Ellie. Didn't see that coming. Was I ready for this? Yes. Hell yes. I needed it. Once I was out there my brain would automatically focus on the task at hand instead of constantly worrying and thinking about her. At least, that was the plan anyway.

"I'm fine." I reached out and patted him on the shoulder gently. "But thanks for worrying about me, you'll make someone a good bitch one day."

He rolled his eyes before stepping to his car door and grinning over at me. "Let's do this."

I grinned too, sliding into my molded leather seat and reaching down to turn the ignition. My car roared to life, the engine loud and predatory as I twisted the key, breathing life into her. I sighed contentedly, tracing my hands on the steering wheel, the growl of the engine enough to make my scalp prickle with excitement. The thrill of knowing that within a few minutes I'd be bursting along at speeds of over one hundred mph made a tingle zip down my spine.

Checking that the street behind me was clear, I left my parking space and headed to the makeshift starting grid, where the other drivers were idling.

I replayed the route in my head, envisioning the turns, the roads, how sharp the corners were. Adrenaline was pulsing through my bloodstream as my foot hovered over the gas pedal, my eyes locked on Rodriguez as he walked ten feet past the starting line and raised an air horn.

I held my breath, my jaw clenched in concentration, my foot twitching in readiness. And then the shrill sound of the horn blasted through the air and my body reacted in an instant. I dropped the car into gear and floored it. Tires screeched, engines roared, and clouds of white smoke and dust blasted up from the back of every car as we all shot forward almost in unison, the force of it shoving us back in our seats.

By the time I'd made it to the end of the short road, I was already pushing eighty mph. My eyes remained locked on the road ahead, watching the orange Mitsubishi and the BMW M3 jostle for position as I skidded around the first turn, my tires scrabbling for traction in a delicious way that gripped my stomach in excitement.

As the streets whizzed by in a blur and I pushed it faster and faster, I felt some of the tension of the last few days start to diminish. Each quick gear change took back a little bit of the control that I'd felt slipping away from me since Ellie had returned.

The streets were deserted. I grinned as the car in front of me braked too soon going into a corner, which allowed me to breeze past him. I was now in second place behind the orange kamikaze. Flicking a quick glance at my mirror, I saw Dodger behind me, overtaking the same car I had seconds before; he was pushing and grappling with the green kamikaze to hold his third-place position. It always came down like this, we four all fighting it out to see who would take the top spot this time.

I gritted my teeth in concentration, twisting my wheel and shooting onto the other side of the road, attempting to get more room to make my move for first. My speedometer showed 121 mph. Orange kamikaze sped up, shooting a quick grin over at me as we zoomed down the road in a flurry of noise, smoke, and fumes that the residents of this street would wake and complain about at any second.

I pulled back onto the right side of the road, now level with the orange kamikaze as Dodger tried fruitlessly to find a way through behind me. I grinned, tightening my grip on the wheel as we approached the next corner at full speed. Leaving it until the last possible second, I braked and turned my wheel, feeling my back tires lose purchase on the road for a split second before I turned into the skid and caught it. The hair on my arms prickled, my adrenaline bumping up another level as I nosed ahead, pressing down onto the gas with all my might. Cars screeched around the corner behind me, the sound cutting through the night air like a knife.

"Two more corners," I muttered to myself, allowing myself another split-second glance in the mirror, seeing all three of them on my six and grappling to catch me. At the next corner, I left it slightly too late to brake, not realizing how sharp it was. I grunted, fighting with the steering to catch the skid before correcting and plummeting on down the straight road.

Suddenly Ellie's face flashed in my mind, and just like that, I wasn't as fearless as I liked to believe. All this time I'd been racing, I'd never once worried about being hurt or killed. I'd never had anything worth living for anyway. But as soon as that little girl's face appeared in my mind, fear clutched my heart with its icy hand. If I were hurt or dead, then I wouldn't be able to be there for her, and that was something that was extremely important to me. I *did* have something worth living for, even if I didn't actually *have* her, so to speak.

I looked over to see the green kamikaze now in second place, almost at my side. I could see his determined look as he clasped his wheel tightly and gunned his engine. The next corner was within sight; the twin was not even yet thinking about applying the brakes. I gulped, thinking of Ellie having to lay her father to rest tomorrow. I needed to be there for that. I had to.

My foot eased off the gas, my car slowing, and almost instantly the green kamikaze and Dodger breezed past me and into the corner as I braked, staying fully in control this time. It wasn't worth it, I couldn't risk it.

Now on the home straight, I held my own, staying in third place as I crossed the finish line, seeing people videoing and applauding the cars as they stopped. When I came to a full stop, I closed my eyes and rested my head back on the headrest. Dodger had been right, I shouldn't have raced tonight. My head was all over the place, and I'd almost lost control. If my reactions had been any slower, I would have rolled my car. At that sort of speed I probably wouldn't have walked away from it.

A loud rap on my window made my eyes pop open. One of the twins stood there, his toothy grin splitting his face. I rolled down my window.

"Almost had you there," I said, forcing a smile so he wouldn't know anything was wrong.

He shrugged and ran a hand through his hair. "Almost. Until you pussied out going into the last turn."

"Oh, whatever," I replied, rolling my eyes with mock annoyance.

He grinned. "See you next time, buddy. Drive safe." He held out his fist and I bumped mine against it.

"Yeah, next time," I replied. But I wasn't even sure there would be a next time; at least, not until Ellie was out of my life again and safely back in England with her Brit. As soon as I thought about it, I realized how much I didn't want that to happen. I didn't want her out of my life; I didn't want her to marry someone else and have his British children; I didn't want her to continue hating me, thinking I hadn't loved her enough.

I didn't want this life. Since I'd been released from prison, I'd just been fooling myself into thinking I was content with what I had, when in reality that couldn't be further from the truth. Maybe it was time I was honest, put myself out there, realized I was maybe worth taking a risk on. Maybe I still could be good enough for her. Maybe.

CHAPTER 14

ELLIE

BEEP. BEEP. BEEP.

The bedside alarm clock was loud and shrill and I instantly regretted setting it instead of the nice bird chirping or soft music I could have set on my cell phone alarm instead.

"Ugh, tell me it's not morning and that thing is malfunctioning," Toby grunted, throwing his arm over his face as I reached out to turn the alarm off.

"Nope, it's morning," I answered, rubbing at my tired eyes. A headache thumped at the back of my skull already. *As if today won't be hard enough.* The headache was a by-product of another night of barely any sleep. I'd spent the wee hours lying in bed, staring at the ceiling in the darkness going over everything that needed to be done today, things I needed to do or say, wondering how I was going to hold it together. Today we would lay my dad to rest, and I was supposed to be the strong one who was there for my family. How in the hell was I supposed to do that? I had no clue.

I turned to Toby, squinting down at him through blurry, puffy eyes from when I'd eventually cried myself to sleep silently so I wouldn't wake him. He sent me a sad smile, his eyes still half-closed, and I lay back down, scooting closer to him and setting my head on his chest. His arms wrapped around me, surrounding me in his warmth as he placed a kiss on the top of my head. Wrapped in a little duvet-Toby cocoon, I felt safe and comfortable, and I didn't just mean the sleeping position. Our whole relationship was like this: lazy and uncomplicated companionship.

"Okay, sweetheart?" he whispered.

I blew out a big breath and lifted my head, resting my chin on his chest so I could look at him. "Toby, how am I going to do this today? I don't think I can," I confided. My heart hurt, my whole body heavy with sadness.

His hands came up, cupping the side of my neck as his soft green eyes met mine. "You can do it. I'll be right 'ere, and you'll get through it. You're stronger than you think."

"Yeah," I croaked, unsure if I believed it. Getting through today was going to be the hardest thing I'd done so far, and I'd barely managed to make it through some of the previous things.

How could I say good-bye? How could I stand there and listen to people talk about my dad and what a great man he was, how he had so much life left in him, and how on earth was I going to do it all without breaking down in front of everyone?

"Will you do me a favor today?" I asked.

"'Course." He nodded sadly.

I smiled gratefully. "Watch out for my nana for me, okay? I'll be fine, I'll get through it, just stay close to her and make sure she's all right. I know we're all going through it, but she's saying good-bye to her son today, and no mother should have to do that."

Toby's hand slid down my back, pulling me closer, hugging me tightly to his body. "'Course I will. I'll watch out for all of you."

"Thank you," I muttered against his shoulder, clutching him closer to me, wishing I didn't ever have to get out of this bed and I could just hide here, away from all my problems. Unfortunately, life didn't work like that, so I pulled away, kissing his cheek softly before swinging my legs out of bed.

It was only seven a.m., but I had lots more preparations to do today before the funeral. To save on money, because I simply hadn't realized how expensive these things were and was already struggling, Nana and I were catering the wake ourselves. We'd prepared a lot of the food last night, baking mini sausages, stuffing pastry shells with a variety of fillings, and cooking all manner of finger foods until well past midnight, but today we needed to make the sandwiches and deviled eggs, sort out the cold cuts selection, and chop vegetables. *At least it will keep our minds occupied for a while*, I thought, slipping on my robe and heading downstairs.

* * *

Hours later we were essentially done, and I was pretty ready to throw the hors d'oeuvres out the window. I didn't want to see another teeny pizza or chicken nugget in my life. The table in the living room was all laid out like we were hosting some sort of party for little people or something. My nana kept saying how much my dad would have loved it and how partial he was to a bit of finger food. She was right; he'd always said there was something about miniature food that made it taste better.

While Toby and Kelsey tidied the house, Nana finished

plating up the cold cuts and I gathered all the trash, tying the bag tightly. "You sure you don't want to come to the hospital?" I asked, walking into the living room and raising my voice a little over the vacuum that Kelsey was pushing around.

"No. I'll stay here and finish up," she answered quickly, turning the vacuum off. Kelsey didn't visit Mom as much as I did. She wouldn't talk about it, but I got the distinct impression that she didn't like seeing our mother like that. I must admit, I didn't, either.

"Okay. I'll be back in a bit," I told her before turning to Toby. "You'll watch Nana for me while I'm gone?"

He smiled, walking to my side and bending to kiss my cheek. "Like an 'awk," he replied.

"A what?" Kelsey questioned.

"An 'awk," Toby repeated. When Kelsey's eyebrow rose and it was clear she still didn't get it, I laughed. Seeing my family trying to get used to his accent was hilarious. "Big bird, excellent eyesight, likes to eat mice . . . an 'awk."

I turned, heading out of the house and leaving them to it, picking up the trash bag on the way out. As I walked down the path, I looked up at the rain clouds brewing in the sky, hoping they'd clear before this afternoon. A funeral in the rain would just about be the icing on the cake for me, though it certainly would suit my dark, depressive mood perfectly.

"Oh, Ellie. Do you need anything done today, honey?" Mrs. Egbert, our next-door neighbor, came trotting across her lawn, her hair still in rollers, her large frame still in her nightdress.

"We've got it all under control, thank you. Though I wanted to ask, would it be possible for a few cars to use your driveway later?" I replied. I'd meant to come over yesterday, but we'd been busy shopping for all the food and drinks for the wake.

"Of course it is, honey. I'll have Derek move our cars into the garage so you can feel free to use the whole drive if you need to," she said, setting her hand on my arm. "It's so sad what's happened. I just feel for you all. And your poor mother..." She clucked her tongue and shook her head sadly. "We're both praying for her."

"Thanks," I muttered. "I'd better go. Heading to the hospital for a visit."

"Oh, give your mother our love," she instructed.

I nodded, sending her a last smile, and then turned toward my car. As I started down the path, a maroon sedan caught my eye and I stopped, glancing over at it. It was parked across the street, opposite my house. It had been there yesterday too, but I didn't recognize it as one of the neighbors' cars. Today the guy sitting in the driver's seat, a handsome twentysomething black guy, was looking back at me, seeming a little apprehensive as we made eye contact. I frowned. Hadn't the guy sitting in the car yesterday been an older white guy with brown hair? *Surely it couldn't have been the same car, though, with two different drivers parked outside my house...*

As I squinted, trying to get a better look at the guy because something about him seemed a little familiar, the car started up and drove off, the driver putting his cell phone to his ear. I watched the car as it rolled down the road and out of sight. Maybe I'd been wrong about yesterday; my mind wasn't exactly focused and engaged lately, I was just cruising along in a bit of a daze still.

I shook it off and headed to my car, trying to keep my mind on anything other than what would happen in four hours' time.

* * *

No matter how many times I was subjected to it, I simply couldn't get used to that distinct hospital smell. It was like the scent of death lingered in the air, covered up with cleaning fluid and bleach. I'd come to the hospital to visit my mother two or sometimes three times a day, and the scent of it, especially her ward, made my throat dry and my nose burn.

As usual, I stopped at the nurses' office on my way in and asked for an update—as usual, I was told no change.

It had been too long already. A week had passed since the accident and she hadn't woken. Her prognosis was getting worse each day. I hated that there was nothing anyone could do but keep her comfortable and wait. I didn't like not being in control of anything.

The uncomfortable chair at the side of my mom's bed creaked as I eased into it, setting my purse on the floor before leaning forward and taking her hand in mine.

"Morning," I muttered. The doctors and nurses had been encouraging us to talk to her, saying it might help. I felt a little stupid doing it, but we all tried anyway, even Kels sometimes. "I can't stay long today, I just wanted to come and say hi." I cleared my throat. "So, um…" I looked around her room for something to talk about. "Looks like rain today." That was all I had. *Pathetic.*

I sighed and leaned forward, resting my chin on the edge of her bed and watching her chest rise and fall with the soft suck and pull of the ventilator.

"I'm so sorry we couldn't wait for you to wake up before having Dad's funeral." And I was sorry, too. I'd considered waiting, but the doctors had been adamant that the best thing to do was to do it now. They'd said that even if she woke up, the stress of it all might cause other complications.

"I wish you could be there." The silence in the room was

deafening to me. "I'm not sure I can do it, Mom. I'm trying to be strong for everyone, but inside I feel like I'm breaking. There's so much pressure and everyone is looking at me to do everything because Nana is struggling too, and I'm trying to keep the pressure of it off her, but it feels like everything is weighing me down and I'm not sure how much more I can take."

I swallowed and closed my eyes. "I think we've done everything, though. I've been busy sorting out food and flowers and songs for today. And don't worry, we've cleaned the house because I know how particular you are about keeping up appearances." I chuckled humorlessly. "Everything should go fine, I hope. I'm just sorry you won't be there."

I squeezed her hand and sat back, watching the rise and fall of her chest again as my thoughts wandered to this afternoon and tears welled in my eyes.

★ ★ ★

When I returned home, the place was sparkling clean yet deserted. I could hear the shower on upstairs, but there was no one around that I could see. I set my bag down and checked the time on my watch. Half past one. There was a little over an hour left until the car would arrive to pick us up and take us to the crematorium.

I set my purse down, following the sounds of life from upstairs. I stopped outside the spare bedroom, the one Nana was using, and could hear the whirr of a hair dryer, so I moved on, meaning to head to my bedroom and shower so I could change. As I walked up the hallway, sounds of quiet crying made my ears prick up. I frowned, creeping over to Kelsey's room, noticing her door was only half-closed. The sound of crying got louder the closer I got. My heart ached, and I wished I could take her pain away.

As I peeked in the door, I saw her sitting at her dresser, hair-brush in one hand, bobby pin in the other. Tears were streaming endlessly down her face as she twisted the front of her hair, pulling it away from her face and attempting to push the bobby pin in to secure it. A groan of frustration left her lips before she hurled her brush across the room; it hit the wall with a loud thunk.

"Stupid, stupid hair!" she cried, standing up and using both arms to roughly sweep the contents of her dresser onto the floor in one quick motion, sending bobby pins in every direction.

I gulped, knowing it wasn't the hair she was upset about.

"Kels, how about I help you style it?" I offered softly.

She jumped, her eyes flicking up to look at my reflection in the mirror. Anger and frustration twisted her usually beau-tiful features as she shoved up from the stool and marched over to me. When her hand came up and caught the door, swinging it toward my face, I was ready and stopped it before it slammed, pushing it back open again and stepping in un-invited.

This needed to stop. I couldn't keep allowing her to use me as a punching bag for her emotions; I couldn't take it anymore.

"Kelsey, stop it, stop shutting me out all the time and being so mean. I'm hurting too, you know! Do you really think this whole thing isn't killing me inside? Do you really think you're the only one suffering? I lost him, too. I miss him and Mom just as much as you do," I cried, my own frustration leaking into my words. "You can't keep punishing me for not being here when it happened. It's not fair." I shook my head, will-ing her to listen and let me in. "I need you, Kels. I can't do all this on my own. You need to stop pushing me away. At the moment, we've only got each other. We can help each other get through this, but not if you keep shutting me out."

Her tears were in full force. This was the first time I had seen her cry since I'd been home. I groaned and stepped forward, wrapping an arm around her and pulling her against me, holding her tightly when she wriggled and tried to push me off. I held fast, not letting go, and after a couple of seconds, her body sagged against mine and her arms looped around my waist, hugging me back.

My eyes fluttered closed as I pressed my face into her hair, holding her while she sobbed onto my shoulder and finally let it all out. I stroked her back, thanking God for this mini breakthrough and just hoping that it wasn't limited to today.

After a few minutes she pulled back and sniffed loudly, wiping her face with the back of her hand. I left my hands on her shoulders and dipped my head slightly, so I could meet her red-rimmed eyes. "I love you lots, like tater tots. You know that, don't you?" I whispered. It was something we'd always said to each other when we were younger; she'd come up with it once because they were her favorite food as a kid.

She nodded. "You, too."

I smiled and reached up to take hold of her hair, tugging on it playfully. "How about you let me do your hair, just like old times?" I offered, praying she wouldn't reject me again now that the forced hug was over.

"Okay." It was a small gesture on her part, letting me do it, but I took it and ran with it.

I smiled gratefully and bent to retrieve her hairbrush from the floor where it had landed after she'd launched it. "How about I braid the front and we curl the back?" I offered. It was a hairstyle Stacey had given me many times.

"Are you sure you have enough time? Don't you need to

shower and get changed?" she asked, looking down at my jeans and sweater.

I waved a dismissive hand. I would be pushing it, but I'd just skip the shower and throw on my clothes after. "Plenty of time."

She sat at the dresser and we didn't speak as I negotiated the front of her hair into a cute little French braid, tucking the ends under the rest of her hair and then picking up her curling iron and getting started on adding some soft curls to the back.

"Are you leaving on Wednesday with Toby?" Kelsey suddenly asked out of the blue.

I frowned, wrapping another segment of hair around the curling wand. "No. What made you ask that?"

She shrugged, picking at the skin around her fingernails. "I just figured that once the funeral was done you'd leave as soon as you could."

I shook my head adamantly. "I'm here to look after you."

"Nana is here for that."

I frowned and set the curling iron on the dresser, squatting down next to her so we were basically eye to eye. "Kelsey, I'm here to take care of you, whatever happens," I promised. "Is that why you've been so pissed at me, because you think I just flew in for the funeral and then was going to flit right off again after?"

She shrugged, her hand going up to her mouth so she could nibble on her nail. I knew I was spot on. She thought I would abandon her at the first opportunity.

"I'm not going to jet off again, I promise."

"What if Mom doesn't wake up?" she whispered, her eyes wide, fearful. I could see the desperation there as her gaze locked on mine.

"She will, I know she will," I replied, trying to be more confident than I actually felt. The truth was that no one knew what would happen, not even the doctors.

"But if she doesn't?" she pushed.

I smiled reassuringly. "If she doesn't, then I'm here. That's all you need to know." I got to my feet, stooping to kiss the top of her head as I softened her curls with my fingers and then smiled at her in the mirror. "There. Beautiful."

A smile twitched at the corner of her mouth as her eyes met mine in the mirror. "Thanks, Ellie."

CHAPTER 15

WHEN THE BLACK funeral car containing me, my sister, my grandmother, and my fiancé pulled up at the crematorium that we'd chosen to hold my father's service, my lungs constricted with finality.

Kelsey's hand gripped mine so tightly it pinched. "I don't think I can do this," she muttered, shaking her head, her tears flowing again. Her words echoed mine of this morning.

I twisted in my seat so I could look at her. "You can. *We* can," I said confidently. "Come on. We got this." I reached out and placed my free hand over my grandmother's crinkly one and gave it a little squeeze. "We all got this."

Nana nodded and Toby opened the car door, stepping out first, then turning to help my grandmother as she scooted up the seat. I smiled over at Kelsey, letting go of her hand as she followed the other two out of the car. I took a deep breath, steeling myself, silently repeating the mantra that I'd been going over and over for the last hour.

Don't cry. Don't cry. Don't cry.

I raised my chin and climbed from the car, heading straight

over to Kelsey, who was staring up at the ominous brick-and-glass building with evident terror. I placed a hand on the small of her back, and she turned and offered me a tentative smile, but I could see the pain in her eyes.

Soft crying to my left gained my attention, and I turned to see that Nana was in bits, crying and dabbing at her face with a hankie. Toby had his arm around her shoulders, his expression solemn. My stomach coiled as I linked my arm through Kelsey's, just needing to get this whole thing out of the way. Maybe once we'd said good-bye we could start to feel slightly better and begin to rebuild.

"Come on, Nana," I said, opening my other arm and beckoning her over to me. Toby's arm dropped from around her shoulders and he mouthed the words "Love you" to me as Nana shuffled toward Kels and me. I smiled, my heart warming slightly at the pride I could see in Toby's eyes as he watched me. Nana came to my side, pressing against me as she looped one arm around my waist, gripping a fistful of the black jacket that I'd changed into for the service. I raised my chin and the three of us walked as a unit toward the arched entrance to say good-bye to the greatest man I ever had the pleasure of knowing.

Toby walked slightly ahead, pausing at the heavy wooden doors, waiting for us to walk in first. I swallowed, repeating my "don't cry" mantra, willing myself to stay strong for them. As we stepped inside, my eyes widened in surprise. There were so many people here, so many of my dad's friends and family turned up to pay their respects that they'd already filled every single bench. Off to the left, maybe another twenty or so people stood, all dressed to the nines. Some I recognized as friends, some were inevitably work colleagues and clients, people from all different backgrounds here for my father. A swell of pride and gratitude rose within me. It was a testament to his character how many people were going to miss him. He would be honored to know he'd touched so many people's lives.

We stopped at the entrance, taking one of the order-of-service cards I'd painstakingly designed from the person handing them out. Before we could get going again, the minister walked over, his smile sad as he reached out and took one of my nana's hands in both of his. "I'm sorry for your loss. I think everyone is already here. We have everything ready, and I can play the first song whenever you're ready."

"Thank you," I replied.

He smiled and let go of Nana's hand, waving us forward. As we walked up the aisle toward the front bench that had been left empty for us, people nodded in greeting, their smiles sad and full of emotion.

Off to one side, nestled among the standing crowd, my eyes lingered on a young black guy wearing a stylish gray suit and black shirt. His face was familiar, but it took me a minute to place him. He looked up and our eyes met, and it suddenly hit me: He'd been sitting in the sedan outside my house.

And standing next to him...Jamie Cole.

My breathing faltered for a second. I'd forgotten how good he looked in a suit. When he'd asked to come to the service, part of me thought it was just for show and that he wouldn't turn up; part of me *hoped* that would happen. But here he was, in the flesh, looking impossibly handsome.

I forced my eyes away, turning my attention to the coffin that sat on a large oak platform. Flowers framed the sides and rested on top. To the left and right of the platform were wooden stands with large photo boards on them.

My legs were weak, but somehow we all made it to the

front of the room and sat on the bench, my grandmother on my left, my sister on my right. Toby squeezed in next to Nana. Almost as soon as we were seated, Frank Sinatra's "That's Life" began playing. My father had said it was one of the greatest songs ever sung by the legend, who just so happened to be my dad's hero, so I'd chosen it to open the ceremony.

When the volume faded, I looked up at the minister and attempted to prepare myself for what was to come.

During the ceremony, I tried to focus but my eyes kept drifting to the crack in the tiled floor at my feet as I fought to contain my tears. My hands stayed gripped in those of the women next to me as the congregation sang hymns I could only mouth and a couple of my father's closest friends gave readings I barely heard. When the minister delivered the eulogy, it garnered a few laughs from attendees, as I had intended when I wrote it. I wanted it to be full of good humor and grace, as my father himself had been.

But during the whole thing, I just sat there silently, numb and devastated. My chest had tightened to the point where it was hard to breathe, like a vise had been clamped around my torso. I was losing my battle to be strong; my strength was crumbling away as I looked up at that photo of my father with that smile that always reached his eyes. I couldn't take it, I needed out, I wanted out of this room and away from the flowers, the hymnbooks, and all these people sitting around. I wanted to scream and shout at the injustice of it all, throw things, smash things, ask why, why, why? My heart was drumming in my ears. I could almost feel my temples throbbing to the tempo of it.

But just as I was about to lose control, Kelsey sniffed and tightened her hand in mine, leaning over to rest her head on my shoulder. Her other arm wrapped around mine, pulling it across her body as if hiding behind it somehow would protect her from what was happening. And in that moment, a calm settled over me and my chest loosened. She needed me. It was that simple. I couldn't lose control because she needed me to take care of her.

I raised my eyes to the dark wooden coffin and made a silent vow to my father that I would always be there to look after Kelsey. Always. No matter what happened with my mom. Then I silently told him it was okay, and that he could rest in peace knowing that we would be fine. Together.

I sucked in a deep breath through my nose, blowing it out through my mouth slowly and deeply, repeating a couple of times, breathing through the anxiety attack that was brewing within me until I felt better.

The ceremony was drawing to a close now; the last reading had just been done and now there was just the closing and the final song left.

"So make sure you talk about him often, share stories about silly things he did, remember him often. For when you do that, a person's spirit lives on through us and they never really die," the minister said before smiling over at us. "Michael's family would like me to tell you that the wake will be at their home and that all are welcome to attend. I'm sure the family joins me in thanking you all for coming today to say your farewell to Michael. As you leave, the family has chosen a song that I'm told is Michael's all-time favorite." He turned, seeming a little hesitant as he nodded to one of his staffers, who must have cued up the song.

A loud, beautifully sung harmony cut through the air.

The person behind me snorted a laugh as they realized what song it was.

Moments later, guitars and loud drums kicked in as Queen's "Fat Bottomed Girls" reverberated off the walls. I smiled despite the pain I was feeling inside. My father had had a bold range of songs in his repertoire. This one, however inappropriate for a funeral, was his favorite song by his favorite artist. I couldn't have *not* played it for him one last time.

Next to me, my nana chuckled, releasing my hand, and started clapping along to the beat. I grinned over at her, seeing people doing the same, smiling, tapping their toes to the beat, their shoulders swaying a little, a few even mouthing the words to the song. All of us had probably seen my dad do air guitar to this song at least once in our lives. No one left the room until the last beat had been dropped.

When it was finally finished and people started to stand, the mood in the room was significantly lifted, as was my own.

My dad's friends, our family, neighbors, and his coworkers all started slowly walking past us to get to the side door, which led to the gardens on the side of the crematorium. Some stopped to say how sorry they were for our loss, some complimented us on the choice of song, and one of my father's friends even laughed and told me that he could almost see my dad whipping his head to that song from heaven. I smiled and nodded, thanking people for coming, telling them I would see them back at the house for a drink and some food.

"Such a lovely service," Great-Aunt Shelly noted. "The eulogy was perfect for Michael. I remember him as a child, such a naughty boy, but he had the cheekiest smile, so you could never tell him off." She laughed to herself and my nana nodded in agreement.

I reached out, placing a hand on Shelly's arm because she looked a little unsteady on her elderly legs. "Thank you for coming. Are you coming back to the house for a bite to eat?"

"Oh yes, I'll be there. I'll have to have Errol follow your car back to the house, though. I can't remember the way and he's never been," she replied, nodding back to her new boyfriend—well, he wasn't exactly a *boy*, he was eighty if he was a day.

My eyes wandered to the left while she told me about how slow Errol drove and how long it had taken them to get here to-day. Jamie was in the line, filing out behind a group of my dad's work friends. I bit my tongue, my eyes meeting his, and every-one else there seemed sort of insignificant as all my attention now went to the boy who broke my heart. He nodded slightly, but I saw it and it was enough for me to get the meaning. He was thanking me silently for letting him attend. I nodded back, praying he wouldn't approach me. With Toby standing just three feet from me, it would be überawkward and some-thing I wasn't prepared to deal with today at all. But true to his word, Jamie silently walked past, heading toward the door with the crowd.

I breathed a sigh of relief and tried to ignore an inappropriate stab of disappointment. Part of me had wanted him to come over, to be close enough that I could smell his cologne and feel the heat radiating from his body. Part of me had wanted him to wrap his arms around me and whisper in my ear that everything was okay and that he'd be here to help me through this. Part of me longed for him like I had when I was eighteen. That part of me, however much I had wanted it to, had not diminished over time.

I forced my eyes away from him as I felt heat flush my cheeks, my mind wandering to the kiss on Tuesday night and how it had created sparks of desire that threatened to ignite us both.

I turned to see Toby, who was offering Nana and Great-Aunt Shelly an arm each so he could help them navigate the wind-ing path back to the parking lot. My heart squeezed painfully at the sight and a wave of sadness and guilt washed over me like a bucket of cold water. Toby was such a good man, and I wished things were different. That *I* was different. That I hadn't been so broken when we'd met, that I hadn't allowed myself to believe I was fixed, because really, seeing Jamie again, I realized I had just been fooling us both. I wasn't over him, not even remotely, and I despised myself for that.

CHAPTER 16

JAMIE

SHAUN'S WEDDING WAS in full swing. The ceremony had gone without a hitch, and it was now the evening reception. They'd opted to go low key with it all, no sit-down meal but a huge buffet and an open bar instead. It was pretty much how I would have planned a wedding too—more emphasis on celebrating rather than formalities. A few people from my crew had already taken advantage of the free bar and were a little tipsy, but then again, most people were, especially Shaun.

"So you don't miss it?" I asked Shaun, watching him lean heavily on the bar and slurp his drink.

He shrugged one shoulder. "I miss some things. The guys. And the money." He sighed wistfully. "But I don't miss prison."

"You sure you don't want back in? I can use you on my team," I offered.

Shaun laughed and turned to me, his eyes glazed over from too much alcohol. "Can't. It's hard being broke and having to live paycheck to paycheck, but I wouldn't change it for the world. I get to wake up every day to my little boy and my beautiful girlfriend...oops, wife," he corrected, glancing down at the new gold ring on his finger. "They're two things money can't buy, so I'll just keep pushing on and saving up for shit I want."

"Good for you, I'm happy for you." I smiled and patted him on the shoulder. I respected that. To be honest, when I'd had Ellie in my life things like money and cars hadn't mattered to me, either. I guess when you love someone more than anything, everything else becomes a little inconsequential. I missed that.

"Thanks, man," Shaun slurred.

Ray and Enzo walked over then, Ray slinging his arm around Shaun's shoulder as he spoke. "You want to take it easy on the booze, there, Shaun. You want to be able to consummate the marriage tonight, don't you?"

"I can consummate anytime and in any state," Shaun boasted, grinning lopsidedly.

Ray turned his attention to me. "Are you ready to leave, Kid? I gotta be up early tomorrow," he lied.

I took the hint. It was time to go. The boost was waiting. "Yeah, sure thing. Thanks for inviting us, Shaun. And congrats again on the ball and chain," I joked, holding out my hand for him to shake. "Come to the club anytime, there's always no cover for you and the missus."

"Thanks, Kid. I will."

After Ray and Enzo had said their good-byes, we headed out to my car and back to the warehouse to get tonight's boost started. It was only a short drive, and the whole way there Ray was talking about Shaun and how good he looked. I had to admit, being a family man suited him. I tried not to acknowledge the jealous feeling that swirled in the pit of my stomach. If I hadn't been arrested, that could have been me and Ellie getting married today. If only I hadn't done that fucking job, my life would be so different.

Dodger, Chase, and Ed were already at the warehouse and

ready to go. Dodger and Chase were busy moving the three shipping container trucks into place, ready for when we brought the cars back.

I grabbed my boosting kit from the workbench and walked over to talk to Ed while Ray and Enzo went to change.

"Listen, when you're outside Ellie's tonight, be extra careful. She saw Dodger yesterday, and I'm pretty sure she made him at the funeral because she was looking at him funny. I don't want her to know anything about this, so park a little farther away and be extra vigilant," I told Ed, setting my bag down and sorting through it, checking that everything I would need tonight was in there. "Oh, and don't take the sedan, take one of the other cars in the lot," I added as an afterthought, nodding toward the front door where five cars sat ready and waiting. I'd purchased them for my crew to use when they saw fit. They weren't anything special, but some jobs were better done with an unmarked car than one that could be traced back to someone. It was prudent to be prepared, and they'd come in handy with the people watching Ellie for me, too.

"Okay, Kid." Ed sighed, plopping himself down onto the empty stool at the end of the workbench. "Are you sure you don't just want to pull the surveillance on this girl? If the Salazars were going to make a move, they would have done it by now."

"Not yet," I answered, removing my bolt cutters from the bag and laying them on the table so I could grease them just in case they were needed tonight. "Have you heard anything from them? What's Mateo up to?" I asked, glancing sideways at Ed.

"Still in Mexico," he answered, shrugging. I'd had a tail on the Salazars, too. Mateo had gone back to the village that he came from in Mexico and was visiting family, from what I'd heard.

"And Alberto?" I prompted.

Ed rolled his eyes. "Alberto wouldn't dare make a move like that. From what I gather, he was the one who sent Mateo away to lie low for a while after the whole rift with you in the club. I don't think the Salazar camp is united at the moment."

"Good. That's good."

Enzo walked over, now fully changed into jeans and a sweat-shirt, blowing air into his cupped hands to warm them. "Cold tonight," he muttered. "You ready? Dodge says I'm with you, and he's going to take Chase with him."

"I just need to change and then I'm ready," I replied, hastily putting all my stuff back into my bag. I turned to Ed. "Go relieve Spencer at Ellie's place. I'll come relieve you once this boost is done."

He nodded and turned for the door. "Hope the boost goes well."

"It will," I replied confidently. They always did.

* * *

The first and second boosts were an easy grab-and-go. Two beau-tiful Rolls-Royce Dawns that screamed elegance and money.

Two down, seven to go.

We arrived at the third car, a dark blue F-Type Jaguar parked in its driveway, at almost two in the morning.

"See you back at the warehouse," I told Enzo, grabbing my bag and checking up and down the street again before I jumped out and jogged toward the car. As I stepped onto the drive, the overhead security light flicked on, shining down on me almost like a spotlight. I froze, my eyes darting around. It was an auto-matic sensor, but you could never be too careful. Cars parked in private driveways were always more difficult, though not as bad as if I had to break into someone's garage and get it.

I looked up at the light; it was just above the garage, within easy reach. *These people never think!* Rolling my eyes, I pulled my bag from my back and fished out a pair of latex gloves, snapping them on before grabbing a black plastic sack from my bag, too. I headed over to the light, going up on tiptoes as I slipped the black sack over the light. It did the job I was hoping for and diffused most of the light, sending the street back into basic darkness again. Light still shined through the bottom and through the airholes at the top of the bag, but it wouldn't cast enough glow to show me stealing a precious sports car if anyone looked out their window.

I grinned back at Enzo, who gave me a thumbs-up, and then headed over to the car. Reaching into my bag again, I got out a booster's most valuable tool and shoved the thin bar down the side of the window. The lock popped open within a few seconds and I jumped in, cutting the wires on the alarm and resetting it quickly. Once the alarm was taken care of, I jimmied the steering column off and cut the wires, sparking them and breathing a happy sigh as the car purred to life.

"Piece of cake," I muttered, pushing it into gear and rolling out of the drive as slowly as I could so as not to arouse suspicion with what was sure to a be a loud, sexy roar of the engine.

When I got back to the warehouse, I passed Dodger on his way back out again and sent him a wave. He'd obviously just finished delivering a car back here. I pulled up outside one of the containers and climbed out. As I closed the door, a huge white scratch down the side of the car caught my attention.

"Mother dick!" I muttered, scowling at it. This hadn't been on the car yesterday morning, I'd scoped it myself for the pack. The stupid-ass owner must have scraped it within the last twenty-four hours. "Ray!" I called, watching him come out of the garage, wiping his hands on a rag. "Fucking big-ass scratch on the side of this one. And before you ask, no, I didn't do it."

His eyes tightened and he walked over to me, bending to run his fingers along the scratch. "Looks like it's just superficial. I can buff this out, no worries," he said finally, just as I was starting to worry that we either wouldn't be able to deliver the full list or would have to deliver this one damaged.

"Yeah?"

He nodded and stood. "Yep, no bother. Go get the last one. Dodger is on his last, too."

Dodger had more cars than me, but all of his were located closer. Hopefully we'd get done within the next hour, then. "All right, see you in a bit."

"Oh, and Kid, try not to scratch the next one," Ray called, winking at me jokingly before heading into the warehouse to get his repair kit.

"Hilarious," I muttered, climbing into the car with Enzo again. My mood was lower now, the high almost entirely worn off. All I wanted was to be done so I could go check and make sure Ellie was all right.

My fourth acquisition was going to be trickier. It was in a private underground parking lot of a luxury apartment building. There were cameras on the entrance and exit barriers, and only owners were allowed to park there. Fortunately, it wasn't hard to get my hands on a building pass. Anything was possible with the right amount of cash thrown at it.

When I spotted the car I was here for, my hands twitched with excitement. A brand-new Audi R8 V10 Plus Coupe, red with black trim. It was beautiful and less than a week old—$180,000 of car just sat there, ripe for the picking. A little excited grunt escaped my throat as I walked over to it, my eyes darting left and right to make sure I was alone.

Seeing no one around, I got to work and had the door open and the alarm reset in less than a minute. When I got the steering column off and sparked the wires, anticipating that growl of the engine, nothing happened. I frowned, trying again. Nothing. My eyes widened as I slumped down in the seat and ran my hand under the dash, looking for the kill switch. A lot of nice cars had them. A kill switch was essentially just a little switch that prevented the gas from getting to the engine. I wouldn't be able to take this one if I couldn't find it. This hadn't been in my briefing package.

When my search returned nothing, I concluded it had to be under the hood. Popping the hood, I slid out of the car, making sure the lot was still clear. Grabbing my flashlight from my bag, I yanked the hood up and ran my hand over the inside of the chassis. *Got it!* I pressed the switch and let the hood down easy. Kill switches were remarkably effective, so long as you kept them out of sight.

I grinned and headed back to the driver's side, shutting the door quietly and sparking the wires again, laughing as the car started up. Tossing my bag on the passenger seat, I tugged my baseball cap lower and drove toward the barrier, pulling my fake security pass from my pocket. One quick swipe and the yellow-and-black barrier rose.

Although everything in me wanted to celebrate, I kept my head down and my face tilted away from the camera as I eased out onto the street. When I was on the main road and home free, I couldn't keep the smile off my face as I decided to see how fast this baby could go. I depressed the gas harder, really letting go. There was no one around, so the road was deserted.

The journey to the warehouse in one of these babies was exhilarating, like there was a demon under the hood, trying to escape every time I touched the gas. I decided on the short drive back that I was going to buy myself one of these.

It didn't take long to finish up once I was back. After I settled up with everyone and paid them their nightly boost fee, Chase, Enzo, and Dodger each drove a truck to the rendezvous point to meet with the client. Ray was going to follow them and bring them all back here again to collect their own cars. I myself had something else planned for the rest of the night. No sleep for me.

* * *

"Hey. How'd the boost go?" Ed asked when I went to relieve him on stakeout duty.

"Without a hitch, as usual," I replied, shrugging. I motioned toward Ellie's house with my chin. "Any problems?" I asked, glancing into his car, seeing an iPad and a couple of magazines piled on his seat and empty candy wrappers dotted over the floor of the passenger side.

"Not a one. She's been inside all night, all of them have. Her friend, the smokin' hot blonde one, came over for a while, but she left around eleven. Lights have been off for the last couple of hours." He yawned and checked his watch before reaching for a can of soda and taking a swig of it.

Nodding, I took hold of the handle and opened the car door. "Okay, thanks. You can go for the night and just take my car back to the warehouse."

Ed climbed out of the car, stretching his back and groaning. "Someone taking you off tomorrow, or do you want me to arrange it?" he asked, and then pointed to his iPad. "Pass me that, would ya?"

"Spencer is coming back to relieve me," I replied, passing him his tablet before taking up his spot in the car. I hated that the seat still retained the warmth from his ass.

He patted the window frame and stood. "All right. Have fun."

As his taillights disappeared into the darkness of the night, I turned my attention to Ellie's house, scooting down in the seat to get more comfortable, and picked up the energy drink I'd brought with me. The house was indeed quiet. No lights on, no signs of life. My mind wandered to Ellie and what she was doing inside. Was she sleeping soundly or tossing and turning, worrying about her mother? Was she talking in her sleep? Was she cuddled up next to her fiancé or was he not a snuggling type of guy? I sighed, wishing I were him, wishing she were mine and that I were huddled against the warmth of her body in her hot-pink bedroom rather than sitting in the cold, uncomfortable car. My life fucking sucked.

CHAPTER 17

ELLIE

TODAY WAS TOBY'S last day here with me in New York. He didn't want to go, and I didn't want him to, but he'd only managed to arrange a week's worth of cover at the pub. It had been great having him here; he took my mind—well, *all* of our minds—off the horrible situation we were in. Having him here to support me relieved some of the pressure.

Of course, he'd managed to charm my nana to the point where she was baking his favorite foods every day, and he even managed to bring my sister out of her shell by teaching her some rhyming slang. Toby had a heart of gold, and I absolutely did not want to watch him jet off and leave me.

During the limited downtime we'd had since the funeral, we'd tried to show him some of the sights. Monday we'd gone to the Empire State Building, Times Square, Rockefeller Center, and Central Park. Yesterday we'd caught a Broadway show. Today was the big one, though, the one he was really looking forward to—Lady Liberty. When given the choice of all the things he could do while here, he put that at the absolute top of his list. Not because it was a historical landmark or anything like that; no, it was because the Ghostbusters had made the thing come to life with pink slime and walk through the streets to the tune of "(Your Love Keeps Lifting Me) Higher and Higher." I was engaged to a geek.

It was early by the time we arrived at Battery Park and stood in the security line waiting for the ferry to start operating for the day. Unfortunately, because we hadn't booked weeks in advance, we couldn't go into the crown, but Toby was still as giddy as a child waiting in line to meet a department store Santa.

"Queue selfie," Toby said, whipping out his phone. "I'm gonna send this to my mum, she'll be well jel."

I smiled and leaned in next to him, sticking out my tongue at the last second and giggling when he poked me in the side with one finger. He draped his arm across my shoulder and looked out over the water. "This is great. I'm gutted that this is my last day, I don't want to leave you." He turned back to me, his mouth turning down in a frown as he pulled me closer to his body.

"I don't want you to leave, either," I mumbled, pressing my face into the side of his neck and breathing him in. His flight was at six p.m., and he had to be there a couple of hours before, so we only had a few hours left together. I was making them all count.

Once the ferry opened, the line moved pretty quickly and we were over at the island in no time. Toby got more and more excited as time passed; his little face lit up when we approached the statue and he shielded his eyes, leaning back to look all the way to the top. We took no end of selfies. After an age of exploring and just sitting and appreciating the vast beauty of the statue, Toby started humming the theme song from *Ghostbusters*, and the forty-or-so-year-old man next to him with the expensive camera hanging around his neck laughed and hummed along, too.

It was official: Toby could make friends anywhere, without even saying a word.

"How many times you seen the Statue of Liberty, then? Bet you're bored of it, aren't you?" Toby asked, leaning his head on my shoulder, his arms wrapped around my tummy as he pressed against my back.

I smiled. "Lots and lots," I replied, turning in his arms so we were face-to-face. "But I can honestly say I've never enjoyed it as much as today." Seeing it through his eyes, how excited and impressed he was, it made me appreciate it on a whole new level.

When my stomach growled, ruining the sweet moment, he grinned. "How about we raid the gift shop and then go get some lunch? Can't 'ave you getting hangry, can I?"

I nodded. "You wouldn't like me when I'm hangry."

"Sweetheart, I've seen it. It was truly terrifying."

Once loaded up with snow globes that he'd never be able to get home in one piece, key rings, bottle openers, and notebooks decorated with Lady Liberty, we hopped back on a ferry and over to the mainland. I led him to a great pizza restaurant I knew and came to often with Stacey.

As soon as we stepped into the restaurant, my mouth was watering at all the delicious smells wafting through the air. It was just before twelve and the place was heaving with people already. I took Toby's hand, tugging him to the counter so we could order. His eyes widened as he looked at all the precooked pizzas in the glass case under the heat lamp.

"Bloody 'ell, they're ruddy 'uge!"

I laughed and sidestepped when the person in front of me turned, carrying his food. "What do you want?" I asked Toby before turning my attention to the young pimple-faced server. "Hi, can I get a slice of pepperoni and a Diet Coke?" I turned to Toby, waiting for him to add his order.

"Same, thanks," he muttered, watching the server put two ginormous slices of pizza into the oven to reheat, before turning to make our drinks. When the hot slices were laid onto paper plates and pushed toward us, the pure want in Toby's eyes made me smile.

"I'll get these, I got loads of dollars left to use," Toby said, waving me off when I dug in my purse to get some money out. I smiled at Toby and picked up the two plates of food, being careful that the flimsy paper plates didn't bend as I walked to an empty booth at the back of the restaurant.

I slid in, the plastic-covered cushion squeaking under my behind. Moments later Toby came over with the two drinks, pushing one to me as he sat down on the opposite side. "You been in 'ere before?" he asked, tugging his plate toward him.

I nodded, picking up my drink and taking a pull on the straw. "Yeah, Stacey and I used to come in here when we were shopping and stuff."

Toby nodded absentmindedly, his hand reaching out to the napkin dispenser and moving it, looking behind it, a frown on his face. "Where's the cutlery?"

I grinned and shook my head. "You're in New York, you have to eat like one of us. Pick it up, you pansy."

His frown deepened. Toby's mama raised him right, and I'd never seen him eat pizza without a knife and fork. "Really?" He picked up his pizza with one hand and it immediately flopped over, drooping toward the plate. He frowned, using his other hand to straighten it so he could take a bite from the end.

"You British people suck at pizza," I joked, winking at him. "Fold it." I picked up my slice, folding the two sides together and taking a rather large bite, the greasy cheese hitting my tongue and making me groan in appreciation.

He grunted. "American weirdos." He did as I did, folding his slice and taking a massive bite, his eyes closing as he savored the flavor. I smiled, chewing slowly, glancing around at the busyness of the place. "It's official, New York 'as ruined me for English pizzas. From now on all pizzas will be compared to this," Toby announced, instantly taking another huge bite. "It's so good," he muttered, his mouth still full as his shoulders sagged in appreciation.

"Much better than that gross pie and mash with the green stuff you Londoners call good food," I agreed. I'd never seen the attraction to the pie and mash shop that Toby raved about—the mash was stodgy and had no butter, the pie was all flat and had a weird pastry, and to top it off, they covered the whole thing in some sort of strange parsley sauce that they called liquor. If that didn't turn your stomach, most people then added vinegar to their food, too. Disgusting.

"Oi, don't knock the pie 'n' mash shops," Toby replied, raising one eyebrow in playful reprimand.

I grinned and chewed in silence, and then the conversation turned to the inevitable—him going home. We'd both been ignoring it all morning.

"Ellie, I'm really sorry I can't stay longer. I feel like a right muppet going 'ome and leaving you on your own," he said, taking a large bite of his pizza.

"I'm not alone, I'll be fine. Promise."

He nodded, setting down the crust of his pizza and sitting back to rub his stomach in appreciation. "So 'ow long do you reckon you'll need to be 'ere? Should I start planning another flight over and arranging cover for in a couple of weeks' time, or do you think you'll be 'ome by then?" he asked, watching me carefully.

I wasn't sure we were ready to talk about this, or that we were ready to deal with it once we said the words.

"I'm not sure. Toby, I…" I swallowed and dropped my eyes to my plate, wiping my fingers on the napkin, no longer in the mood for food. My stomach clenched, a sense of dread and trepidation settling there. "I don't know what's going to happen. If my mom doesn't wake up…" I closed my eyes, hating that I now doubted she would, but it had been a week and a half; her chances were slim. "There's Kelsey to think about," I finished.

He nodded, tapping one finger on the table, clearly unnerved by the direction this conversation was taking, too. "If the worst 'appens and your mom doesn't wake, what will you do?"

Hating the nervousness in his voice, I looked up at him. "I'll be Kelsey's guardian," I whispered. I wouldn't leave her again. I'd promised.

He nodded slowly and sat back in the booth; his posture seemed deliberately relaxed, like he was working to make it that way. "And do you think she'd want to come to England?"

I blew out a slow breath. I hadn't spoken to her about it because that would mean admitting that I had doubts about our mother's survival, but I didn't think she would want to. It would mean giving up her friends, her home, her education, all to follow her sister to a foreign land where she didn't know anyone. I was almost certain, without having to ask, that wouldn't be something she would want to do at all. And I would never make her. This was her home; I had no right to make her leave it for my own personal gain.

"I don't think so," I muttered.

His eye twitched and his Adam's apple bobbed as he swallowed. "I don't think she would, either."

"Would you move here?" I asked, but deep down I already knew the answer. Toby had his kids at home, he was a great dad, he loved having his kids as much as possible, and he would never move to another country. And, to be honest, I wouldn't really want him to. I loved his kids too, and I would never want to deprive them of him.

He shifted on the bench, his shoulders hunching as he leaned forward and took my hand on the tabletop. His eyes narrowed in apology, his mouth tight. "Ellie, I . . . I got the boys," he whispered.

I nodded quickly. "I know."

He blew out a big breath and raked a hand through his hair roughly. "I'm not sure where it would leave us. We'd 'ave to find some sort of middle ground, compromise, if there is any."

There was no middle ground here—we both knew it, but neither of us wanted to say it. "Long-distance relationships . . . they don't work," I muttered, my voice breaking as I spoke. My heart was sinking, sadness already building in my chest.

Toby swallowed and my words hung in the air for a long minute as we just looked at each other silently. He was a smart man; he knew the score and what this meant.

Suddenly he shook his head and his hand tightened on mine, squeezing gently. "Look, let's not get our knickers in a twist 'bout it now. We're worrying 'bout something that may never 'appen. Your mum could wake any day, and then once she was better, she'd be able to take care of Kelsey and you could come 'ome."

Home. The word made me feel worse because now that I was back here, I already knew I *was* home. I'd just been fooling myself in England, hiding from my problems, trying to be a different version of myself. Now that I was back, after losing my dad and all that we were going through with my mom, I knew, deep down, that I didn't want to leave them again, even if my mom did recover. I'd left before and wasted time I could have had with my family. I wanted to be near them again, be here for them, always. But that meant that I couldn't be near Toby. It was a horrible choice, but one my heart and soul had already made, however much it hurt. And I think he knew it, too. His eyes held mine, his gaze understanding, but I could see the pain there.

Toby cleared his throat awkwardly. "Let's just stick a pin in it for now. We'll cross that bridge if we come to it. Your mum might be fine, and then we're getting all worried over nothing. It's another day's problem." His tone held forced cheer that I could detect a mile off.

He knew, he just didn't want to admit it. Neither of us did. We'd had a good thing, and with one accident and phone call, our relationship was basically destroyed. We could never go back to what we'd had, and that was like a punch to the stomach.

I forced a smile too, trying to make it look genuine as I nodded. "Yeah, we'll just focus on now and see what happens," I agreed. I checked my watch, seeing it was almost one. "We'd better go."

After taking another swig of his drink, he nodded and stood, picking up the bag containing his souvenirs and then holding his hand out to me. I smiled and slipped my hand into his larger one, stepping to his side and following him out of the restaurant and down the busy street toward the bus stop.

The ride back to my house was mostly silent apart from the low rumble of the engine and the soft chatter of the other passengers. It was a little awkward. We were both hurting, but instead of confiding in each other, we were both choosing to deal with it separately.

When we arrived home, Toby packed the snow globes and other trinkets into his case and then said his good-byes to my family. My nana looked extremely sorry to see him go; he had definitely won her over in a short space of time. Kelsey hugged him tightly and told him to make sure to call or there would be "ruddy 'ell to pay"—she'd definitely mastered the English terms. I watched it all with a lump in my throat. I watched how easily he conversed with my loved ones and how much camaraderie he had with my little sister, and my heart started to break. I blinked back tears, sorrow and despondency swirling in my stomach.

"Ready?" I asked, clearing my throat.

He turned back to me and nodded. "Yeah." He turned back to my nana and smiled that charming lopsided smile that made his eyes crinkle at the edges. "Thanks for 'aving me. And for packing me food for the flight." He patted his flight bag and grinned.

"You're welcome, dear. You come back soon, all right?" Nana said, leaning in and planting another kiss on his cheek. I walked out of the house, heading to my car, needing to be away from their final good-bye. In a way, I was already trying to distance myself. Toby had been such an enormous part of bringing me back to myself after Jamie, I owed him so much, and now it was coming to an end, and I didn't want it to.

He followed me out to the car a minute later, slinging his case onto the backseat and sliding in the passenger door. "Your nana just made me take some more of her banana cake for the flight."

I smiled, gripping the wheel tightly as I started the engine. "You do know you can't take food through customs, right?"

He nodded. "I know. I think she just wanted to feel useful; she's a carer that one, not 'appy unless people are fed."

He'd nailed her personality traits in just one short week. I smiled and nodded, and silence fell over us again. I tried to keep my mood up, but by the time we got to the airport I was just a fraction short of tears and barely holding myself together.

When we got out of the car, Toby looked off to one side and smiled before digging in his backpack and pulling out the brown bag chock-full of sandwiches, cake, chips, and cartons of juice.

"Be right back," he muttered, jogging off. I shielded my eyes and watched him approach a homeless man who was rooting through one of the trash cans. When he handed over the package, the toothless homeless man's gratitude was clear to see, even from where I stood a hundred or so yards away.

My heart throbbed, and again I wished things were different, that I could somehow keep him.

When Toby came back to my side, he smiled, taking my hand in his and dragging his suitcase in the other as we headed into the busy airport. I frowned, a little uncomfortable to be in the terminal again. The last time I took a flight out of here I had been alone and heartbroken. Now as I stood there again, preparing to say good-bye to the person who had helped fix me, my heart was splintering all over again.

After he'd checked in for his flight, we walked over to the security line where I wasn't allowed to go. When he turned to me and offered me that lopsided smile, I lost the battle I was having with my tears and they started to flow relentlessly down my cheeks. He groaned and wrapped his arms around me, pulling me in for a tight hug, almost crushing me in its ferocity. The hug lasted way longer than a comforting one would—it was as if he didn't want to let go either. We were clinging to each other as people just got on with their lives around us, unaware of the pain we were sharing.

He finally pulled back, sliding his hands up my back until he cupped my neck. His watery light green eyes locked onto mine and I could see it there: understanding, acceptance, anguish. The unspoken breakup lingered in his eyes. He somehow knew I wouldn't be going back to England, and he understood why.

"I really love you, you know?" he murmured.

I nodded, my body hitching with a sob. "I love you, too."

And I did; it might not be the all-consuming, weak-at-the-knees, swoon-worthy love I'd had in the past, but I loved him deeply.

He smiled weakly and leaned in, planting a soft, lingering kiss against my lips. Featherlight, but it held so much emotion that it almost knocked me off my feet. I whimpered against his lips, gripping fistfuls of his shirt as I pressed against him, savoring every last detail, categorizing it, storing it so I would never forget what that one last beautiful kiss felt like. It wasn't a lust-filled kiss, it was a sweet good-bye kiss.

I watched him until he was out of sight, feeling like I'd just said good-bye to my best friend. I felt hollowed out, empty, and everything was getting on top of me.

But I couldn't afford to let myself sink into depression or I would never get out of it again. Plus, staying busy would keep my mind occupied. There would be time for tears later when I was alone in bed; I couldn't allow myself to fully feel it now.

Instead of going straight home from the airport, I decided to make a quick stop at the funeral director's to let him know I was on top of the invoice. I just needed a few more days to get it sorted out and wanted to explain.

I parked in the little lot next to Mortimer and Witcombe Funeral Directors and grabbed my purse, heading for the entrance. As I stepped in the door and the little bell above it announced my presence, a plump lady with blue-rinse set hair looked up, her lips stretching into a warm smile. "Good afternoon. Can I help you?"

"I was wondering if I could have a quick word with Mr. Mortimer? My name is Ellie Pearce. Mr. Mortimer was the one looking after my father last week," I said, wringing my hands because I was a little nervous. I didn't like this place. It reeked of death and sadness. Just being in here I could feel my mood sinking even lower than when I'd said good-bye to Toby less than an hour ago.

"Of course. He's between appointments right now. Follow me and I'll show you to his office," she replied, standing and brushing down the skirt of her pale pink suit. I followed her slowly, stopping outside the office that I knew belonged to Mr. Mortimer because I'd been in there numerous times over the last week. She knocked gently. "Maurice, I have Miss Pearce here to see you."

"Oh, show her in, Beryl."

She turned and waved me in, pushing the door all the way open. I smiled in thanks and stepped into the room, looking over to Mr. Mortimer, who was sitting behind his desk. He stood and walked around to greet me, his hand held out in front of him.

"Hi, Ellie, how are you doing?" He shook my hand and gripped my forearm at the same time with his other hand, a handshake he'd no doubt perfected over the years, one that conveyed just the right amount of sympathy—if a handshake could do such a thing.

"I'm doing well. I wanted to thank you in person for all your help with the funeral. It went off very smoothly," I said, but he already knew it had because he'd been there to oversee it all.

"You're very welcome." He waved me into a seat, and he perched on the edge of his desk, facing me.

"I also wanted to let you know I'll be paying your invoice soon. Things have just been a little difficult, what with me just returning home from overseas. It's been a bit of a struggle, but I promise I'll get it sorted out in the next couple of days. I've put in a call to my UK bank to get money transferred over to my old U.S. checking account so I can withdraw it, but it's taking a few days. I hadn't anticipated that getting money from a UK savings account would be so difficult from here," I explained.

Luckily, I'd been saving money to pay for the wedding. But it looked as though it would be spent a different way now.

His eyebrows knitted together in confusion. "But the invoice has already been paid."

I shook my head. "I haven't paid it."

He smiled, the kind of smile that implied he felt sorry for me in some way or that he thought he was talking to someone who wasn't all there mentally. "The invoice was paid in full Friday morning over the phone."

I reeled back. "Excuse me?"

He nodded. "Your account is clear. A man called up on the morning of the funeral to make sure everything was on track for the service. He paid the full amount on his debit card. He said he was a friend of the family and that you'd asked him to do it for you."

My mouth dropped open in astonishment. I owed thousands; there's no way someone had just called up and paid it off. Unless... was it Toby? Had he done it without telling me so I would have one less thing to worry about? But why wouldn't he have told me already? Then I realized it couldn't be him because he'd been sitting next to me when I'd put the call in to the bank on Monday asking for them to get the money moved into my U.S. account.

"Who was it that paid?" I inquired.

He frowned, standing up and heading back around to his desk chair. "I think it was a Mr. Colt or Cole or something like that. I can't remember off the top of my head. Let me check," he replied, already pulling open a filing cabinet drawer and searching through it.

Mr. Cole. Jamie Cole. My whole body stiffened and my eyes

widened at his name. Jamie had paid for my father's funeral? Had he known I was struggling for money and barely had enough to cover the fees for it? I was stunned into silence.

The thought, the sentiment hit me hard and my heart squeezed. That was the kind of thing that had caused me to fall in love with him in the first place, that thoughtful, compassionate side of him that shined so brightly.

"Ah, here it is," Mr. Mortimer said, pulling out a light green sheet of paper and scanning it. "Yes, a Mr. J. Cole. Paid in full." He set the piece of paper on the desk and slid it toward me. "Was I not right to accept? Do you not know who this person is?" He now looked a little worried, his eyes narrowed in concern.

"I do," I replied quietly.

I pressed my lips together, unsure how to even begin to process this information. I swallowed the lump in my throat and looked down at my hands, my mind reeling. Had he done this on purpose, knowing I would find out he'd paid so I would owe him something in return? No, that wasn't who he was. But then again, I didn't know him as well as I'd thought I had. One thing I knew for sure, though: I would have to go and see him now and find out what the hell he thought he was doing interfering in things that weren't his business anymore. I wasn't looking forward to that at all.

"Is everything all right, Ellie?" Mr. Mortimer asked, touching my elbow.

I jumped. I hadn't noticed he'd come around to my side of the desk again and had crouched down beside me, his face a mask of concern.

I forced a smile and nodded. "Everything's fine, thanks. I just hadn't realized Mr. Cole had paid, that's all. I'm glad you've got your money, and I apologize for taking up your time today." I stood, needing to get out of the room.

He used the arm of the chair to push himself to his feet, too. "Are you sure everything is all right? You look a little shaken up."

I nodded quickly, fixing a smile in place as I held out my hand to him. "Thank you again for a beautiful service." I shook his pudgy hand quickly and turned for the door, walking quickly down the hall and out the front door without stopping, even though the receptionist called a good-bye to me on my way out.

I stopped once I was through the door and stepped to the side so the receptionist couldn't see me, leaning against the wall, taking deep breaths. My chest was closing up again, an anxiety attack looming.

Why? Why had he done this to me? Why couldn't he just leave me alone instead of making me dredge up feelings from the past that should stay exactly where they belonged—in the past?

CHAPTER 18

AS I SAT in the uncomfortable hospital chair by my mother's side, I wasn't sure how much more I could take.

Everything was piling on: losing Dad, his funeral, the prospect of having to be Kelsey's guardian if the worst happened, saying good-bye to Toby yesterday and realizing our relationship was basically over because of a decision I'd already unconsciously made, and to top it off, Jamie paying my debt. Apparently diamonds are made under pressure, but I was pretty sure the pressure would just gradually grind me down to nothing. Nope, no diamonds here.

I sighed and sat forward, taking Mom's hand carefully. "Mom, I don't know if you can hear me, but if you can, please wake up," I whispered. My eyes fluttered closed and I pressed her hand to my face. "I need you. Kelsey needs you. I don't know if I can carry on like this; there's so much going on, too much sadness and heartache. I'm trying to put on a brave face, but I'm really struggling to keep everything together. It feels like I'm drowning, and I don't know what to do. I'm trying to remain hopeful, but every time I sit here, I fear that you're going to leave too and I don't think I could bear it. I don't have much more fight left in me, so please, if you can hear me please come back." I opened my eyes and looked at the steady blip of her heart rate monitor. No change. Nothing. If she could hear me, then surely there would be something to show for it, some sign?

"Mom, please. I can't arrange another funeral, I can't lose another parent and neither can Kels. We need you, so please fight this. Please wake up," I begged, looking again at the heart rate monitor. Nothing.

I gulped, disappointment settling in my stomach. I just wanted to sit in a dark room and hug my knees to my chest in silence. Depression was ebbing over me slowly, casting its spell and dragging me down. If I allowed it, it would take over and cloak me in darkness. But I couldn't let it. I had to keep going for Kelsey. Keeping my spirits high, or at least pretending to, was the hardest thing I had ever done, but I owed it to my little sister to push through and not give up.

"I gotta go. I'll be back later with Kels and Nana." I stood and leaned over my mom, kissing her cheek. "Sleep tight but wake up soon." I pulled back and gathered my purse and magazines before heading out of the hospital, wondering how many more times I would have to come here before we knew one way or the other what her fate was.

On the way to my car I pulled my cell phone from my purse, switching the airplane mode off. Just as I was about to put it away, a message came through from Nana.

Please can you pick up some ground beef, tomatoes, and eggs on your way home?

I sent back a short yep reply and climbed into the car. Closing my eyes, I gripped the steering wheel so tightly my knuckles ached.

"I don't want to adult anymore," I muttered into the emptiness of the car.

After a few deep breaths to try to calm my frazzled nerves, I twisted the key in the ignition, pumping the gas and hearing how much the engine was struggling to catch. My car had never been the most reliable at the best of times, and apparently using it so much in the last couple of weeks had taken its toll on the poor old girl. On the second try, the car started, a large plume of black smoke fluttering up past my back window that didn't look healthy at all. I would most likely have to buy a new car soon. If I was going to be responsible for Kels, I couldn't have an unreliable car.

Another thing to worry about...

I drove to the convenience store halfway between the hospital and my house and jumped out, grabbing Nana's requested items and also choosing a chocolate bar to eat on the way home. I needed a sugar pick-me-up.

As I was standing in line to pay, I noticed a tall, olive-skinned guy standing just outside the main exit. He was probably in his early thirties, dressed in dark jeans and a black long-sleeve tee with a leather biker's vest over the top. He seemed to be staring straight at me. As I looked over, our eyes caught and he quickly looked away, dropping his cigarette butt on the floor and stubbing it out with a chunky black boot. There was something about his posture, something about the way he appeared to be watching me and quickly looked away that made the hair on the back of my neck prickle with unease.

"Nine eighty-five."

I jumped, startled, and looked at the cashier, a young girl

chewing gum loudly who was waiting with her hand extended, her expression bored. I hadn't even realized I was at the front of the checkout. Opening my purse, I pulled out a ten and held it out to her, then quickly bagged my items. When I looked up at the door again, the guy was gone and the uneasy feeling in my tummy vanished.

I was just being stupid.

Shouldering my purse, I picked up my goods and used my teeth to savagely rip open my candy bar wrapper. As I walked around the back of the store and across the empty parking lot, I took large bites, not even bothering to savor it. I just needed the sugar. When I stopped next to my bug, I struggled to get my keys out, juggling the bag and my candy bar as I dug in my pocket for them.

When something shoved me from behind, I didn't even see it coming. My stomach and chest slammed against the side of my car; air left my lips in a grunted *"oomph"* as everything I was carrying slid from my arms, hitting the ground. Something hard pressed against my back, pinning me against the car.

"What?" I cried, panic gripping my heart.

A hand grasped a fistful of my hair, shoving my head down so all I could see was feet, concrete, the contents of my purse scattered everywhere, and the eggs that were oozing out of the bottom of the paper bag. "Keep still! If you make a sound, I'll slit your throat," a guy growled into my ear as his body pressed harder against mine, pinning me in place.

My breath was coming out in quick, shallow gasps as I tried to comprehend what was happening and what the hell I should do. Self-preservation kicked in and I shoved backward, struggling and wriggling to get free. As I opened my mouth, intending to scream blue bloody murder, something cold and sharp pressed against the skin at my neck, digging in to the point of stinging, but not pain. I whimpered and squeezed my eyes shut, my struggle stopping immediately.

I'm going to die. I'm going to die. That was all I could think, over and over.

When a car sped into the parking lot and squealed to a stop behind me, I was roughly yanked backward, the knife nicking the skin at my throat. I gasped, immediately reaching up to grasp at the guy's hand, attempting to pull his arm from my throat as my eyes began to water. My gaze darted left and right, looking for help, praying for someone else to be in the parking lot and to come and help me. But from what I could see, it was deserted. Because it was at the back of the shop, there was no way people could see me being attacked from the street, either.

"Get her in the back," another man ordered from somewhere behind me. I heard the click of a car door opening. Panic was taking over, and my heart was hammering in my ears as the guy's arm wrapped around my middle, practically lifting me from my feet as I was half dragged toward the dark blue car that had just arrived. Knowing there was no way I could let him get me into the car, I kicked my legs out roughly, scratched with my nails, flailed my arms—anything in a bid to get free.

I heard the new guy hiss, "Oh, fuck. Is that...?" And suddenly, the man who was holding me loosened his grip around my waist, his hand dropping away from my throat, and I was bumped roughly back to my feet. I fell forward, sprawling face-first onto the ground and scratching my hands and knees in the process. Something was pressing down on my legs, pinning me heavily.

I gulped for air and whipped my head around to see what had happened, at the same time preparing myself to wriggle free, get up, and run as fast as I could toward the street.

What I saw took a couple of seconds to comprehend. The guy holding me, whom I now recognized as the same man who had been watching me outside the store, was slumped heavily across the lower half of my legs. His eyes were closed and his body slack. Blood trickled slowly from the back of his head down around his ear and across his cheek.

My eyes caught a movement three feet away. When I realized what it was, my panic marginally subsided. Jamie. I recognized him immediately even though he was wearing a red cap. I would know him anywhere. He stood there, his posture relaxed as he held a baseball bat in one hand, twirling it around like the players do when they're showing off. His attention wasn't on me, though; his eyes were locked on the second guy, the one who'd arrived in the car.

"You totally fucked up," Jamie spat, stepping toward the other man, raising the bat at the same time.

The other guy shook his head quickly, his hands going up in an *I surrender* gesture, but Jamie either didn't care or didn't see because he swung the bat anyway. A sickening thud of wood hitting flesh and bone caused me to flinch as the bat collided with the side of the guy's knee. A scream of pain cut the air as he immediately slumped to the ground, one hand going behind his back, fumbling for something as his other arm came up to shield his face. I saw Jamie bring the bat down again, this time smashing into the guy's arm at full force, eliciting another scream of agony.

I wriggled free of the unconscious guy and pushed up to my feet. What I hadn't banked on was that my legs would be so uncooperative. I stumbled forward again, hitting the side of my car and managing to keep myself upright as I turned back to see that the second guy was now lying on his side, his arm at an odd, horrifying angle that made bile rise in my throat. His good hand was still fumbling behind his back. My heart raced as I watched the scene, morbidly transfixed.

The guy pulled his good arm free, a black handgun gripped in his fist, and whipped it around so quickly it was almost a blur as he pointed it at Jamie.

"Look out!" I screamed. But of course, Jamie was already prepared and aimed a swift kick at the guy's outstretched hand, knocking it sideways before he had a chance to pull the trigger.

When the man righted himself and went to aim the gun again, Jamie raised his foot, bringing it down on top of the guy's wrist in a hard stomp, pinning it in place as he leaned down and quickly plucked the weapon from the other man's hand. Jamie's back was to me now, but I could tell by his posture that he was furious; his shoulders were stiff, his muscles taut as he raised the gun and smashed the side of it straight into the man's face, his nose instantly gushing blood as his body stilled.

Jamie didn't turn back to me; instead, he crouched down, tugging at the man's sleeve, pulling it up to expose a tattooed forearm. I heard a sharp intake of breath from Jamie's direction. "Motherfucker," he muttered quietly before standing and pushing the gun into the back of his pants.

I looked down, seeing the two unconscious men, the blood, their broken bodies lying there next to a puddle of smashed eggs, and my vision started to cloud at the edges. I leaned back heavily against the car, hearing the rush of blood in my ears as my hands began to tingle.

My whole body was heavy as Jamie walked toward me, stooping to pick up the large silver knife that had been held at my throat. He pushed that into the waistband of his pants, too. My knees wobbled and I tried to take deep breaths. I could feel unconsciousness pulling at me. I knew it was because I was hyperventilating, but I could do nothing about it, I was in a total meltdown state.

"Ellie, it's okay," Jamie whispered, dropping the bloodstained bat at my feet with a loud clatter. He stepped closer to me as his hands cupped my face, tilting my head up, dragging my attention from the broken bodies and forcing it onto him instead. His brown eyes were soft and concerned as they met mine. "It's okay, little girl. Shh. I got you. Everything's okay now," he cooed, moving closer and wrapping one arm around me, holding me up as my legs gave out and I began to fall. My head slumped forward, my forehead against his neck. My eyes fluttered closed. His smell surrounded me in an invisible cloak of protection, the scent so recognizable it was as if I'd never been away from it; that, coupled with his whispered words, slowly brought my breathing under control, and my heartbeat calmed to a fast gallop instead of a sprint.

We stood like that for a minute or so before a groan from the ground made Jamie pull back. His face changed in an instant. No longer soft and concerned, now it was fury personified. I'd never seen anyone so murderously angry—his eyes tightened, his lip pulled into a sneer. Looking around him, I saw that the guy who had grabbed me was waking up. He was clearly groggy as he blinked rapidly, struggling to get to all fours.

As soon as Jamie's body left mine, I was instantly cold and felt a shiver run up my spine. His fists clenched so tightly his knuckles whitened. The man didn't even see the first blow coming. Jamie aimed a swift kick into the man's stomach, sending him rolling onto his back and causing a guttural cry of pain to leave his lips.

What followed next was like something from a movie. I'd never seen such violence in real life and I never wanted to again. Jamie straddled the guy's chest, throwing punch after punch into his face, his head jerking with each blow. Blood spurted from cuts and welts, his eyes swelled to the point of closure, instant bruises covered his face, and his movements stopped as his body went limp.

"Jamie?" I shook my head, unable to look away. "Jamie, stop," I pleaded, my voice barely above a whisper. Setting my hands on my car behind me, I pushed myself upright, praying my legs would support me. "Jamie?"

As if he'd heard me, he ceased his savage assault and stood. I huffed a sigh of relief that quickly got stuck in my throat as he gripped the gun in his pants and pulled it out, aiming at the now-unconscious man's face. I whimpered and staggered forward, my hand closing around his shoulder, pulling with what little strength I could muster. "No!" I cried desperately. "Jamie, no, don't. Please don't." I knew his past—I knew he'd killed before, he'd told me that he'd lost control when his sister was killed—but that was entirely different. I could see he was in control of himself; this would just be cold-blooded, revenge-fueled murder, and I couldn't condone that.

When he turned back to me, his eyes were murderous, his face set. He wanted to kill this man, probably kill them both. He'd changed so much from the boy I knew—so, so much. It hurt to see it. "Ellie, I have to. I have to make you safe." His eyes tightened, and I could see the anguish there, the desperate need.

I shook my head and stepped closer to him, my eyes locked on his. "Don't, Jamie. This isn't you, this can't be you," I whimpered.

His jaw tightened, and he looked back at the man on the ground, a vile hate plastered on his features.

I swallowed, unsure if I was fighting a losing battle. "I'm safe now," I assured him, reaching out and setting my hand on his cheek, pulling his gaze back to mine. "I'm fine. See?" I begged him with my eyes, silently pleaded with him not to take away the good that I'd always seen in his heart, that I *still* saw in him even though it was hidden by a cloud of rage.

He closed his eyes and nodded, his hand dropping to his side, and I breathed a sigh of relief. I stepped closer to him, wrapping my heavy, uncoordinated arms around his waist and pressing myself against him.

His arms folded around me, holding me tightly as his lips pressed against the side of my head. "I was almost too late. I don't know what I would have done. I don't know..." he muttered into my hair, his arms tightening around me almost desperately.

"I'm fine," I repeated, knowing he needed comforting, too.

We stood like that for a good minute, me clinging to him like he was a life raft on choppy waters, before he pulled back and held me at arm's length. "We should go. My car is just there," he said, nodding his head toward the black BMW I'd been driven home in after I saw him at his club.

I nodded, dumbly following as he led me forward. He stopped by my car and bent to collect my purse from the ground, hastily shoving things back inside it. When he had everything, we started for his car again, his arm firmly looped around my waist because I was so unsteady on my shaky legs. He opened the passenger door, helping me inside and setting my purse at my feet.

"What about my car?" I croaked, leaning my head back against the headrest and closing my eyes for a few seconds as his hands took mine, inspecting the grazes I was sure to have there from falling.

"Don't worry about it. I'll take care of it." He let go of my hands abruptly, and I cracked my eyes open to see him opening the glove box and then reaching behind him to get the gun and knife, depositing them in there and closing the compartment again swiftly.

He turned his attention back to me, taking my seat belt and pulling it across me, clipping it into place before he leaned out of the car and closed my door. As he sauntered around to the other side of the car, I could hear muffled talking but couldn't focus on it. When he climbed into the driver's side, he pulled his cell away from his ear, disconnecting the call and dropping it into the middle cup holder on his car. I didn't even have the energy to ask him who he'd called.

When his engine roared to life and he started rolling out of the parking lot, I glanced back at the bodies. "What about them?" I croaked. Shouldn't we call an ambulance or something?

"Do you really care?" he replied tartly, his eyes flicking to the rearview mirror, his jaw tightening at the sight of the bodies.

Did I really care? "No," I answered honestly, shaking my head.

"Exactly."

As he drove, the streets blurred through the window, my mind unfocused. I glanced down at my tingling hands. They were visibly shaking. I clenched my fists a couple of times, trying to stop them, but couldn't. Giving up, I pushed them under my thighs to hide them from view.

As the minutes passed in silence, my mind kept wandering back to what had just occurred. Those men had attempted to push me into their car. I tried not to think about what might have happened to me if Jamie hadn't turned up. He'd saved me. He'd beaten the ever-loving shit out of them.

Turning toward him, I saw his bloody knuckles wrapped around the steering wheel, how the muscles in his forearms were tight, his biceps bulging with stress, his whole posture alert. Fury rolled off him in waves. I gulped, thinking about the murderous intent I'd seen swirling in his eyes.

If I hadn't grabbed his arm and asked him to stop, would he have killed those guys? Would he have actually pulled the trigger? His eyes told me he would have. I'd never seen him like that; it had been kind of terrifying to witness the storm of murder in his eyes. I knew I should be scared, I should be questioning why I let him put me into his car after what I'd just witnessed, but I'd never been scared of Jamie. He would never hurt me. I'd glimpsed the damaged, broken soul inside him. I knew his demons, and I also knew that there was no malice in his heart.

Well, at least that's what I thought of the Jamie I used to know. This new man sitting in the car with me was different. There was an out-of-control, hard edge to him, some shift in his personality that had hardened itself and become desensitized to violence. I'd known he'd done violent things when he worked for Brett. I'd seen him sporting knuckles like that before, cleaned them for him even, but he had always been sorry about it. I'd seen the regret within him and how he would get quiet and distant sometimes, a look of mortification on his face. Now there was no sorrow or remorse, only blazing anger. What had happened to the boy I'd loved; where had he gone?

"Hey, you okay?"

I jumped, my mind jerking back to the present as I turned to look at Jamie. His concerned eyes met mine as he pushed a stray lock of hair behind my ear, his fingers brushing against my cheek gently and lingering there for a split second. Heat crept over my face, burning in a pleasurable way, my skin tingling where he'd touched me.

It took me a few moments to realize he'd half turned in his

seat and that the car had stopped. Frowning, I looked around at our surroundings. An underground parking lot.

"Where are we?" I asked, my voice croaky because of my dry throat.

"Um...this is my new place," he replied, his hand dropping back into his lap. This version of Jamie was more like the one I knew—the one I met at first, before we got comfortable with each other; the nervous, shy guy who didn't feel that he deserved to be treated nicely. It hurt my heart to see he still felt that way.

"Oh," I answered, but then grew confused. "Why would you bring me here? Why didn't you just take me home?" And why was that thought only just now occurring to me?!

Another car entered the parking lot then, pulling up alongside Jamie's. "Good, he's here," Jamie muttered as a lone figure got out of the car. Jamie didn't answer my question, just exited the car and closed his door, talking to the new guy.

Instinct told me I wanted to hear this conversation, so I fumbled with my seat belt with shaky hands, finally prying it open after a couple of attempts, and climbed out, turning to look over at the two men. When the newcomer's face came into view, my frown deepened. I knew this guy, we'd met a few times before. Ray. The one who had come to the airport in Jamie's absence and forced me to see reality.

"Jamie?" I muttered, leaning on the car door heavily because my knees were weak and I felt a little unsteady. I knew I was probably in shock. I'd read about it but had never experienced it before.

He said something else to Ray as he twisted a key from his key ring and handed it to him, then turned to me with a smile that didn't reach his eyes. "Ellie, do you remember Ray?" he asked.

I nodded, glancing over at Ray again, unwillingly replaying memories of the airport and the immense disappointment I'd felt at seeing him, not Jamie. My feet seemed glued to the ground as he and Jamie walked to my side.

"I just have to go take care of something. I won't be long. Ray is going to take you upstairs and watch out for you while I'm gone," Jamie said, leaning into the car and picking up my purse, handing it to Ray.

"I just want to go home. I don't need someone to watch me," I replied, trying to put some authority into my voice but failing miserably when it shook with emotion.

Jamie sighed deeply and stepped closer to me. Too close. I could take one step and melt into his body, wrapping my arms around him and hiding there until everything went away. The pull to do that was almost overwhelming.

"I can't take you home, not yet. Ellie, those guys were after you because of me, so I need someone to protect you while I go take care of the thing I need to do. This is important," he explained.

Those two guys had been targeting me? It wasn't some random attack? And it was because of Jamie? None of this made sense. I glanced back at the dashboard, thinking about the gun and knife housed within, and swallowed awkwardly, a shiver running through me.

When something touched my shoulder, I started, my eyes darting back to Jamie. "I'll be back soon and I'll explain everything, I promise. Please just go upstairs with Ray, so I don't have to worry about you. I need my mind focused right now. Please? Can you just do this for me?" His eyes implored me, the rich color hypnotizing me into submission, just like he'd always had the ability to do.

I nodded. I didn't really have much choice in the matter. It was clear he wasn't going to back down, and I didn't have the strength left in me to continue standing, let alone argue my point.

Jamie smiled. "Thank you. I'll see you soon and I'll explain."

Ray stepped forward, his hand wrapping around my upper arm, taking some of my weight as I stepped forward on wobbly legs. "Let's get you upstairs and I'll make you some tea. It'll calm your nerves," he said softly as I let him lead me blindly along.

As Ray stopped by the elevator and pressed the button to call it, I glanced over my shoulder and saw that Jamie had already climbed into his car. Our eyes locked through the windshield. I gulped at what I saw. Terrifying, murderous Jamie from the parking lot was back, and this time I wouldn't be there to stop whatever he was planning to do.

CHAPTER 19

JAMIE

I COULD BARELY sit still as I drove away from my apartment, leaving Ellie with Ray. My hands flexed on the steering wheel as I scowled out the window, thinking about just how close I'd been to not saving her. I'd parked on the street at the side of the parking lot; I hadn't thought there was any danger to her, so I'd let her park in the lot alone so she wouldn't see me. If that second guy hadn't sped past me and rushed into the lot, I never would have known anything was wrong.

"Stupid, stupid, stupid," I growled, slamming my palm down on my steering wheel a few times in frustration. Rage burned through me at the memory of pulling into the lot to see that guy's hands on her. I groaned, clenching my jaw and unclenching it, fidgeting in my seat and pressing my foot down harder on the gas. My anger was like a monster, clawing at my insides, demanding to be let out. And I would let it out, I didn't care what she'd said. Mateo would die for this.

I drove in silence for a while, letting my rage simmer, and then I hit a couple of buttons on my car dash and the speaker started calling Dodger. He answered on the third ring. "Hey,

Kid," he said, his voice cheerful as always. Sometimes it pissed me off to high heaven.

"Dodge, two of the Salazars' men just attacked Ellie and tried to kidnap her." I almost spat the words, the acid of them tasting foul on my tongue.

"What the fuck? Is she okay?"

"She's fine." *Thank God.* "But the two assholes who attacked her aren't."

"Who were they?" Dodger asked.

"I don't know, but they were definitely Salazar crew. They had the ink." My mind flicked back to the scene and the snake-and-dagger crew ink on the guy's forearm. "Listen, I need you to do some things for me." I checked my mirrors and signaled, heading south toward the nearest of my clubs.

"Sure. What?" I could hear him moving around in the background, probably getting to a place we could talk.

"I need you to call Detective Lewiston, tell him you have a couple of points of interest for him, but he needs to find his own source for the record to back up the story."

I'd already thought through everything—I couldn't hit everywhere at once—but I wanted the Salazars ruined, run out of town, or dead. To do that I'd need help. Detective Lewiston had proven useful before, and he would come in extremely handy for the next few hours.

"Okay, what am I telling him?"

"Tell him you know of three drug labs in connection with the Salazars. Give him the addresses of their labs in Greenwich Village, the Lower East Side, and the Bronx. Tell him the police should raid them as soon as possible because you've heard they're packing them up and moving to new premises in the next couple of hours," I instructed, pulling into the parking lot of one of the smaller clubs I owned. It was only an evening and weekend club, so would be closed this time of day. *Perfect.*

"Meantime, I'm heading to their meth lab in Long Island. I have a feeling Mateo might be there." Reaching into the back of my car, I picked up my gym bag and opened it, pulling out an old tee that I kept in there to work out in. As I spoke, I ripped it in half with a loud shredding sound, and then in half again, my mind already focused on what I was going to do.

"If you're going there, then pick me up," Dodger affirmed. "I'll come with you in case there's trouble."

I smiled at the gesture but shook my head, dismissing it. "There won't be many people there, and the ones that are will most likely be high, anyway."

"And Mateo," Dodger added, his tone concerned.

"I can definitely handle that fuck stain," I hissed. "Look, I gotta go. Make the call but tell Lewiston he'll need to pay some hooker or druggie to validate his story and go on record saying they gave him a tip. It can't come from us," I instructed, impatient to take action.

"All right, I will. Give me the address where you left the two guys," Dodger said. I reeled off the place where I'd left them and Dodger asked, "Are they dead?"

I closed my eyes, wishing they were and that Ellie had let me finish the job. "No."

"Okay, I'll have someone find them, too."

"And have someone take Ellie's car to her house. It's the green bug."

"Will do. Where is Ellie now, want me to have someone pick her up?" he replied.

"She's at my place with Ray. He'll watch her until I get back."

"Okay, that's good. I'll go make the calls now. And, Kid, be careful, all right?"

"Yeah." I disconnected the phone, climbing out of the car and heading to the back door of the club. I let myself in and stomped up the stairs straight to the bar, pulling out four bottles of whiskey. As I suspected, at this time of day no one was around.

That'll be plenty, I thought, setting about customizing the bottles and then carefully setting them upright in my knapsack. Once satisfied I had everything I would need, I drove to my warehouse, swapping my car for one of the unmarked ones registered to a fake address and name so it couldn't be traced. I quickly changed clothes too, putting on a hoodie and tugging the hood up over my cap just in case.

From there, I made the drive to the abandoned building where the Salazars cooked their shit, hoping Mateo was there so I could end it quickly. I wanted to get back to Ellie and tell her she was safe—and fucking mean it.

Pulling up at the end of the road, I got out and jogged down the street, hiding behind a small crumbling wall opposite their lab, edging up to get a good view of the place, stopping next to a large scorch mark on the grass. Their burn pit, where they disposed of their chemicals. I turned my nose up in disgust and looked over the wall, surveying the area.

The large building opposite me was derelict looking; basically an old graffiti-covered tin shack with blacked-out windows. At one point this would have been a storage unit for an industrial company or something, but now it was used to make hundreds of pounds of crystal meth, or "ice," as it was known on the streets.

Staying hidden, I looked left and right, seeing the other buildings in this small industrial-type compound. One was half fallen down, one side missing and panels of the roof hanging precariously like they could fall any second. The only other building in the area was a small brick-built hut that could have once belonged to the security guards who would have watched over this place. There were holes in the roof and the windows were smashed in—clearly no one was using it now. Three cars were parked on the abandoned space off to my right, none of them nice enough to belong to a Salazar.

Remaining still and quiet, I watched, waiting for my opportunity and deciding if I was just going to burst in. Less than three minutes later, my opportunity presented itself. A guy walked around the corner of the building, staring at the screen of his cell phone, clearly engrossed in whatever he was watching. The security guard making his rounds. I smiled to myself, pushing the strap of my bag across my body so it wouldn't fall off and pulling out the gun I'd confiscated from the guy who'd attacked Ellie earlier. I had untraceable guns of my own I could use, but I found it amusing that I might get to kill Mateo with one of his own crew's weapon—I did love a bit of irony.

The security guard stopped, his back to me, put one hand on the door handle, and then let it drop back down to his side as he leaned against the wall, deciding to finish watching what was on his cell instead of going back to work.

I stood, holding my bag steady against my hip as I ran the short distance across to him. He was so engrossed in the TV show, he didn't even hear me approach until I pressed the barrel of the gun against the back of his head. His whole body stiffened, his hands coming up in a reflexive action, and I saw that he was watching *The Walking Dead*.

"Don't move and you'll live through this," I ordered, pressing the gun harder against his scalp as I leaned forward and took his cell phone, turning off the video and shoving it into my bag. "Put your hands behind your head," I instructed, stepping back and moving the gun to dig between his shoulder blades instead. He did as he was told, interlacing his fingers behind his head, his

Salazar ink now in full view on his forearm. "Good. How many other guards are there?" I patted down his body, finding a knife and a small handgun strapped to his waist. I removed both, carefully putting them into my bag.

"Just me," he answered, his voice a lot younger than his face suggested.

"If you're lying..." I pushed the gun harder into his spine.

"I'm not, I swear," he replied quickly. He turned his head and his eyes widened. "Oh shit, you're Kid Cole."

My reputation precedes me again.

I nodded slowly. "Uh-huh. Is Mateo inside?" I almost growled his name, my anger flaring again.

He shook his head. "No, he hasn't been here for a couple of days."

A groan of frustration left my lips. I'd really been pinning my hopes on him being here. "How many people are inside?"

"Three, just three."

"And are you expecting any deliveries or collections anytime soon?" I asked, glancing up the road, seeing it was still clear, not a passerby in sight.

"No, we had a delivery this morning," the guy answered. Part of me believed him, but I still needed to be careful. I didn't know what or who would be inside.

"What's your name?"

"Stan," he replied.

"Okay, Stan. Slowly open that door so I can see in"—I nodded to the door he was going to go through earlier—"and remember, if anyone starts shooting, you'll be the first to die."

He gulped and nodded. "There's no one else here apart from the chefs." He slowly opened the door wide enough that I could see it led to a little security office with a desk and a monitor on it.

"Go in," I ordered, shoving him forward a little to get him moving because his feet didn't seem to want to cooperate. He stepped into the office and I cautiously looked around, seeing that it was empty. "Go over to the desk." He did as he was told again, walking around to the desk with me in tow, the gun on him at all times.

On the monitor were three grainy black-and-white moving pictures—one of outside behind the building, which was clear and empty; another of the front of the building, where we'd just been standing; and the last inside the lab itself. Three people wearing white lab coats, rubber gloves, goggles, and masks were inside, just as Stan had said.

"Okay, we're going to go in there nice and slow. You're going in first." I reached out, putting my hand on his shoulder and holding him at arm's length ahead of me as I raised the gun, aiming over his shoulder, ready for anything.

Stan nodded, walked to the door slowly so I could keep pace with him, and opened the heavy-looking metal door, letting it swing inward, allowing access to the vast lab. As soon as the door opened, the scent of ammonia and solvents burned my nose and made the back of my throat itch.

The chefs didn't even look up from their work as we entered. I glanced around quickly, seeing all manner of things piled high in the room: stacks of cold pills, bottles and bottles of bleach, large bags of salt, empty soda bottles, cans of drain cleaner, and compressed gas cylinders along with so many other household items that it looked like the cleaning aisle of Walmart.

Chemical stains marred the walls, and large, long tables had been set up along the center of the room where the chefs actually did the cooking. On another table to the right, their finished product lay in plastic bags, tied securely. There was easily a couple of hundred thousand dollars' worth of ice sitting on that table. As I stepped farther into the room, using Stan as a shield, my eyes started to water from the stench of cleaning fluid, and I wondered how these guys stood it all day. They had flimsy cloth masks over their mouths and noses, but that wouldn't do much to keep the chemical burn from reaching their throats, surely. Stan clearly felt it too, because he coughed, hacking loudly, and then spat on the floor, making a disgusted sound in his throat.

That caught the attention of the chefs, and two of them looked up at once. The other continued to work, humming a little tune that sounded suspiciously like the Disney song "Bare Necessities" while using a turkey baster to suck up ingredients and add them to a Pyrex dish.

"Nobody fucking move," I ordered, pointing the gun at each one in turn. The third guy stopped humming when he looked up and saw the gun.

All three of them stood stock-still, their eyes wide and terrified; they weren't gang members or anything sinister, just junkies who made the product so they could get their fill.

"Put your hands on your head and spread your legs. No one moves a muscle." I reached into my bag, my hand searching for Stan's cell phone, then pulled it out and handed it to him. "I want you to call Mateo; tell him I'm here and that I want to talk to him."

He gulped and took the phone slowly, using one hand to unlock it and scroll for his contact. When he put the phone to his ear, I pressed the gun into his side again, watching. "Mateo, I'm here at the Long Island lab. Kid Cole just turned up with a gun and wants to talk to you." His face paled at whatever Mateo said and he held the phone out to me to take.

I smiled, taking the phone and pressing it to my ear, keeping my gun trained on Stan and glancing at the others to see that they were standing with their hands on their heads and legs spread as I'd instructed.

"Mateo," I snarled.

"Kid, what are you doing?" I could hear a note of panic in his tone.

His voice made the anger spike inside me; rage clouded my vision and I fought to remain in control of it. "You made my shit list sending people after Ellie. I'm about to burn your fucking lab to the ground, just like I promised you I would. Next, I'm coming for you. I'm going to hunt you down and kill you so slowly you'll be begging me to end it long before I do. You'd better get the fuck off my streets and start running, Salazar; you have a small head start, but it won't do you any good. I'll find you." It was a promise. I'd killed one man in my life; I would make Mateo the second for daring to harm her. I disconnected the call without waiting for any reply, tossing it to Stan.

Everyone was watching me with wide eyes as I reached into my bag, pulling out the first bottle of whiskey with the ripped portion of T-shirt stuffed into the top. I set it on the table, pulling the lighter out next.

A sharp intake of breath from Stan made me look at him. "What the hell are you doing? This whole place will go up, there's propane in here!" he cried, his eyes darting to the gas tanks and all the chemicals.

"I know." I sparked the lighter and held it against the cloth. It caught effortlessly and I picked up the bottle, smiling wickedly. "If you want to live, you better start running," I said, pulling my arm back and launching the firebomb across the lab. It smashed, splattering fiery liquid all over the far wall. None of the ingredients were stored over there, which was why I picked it as my first target.

I stepped back, grinning as all four of them turned on their heels and started sprinting for the door. I pulled out the second bottle, lighting the makeshift fuse and throwing it directly at the table with all the drugs on it, watching the fire come to life, engulfing the table and the wall, creeping over the floor, swallowing the Salazars' drugs with it. I hefted the third at the back wall again, seeing the fire rapidly expand, the flames now licking up toward the roof. The heat in the room was almost unbearable, and I could feel my skin tightening and had to squint against the brightness of the flames.

I laughed, actually enjoying myself as I plucked out the next bottle, walking backward toward the open door, knowing this one was going to be the killer blow, the one to bring the house down.

Checking over my shoulder, seeing the last guy disappear out the door and race for the exit, I lit the bottle and threw it directly at the compressed gas bottles and all the highly flammable chemicals piled high in the corner, then turned and ran as fast as I could out of the building and into the fresh air, following the four men as they dashed across the lot and over toward the grassy knoll I'd hidden behind earlier.

When I was halfway across the lot, an explosion from behind me threw me forward, debris and bits of the building flying through the air and landing around me, flames devouring them already.

I landed with a thump and turned my head to see the whole place practically leveled. Flames licked up into the sky about ten feet high. A plume of black smoke rose into the air, covering the blue sky in a shroud of darkness.

Getting my hands under me, I pushed myself up to my feet, dusting off my jeans, and looked at the burning building with a satisfied grin on my face.

One down, and hopefully Detective Lewiston will take out the other three.

The Salazars would be out of business, out of money, and out of places to hide. A laugh built in my throat, kind of like an evil cackle as I turned and headed for my car. The four men were standing on the grass opposite, watching me with wide eyes and slack, hanging mouths.

I gave them a little salute as I walked. "Kid Cole out," I joked, sending a wink in their direction. This would just form another part of my legacy, something else for people to talk about when my name was mentioned.

My next and only thought as I climbed back into my car was Ellie.

CHAPTER 20

ELLIE

AS RAY AND I stepped out of the elevator and headed for the apartment door, I couldn't stop my mind from returning to the vengeful look on Jamie's face. Was he going back to the parking lot to do what I'd begged him not to? What other possible thing could he have to "take care of"?

Ray opened the door and stepped inside, giving my elbow a little tug in prompt.

"What has Jamie gone to do?" I asked, holding my ground. He must have explained and told his friend the reason he had to stay here babysitting me; he just didn't want me to know.

Ray's eyes tightened. "Just come inside. He said he'd explain everything when he's back, so I'm staying out of it." He tugged my arm again, and because of my weakened, shaky state, my body obliged even though my mind was still reeling.

The door clicked shut behind me and Ray locked it, leaning forward to look through the peephole, checking for some bizarre reason even though we'd just been the only ones out there.

I folded my arms around myself, tucking my hands under my armpits in a bid to quell their tremor. As Ray stood guard at the

peephole, I turned and walked farther into the apartment, my
eyes taking in everything and nothing.

The apartment was nice—a lot better than Jamie had ever
been able to afford when we were together. A large picture window stretched the length of the living room and the open-plan
kitchen area, showing a beautiful city skyscape that I would bet
looked incredible at dusk or at night when all the lights of the
city glowed against the darkness.

Finally, Ray pushed away from the door, his shoulders loosening marginally as he turned to me. "Right, tea with plenty
of sugar. You sit," he instructed, pointing toward the large,
expensive-looking brown leather seating area all arranged
around a gorgeous fireplace with the biggest TV I'd ever seen
mounted above it.

I took his advice, sitting down before I fell down, and Ray
set my purse at my feet before heading to the kitchen area. I
sighed and looked around, my mind whirling, wondering what
this beautiful, expansive apartment really said about Jamie Cole,
because I couldn't see one ounce of his personality here. Everything was sleek, clinical, cold, with an emphasis on money—
unless that *was* the new Jamie of today...

Ray came in a few minutes later, setting a mug of tea on the
coffee table along with a plate of cookies. "I figured you should
eat something; it might help with the shock." He eyed me worriedly as I leaned forward mechanically and picked up my cup,
sipping at the tea until it was gone and then taking a cookie,
nibbling on it but not tasting it. The tea really helped, and my
trembling eventually subsided.

I wasn't sure how much time had passed—long enough for
me to drink my whole mug of hot tea. When Ray's phone rang,
he looked down at it and then back to me before stepping into
the inner hallway and answering it.

When he walked back into the living room and sat down, his posture was rigid and tight. He leaned forward and snagged a cookie, munching on it, not meeting my eyes.

"Was that Jamie?" I asked.

Ray shook his head.

I huffed angrily, my temper rising again now. "How long is he going to be?" I asked. "How long is he expecting me to sit here and wait for him? I want to go home! Why can't you just tell me what's going on? Do you know who those guys were? Is Jamie going to be in trouble or something for that? I mean, they had guns and . . ." It was all too much. Now that my shaking had stopped and my mind seemed to be going back to normal, rational thought kicked in, and so did my anger. I needed answers.

Ray sighed deeply and finally looked up at me. "Ellie, you can't go home right now. Please just wait for Kid to come back and explain. I'm not going to get involved, so please stop asking me."

I scowled angrily, but he just shrugged one shoulder and gave a little shake of his head, so I knew he wasn't giving in anytime soon. I huffed angrily. "Fine. Can I use the bathroom?" I asked, needing to do something other than sit and wait and stew.

Ray nodded and motioned his chin toward the only other door in the apartment. "It's through the bedroom and on the left."

Bedroom. My stomach gave a little quiver thinking about the place where Jamie slept. But then something else occurred to me. Jamie would have had other girls in his bed.

As soon as that thought entered my head, something very unwelcome took root in my stomach. I refused to acknowledge it as jealousy, but as I stepped into the room and closed the door behind me, my eyes searched out signs of a girlfriend—throw pillows, girls' clothing, makeup, anything.

I was more than a little relieved to see that this room was just as cold and clinical as the living room, with one exception. There were a few photo frames on his bedside table and dresser.

Without my permission, my legs carried me over there as I picked up the one next to his bed: his sister Sophie. The same photo I had fixed for him after it had been ripped. A smile tugged at the corners of my mouth as I looked at it. She really was a gorgeous little thing.

Heading to the dresser, I looked at the next one: Jamie holding a baby girl wearing a white christening gown. He looked much the same as he did now, a little more unkempt than he had when I knew him before. He was smiling, but it didn't quite reach his eyes. The last photo on the dresser was of a group of people. Jamie was still holding the baby, but Ray and two women were in this one. My hand reached for it, then stilled as my gaze settled on the younger of the two women.

Her face was familiar.

It hit me all at once. Natalie.

But it couldn't be, could it? How would Natalie know Jamie? I'd met her in Rome; it couldn't be that much of a small world, could it?

My mind whirled as I picked up the photo, inspecting it more closely. But yes, it was definitely her. Natalie Rowson. My traveling companion. Her hair was shorter, chopped into a cute pixie cut now. She was smiling down at the little girl in Jamie's arms.

Wait, was Jamie now dating Natalie? Was that...their child?

My stomach clenched, fiercer this time, churning like fire.

Natalie and I had kept in touch after she came back home and I decided to stay in England. We weren't really close anymore, but we sometimes chatted via Facebook Messenger and liked each other's tweets and statuses, things like that. I'd seen no mention of her dating anyone, let alone Jamie. Surely that would be something she would mention, brag about even? And surely she would have recognized his name—I'd cried over him enough, hadn't I? We toasted to his demise enough times for her to know his name and realize he was the guy who'd shattered me, wouldn't she? Yet here she was, right here in the photo and standing next to him with a proud smile on her face.

My throat seemed to close up as I tightened my grip on the silver photo frame and turned, heading out to the living room again. Ray looked up as I thrust the photo toward his face.

"Who is that?" I pointed to the pixie-cut girl, trying to keep my voice level, still praying I'd made a mistake. If I hadn't, then none of this made sense. There was no reason for her to be in this photo, no possible reason I could think of, anyway.

Ray smiled as he looked at it. "That's Nat, my sister-in-law."

Nat. It is her! And wait, did he just say sister-in-law? What. The. Hell?

I sucked in a sharp breath at his words. Ray's sister-in-law. So Jamie knew her? Had he known her when I met her or after? He and Ray had been friends a long time. Wouldn't he have met her before? And I'd just so happened to run into her at a market in Rome? There was no way it was a coincidence. My brain struggled to catch up as thoughts rushed over me at once.

Judging by the widening of Ray's eyes and the throbbing muscle in his jaw, he regretted answering so casually. He stood, taking the photo from me and setting it facedown on the coffee table. "Look, I'm not saying anything about that either, so don't bother asking. That's something else you'll have to ask Kid about. Just don't be too hard on him when you do, all right?"

"Just answer me one thing before you clam up," I bargained. "Are they dating? Is that their baby?" I pointed to the back of the photo, holding my breath. *Please say no. Please say no.*

Ray smiled almost sadly. "No, they're not dating. That's my youngest daughter. Kid is her godfather."

"Then why—" I started, but he cut me off.

"You really have no idea, do you?" He shook his head before straightening his shoulders. "I'm not saying anything more. Speak to him about it when he comes." His tone was final as his eyes locked onto mine.

They were the last words we spoke about it. No matter how many times I tried to ask, he shot me down every time, leaving me in confused, stunned silence, my brain a mess, my thoughts all over the place; my worry about what Jamie was doing and if he was in trouble was front and center. The one comforting thought...Jamie and Natalie weren't dating. That wasn't his baby. I hated that I cared about that information so much.

Well over an hour of silence had passed when a knock at the door made Ray spring to his feet and rush to answer it. I swiveled on my seat, seeing Ray leaning in and checking the peephole before quickly yanking open the door. Jamie stepped into the apartment, his eyes darting to me. I noted a small margin of relief flicker across his features before he turned back to Ray. They had another quiet conversation and then Ray nodded and left the apartment, closing the door behind him, leaving us in silence.

Jamie stepped into the room, raking one dirty, grime-covered hand through his hair, pushing it back into place. "Hey. Sorry I took so long." He sat down on the opposite end of the sofa from me, turning to face me, his eyes narrowed in concern as they scanned over me slowly. "You okay?"

The heavy scent of smoke lingered around him, assaulting my senses and making me wrinkle my nose in distaste; when I detected another smell coming off him, my anger spiraled. Alcohol: He reeked of it, like he'd bathed in the stuff. "Have you been to a bar while I've been sitting here on my ass waiting?" I snapped disbelievingly.

He recoiled visibly, a frown lining his forehead. "What? No!"

"Oh, come on, I can smell the alcohol on you!" I cried, getting to my feet and snatching up my purse from the floor. "I can't believe I was naive enough to sit here and be concerned about you while you were off bloody drinking!" I snapped, well aware that I'd just used an English term. "I want to go home. Now. Will you take me or should I call a cab?"

Jamie jumped to his feet and shook his head, his hand reaching for mine as I unzipped my purse, meaning to find my cell phone. "I wasn't drinking, I swear. Ellie, please, will you just hear me out?"

I ground my teeth, looking up and seeing that his eyes were doing that begging thing that I'd always been a sucker for.

I snatched my hand from his grip and stepped back. "Fine."

He sat on the edge of the sofa, looking up at me with pleading eyes. "The guys who attacked you earlier, they work for the two Salazar brothers. They have a sort of gang here; they're not good people. The Salazars sent those guys after you."

I frowned, trying to take it in, but it didn't make sense. "Why would they care about me, though?"

"Because *I* care about you," he answered quickly.

I scoffed and shook my head adamantly, folding my arms over my chest defensively. "No, you don't. You never did."

He groaned and put his head in his hands. "Ellie, please don't think that. Don't ever think that I don't care."

I recoiled, my anger peaking. "That's what you basically said to me that night, Jamie! You remember the night I'm talking about? The one when you cheated on me, then called me up and broke my fucking heart the day we were supposed to be starting our future together?" I roared, pointing an accusing finger at him as three years' worth of hurt and bitterness leaked into my words.

His eyes closed and his shoulders sagged. "I lied," he whispered.

"What?" Confusion washed over me. "Lied about what?"

"Everything." His eyes opened, locking on mine. He reached out, taking my hand in one of his rough, calloused ones and tugging gently, guiding me to sit down next to him. "I didn't cheat on you; I never would have. You were my world, Ellie."

"*You were my world.*" Exactly how I'd felt about him. His words made my stomach clench and my scalp prickle. My mouth had gone dry. "I don't...wh-what?" I stuttered.

He sighed, a muscle in his jaw throbbing as he clenched and unclenched his teeth. "I wasn't honest with you, and I hate myself for that, but I still believe I did it for the right reasons." He scooted closer to me, so close that his knee pressed against mine, his thumb stroking over the back of my hand, which he hadn't released from earlier. I hadn't even noticed. "That night...I had one more job to do for Brett, you remember?"

I nodded, dumbstruck.

"It was a meeting with some drug dealers from another state, the Lazlos. The meeting was basically negotiating terms and talking about how the two organizations could help each other. It turned out the police had been surveying the Lazlos for some time. They heard everything that was said and then they raided the joint. There was a huge firefight, and some people were killed. Brett was killed." The sadness in his tone when he said that last bit was evident. "And everyone else was arrested." He looked up at me, his expression forlorn.

"You were arrested?" I muttered, my brain working overtime now.

"Yeah. I had a gun on me at the time, just for a show of force for the meeting. I didn't use it or anything. They charged me with possession of a firearm. My lawyer managed to get me off practically everything else they could have charged me with, but I was still going to do time for it, plus the time I had remaining on my previous sentence when I was let off for good behavior."

I shook my head. "Are you lying to me now, Jamie? I can't even tell with you anymore."

He sighed and his eyes pleaded with me to listen. "I'm not lying! I'm telling you the truth now. Call my lawyer if you don't believe me. It's Miles's father, Arthur Barrington. Check with the prison board or something, or just fucking Google it. The Lazlo raid made headline news; it mentions in there about Brett being killed in the gunfight. Google it. Here." He pulled out his cell phone, offering it to me.

I didn't take the phone. His eyes were telling me everything I needed to know. I could see the honesty there. When I'd said earlier I couldn't tell if he was lying, that wasn't the truth. I had always been able to read him.

His confession made so much sense. I'd never been quite able to understand why he'd broken up with me.

I'd always struggled to accept the fact that he'd cheated; Jamie wasn't that type of guy. I'd always felt there was more to it, but had never been able to figure out what. Hearing these words from his lips now, everything clicked into place and finally made sense.

My brain was whirling, trying to connect the dots, scratching out everything I'd believed for the last three years. Jamie had been arrested. Jamie had lied to me. Jamie hadn't cheated on me. "Why didn't you tell me any of this? You were in jail, and you decided to use your phone call to break my heart instead of just being honest?"

His eyes met mine. "No. I decided to use my one phone call to set you free."

"I don't understand," I whispered. "Why did you do that? Why did you lie to me? You hurt me so badly." My tears had started now, tumbling down my cheeks and wetting my sweatshirt.

Jamie groaned, his grip on my hand tightening to the point of it being uncomfortable. "I was going down for at least a year, Ellie. It was inevitable, a done deal. I loved you so much, more than anything, and I didn't want you to have to go through waiting for me. You deserved better than me, you always did."

Everything had been a lie. All the pain I'd felt, the grief, the crushing heartbreak because the man I loved had betrayed me came rushing back to me at once. And all of it could have been avoided. He'd put me through that heartbreak because he didn't want me to have to wait for him, because I deserved better? Did I deserve to feel like my heart had been ripped out? Did I deserve to cry myself to sleep for a year? Did I deserve to always feel like something was missing inside me, even now?

Anger, burning like lava, coursed through my veins. "Wasn't that *my* decision to make?" I shouted, yanking my hand from his and getting to my feet, needing some personal space. He'd hurt me so badly and my hand was itching to ball into a fist and smash into his face, just so I could cause him a fraction of that pain in return. "This was just like when you kept your past from me and didn't tell me about your sister. Yet again you took the decision away from me, thinking you were doing what was best. You were wrong again, Jamie! I went through hell because of that phone call. It took me ages to get over you and what you said to me!"

Maybe I still wasn't over it—it sure felt like I wasn't. The pain was still there; looking at him, I could feel it washing over me. And now to know I hadn't even had to go through it—I was so livid I could barely stand still. For three years I'd believed this was all my fault, that me doubting him over whether he'd killed his sister, Sophie, was what made him realize he didn't want to be with me, and now I found out it wasn't anything I did or didn't do. I wasn't even sure how to come to terms with this new piece of information.

He stood too, holding his hands up in a *calm down* gesture. "I'm sorry. I really thought I was doing what was best for you."

"Well, you weren't!" I screamed, throwing my purse onto the sofa roughly just for some sort of release. I pointed an accusing finger at him. "You didn't want to fight for our relationship, that's what it was. You were afraid to ask me to wait. What happened? Was I not worth fighting for?" My voice broke, my breath hitching with sobs.

A look crossed his face, a fierce determination flashing in his eyes as he stepped forward, cupping my cheeks, our bodies brushing gently where he was so close, causing my heart to jackhammer in my chest. His thumbs brushed across my cheeks softly, wiping away my tears as they fell. "You're worth dying for," he whispered, his eyes soft and tender as they met mine.

A lump formed in my throat. That kind of sweet, corny line from his lips used to make me swoon, and if I was honest with myself, it still kind of did.

His words hung in the air as we looked at each other, inches apart, his hands cupping my face. So many unspoken thoughts and feelings transmitted between us as I stared into his eyes, losing myself there as my body's urges slipped back to the past, longing for him to lean that little bit farther in, to place those soft lips against mine and claim my mouth in a scorching-hot kiss that set my body alight.

"So you did want to come with me?" I asked, my mind finally wrapping around what had happened.

He nodded quickly. "More than anything."

I sighed. "You hurt me so much." Somehow those words didn't even cover the grief and loss I'd suffered.

"I know, and I'm so sorry for that. If I could take it back..." He trailed off, tearing his eyes away from mine and staring down at the floor.

"Would you?"

One of his shoulders lifted in a small shrug. "I don't know. The selfish part of me says yes straightaway. The part of me that loved you so deeply it was painful, the part of me that still would die for you in an instant, wants to go back in time and tell you the truth, beg you to wait so we could make the life we wanted when I was released. But the reasonable, caring part of me that wants the best for you would probably still make the same call. I don't deserve you, Ellie. I never did. Even if I had a thousand years to repent for all the shit I've done, I *still* wouldn't deserve you." He looked up at me, his eyes showing his sincerity.

And God help me, just like that, I swooned internally. "That was so corny," I said. I couldn't help myself.

"I still got it then, huh?" He grinned, the beautiful smile that I always used to think was reserved only for me, and that dimple appeared on his cheek. And oh, how I'd missed that dimple. My finger twitched, longing to reach out and trace my finger over it, but I resisted. Despite everything, I smiled and rolled my eyes.

Knowing I needed to get control of myself and stop letting him turn me into a giddy little schoolgirl, I stepped back, and his hands dropped down to his sides. His eyes never left mine, stripping my defenses, melting my anger and hurt into a puddle at his feet. I wanted to stay mad at him, to blame him for hurting me so much when he should have let me make the decision myself as to what I wanted to do.

I could understand why he had done it, though. Jamie was selfless. He'd also never seen the good inside himself or felt he deserved anything good in life. Not wanting to ask me to wait for him all stemmed from his horrible childhood and not feeling worthy of love or affection. He'd already said it himself—he thought he wasn't good enough for me. He was wrong, oh so wrong. I thought I'd convinced him he was worthy of loving and being loved in return, but clearly I hadn't or he wouldn't have taken it upon himself to make that decision for me.

"I still don't understand why those guys tried to grab me, though. Who are they to you?" I asked.

He sighed and sat down, patting the seat next to him. "It's kind of a long story. You want to sit?"

I sighed and perched on the edge of the cushion, keeping enough distance between us that I could keep my concentration firmly on what he was saying and not have flashes of us writhing together while hot and sweaty.

He cleared his throat, looking down at his hands as though he didn't want to look at me. "I was in jail for a year and a half, and at first I had every intention of finding you and telling you the truth once I was out; I held on to that for a long time before I finally accepted that things would never work out how I wanted. But as time went on and I was in there day after day with all those people, I realized that you were just better off without me. You were away traveling, living your life, and I had no right to come in and be a part of all that again. By the time I got out, I figured I had nothing left to be good for. You were gone, Sophie was gone, and I had no qualifications and nothing going for me other than my reputation. I guess when I was released I just used what I knew best. Brett had left me some money in his will, so that helped, and my reputation made people want to take a risk on me. Over the last year and a half I've built my organization to be one of the biggest of its type in New York. The Salazars are one of my rivals. They were at the club last week when we had our...*exchange*." He chewed over the word, struggling to find the best one. "I guess they saw you as a way of getting to me."

My mouth had gone dry. Jamie was now leading his own crew, even though he'd fought so hard to leave all of that behind him? I hadn't expected that to come out of his mouth at all. I knew he had changed, that was easy enough to see. But to abandon everything he'd said to me and immerse himself in a life he claimed he hated? I hadn't realized he'd changed quite that much.

He looked up at me, his eyes pleading with me to understand. I could also see regret and shame, like he was embarrassed to be admitting it to me. "These people, the Salazar brothers and their organization, they've got no morals. They don't care who they hurt to get what they want."

"And you're different?" I asked, my voice barely above a whisper.

A frown lined his forehead as he nodded. "Yeah. I mean, most of my work tends not to be violent. There are times when I have to do things I don't want to, but we're *nothing* like them. Our main priority has always been the cars."

I shook my head in disbelief. "This can't be the real you, Jamie. You can't have changed that much in a couple of years."

He smiled boyishly. "I love it when you call me Jamie. No one calls me that anymore." He sighed sadly. "In a way, Jamie went into prison, but Kid Cole came out. This is who I am now." He gave a resigned shrug, but his eyes betrayed him. I could see the sadness there, the longing for something different that he was trying so hard to hide—even from himself.

"I don't believe that, I see it in your eyes. There's good in you. You're a good person, you always have been. It's just that circumstances have always been against you," I protested. "Before, you had a reason to fight against what people thought of you; I think you've just lost your way. It's easier to conform and be what's expected than to change, I know that. My whole life through high school, I was trying to be someone I wasn't just because it was what was expected of me. Then I met you and I realized I could be the person I wanted to be, screw expectation or reputation, I could do whatever I wanted."

His frown deepened. "And what exactly did you want that was so against what people expected?"

I shrugged one shoulder. "You."

Silence followed as his eyebrows rose in surprise.

"I fought for you. I fought against people who believed I was better suited to the school jock. I fought against my mother, who told me over and over you weren't good enough for me. I fought so hard for you because I saw the good in your heart. I still do, even if you don't. You should have fought for me, too. Things could have been so different. I loved you; I would have understood, and I would have waited for you to get out. We could have made a life together, Jamie." That hurt to say because it was so true. I would have waited until the end of the world for him, and then we could have had our happily-ever-after.

"It's too late now, I suppose?" he asked, his hopeful eyes boring into mine.

I wasn't expecting that response, and my body automatically recoiled from shock. "I…I'm…" I wasn't even sure what I wanted to say to finish that sentence.

"Engaged. I know. And he's a good man," he finished my sentence for me, and then a fierce determination crossed his face. "But do you love him like you loved me?"

Did I? No. I knew it, deep down; I had never loved another like I loved Jamie, and I most likely never would. "No." I felt like I was betraying Toby by saying the word out loud.

Jamie, ever the gentleman, didn't gloat over my admission. I saw a smile twitch at the corner of his mouth, but he hid it as quickly as it had come and then changed the subject. "I bought you a ring once. I was going to propose. I'd asked your dad and everything, but then..." He frowned. "Then shit happened."

I couldn't mask my shocked expression; my mouth dropped open with an audible pop as my eyes widened. "What?" My father had never revealed this piece of information. I'd gone off, heartbroken, and he'd never told me that Jamie had spoken to him about taking the next step. "What did my dad say?" Somehow that was important. Having just lost him, I needed to know his opinion—would he have given Jamie and me his blessing?

Jamie smiled sadly. "He said as long as I kept making you smile, then yes, but he made me promise to wait a few years before I took you down the aisle."

My emotions overcame me again and I burst into tears, covering my face with my hands. And then Jamie was there again, wrapping his strong arms around me, crushing me against his body as his face pressed into my hair, his breath fanning down my neck. I cried harder, clinging to him, grieving for the loss of us as a couple and for my dad.

"Would you have said yes?" Jamie asked, stroking my back soothingly as my body shook and hitched with sobs.

I nodded awkwardly against his shoulder, my fingers digging into his back, clutching him closer. I definitely would have said yes, I would have practically snatched the ring from his hand and screamed the word yes. I would have been proud to wear his ring on my finger.

His body sagged against mine, and he let out a long, slow

breath as he bent his head and pressed a soft kiss to the base of my shoulder. My whole body prickled with need and my heart stuttered as lust ignited within me. I gulped and closed my eyes, enjoying the sensations building within me at an alarming rate.

I didn't move, afraid of what would happen if I did. Maybe he would pull away and apologize, or maybe he wouldn't pull away at all, maybe he would clutch me closer and the flames of passion would burn us both to the ground. I wasn't sure which I wanted more.

"Why do you smell like smoke?" I asked after a minute or so, when I'd managed to calm my body and my tears. The smell clinging to his clothes made my throat itch a little.

"Uh...I went to see the Salazar crew," he answered, his tone sheepish.

I pulled back quickly, wiping my nose with the back of my hand. "What? What does that mean?"

He shrugged, reaching up to scratch at the back of his neck as he looked away from me. "I couldn't let them get away with touching you."

"So you did what exactly?" I asked, not sure if I wanted to know.

He stood, brushing down his shirt, and shrugged. "Do you want a drink or something? Maybe something to eat? I still can't cook, but I try sometimes." He turned and walked off toward the kitchen, leaving me sitting there in stunned silence. He'd flat-out refused to answer my question. What exactly was I supposed to take from that?

I stood too, turning to see him leaning into his fridge, his back to me. "Jamie, what did you do?" I repeated hesitantly.

His back stiffened, but he didn't turn to face me. "Less than I wanted to do."

I could see I wasn't going to win this one. He wasn't going to answer, no matter how much I pushed. My frustrated gaze fell onto the table and the upturned photo, and suddenly different questions formed in my head.

"Jamie, who is Natalie to you?" I asked, watching as his hand stopped midway through reaching into the bag of bread.

"What?" He cleared his throat awkwardly. "I don't know any Natalie." He turned back to me then, his eyes wary and guarded.

"More lies," I muttered, frowning. I reached down for the photo, holding it up, watching as resignation flitted over his features.

He sighed deeply, reaching up to rub at the back of his neck. Silence hung in the air, almost palpable, until he finally spoke, "She's Ray's sister-in-law. I didn't want you traveling alone. I couldn't be there and I knew you were upset, so..." He swallowed. "I paid for Nat's trip so she could keep you company and try to cheer you up a little."

My eyes widened. I hadn't expected that answer. That possibility hadn't even entered my head when I was turning over scenarios while I waited for him to return from wherever he went earlier. "You what?" I gasped.

His eyes tightened, his posture tense. "I wanted to look out for you, even if I couldn't be there with you. I couldn't just cut all ties. I needed to know you were okay," he explained.

I wasn't sure how to respond. In a way, knowing that he had still been looking out for me, still protecting me, even from prison, kind of took a little of the hurt away. Jamie always was overprotective, but this was extreme even for him. The gesture made my heart ache, but it also made me a little angry.

"I can't believe this," I said quietly. "I was traveling with her for almost a year. She never said a thing to me about you. I thought she was my friend." Now I understood how she seemed to have a never-ending supply of cash—it was Jamie's dirty gang money that he'd worked so hard for. Finding this out about her was like a punch in the gut. I'd opened up to her about the breakup and all the time she was playing me for a free trip?

Jamie shook his head and walked back to me, reaching out and taking my hand, squeezing softly. "She *is* your friend. She just lied about how you met, that's all. Everything else about your relationship is real. Don't be mad at her for it, Ellie. She helped you through a tough time, she was there for you."

True. I don't know what I would have done without her.

He bent so we were at the same level, his eyes latching onto mine, the beautiful shade of them catching me off guard and making my heart stutter. "She helped me through a tough time, too," he continued. "She gave me updates on how you were." He smiled sadly. "If it weren't for those, I'm not sure I would have made it, to be honest. I was miserable and just as heartbroken as you were." Reaching out, he snagged a lock of my hair, pushing it behind my ear, his fingers tracing the sensitive skin at the side of my neck, causing goose bumps to break out on my body.

I opened my mouth, unsure what I even wanted to say. I wanted to thank him for looking out for me, I wanted to scold him for invading my privacy, I wanted to step closer and press myself against him, I wanted to slap him in the face. I didn't know what I wanted.

I decided to go for honesty.

"When I saw the photo in your room, I thought that maybe she was your girlfriend," I said, hating that my voice shook a little on the word *girlfriend*.

One side of his mouth rose into a sad smile. "She's not my girlfriend. There's been no one since you."

My mouth popped open in shock. "No one?" That couldn't

be true. Three years I'd been gone, and it wasn't as if a guy like him would be short of offers!

Before he could answer, my cell phone began to ring, saving him from more probing questions. We both looked down at my purse, and I debated leaving it so we could get everything out in the open once and for all, but then figured it was probably my nana wondering where I was because I should have been back hours ago with the food she'd asked for.

I pulled away and picked up my purse, shoving my hand in and fishing out my cell. I groaned when I saw several large cracks covering my screen. The phone itself was thankfully functional, though, because it was still illuminated and vibrating in my hand and I could just make out that it said a private number was calling. I pressed the Answer button, being careful not to cut my finger, and put it to my ear.

"Hello?" I answered.

"Oh, good afternoon, is this Ellison Pearce?" a lady asked, her voice curt but polite.

I frowned, wondering who it was. "It is."

"Hello, Ellison. This is Nurse Partridge from the ICU ward that your mother is on."

My heart stopped, my mouth going dry as I imagined the worst. "Is everything okay?" I croaked.

"Actually, I'm calling with some good news. Your mother just woke up," she replied cheerfully.

I gasped in shock. "Really? Oh my God," I murmured, my hand coming up to cover my throat. I couldn't contain my grin. "Is she okay?"

"She's doing well, her pressures are all steady and she's breathing on her own. She's even taken a drink. She's drifted back to sleep now, but that's expected. She'll probably sleep on and off for the next day or so," the nurse explained. "I know you've already been in this morning, but I thought I'd give you a call in case you wanted to come back to see her."

I nodded eagerly, my heart lifting. Maybe she really had heard me this morning; maybe there was actually something in this talking-to-coma-patients crap that the doctors spouted.

"I'll be there soon! Thank you so much for calling." I grinned, disconnecting the phone and looking up at Jamie, who was watching me curiously. "My mom just woke up," I gushed excitedly.

His face split with a grin as he pulled his car keys from his pocket. "That's great news. Come on, I'll take you to the hospital."

I nodded gratefully, the conversation between us immediately forgotten because all I could think about was hugging my mother and telling her I loved her.

Maybe, just maybe, things were looking up for the Pearce family now.

CHAPTER 21

ON THE WAY out of Jamie's apartment, I called home and told my nana the good news about Mom. As expected, she was over the moon and almost burst my eardrum with the earsplitting scream of joy she emitted. Luckily, it was now after three p.m., so even Kelsey was home. Jamie was taking me to my house now so we could meet up and all go together. On the drive, I couldn't keep the broad grin from my face. After everything that we'd been through, this news made a whole world of difference and uplifted my heart.

As we approached my house, I saw that my beloved green-and rust-colored monstrosity was parked in my drive. I frowned at it, confused. "How did my car get here?"

"I had someone pick it up from the convenience store and bring it back for you," Jamie answered casually.

I patted my pockets, feeling the lump of my keys against my hip. "But how? I have my keys..." I turned to look at him in time to see a smile pull at his lips.

"Me and my associates don't need keys to start cars, remember?" he joked.

My frown turned into a scowl of disapproval. "Right," I muttered quietly as he pulled up at my house and killed the engine. "Well, thanks for the ride and for, you know, saving me from those guys even though it was your fault they were after me in the first place." I smiled awkwardly. "I'll see you around."

I didn't know what else to say, and that had sounded a lot more final than I had intended. We still had things to talk about; he still had explaining to do, but I wasn't entirely sure I wanted to hear it. It would be a lot easier for me if I just got on with things and didn't dwell on the past.

As I reached down to unbuckle my seat belt, his hand stretched out, covering my knee. "Ellie, the Salazars might still be after you. I have people trying to find them. They shouldn't be stupid enough to come and try anything again, but just in case, I need to have people watching you for the time being."

I turned in my seat, regarding him curiously. "What do you mean, watching me? Like someone following me around? I don't want that."

One side of his mouth quirked up into a knowing half smile. "You haven't seemed to mind it so far."

So far? What is that about? "Huh?"

He looked away from me out through the windshield; his eyes fixed on my house. "Since the club last week I've had people watching you around the clock, just making sure you're safe and that you're not being followed or anything."

I gasped as everything clicked into place. "The guy in the sedan! He was at my dad's funeral, too!"

Jamie nodded once in agreement. "That was my friend Dodger. I've been taking a lot of the shifts myself, but a guy's gotta sleep and eat..."

Jamie had been parked outside my house; he'd been that close the whole time and I hadn't known? A little stab of something twitched in my gut. "You've been sitting outside my house watching me?"

"Well, that doesn't make me sound like a stalker much," he joked, smiling wryly.

I smiled too and shook my head. I couldn't deal with all of this now. I had somewhere to be. "Anyway, whatever. Thanks again for the ride." I put my hand on the door handle, cracking it open.

"Wait, let me put my number in your phone," he ordered, holding out his hand for my cell. I frowned but reached into my purse and pulled out my broken phone, passing it to him. He punched in his number, then used my phone to call his own so he could store mine, too. When he handed it back, he smiled sheepishly. "You know, in case anything happens and you need to get hold of me."

"Okay." I nodded. "Bye, Jamie."

"I can drive you to the hospital if you want," he offered as I stepped out and shouldered my purse.

I pointed to my little bug sitting in the driveway. "I got transport." I closed the door and waved, expecting him to drive off up the street, but his car didn't start; instead he continued to sit there and watch as I jogged into the house excitedly.

"I'm here. Who's ready?" I called as I burst through the door.

Kelsey immediately bounded down the stairs, a huge grin on her face, and Nana came from the kitchen, her coat already on. I raised one eyebrow at Kelsey. "I'm telling Mom you had your sneakers on upstairs," I teased, nodding down at her feet.

She didn't answer, just threw herself at me and hugged me so tightly it almost cut off my circulation. I grinned and hugged her back before pulling away. "Come on then, let's go."

I stepped back outside again, noticing Jamie was still parked there. I sent a little frown in his direction, but couldn't see inside his car because of the tinted windows, so I wasn't sure he was watching. We all piled into my car and headed to the hospital. I noted, with some level of unease, that Jamie had pulled out behind me and was following along. Had he been serious when he said someone was going to have to watch me? Did he actually think those Salazar guys would come after me again?

When we arrived, we all speed-walked the familiar path through the hospital, my nana tutting in annoyance at the slow ambling of the noisy elevator as it took us to the correct floor.

My excitement to see my mom faded a little when we stepped into her room only to find that she was asleep. Kelsey frowned, her hand slipping into mine and squeezing tightly. "I thought you said she woke up?"

My eyes roamed the room, seeing the subtle differences from this morning. Although the heart rate monitor continued its steady rhythm, spiking and falling gently as usual, the IV pole didn't have a bag attached to it and was pushed against the wall, the drip in her hand had been capped off, and no tubes were coming out of her mouth or nose.

"She's just sleeping," I whispered, stepping farther into the room and pulling Kelsey along with me. With her pressed against me so tightly, I felt the tension leave her body as she took in my words. I smiled over at her and nodded toward one of the chairs. "You and Nana sit, I'll stand."

I walked to one side of the bed, letting them occupy the two visitor chairs on the other side. We waited in silence for a good five minutes before we started whispering to each other, planning ways to subtly wake her up and considering the consequences. And then her eyes fluttered open and closed again, and it was one of the most beautiful things I had ever seen. I stepped closer to the bed as she fully awoke, her eyes settling on me.

She blinked a couple of times, her forehead scrunching up as if she was confused, and then her mouth popped open and she gasped. "Ellison?"

I nodded, beaming down at her. "Hi, Mom."

A little strangled cry left her lips as she reached out and touched a tentative hand to my cheek. "Oh, Ellison! It's so good to see you; I'm so glad you're here." Her voice was weak and hoarse from the breathing tubes.

"It's good to see you, too," I replied honestly.

Her hand moved from my cheek to my hair as she caught a lock of it between her finger and thumb. "You cut your hair since we last video called." Her smile was warm and tender; her eyes shined with affection that I'd never really associated with my mother when I was younger. "It's shorter than mine now. I don't think you've worn it this short since you were a baby. You always liked it longer."

Kelsey stepped to the other side, her hand reaching out and taking Mom's. My mom turned in her direction and her smile grew wider. "Kelsey," she whispered, and then her eyes settled on Nana, who had stood up but stayed a little behind so Kelsey could get to the bed. "Betty, hi," Mom greeted her.

"Hi, Ruth. It's lovely to see you awake; we were beginning to wonder how long you were going to sleep for," Nana replied, smiling softly at her daughter-in-law.

Mom tugged on mine and Kelsey's hands, pulling them to her tummy as she held them tightly. "What happened? They said I was in a car accident." She frowned, seeming confused about the whole thing. "But I don't remember any accident."

I nodded, silently grateful because no one should have to remember things like that. "You and Dad were in a car accident. You've been in a coma, Mom."

She gulped, her confusion growing. "How long for?"

"Almost two weeks," Kelsey chimed in. "The doctors weren't sure you'd wake up."

Mom looked at me for confirmation and I nodded. "You had extensive head injuries and a brain bleed."

She seemed shocked to hear this; her eyes widened and her grip intensified on my hand. Silence hung there for a few seconds before she looked around the room at the three of us again and her eyebrows knitted together. "Where's Michael?"

An instant jolt of grief hit me like a punch in the gut. The doctors hadn't told her. She didn't know. She'd slept through the whole thing and didn't know her husband of twenty-two years, her college sweetheart, was gone. I remembered how hard it was for me when I heard the news; surely it was going to be ten times worse for her.

I gulped and opened my mouth as Mom's voice rose in a slight alarm as she looked at my nana. "Betty, where's Michael?"

Kelsey had begun to cry, big, fat tears rolling down her cheeks. I cleared my throat, willing my voice to come out strong as I looked at Nana. Her panic-stricken eyes met mine as her wrinkled lips pressed into a thin line. "Nana, why don't you and Kels go get some coffee, and maybe buy Mom some magazines and candy for later?" I suggested.

Nana nodded, her expression almost grateful as she stepped to Kelsey's side and draped an arm around her shoulder. "That's a good idea, let's go get your mom some things she'd like, all right?"

Kelsey looked at me and then down at my mom, whose eyes were now wide with panic as her gaze flipped between the two of us; she was gnawing on her lip so much that it was beginning to bleed.

"Go on, Kels," I encouraged her, nodding toward the door.

As she let Nana lead her out of the room, an intense feeling of foreboding gripped my stomach.

"What's happened?" Mom rasped as soon as the door closed.

I gulped, unsure how to even word it. "Mom, I'm so sorry," I croaked, reaching out and putting my hand on her shoulder, squeezing gently. "Dad, he..." I shook my head, my vision swimming slightly from the tears that pooled in my eyes.

She drew in a sharp intake of breath, her whole body becoming rigid. "No," she cried. "No, it can't be. He wouldn't leave me, he wouldn't. There must be some mistake, someone must have messed up somewhere along the line, it can't be true." Her voice broke several times as she spoke; her eyes stayed locked on mine and I could see a full range of emotions flickering across her face as she silently pleaded for me to tell her it wasn't true.

"I'm sorry, Mom. I'm so sorry," I whispered, dipping my head and planting a kiss on her cheek.

Her mouth popped open as she shook her head violently. "No," she whimpered. "He's dead? Your father is dead?"

I nodded once, watching as her heart fragmented. Her chin trembled and her whole face crumpled. "But I can't...He can't be." Her heart rate monitor jumped all over the place as she covered her face with her hands and cried so hard her body shook. "I want to die too, why didn't I just die, too?" she moaned through her fingers, the sound harrowing and guttural.

I groaned and felt a stab in my heart as I reached out, stroking her hair back from her forehead. "Mom, it's okay, I'm here, and Kels, we'll take care of you." I didn't have the right words; there was nothing that would lessen this pain she was going through, so all I could do was watch and support. I hated the helpless feeling.

"Oh, Michael!" she cried.

I looked at her heart rate monitor worriedly, seeing the

numbers in the corner creeping higher and higher. She needed to calm down. She'd just awoken from a coma; she shouldn't be so worked up because it wasn't good for her. Silence filled the room, the soft sounds of weeping all that could be heard over the erratic pounding of my own heart.

Her hands came down from her face, one pressing against her chest as her tears continued to flow. Her bloodshot, watery eyes met mine. "Your father was my soul mate, the other piece of my puzzle. I wish I'd told him more before it was too late." Her lip quivered and she bit into it roughly, her breath hitching.

"He knew, Mom." Of that I was sure. All the adoring looks I'd caught him shooting her over the years, all the secret smiles, all the heartfelt *I love you*s he'd said to her when he thought no one was listening. He'd worshipped the ground she walked on, even on her off days, and he knew she felt the same.

"I should have shown it more, sometimes I was so horrible to him," she whimpered. She started crying harder. I had no idea what I could do or say to make her feel better, so I just leaned down and hugged her awkwardly, pressing my face into the crook of her neck as I wrapped my arm over her body, holding her as best I could in light of the awkward position of her lying on the bed. Her hand came up, tangling into the back of my hair as she gripped my other hand so tightly it was almost painful.

Her body trembled and hitched under mine. Her tears wet my hair and dripped onto my face as she clung to me, lost in her grieving. I gulped, trying to remain in control as her heartbreak threatened to swallow me, too. In that moment, I had never felt closer to her as I shared her mourning. This was the first time I had ever seen her cry—the dust-in-the-eye crying of my traveling departure was nothing compared to this all-out, soul-crushing heartbreak.

Eventually, her breathing evened out. My eyes stayed glued to the heart rate monitor as time passed, seeing the numbers in the corner slowly creep back down to a normal, steady rhythm. I pulled back carefully, looking down at my mother, now deep in sleep, her forehead and cheeks blotchy and splotched with red from all the crying.

I swallowed, reaching up to wipe my own puffy, tearstained face as I sat down in the chair by the side of her bed and took her hand. As I watched her sleep, I actually dreaded the time when she would wake again and have to deal with the loss and grief of losing her soul mate. In the silence of her room, I actually began to wonder if it would have been kinder and fairer to her if she *had* died.

A few minutes later, the door creaked behind me and I looked up to see the doctor step in. "She's gone back to sleep. Is that normal?" I asked quietly, my voice raspy and dry.

He nodded, picking up her chart and scribbling some notes. "Perfectly normal. Her body can heal itself better while she's sleeping. She's been through a lot; she's very lucky. It was touch-and-go for a while there."

"I know," I replied. I didn't want to admit that along the way I'd kind of given up hope of this moment ever coming.

"How long until she's well enough to come home?" I inquired, stroking my mom's hair back from her forehead.

The doctor smiled. "There's a long road ahead and I'm afraid it may be a little bumpy. Your mother will need to stay in at least a few more days. After that she'll most likely need a wheelchair for a couple of weeks because of the extent of her injuries. There's quite a bit of rehabilitation and physical therapy that's going to be needed before she's up and about and back to normal, but she'll get there. With any brain injury, you can expect some good, lucid days and some bad days. She's going to need extensive physical and emotional support."

I nodded in understanding and lifted her hand to my lips, kissing the back of it gently. "That's okay. I'll be there." And I would. Always.

CHAPTER 22

THE MOOD ON the drive home from the hospital was distinctly more somber than on the way there. We'd all been so excited when we got the news she was awake; everyone was so happy, it hadn't even occurred to any of us that Mom was two weeks behind events and wouldn't know about my dad's death. If anything, our moods were lower than before; we were all sharing in my mom's newfound grief.

She'd woken and drifted off a couple more times during the visit, and each time had been just as heartbreaking as the first when she remembered and burst into hysterical sobs. The worst was when I told her we'd already held the funeral. She'd been devastated she hadn't been there to say good-bye, and wailed about what Michael would have thought of her not being there. There had been no consoling her. The guilt I felt surged within me, twisted in my gut like a knife. But the more rational part of me knew I was punishing myself for nothing. The doctors had told me not to wait, that they weren't confident she was going to wake. We could have been waiting forever for something that might never have happened; no one could see into the future.

Another part of me decided it was a good thing my mom had missed it. Her last memories of Dad were untarnished; she couldn't remember the crash, so the last thing she said she remembered was being in the car and my dad singing—badly—to some Spandau Ballet song on the radio, trying to make her laugh.

I envied her. Whenever I thought of my dad now, all I saw was the funeral, the groups of crying people gathered, and the coffin sitting on the little raised platform. So maybe it was a good thing she'd slept through it; I kind of wished I had.

Leaving my mom had been hard. She was so broken and weak, miles away from the strong and in-control woman I'd come to know and love. It was like she was a little girl lost in a storm; the hospital staff had eventually given her a sedative to help her sleep because her heart rate was all over the place again. Once she was asleep again for the night, we all headed out and piled into my car to make the short drive home.

The visit had taken its toll on everyone. Flicking my eyes to the rearview mirror, I saw that Kelsey had her head resting against the window, her eyes vacantly staring at nothing as she twisted her hands in her lap. She hadn't spoken a word since we left the hospital.

When I pulled into the driveway, I saw a car roll to a stop at the curb, killing the lights. Jamie. As I climbed out of the car, I looked over to see that he'd parked more obviously outside my house this time, just at the curb at the end of the yard rather than a few houses down as the other car had. Maybe it was because I knew he was watching now, so he didn't need to hide.

Kelsey's eyes flicked in that direction and a small frown lined her forehead. I held my breath, hoping she didn't recognize my ex-boyfriend or ask questions. I really didn't need any more drama tonight. If I was honest, all I wanted was a stiff drink.

Thankfully Kels didn't say anything; Jamie's car only held her attention for a second or two before she headed to the front door with Nana.

I held my hand up in a quick wave—acknowledging he was here was the polite thing to do, after all—before heading into the house.

"I'm going to make us a late supper," Nana said, immediately walking into the kitchen and opening the fridge. At the mention of food, my stomach growled and I suddenly remembered that I never did bring home those groceries Nana had asked for. They were probably still smeared across the store parking lot where I'd left them. Thankfully, in the excitement of everything, Nana hadn't mentioned it. I glanced at my watch and saw it was just after eight p.m. Today had been an extremely long day.

Kelsey and I sat in the living room, both of us pretending to watch TV so we wouldn't have to make conversation, while Nana banged around in the kitchen. When she came in fifteen minutes later with three plates loaded with cheese-and-tomato quesadillas, my mouth watered. Eating them was a different story, though; I couldn't concentrate and ended up just pushing most of the food around my plate while I replayed things my mom had said tonight. Eventually, I gave up trying.

"I'm going to take a bath," I announced, standing and carrying Nana and Kelsey's mostly full plates to the kitchen. After scraping the contents into the garbage disposal, I slinked upstairs and headed into the bathroom. I turned on the water, tipped in some of the bath salts that were in a jar on the side of the tub, and then sat on the edge, staring into space as steam swirled around me and fogged up the mirror.

I stripped off my clothes and sank down in the hot water, closing my eyes as it lapped around my neck and chin, the flowery scent of the bath salts tickling my nose. I lay there for a long time, the water turning lukewarm as my mind was on my mother and what her future held, and how that tied in with my own. Conversations with Toby infiltrated my thoughts, the unspoken words that had hung between us at the airport, the understanding in his eyes when he'd kissed me good-bye.

I sighed and sat up, pushing my wet hair off my face, staring up at the ceiling. I needed to speak to him; this uncertainty was weighing on me, and I couldn't take much more pressure without breaking. I wanted to stay here with my family, and he needed to stay with his family, which left us in an impossible situation that just caused more pain than it needed to.

After quickly shampooing my hair and washing my body, I climbed out of the bath, wrapped myself in a big fluffy towel, and padded to my bedroom. After a quick dry and dragging a comb through my unruly red hair, I picked out my most comfortable pajamas, the ones with the sleeping panda bears on them, and then snagged one of my old high school team hoodies from the closet. As soon as I pulled it over my head, I realized it didn't fit, but I went with it anyway, wriggling to get into it and tugging it down over my body. It was slightly too small now, especially across my tummy and breasts. I remembered a time when I was in high school that it would have flattered my toned stomach and sat perfectly on my hips. I wrinkled my nose and pondered going on a diet so I could drop the fourteen or so pounds I'd put on in the last couple of years, but then I remembered I liked chocolate cake too much and dismissed the thought. I wasn't overweight, I just wasn't the perfect lithe cheerleader I used to be.

I smiled to myself and picked up my damaged phone, carefully scrolling through to find Toby's number. It wasn't until it started ringing that I remembered the time difference. Wincing as he answered in a croaky, sleep-filled tone, I looked at the clock. It was almost ten here, which meant it was nearly three in the morning there.

"I'm so sorry! I forgot about the time difference," I said quickly, perching on the edge of my bed.

He cleared his throat and I heard bedcovers moving and rustling in the background. "S'okay, don't worry."

"Sorry, Toby," I whispered.

"'Onestly, it's fine, I love speaking to you so it's all good," he replied, his voice soft and sensual since he'd just awoken. "'Ow are ya?"

"My mom woke up." I smiled.

"Bloody 'ell, that's great news!"

"Yeah." I nodded, and even I heard the sad tone to my voice, so I wasn't really that surprised that he picked up on it, too.

"What's wrong, then? You don't sound like your usual cheerful self."

I sighed and leaned forward, resting my head on my hand and my elbow on my knee. "It was just hard, that's all. She didn't know about my dad, so I had to tell her and stuff." I chewed on the inside of my mouth, trying not to picture her crushed expression again.

"Damn, that's rough," he answered, his tone sympathetic. "You all right?"

I have to be. "I'm getting there." We would all get there together.

"So if she's awake that means she'll be 'ome soon, right?" Toby asked.

I closed my eyes. This was the start of the conversation; this was my in to telling him I wasn't coming back. Although I knew I had to say the words, I didn't really want to. I'd just never expected it to end this way. In fact, I hadn't expected it to end at all. If none of this had happened, I would have lived out the rest of my life with him, content to be a mother to his two boys when they came to stay on the weekends, running the pub with him, and crawling into bed with a good man every night. Fate had other ideas, though.

"They said she'll be in the hospital for a few more days, and then when she's out she'll need extensive support to rehabilitate after the accident." I cleared my throat and then took a deep breath. "Toby, we need to talk about something," I started, struggling to find the words. "I...I..." *Oh God, why is doing the right thing always so hard?*

He sighed deeply, his breath making static down the line. "I know what you're going to say."

My breath caught. "You do?" My voice was barely above a whisper.

He sighed again. "Yeah. I saw it in your eyes. You don't want to leave your family. You want to stay there and not come 'ome."

I nodded. He had it right apart from one thing—I was home *here.* London had never really been my home, and neither had he. I just hadn't wanted to admit it to myself. "I'm so sorry," I croaked. And I was. I never wanted to hurt him, but there was no way around this. We were from opposite sides of the world.

"It's okay, Ellie. I understand, 'onestly I do. I'm gutted, don't get me wrong, but I get it. I know 'ow much your family means to you, and after everything that's 'appened, I can see why you'd need to make this decision."

"I never wanted to hurt you," I said solemnly.

"I know that, sweetheart. It's just geography, it fucked us up. We never stood a chance, not really." He was putting on a brave face, forcing cheer into his tone, but I could hear the underlying sadness there. He understood, but it still hurt him. "I love you. I wish things could be different, but you know, once geography speaks, everyone listens," he joked.

"I love you, too." The words were true, I meant them with all of my heart. In a way, he'd saved me; I'd been a different person when we first met, and he'd helped me back onto my feet and supported me while I found myself again. I owed him more than I could ever repay for that. I'd always thought that was enough to base a relationship on, but now I realized that wasn't true. "I'm going to miss you so much." I'd miss his jokes, his infectious laugh, his errant goodness, and the whole cheeky-chappie easygoing Londoner thing he had going on.

"We can stay in touch and stuff, talk and catch up. I don't want to lose you altogether." His words were heartfelt, and I could hear the sadness in his tone that he was trying to mask.

I nodded in agreement. We'd remain friends, of that I was sure. Toby was friends with everyone, even his ex-wife, so I knew we could stay in touch. "You won't," I promised.

"Good, because I'd 'ate that." He cleared his throat. "Look, I'd better get some sleep, I 'ave an early start tomorrow. We'll chat later in the week, yeah?"

I knew he was just trying to end the call. Breakup calls weren't exactly the most comfortable of conversations. "Yeah," I agreed. "I'll give you a call in a couple of days."

"Okay, but if anything changes or you need to chat before that, then 'it me up. I'm still 'ere for you if you need someone to talk to or whatever."

I smiled. Toby's goodness was one of the things that I loved about him—that and his ability to make a joke out of anything, even if it was a terribly unfunny pun in the supermarket. "Thank you, and same goes for you. Say hi to the boys from me next time you see them," I replied. Thinking about not seeing him again, his kids again, made my heart drum wildly in my chest. It hurt. But not as much as I'd expected it to.

He disconnected the call and I lay back on my bed, knowing

I'd done the right thing. I'd made the right decision for me, and it might not feel like it at the moment to Toby, but eventually he would see it was the right decision for him, too. I loved him, but I had never been *in love* with him, and he deserved that. He was such a good man; he deserved someone whose heart would flutter when he walked into the room wrapped only in a towel, a girl whose thighs clenched in excitement when he touched her, someone who swooned when he smiled. That girl just wasn't me—it never had been—and for a long time I'd thought that was okay, but I'd been fooling us both. We were settling for each other, and people like Toby deserved better than to just settle.

I was happy it was finally out in the open. Now we could each get on with our lives and I could focus on mending my family one little piece at a time. Slipping on the pink fluffy slippers that Kelsey had bought me for my eighteenth birthday, I padded out of the room and down the stairs, deciding to make some hot cocoa.

At the bottom of the stairs, I headed to the front door, moving the curtain out of the way and peeking out. Jamie's car was still parked there in the same spot. I frowned, wondering how long he was going to be camped outside my house, watching my every move. It was a little weird, but I could understand why he was protective.

My thoughts drifted back to his apartment, how he'd wiped my tears away and told me he'd once planned a life for us. How he'd asked me if it was too late for us.

I gulped, my heart swelling at the memory. My decision to stay here and not return to England had nothing to do with Jamie. It had already been subconsciously made before I'd even seen him in that club. I wanted to be close to my family; I wanted to stay in my home instead of a place I lived in with

Toby. Jamie hadn't been a factor at all…at least, not at the start—I wasn't so sure about now.

I shook the thoughts away as I walked into the living room, seeing Kelsey and Nana curled up on the sofa together watching TV. "Anyone want hot cocoa? I think I saw some marshmallows in the cupboard earlier," I tempted.

They both nodded eagerly and I stepped into the kitchen, grabbing the milk from the fridge and pouring some into a pan. As I leaned down to put it away again, I saw the leftover chicken from yesterday's dinner. My mind immediately flicked to Jamie again. Had he gotten anything to eat? I chewed on the inside of my mouth and then pulled the chicken and mayonnaise from the fridge, setting about making him a sandwich while the milk bubbled lightly in the pan.

When everything was done, I took the two girls' drinks into the living room and set them on the table before heading back to get the plate of food and the cocoa I'd made for Jamie. Being as quiet as I could because I didn't particularly want to answer any questions about my actions, I tiptoed out of the house, closing the door carefully behind me.

As I walked across the front yard, my hair whipping everywhere in the wind, Jamie rolled down his car window. I smiled weakly and offered the plate and mug, which he took gratefully. "Thought you might be hungry. I haven't seen you go get any food yet," I said as he picked up the sandwich and took a huge bite, chewing quickly.

"Starving," he mumbled with his mouth full. "Thank you." His eyes flashed in the darkness as I squatted down by the side of his car so I could see in better.

"Jamie, how long are you going to be watching me for?"

He shrugged one shoulder, setting the cup on his dashboard, where it was sure to leave a ring stain on his expensive interior. I silently scolded myself for not bringing a mat or something for him to use. "I'll be going in a couple of hours. I have someone else coming to watch the house tonight, but I'll be back tomorrow."

"That's not what I meant."

He sighed deeply, half turning in his seat so we were almost face-to-face. "I don't know. I have people trying to find the guy who put the order in for you to be grabbed, but I'm not sure how long it'll take." His eyes were tight with both anger and worry.

"Oh," I muttered. I hated the fact that I had to be babysat. I shoved my hands into the pocket of my hoodie, linking my fingers together over my stomach. "We need to talk some more about, you know, earlier."

He nodded, setting his plate on the dash next to his mug. "Now? We could go get a coffee," he offered, his voice ridiculously eager. I tried to ignore the flutter in my tummy. I secretly loved that he wanted to spend more time with me.

I looked down at my pink fluffy slippers, pajamas, and too-small hoodie and raised one eyebrow. "I'm not dressed." I shrugged.

The corners of his mouth quirked into a smile as his eyes raked down me so slowly that I felt heat creep across my cheeks from the intimate inspection. "I don't care. I think you look beautiful."

I had to smile at that. *Corny.* I sighed and shook my head, my body overcome with tiredness. "Not tonight, all right? I'm exhausted." I looked back at the house, lifting a hand and trying to tuck some of my still-damp, flyaway hair behind my ear. The chilly wind whipped it right back out again. "I should go in. Good night, Jamie." I turned toward the house, not waiting for a reply as I stalked off.

"Ellie?"

I'd only gotten a few steps before he called me back. I stopped, turning to see him climbing out of the car, his long, toned body looking sleek and gorgeous as he strode toward me. He didn't speak as his arms folded around me, engulfing me in a hug and holding me tightly against him. My breath came out in one long, deep sigh as I melted against him, my eyes fluttering closed as I wrapped my arms around his waist. We were so close I could feel his heart beating against my chest, and a feeling of safety washed over me as his smell filled my lungs.

I tucked my face into the side of his neck, my nose brushing against the skin there, eliciting a soft moan from his lips. His fingers dug into my back gently, clutching me closer as I just reveled in how wonderful it felt to be in his arms again, how right it felt. It was like, in that moment, I was finally home.

His face pressed against the side of my head, his lips grazing against my scalp, causing cells within me that I thought long dead to awaken and tingle. The desire that pooled in my belly bumped from embers to a slow delicious burn that tightened my skin and made my mouth water. I wanted to be closer; I wanted to melt into him and stay like that forever, my problems a distant memory.

He pulled back slowly, his arms still around me. I could see the desire in his eyes, his need maybe as great as my own. I smiled gratefully. I'd desperately needed that hug and I hadn't even known it.

With herculean effort, because I wanted to stand there in his arms forever, I stepped back, putting some space between our bodies. "Good night, Jamie."

The dimple appeared, his smile reaching his eyes as his arms dropped to his sides. "Good night, little girl." His voice was husky and thick with desire that made my womb clench, the pet name from years ago just adding to the smoldering hotness of the moment.

I grinned, hoping the darkness would mask my burning cheeks so he wouldn't know how much I still loved that nickname. Turning, I headed toward the house and thought that for the first time in two weeks, I might actually be able to sleep.

CHAPTER 23

AS I WAS slipping my sneakers and coat on at the front door, I reached out and peeked out through the curtain, seeing the same blue Astra parked at the end of my drive with the young blond guy sitting behind the wheel, looking bored. My heart sank, as it had the last three times I'd looked out to see it wasn't Jamie sitting there watching the house. He'd been gone this morning, replaced by this guy I hadn't seen before. The disappointment that Jamie wasn't the one outside hit me a lot harder than I thought it would. I hadn't been able to stop thinking about him since last night when he'd hugged me on the grass just ten feet from where I was standing now. I'd fallen into a peaceful sleep, thinking about how nice it felt to be wrapped in his arms again, how incredible he smelled, and how that dimple in his cheek when he smiled made my heart ache.

Sighing, I called a good-bye to my nana and stepped out the door, walking to my car, ignoring the guy who was also starting his car, ready to follow me to my destination—the hospital.

We'd been trying to stagger visits to my mother so that she had someone at each visiting time. Nana had gone this morning while Kelsey was at school, I was going this afternoon, and tonight we'd most likely all go together.

When I arrived, Mom was sitting up in bed, her TV turned down low, but she wasn't really watching it, just staring off into space absentmindedly. Nana had told me she was a little better today, that she wasn't drifting in and out of sleep like she had been yesterday and that she hadn't cried as much. This was the first time I'd seen her since I'd had to tell her my father was gone.

"Hi, Mom," I greeted her, walking in and setting the grapes Nana had sent on her little table.

Mom looked up and gave me a half smile. "Afternoon, Ellison."

I walked over and kissed the side of her head. "How are you today?" I asked, perching on the edge of her bed and watching her worriedly. Her eyes were red rimmed, her cheeks a little blotchy, like she'd been crying recently.

She reached up a shaky hand and brushed her hair away from her face. "I'm better. They gave me some different pain meds today; they've made me feel a little woozy, but the pain in my hip and leg isn't as bad as it was."

I nodded. "That's good. Well, not about being woozy, but about less pain."

"Yes," she replied, eyeing me curiously. "Are *you* all right?"

"Sure I am," I answered robotically, reaching out and opening the bag of grapes, helping myself to a few. I glanced up at the TV. "Whatcha watching?"

She sighed deeply. "Some terrible soap opera. I forgot how much I dislike daytime TV."

I smiled, staring at the screen, my mind wandering to Jamie again without my permission. Mom reached out and touched my arm softly, catching my attention, and I realized she must have been talking to me and I'd been off in my own little world.

"Ellison, is something wrong? You seem a little distracted."

I shrugged one shoulder, reaching out and plucking another grape from the bunch. "Nothing's wrong. Sorry, what were you saying?"

She sighed, her eyes concerned as she watched me. "I said, when are you leaving to go back to London?"

I shook my head slowly. "I'm not. I've decided that I want to stay here. My home is here with you guys."

She recoiled, her mouth dropping open in shock. "You're staying here?"

I nodded, popping the grape in my mouth. "Yeah. I spoke to Toby about it last night, it's all decided."

"But what's going to happen between you two?" she pressed, her eyes boring into mine.

"We broke up," I replied. "It was amicable. There's not much else to do, really. I want to stay here, and he can't move because of his kids."

She paused before she spoke, as if she couldn't quite find the words. "Ellison, don't think I'm not thrilled to hear you're staying here, because I am. I missed you so much while you were gone, it felt like a piece of me was taken away with you. But if this is about me and the accident, I'll be home soon and can look after Kels. You don't need to do this. I just want you to be happy, I don't want you to put your life on hold."

I sighed, fingering the edge of her bedsheet. I hadn't spoken to anyone else about this; I hadn't even really fully accepted it myself. "Thing is, Mom, I'm not sure if that was meant to be my life. I'm wondering if maybe I was just running away from things and settled there because it was easier than coming back and facing everything."

"What do you mean?"

I gulped, Jamie's smile immediately flickering into my mind. How could I ever have thought that my life was supposed to be with Toby when I still had this space in my heart that was reserved only for Jamie? I frowned, voicing the question I'd asked myself over and over this morning. "Mom, do you ever get over your first love?"

"Is this about Miles?" she asked.

I snorted a laugh and shook my head. "No."

Her lips pursed. "Jamie?"

I nodded. He had been my first love and, I had come to realize, my only love. "Yeah. I saw him the other day and we talked. It brought back all the feelings from years ago. We spoke about what happened and why we broke up. He told me some stuff that made me see the situation a little differently."

She settled back against her pillows, watching me like a hawk. "Like what?"

I frowned down at the bedsheet. I couldn't tell her what he'd said. She didn't know anything about his past. I had always kept his secret because he didn't want anyone else to know. I couldn't admit to her now that he'd been arrested that night. Chewing on the inside of my cheek, I wondered what I could say to explain without having to actually tell the truth. "He said that he'd made a huge mistake breaking up with me and that he had actually wanted to come traveling with me, but he was..." I tried to think of a word to fit that wasn't *arrested*. "Scared," I finally settled on. "We were moving so fast that he got a little scared and that's why we broke up. He regretted it, but by then it was too late to take it back because I'd already gone, and I didn't come back, so..."

My mother had fallen silent. I looked up at her now, expecting her to be angry about it, but instead she looked deep in thought. "I always thought it was weird. That boy was so in love with you, even I could see it. I never saw anything like that coming. I thought you two were solid. Your father even said that he thought you two would be married within a year or two. I always wondered what prompted the breakup, and you would never tell us the entire story," she said thoughtfully. "Do you still love him?"

I gulped. "I'll always love him, that's the hard part," I admitted.

She nodded. "What about Toby?"

"We had a different kind of relationship. I love him, I do, but…it was different. I'm beginning to wonder if maybe I latched onto him just because he treated me nicely and because he was the first one I felt close to after Jamie," I said. "I don't think I ever really got over Jamie." There was no real confusion about it for me; I *hadn't* gotten over it and probably never would.

My mom cleared her throat awkwardly. "Does Jamie feel the same?"

I shrugged in answer. "I don't know. I think so, maybe, yeah."

He hadn't said he still wanted to be with me, but some of the things he'd said had led me to believe we had a chance as a couple.

Mom sighed deeply, pulling the sheet up higher around her as her eyes became a little dreamy. "Ellison, did I ever tell you about when I met your father?"

A corner of my mouth twitched up as I shook my head. "I know you met him in college, but that's about it."

She smiled sadly, her eyes glazed over with tears. "When I met Michael, I never would have imagined that just a couple of years later I would marry him. He was everything I never wanted in a man, everything I always thought I hated and would never settle for," she started.

I sat enraptured, listening to her every word because I'd never heard her speak of my dad this way.

She smiled. "As you can probably imagine, I was very prim and proper, my clothes pressed and hair perfectly styled. Your father, he was grungy, there's no other word for it. He played guitar in a band that was simply terrible. He would wear the same raggedy *Star Wars* T-shirt for three or four days in a row without washing it, he barely styled his hair, and he liked going to festivals and camping in tents, for goodness' sake."

She laughed and shook her head. "I guess before that I'd been a little sheltered. The boys I knew from high school were nothing like your father. They were snobby, self-righteous trust fund babies who thought the world owed them a living because of their family name. Your father opened my eyes to possibilities I'd never considered, made me see the lighter side of life that I'd never appreciated. I'd never met anyone like him before. Within a few weeks, I fell so deeply in love with him that I basically gave up everything to be with him. My parents never approved of Michael. They never saw what I saw in him, but that didn't stop me. You can't help who you fall in love with. When you find the one you're supposed to be with, everything else just clicks into place and you'd do anything for them."

Her sad smile made my heart ache. I always suspected there was something off between her and her parents; there was always an unease and an awkward atmosphere when we would visit them—which wasn't very often. Now I knew why. My heart swelled with love for my mother because she'd loved my father so much she'd basically turned her back on the life and society she was expected to go into. This new information also went a little way toward explaining why my grandparents hadn't come to visit their daughter who was critically ill in the hospital, or made it to their son-in-law's funeral—they'd blamed poor health, but if they really wanted to, wouldn't they have moved heaven and earth to be there for her, poor health or not? Maybe the old resentment was still there, just not admitted. It was their loss, not ours.

Mom reached up and swiped a tear away as it slid down her face. "I guess what I'm trying to say here, Ellison, is I know I never gave you and Jamie an easy time of it, and I apologize for that. I guess I kind of forgot what it felt like to fall in love but have expectations on you from your parents. I'm sorry I put such pressure on you to be someone who you didn't want to be. I never should have done that. I should have trusted your judgment and treated you with more respect than my parents afforded me. You're a good girl, Ellison, and all I want for you is to be happy."

"Thanks, Mom," I croaked, tearing up myself now, too.

She smiled and reached for my hand, holding it tightly as she looked directly into my eyes. "If you love someone, don't ever be afraid to show it. Shout it to the world if that's what you want to do. Life is fleeting, Ellison. True love is rare, so if you find it, you hold on to it so tightly and never let anything or anyone get in the way."

True love. That was what I always felt Jamie and I had. "So you think I should talk to him about it?" I asked, unsure how this conversation even got started, it had escalated so quickly.

She nodded. "I followed my heart and I never regretted it, not for one single day. That's all I want for you, too. I just want you to find someone who makes you feel that kind of heart-stopping, epic love, even when he hasn't shaved or leaves the toilet seat up or can't manage to put the milk carton away after using it. All of those things, they don't even matter, because once you've fallen for someone, you love the person within unconditionally. Flaws and all."

She was right, I knew she was right. Jamie was the other piece of my puzzle, just as my dad had been hers. "But what if he doesn't feel the same? What if he hurts me again?" I said the words before I'd thought them through.

Mom smiled sadly and patted the back of my hand. "That could happen, but if you don't try you'll never know what you could be missing out on. If you love him, Ellison, you need to be brave enough to give him that chance."

Again, I knew she was right. She'd spoken nothing but the truth, and it echoed my feelings of the last day or so, too. The trouble was, this situation was more complicated than I could ever explain to her. Jamie's flaws I could live with, but his new-found career as some sort of local gangster was a different story. I wasn't sure I could be with him, always wondering if he was going to be taken away from me because of his job. I didn't want to forever have that fear hanging over my head. It would eventually drive me crazy, I knew it would. It would be something we would need to talk about before we could even think about moving forward—if he even wanted to move forward from here, that was. He'd been willing and eager to get out of that lifestyle once; maybe he would want to again. Like my mother said, I just needed to be brave enough to open up the conversation and see where it led.

I sighed. "You're right. I need to talk to him," I agreed. "When did you get so wise?"

"Must have been the bump to the head," she joked, reaching up and touching the healing scar above her right ear. "Whatever you choose, I'll always support you. I'm just sorry it's taken me all this time to see things clearly."

I leaned in and wrapped my arms around her, hugging her tightly, some of the tension leaving my shoulders. I hadn't realized what a weight I'd been carrying around with me, and how much I had desperately needed to talk it through with someone. She was right, I owed it to our memory to be brave enough to give him that chance.

Mom hugged me back, her arms tight around me as her breath fanned down my neck and I felt her tears wet my shoulder. "Seriously, though, talk to him soon. Don't waste a single moment. Enjoy every precious second of your life and make it count, because you never know when it could all be ripped away from you."

I pulled back and planted a kiss on her cheek as a rush of adoration for her washed over me. I'd never had this kind of conversation with her before, and her baring her soul about my father made me see a completely different side of her than I'd seen growing up. "I love you," I said softly, meaning every word. It was probably the first time I'd outright said that to my mother, but somehow it just felt right confessing it now.

Her lips pulled up into a grin as she reached out and stroked the side of my face. "I love you too, and I'm sorry I never told you enough. From now on, that'll change. I'll change. And I'll always support you in everything you do. I'm so proud of you, Ellison, and the beautiful young lady you've become. You remind me of your father in so many ways." She sniffed and her smile grew. "And I'm secretly over the moon that you're staying."

"Me, too," I admitted, hugging her again.

CHAPTER 24

JAMIE

WHEN I PULLED up outside Ellie's house on Saturday, it was almost midnight. Someone was still up, though. I could see the hazy glow of the TV flickering through the drapes. I wondered if it was Ellie who was awake and what she might be watching.

I hadn't seen her for a couple of days, not since I'd told her the truth about what happened on that day we broke up. I'd been trying to keep my distance, give her some space. I figured she'd need it after I dropped that bomb on her. I'd been hoping she'd call, but nothing so far.

The car in front of me started up, and Spencer, the one I'd had guarding her for me this evening, waved his hand in acknowledgment and then took off down the street, leaving me to take the next watch. He'd been doing a lot of the shifts for me; he was one of my most reliable workers and I knew he would take the job seriously. Between him, Ed, Enzo, Dodger, and me we managed around-the-clock surveillance on her. Not that she ever really went anywhere other than the hospital, the grocery store, or Stacey's apartment. The last two days I'd left her safety in the hands of the other three while I'd occupied my time with trying to find Mateo. So far, my search had been futile. He was nowhere to be seen; he'd vanished into the night like a ghost.

While I was watching the house, I noticed a twitch to the drapes, light beaming out for a split second as someone looked out, and then it was gone. Reaching into my glove box, I pulled out my iPod, just about to stuff one of the earbuds into my ear when the front door opened. Ellie stepped out and turned to quietly close the door behind her.

I frowned, tossing my iPod to the seat and climbing out of the car, wondering if something was wrong for her to suddenly appear like this. As she made her way across the yard in a tight pink tank top that showed off all her delicious curves and a pair of short shorts emblazoned with Miss Piggy that ended just barely an inch below her bottom, I couldn't stop my eyes from roaming her body. My teeth sank into my lip as my gaze trailed over her breasts and thighs, imagining how her smooth skin would feel under my fingertips. She was amazing, even with her hair whipping across her face from the breeze.

Her eyes dropped to the ground as a small smile twitched at the corners of her lips. Maybe she liked the fact that she still drove me wild. Maybe she came out here wearing that tiny, sexy outfit just to show me what I was missing. As quickly as the thought came I dismissed it. She hadn't known I was coming here tonight. These were simply her pajamas, which just happened to be the hottest things I had seen in a long damn time.

"Hey," she muttered, wrapping her arms around her body and rubbing herself for warmth.

I cleared my throat, hoping my voice wouldn't betray my desire as I immediately unzipped my jacket, shrugging it off. "Hey, you shouldn't come out here with no jacket. You'll catch pneumonia or something," I scolded, reaching out and draping my jacket around her shoulders.

She smiled gratefully and pulled it closed around her, hunching her shoulders inside it. "Thanks." She nodded back toward the house. "I just wanted to see if you wanted to come in and have a drink or something. I can make you some food if you're hungry."

"Um...yeah, sure," I replied, unsure what this was really about. As soon as I answered, she turned and marched off toward the house, and my eyes instinctively dropped to her legs peeking out the bottom of my jacket. I'd never be able to wear it again without thinking of them, I was sure of it.

I followed, pressing the button to lock my car as I stepped into the house behind her. I stopped, a blast of memories hitting me at once. I hadn't been here for a long time, but the place looked just like I remembered. Ellie kicked off her shoes and I did the same, watching as she hung my jacket up on one of the coat hooks mounted on the wall.

My eyes landed on the family photo that sat on the sideboard, and a pang of sorrow hit me when I looked at her smiling father. "This place hasn't changed," I commented, unsure what else to say as I followed her through the living room. My eyes landed on the couch and I stopped, setting a hand on the back of it. Just the feel of it under my palm made my pulse quicken. I raised one eyebrow and smirked at her. "I definitely remember this couch." The suggestion in my voice was evident. We'd had many a cuddle session that turned into a lot more on that sofa on a Saturday morning when everyone else went to visit her nana.

Her cheeks turned pink as her teeth nibbled on her bottom lip. "Yeah, it's a very good couch."

I couldn't contain my smug grin. Her eyes bored into mine as memories of dirty things I'd done to her on this couch surfaced in my mind. I wanted her so much, the intense desire was almost painful. She gulped and then shook her head a little as if to clear it.

"Do you want coffee or a soda or something else?" she offered. Her voice betrayed a slight tremor, so I knew she was probably having the same filthy flashbacks as I was.

I grinned. "Coffee is good, thanks."

She nodded, immediately turning for the kitchen, her ass wiggling in such a delectable way that it made my dick twitch. I bit back a moan.

"Is your mom still doing okay?" I asked, wanting to change the subject and clear my lust-filled mind as I trailed behind her into the kitchen and sank into one of the dining chairs.

She went straight for the kettle, boiling water. "She's good, getting better every day."

"I'm glad. I can't imagine how stressful that was for you, waiting for her to wake up."

"Yeah. Wasn't a fun time," she answered.

"I bet." Silence filled the air as my foot twitched. I was nervous because I wasn't sure why she'd asked me in here and how this conversation was going to go down.

"Jamie, I wanted to ask you something. I didn't get a chance the other day what with all the other revelations," she started, turning around to face me and leaning on the edge of the counter. "Why did you pay for my father's funeral?" Her eyes tightened as she said it, and it was clear she was still struggling with the loss of him.

I shrugged. I hadn't been expecting this question; I'd almost forgotten I had paid for it, actually, what with everything else going on. "I wanted to make sure you weren't struggling with money or anything. You had enough to deal with and the invoice was unpaid, so I paid it." There were no other motives. "I just wanted to make things easier for you and take the pressure off a little. There didn't seem to be any other way I could help."

She gulped, and her shoulders sagged as she frowned down at the floor. "You didn't need to do that. But it was a very nice gesture. Thank you, I appreciate the thought. You always were thoughtful like that," she said, turning back to the kettle, which was starting to whistle on the stove. "I'll pay you back, of course. I have money." She glanced shyly over her shoulder.

I smiled and shook my head. "Keep it. I don't need it. Money isn't an issue for me."

"Yeah, I gathered that from the expensive car and penthouse apartment," she muttered, reaching up for the mugs from the top cupboard. I opened my mouth to reply, but as she raised her arm, the movement caused her tank top to rise a little. A strip of skin was exposed across her midriff and my mouth watered, wanting to trace that line with my tongue and head lower, tasting her and making her moan my name in that breathy way she used to.

Focus, Jamie!

She looked over her shoulder then, and her eyes twinkled as her mouth kicked up at the corner in a smug smile. She'd caught me looking. I didn't even care.

"Sorry, what?" I asked, my voice husky and full of lust.

"Busted for staring at my ass," she teased, raising one eyebrow.

"It's a nice ass," I replied.

Her eyes sparkled from the compliment, and she picked up the two mugs, carrying them to the table and seating herself in the chair next to mine. "Well, thank you. For the compliment and for paying the invoice."

"You're welcome for both." I turned in my chair slightly so our knees were just a hairsbreadth away from each other. "So, how you been the last couple of days?" I asked, wanting to change the conversation from money. I had a feeling that wasn't why she'd asked me in here tonight.

She picked up her mug, blowing the swirling steam from the top, watching me over the rim. "I broke up with Toby."

My eyes widened and my mouth dropped open in shock. "Yeah?" I could feel the smile fighting to break out, so I tried to stifle it and not show how fucking happy that made me. No more imagining that asshole's hands on her and his mouth on hers. I was ecstatic.

She nodded. "Yeah, I decided I would be leaving too much behind if I went back to England."

"Ah, well, I'm sorry to hear about you two not making it." I wasn't sorry at all, but felt I needed to say the words anyway.

She smiled knowingly. "Liar."

I grinned down at my hands and shrugged one shoulder. *Obviously didn't mask my expression as well as I thought.* "All right, I admit it. Did I like the thought of you with another man? Hell fucking no. Did I find it hard not to come over and punch him in the face when I saw you two together? Yes, yes, I did; but I am sorry if this breakup has hurt you in any way." That was the truth. I didn't want her hurt, and if the guy had made her happy that was all I wanted for her.

She set her mug on the table. "Why did you hate the thought of me with another man?" she asked, cocking her head to the side in that adorable way she did and regarding me curiously. I had the distinct impression I was being tested. I hoped I got the answer right.

"You know why, Ellie." *Because I'm madly in love with you, that's why.*

She shook her head, straightening in her chair. "I don't, actually." She seemed to hold her breath as her eyes met mine. I could see a hopeful glint in them that made my heart stutter.

"Because you were supposed to be mine. And you were until I fucked it all up. I should have asked you to stay and wait for me." Honesty was always the best policy.

Her eyes widened a fraction, her mouth quirked up into a smile. "You should have," she agreed.

I cleared my throat, deciding to just spit it out. She was obviously trying to coax me into admitting I was still fucking nuts about her. "So do you think that maybe I'd get another shot? Take you out one time?"

She grinned now, her eyes playful. "Just one time?"

"Okay, maybe a lot more than one time."

She blew out a long breath, seeming to steel herself as she set her mug on the table and twisted in her seat to look at me. "Look, why don't we cut the playful act, we just need to be honest with each other because up until now there's been a lot of lies that have kept us apart. Do you still love me, Jamie?" Her eyes dropped to her lap as soon as the words left her mouth. Her jaw clenched and she frowned, seeming unsure of herself.

My hand stretched out, hooking a finger under her chin. I tilted her head up and made her look at me. I wanted to look into her eyes when I said the words so she would see the truth of them. "I'll never stop loving you, Ellie, not until the day I die. If you let me, I will take care of you forever. All I ever wanted was to be with you and have a life with you," I said honestly. Her face softened, the stress leaving it as her eyes bored into mine, but then just as quickly as the happiness crossed her face it was gone and she was guarded again. "What's wrong? That wasn't the answer you wanted?"

She shook her head, pushing my hand away gently. "It's not that. It was the answer I wanted." She swallowed, looking at me helplessly. "I could love you; I *do* love you. And I want to be with you again," she replied.

My heart soared for a second before bumping back to earth with her next word.

"But..."

I groaned and let my hand drop from her chin. "There's always a but."

She nodded, her expression almost apologetic. "But... the life you lead, I can't..." She frowned, seeming to be choosing her words carefully. "How can we even think about the possibility of a future when every day there's a chance of you being hurt or killed or that the police could show up and arrest you? I can't live like that. I love you, I do, but..."

That was it? That was her *but*? That wasn't a *but* at all, it was barely even a *b*... If my job was the only thing holding her back, then this was easy. Before I could stop myself, I reached out and cupped her face in my hands, leaning over and crashing my mouth to hers. She whimpered against my lips, kissing me back immediately, her arms looping around my neck. When her lips parted everything in me rejoiced and the kiss deepened, setting my very soul on fire. I needed her closer, I needed her so close we'd meld together and never be apart again. My hands slid down her sides to her waist, gripping as I lifted her easily, setting her on my lap. Her chest pressed against mine, her smell surrounded me, and her arms tightened on my neck as the kiss grew, changed, morphed into something magical and all-consuming.

I pulled back when we were both breathless and rested my forehead against hers. My heart was hammering in my chest in celebration as she pressed herself tighter against me, her eyes gleeful as they met mine.

"You don't have to worry about my job," I promised. My hands slid down to her ass; the material of her shorts, sleek and sexy, made my excitement bump up another level. "I'll stop doing it. I'll stop all the illegal shit. I'll do anything it takes. I'll leave everything, get a normal job, be an ordinary guy, just like we'd always planned. I only got into this life because I had no reason to be good, no one to be good for—now I do." I moved her hips, and her crotch rubbed across mine in a delicious way that made my mouth water. Ellie had always had the ability to make me hard in an instant.

"Are you serious?" Her eyes searched mine. "Look, I know I'm being unreasonable, I should love everything about you and not care what you do, but I can't love something that could one day take you away from me again. I can't let myself be with you only to hear you've been shot or stabbed or some other horrific thing that's going to rip my heart out. I can't do it."

I smiled at that. "You're all I need. None of this ever meant anything to me anyway."

Ellie shook her head, clearly not convinced as her fingers toyed with the hair at the nape of my neck, making my skin prickle with desire. "But it shouldn't be that easy for you to just decide. I'm asking you to give up your life for me, Jamie."

"No, you're not. *You're* my life, little girl. Everything else is just existing, not living." I shook my head, tracing my fingers up her back softly, so happy I could barely contain my exhilaration that this girl still loved me, that she wanted to give me another chance, that she wanted to give *us* another chance.

Her mouth popped open in shock and her eyes flashed with

intensity before she squealed and pressed her lips to mine, kissing me almost desperately. My whole body was rejoicing, reveling in the weight of her on my lap, the feel of her in my arms, her warmth. All of it combined frazzled my senses and made me so excited that I could barely sit still.

My hands slipped up her back, tangling into her hair, holding her against me as the kiss deepened, and this time when it changed, it morphed into something darker, something desperate, something needy.

The mood in the room thickened as she wriggled on top of me, rubbing against places that were already awake and straining for attention. Her hand fisted into the back of my hair as I pulled away from her mouth and peppered little kisses down the side of her neck, stopping to nip gently at the creamy skin, breathing her in. "I love you," I murmured against her neck.

She gasped, tilting her head back to give me better access. "I love you, too," she whispered.

Those words. I'd never expected to hear them again in my life. Those four words made my desire blaze inside me. My hands trailed down her body, cupping her breasts through her top, and I couldn't hold back a groan of appreciation. I'd forgotten how good this was, how amazing it felt to be close to her, to taste her. Her hips moved, grinding on my crotch through my jeans. She moaned in pleasure and that moan was my undoing. I wanted more, I wanted it all. I just about lost control of myself as lust consumed me. She must have felt it too as she breathed my name, her hands sliding down my chest, rubbing the outline of my shaft through my jeans.

"Fuck, I want you so bad," I groaned, dipping my head and nipping at her shoulder as I slipped my hand under her top and felt her soft, heated skin under my palms.

She fumbled with my belt, her hands shaky with excitement. "Take me, then," she said, grinding on me.

I stood, lifting her, setting her ass on the edge of the dining table as I stepped between her thighs, my mouth claiming hers in a kiss that made my balls ache. Without breaking the kiss, I pushed her hands away and yanked open my fly. Ellie's breathing hitched as her legs wrapped around my waist, pulling me against her. The kiss broke, and her eyes followed my hand as I shoved my jeans down around my hips, releasing my painfully hard erection.

As her hand fisted around my shaft, my eyes dropped closed and my breath came out in one long groan. "Fuck," I hissed, thrusting gently into her hand as my mouth claimed hers in another scorching kiss.

I pushed her shorts to the side, my fingers delving inside her folds. My dick hardened even more at the feel of how wet and ready she was for me. My mouth watered at the thought of going down to taste her, but that would have to wait. I needed to be inside her, needed to feel her body wrapped around mine while I fucked her and showed her that the three years apart meant nothing, that I loved her more than anything, and that we were always meant to be together.

"Fuck. So wet," I gasped, pumping two fingers inside her slowly, watching her face contort with pleasure. "Ellie, I need you. Do I need a condom?" *Please say no, please say no!* I wanted to feel her, all of her, not have something between us.

She shook her head quickly. "Implant," she breathed, moving her arm to show me a tiny little scar on the inside of her bicep. I grinned and withdrew my fingers, fisting my shaft and moving toward her entrance.

"Okay?" I asked, wanting to check that this was what she really wanted.

Her eyes flashed with impatience. "Do you want me to beg or what?" she asked, chuckling and tightening her legs around me, tugging me impossibly close.

I raised one eyebrow. "Begging could be fun," I teased.

"Jamie! Seriously, bloody just..."

Grinning, I thrust inside while she was still speaking, and her words died on her lips as her head tipped back and her eyes fell closed, her breath coming out in one long moan. I gritted my teeth against the sensations and groaned at the pleasurable feeling as her walls gripped me tightly. I'd forgotten how damn good this was with her.

Her fingers bit into my skin as I started to move, slowly at first, but then losing control of myself. It had been too long since we did this. Her eyes met mine as she kissed me fiercely, her body taking me to places I'd dared not even think about for the last couple of years. It was hard, fast, and intense, both of us desperately chasing our end. This was just a joining of bodies, a desperate need to be closer to cement our rekindled relationship.

She sank back on the table, her hips moving in time with mine, matching me thrust for thrust as our passion turned us a little animalistic. When she came, her back arched off the table and her thighs shook as she gasped my name, her fingers scraping at the skin of my back through my shirt. Her tightening around me sent me to my end soon after.

As we both caught our breath, I pinned her down against the table, my body covering hers as I looked over every inch of her flushed face. My love for her was overwhelming. It had always been powerful, but now it felt like it had grown. This second chance she had given me had moved it onto a whole new level. I hadn't thought it possible that I could love her any more. Her eyes shined with emotion as she looked up at me, stroking my hair away from my sweaty forehead, a contented, lazy smile on her lips.

"I love you," she whispered, her eyes shining with truth. I was on cloud nine, still flying after my orgasm, and her words just made me soar higher.

"I love you more." I dipped my head and planted a soft, tender kiss on her lips. "Can I take you upstairs?" I asked, trailing my finger across her collarbone, drawing a little pattern there. "I want to take my time with you. I didn't get to do all the things I wanted to," I murmured.

I definitely hadn't done even a tenth of the things I wanted to do to her; I hadn't even managed to get her damn clothes off because I was so desperate.

She nodded as her arms slid around my neck. I grinned, holding her against me as I pulled back, bringing her body with me because I didn't want to lose the connection between us. She squealed, tightening her arms and legs around me as I strode out of the kitchen and toward the stairs.

Her eyes sparkled with excitement. "We'll have to be quiet, my nana and sister are sleeping."

I nodded in acknowledgment and bounded up the stairs and into her bedroom, stopping to twist the lock on the inside so we wouldn't be disturbed—just like old times. I didn't turn on the light; the drapes were open and there was already a soft hue in the bedroom to see by, so I walked her to the bed and set her down, my arousal already spiking again. Hopefully I'd be able to take my time with her this time.

I pulled off my T-shirt in one swift movement while she watched me. As I started to push off my jeans, she switched on the bedside lamp. Soft light filled the room and I froze, my body stiffening all over as my old insecurities surfaced full force. My jaw tightened and I looked at her face, watching her eyes drag over me slowly, taking in the scars again for the first time in three years. My stomach clenched, waiting to see what her reaction would be again. I was actually terrified— Ellie was the only one who had the power to frighten me like this. What if she didn't accept them like she had before, what if they turned her off, what if she changed her mind? How would I cope with that?

"Does the light have to be on?" I asked, swallowing my anxiety.

Her head cocked to the side and she raised one eyebrow in question, and then her frown dissipated and understanding crossed her face. A sad smile graced her lips as she pushed herself up onto her knees on the bed, reaching for my hand.

She tugged me to her, her eyes not leaving mine as we were almost on the same level. "Yes, the light has to be on." My eyes dropped to the bed as her free hand touched my chest, trailing down slowly, feeling the bumps and ridges of scars and welts that would never fade. I shivered, my jaw tightening at the disgust I felt for my body. "Please don't start this whole thing again. I've told you before, your scars make you who you are. They're nothing to be ashamed of," she said softly. She bent her head, her eyes catching mine. "I love you, Jamie Cole. I love every part of you, scars and all." Her fingers traced the longest scar across my stomach and to my hip as her eyes stayed locked on mine, unwavering.

"Scars and all?" I repeated, rubbing the back of my neck.

Her hand snaked around to my back, gripping my ass as she pressed her body flush against mine, her hard nipples rubbing my chest through her shirt. "Scars and all," she confirmed, her eyes showing the truth of her words.

That was exactly what I needed to hear. Another rush of love hit me full force and I crashed my mouth to hers, vowing to be slow and sensual this time as I made love to her on her bed.

When we finally broke apart, my body was covered in a thin sheen of sweat and I struggled to catch my breath. I was totally and utterly satiated, and I was pretty sure she was too because she flopped to the side, her hair a mess, her lips swollen from so much kissing and her cheeks flushed with a post-orgasm glow.

"Oh God, I'm exhausted. I'd forgotten how good you are at that," she mumbled, throwing one arm up to cover her eyes, breathing heavily. "How many calories does sex burn?"

I laughed at the randomness and rolled to the side, draping my arm across her stomach. "I don't know, why?"

She shrugged one shoulder. "I've put on a bit of weight recently. If we keep going like this, I won't even need to diet, I could fuck those extra fourteen pounds away."

I frowned, pulling back to check if she was joking, but I didn't see any humor there. "What? You don't need to lose weight! You're perfect." To really ram my opinion home, I dipped my head and let my tongue make a slow, lazy sweep of her body, starting at her throat and going all the way down over her breasts and across her stomach, stopping to nibble at her hip. To me, she was sheer and utter perfection, and I wouldn't change a single thing.

"If you feel that way, I guess eating chocolate cake can stay." She giggled and shied away, looking down at me playfully.

I crawled up her body, settling myself at her side as one of my hands tangled into her hair and the other made a gentle, appreciative sweep of her body, memorizing all the curves. She smiled over at me, her eyes so adoring my heart was fit to burst. "I love everything about you, little girl. Don't ever think that you're less than the most beautiful thing I've ever had the good fortune to lay eyes on," I promised before slanting my mouth over hers and kissing her deeply.

The kiss was so achingly good, it made my whole body tighten with excitement. When she pulled back she smiled, a look of complete contentment on her face as she snuggled against me.

"Go to sleep, little girl. You look exhausted." I curled around her protectively and sighed with relief at the feel of her in my arms again.

She pouted, tilting her head back so she could look at me. "I don't want to."

I frowned, brushing one finger across her cheek. "Why?"

She gulped, looking away from me. "I'm scared I'm going to wake up in the morning, and you'll be gone and this will have all been a dream."

A smile twitched at the corners of my lips. "You don't have to be scared of that. I'm in this for the long haul."

She smiled at my assurances, her eyes turning playful and losing the fearful edge. "The long haul? How long were you thinking?" she asked, raising one eyebrow in question.

I pursed my lips, pretending to think. "At least eighty years."

She snuggled closer. "Eighty years? You think you'll still want to be with me when I have no teeth, gray hair, and I step on my own boobs in the shower?" In the dim glow of her bedside lamp, her eyes twinkled with amusement.

I nodded in confirmation. "Yeah. But do you think you'll still want to be with me when I'm bald, have a potbelly, and I step on your boobs in the shower?" I replied, tilting my head so our foreheads pressed together while we both laughed quietly for a minute or so. Secretly, I hoped it happened just like that, potbelly, saggy breasts, and all. I wanted to grow old with her; that was all I wanted in life. "In all seriousness, though, I'm not going anywhere. It's Team Jellie forever," I concluded.

She snorted and rolled her eyes. "Team Jellie, did you just

come up with that?" She reached out, brushing her fingers over the scar on my eyebrow that I'd gotten in prison.

"Nah, I came up with it ages ago, I've just been waiting for the perfect opportunity to use it."

She grinned wickedly. "This wasn't that moment, baby."

I rolled my eyes and pressed a kiss to her forehead, about to get comfortable and ready for sleep when I suddenly remembered I hadn't arranged for someone to take over my shift in the morning. I groaned and pulled away, sitting up and reaching over the side of the bed for my jeans. When I found my cell, I typed out a quick message and sent it to Ed, telling him I was inside Ellie's house and that was why my car was empty, and told him to come here at nine.

Ellie rolled to her side, tracing her fingers across my back softly. "Who are you texting? Your other girlfriend to tell her you won't be home tonight?" she teased, biting the skin at the side of my hip and making me jump from the feel of it.

I grinned over my shoulder at her and pressed Send, pushing my phone onto the side table. "No, I told you. There's no other girlfriends, I promise. I was just messaging one of my crew. Ed. I've asked him to come here at nine and watch over you tomorrow morning. There're a few things I need to go and sort out, and I don't want to leave you unprotected."

"I thought you were done with all of that stuff," she said with a frown.

I nodded quickly, reaching out and touching her pouty lip. "I am. Don't pout," I joked, leaning down and replacing my finger with my lips, kissing softly. "I can't just walk away and never go back, though. I need to explain to my crew, hand things over to someone else, pass the baton, and all that. I'm done with the illegal stuff, I swear to you. I wouldn't jeopardize our relationship again now that I've just gotten you back. You're my life, Ellie."

She sighed happily and nodded in understanding. I grinned and settled against her side, reaching out to turn off the bedside lamp before curling around her protectively. Having her in my arms, knowing she loved me and that we would face the world together, was all I'd wanted since I met her. And now, it looked like everything we'd planned for our future was finally beginning to come true. I fell asleep that night wrapped snugly around her with a broad smile on my face.

CHAPTER 25

ELLIE

WHEN I WOKE in the morning Jamie and I were a tangle of limbs, our naked bodies pressed together so intimately that memories of last night made my cheeks flame with heat as my insides sizzled with lust. It had been beautiful—adoring, sexy, sensual, everything I had wanted and much, much more. I'd forgotten just how great sex with Jamie was and how attentive he was. Last night proved that even after all this time, he was still in tune with my body. I'd felt every touch and kiss down in my soul. I hadn't been able to get enough of him, and maybe I never would.

My head was nestled on his arm, tucked in the crook of his neck as we lay facing each other. Smiling, I scooted closer, pressing my lips against his neck, kissing softly. A contented sigh left my lips as I closed my eyes and just enjoyed being close to him again. It had been so damn long since I'd woken in his arms—and this lived up to every fantasy I'd envisioned in the last three years.

His words from last night danced in my mind and I couldn't contain my grin. *"Team Jellie forever."*

I'd joked that it was silly last night, but I actually really loved it.

Jamie gave a breathy little moan and his hand slid down my back, coming to rest on my rear, his touch leaving a burning trail across my skin that made my toes curl. A lust built within me so intense that I had to clench my thighs together to relieve some of the pressure. I remembered this feeling; he had always made me wild and desperate. I was glad to see that three years on he still had the same effect. I snuggled closer, feeling his arms tighten, his hand sliding down my thigh and curling around the back of my knee, pulling gently so my leg hooked over his hip. I gasped as the new position made us rub together in places that already ached in a delightful way from last night.

"You wriggling like that against me brings back good memories," he muttered, a sleepy half smile pulling at his lips.

I grinned and wriggled some more, basking in the way his eyes closed in pleasure. "Oh yeah? What kind of memories?" I flirted, leaning in and capturing his lips with a soft kiss.

"The hot, sweaty kind," he replied, grinning over at me as he rolled, the top half of his body now draped over mine as his fingers traced across my cheek and down my neck, his eyes following their path as they traveled across my chest. He sighed deeply and placed a soft kiss on my shoulder. "I wish I could stay in this bed with you all day," he murmured against my skin.

"Me, too." I cupped his face and guided him to look up at me. "But you can't. I have to get dressed and go see my mom." My eyes flicked to the bedside clock, seeing it was after nine thirty already; I actually needed to move my butt soon and get in the shower or we wouldn't have long for morning visiting. "Didn't you say your friend was coming here at nine to replace you on babysitting duty? It's already half past."

He groaned, his eyebrows knitting together as he pulled away and sat up. I felt the loss immediately, my body yearning for his touch.

"Yeah, he should be outside already." He picked up his cell from the bedside table, sending off a quick message, and then dropped his phone back down and turned to look at me.

A slow smile spread across his face as he leaned back over me. "Thank you so much for giving us another shot. I promise I won't let you down. I'm going to make you so happy that you'll crap rainbows for the rest of your life."

I burst out laughing, shaking my head at his absurdity. But when his mouth closed over mine, swallowing my laughter and stealing my breath, I felt the truth behind his words—I might not crap rainbows, but he was going to make me happy for the rest of my life for sure. He kissed me until my head spun, then pulled away.

"I love you, so, so much," he whispered against my lips.

"I love you, too." The words were natural and honest; they felt so right coming out of my mouth that it made my heart flutter in my chest. But somehow, it just didn't feel like enough—one word, *love*, it barely even scratched the surface of what I felt for this boy.

When we were both fully clothed, I headed over to my door and peeked out, grinning to myself because this was just like old times when I'd have to sneak him out of my room. He stayed close to my back as we edged quietly down the stairs and to the front door. As he grabbed his jacket and slipped on his shoes, I pried the door open quietly, just enough for him to slip out. A car was parked behind his, and a guy in his midforties sat behind the wheel, watching us with a cigarette wedged between his lips. Jamie gave him a little nod before turning his attention back to me. His arms looped around my waist, capturing my lips in one last kiss before he turned and walked toward his car.

I sighed dreamily and leaned against the doorframe, pressing my finger to my lips as I watched him walk off. I'd never imagined that I would be able to feel this happy again, not after being so low for the last three years. Funny how one person can come into your life and turn the whole thing upside down.

About halfway to his car, Jamie turned. "Hey, want to get a late lunch or something after you've been to the hospital?" he called out, walking backward to his car.

I nodded eagerly. "Sure."

"I'll call you," he replied. I waved good-bye and closed the door as he leaned down and began talking to Ed. As I turned, I came face-to-face with Kelsey, who was standing at the bottom of the stairs with her arms folded across her chest, one eyebrow arched knowingly.

I jumped and let out a little squeal. I thought we'd been incredibly stealthy. Clearly not.

"Morning." I hoped she'd just arrived and hadn't seen anything.

"Was that Jamie I just saw sneaking out of your bedroom?"

Well, shit. "Um...yeah," I answered, not wanting to lie. "We got back together." She frowned, her eyes dropping to the floor, and I wondered how much she knew from before and how much she had overheard about our breakup. She'd only been ten at the time, but she understood and heard a lot more than she let on. "He makes me so happy, Kels. I love him, I always have."

Her lips pursed in thought, and then she nodded in acceptance. "He's your zing."

I raised a quizzical eyebrow. "My zing?"

She nodded, smiling now. "Yeah, have you not seen the movie *Hotel Transylvania?*"

I smiled in understanding. I had seen that movie with Toby's kids, who had it on DVD. A "zing" was what they called it when you met the one you were supposed to be with, your soul mate. According to the movie, you only zinged once in your life. "He *is* my zing," I confirmed, nodding.

She nodded, too. "I'm happy for you if he makes you happy."

"He does," I promised, even though *happy* didn't even come close. *Complete* was more like it. I stepped forward and wrapped my arm around her shoulder, nodding toward the kitchen, where the smell of bacon wafted out tantalizingly. "Let's go get some food and then visit Mom, yeah?"

* * *

At the hospital later that morning, Mom was already up and in a wheelchair, sitting by the side of her bed staring absentmindedly out the window that overlooked nothing but the brick wall of another building. My heart went out to her, seeing her so still, so lost in her thoughts like that. She didn't even look up or notice when we entered the room.

"Mom?" Kelsey said, walking to her side and crouching so they were almost at the same level.

"Hi," she said stiffly, dragging her eyes away from the window and looking around at each of us in turn as she shifted in her wheelchair, her broken leg jutting out in front of her on the footrest. She looked so different from the woman I'd had a heartfelt conversation with just a couple of days ago. She looked lost and so sad that it hurt to witness. The doctor said there'd be good days and bad, but I hadn't expected her to go from the open and loving woman to this zoned-out emptiness in just a matter of days.

"Morning, Ruth. Are you hungry?" Nana rustled through her tote bag, pulling out cartons of food she'd prepared and setting them to the side. She popped the lid off one and held it out to my mom, offering her one of the freshly baked cinnamon rolls that were inside. "I know hospital food isn't up to scratch, so I've made you a few things you like," she said, smiling warmly at her daughter-in-law.

"Thanks, Betty." Mom's hand came out, taking one, her eyes still glazed over and vacant. A smile twitched at the corner of her mouth, but it wasn't a genuine one. It was like she was trying to put on a brave face, pretend she was fine, but everyone could see she wasn't. The light in her eyes had gone out, the life in them deflated and lost. I had no idea how to help her.

While Mom absentmindedly picked at her pastry, shredding it into little pieces and dropping them into a napkin Nana had given her, the door opened and the doctor stepped in. He smiled at us as he walked over to Mom's side, picking up her chart on the way past.

"Good morning, Ruth. How are we feeling today?" he asked.

"Fine," she answered flatly.

He didn't seem affected by her tart answer. He pulled out his penlight and leaned in, checking her pupil dilation, making her follow the light. He took her blood pressure and checked the wound on her head and then announced that she was doing great and healing up nicely.

He was right, she was getting stronger every day. Her bruises had now all but gone, so it was just the broken bones and emotional damage that were left in the accident's wake. I nodded, watching him scribble on her chart.

He turned to me and smiled. "I was speaking to Ruth about it earlier, and I think she'll be well enough to discharge tomorrow, or certainly the day after if you have preparations to make at home to accommodate the wheelchair," he said, hooking the chart onto the end of the bed and turning back to my mom. "I'm sure you're eager to get home and sleep in your own bed, right, Ruth?" he asked, his tone warm as he winked at her and then turned for the door.

I watched him leave, a smile in my heart because she would be coming home and I could take care of her properly instead of having to leave her here on her own each day. "That's great news," I said, turning to smile at my mom, expecting her to be happy about it. But when I looked at her, my eyes widened in surprise.

She was shaking her head adamantly, her hands clenched into tight fists, tears leaking from her eyes.

I gasped and rushed to her side, dropping to my knees next to her. "Hey, what's wrong?" I asked, reaching out and placing a hand on the side of her face, wiping a stray tear away.

"I don't want to," she croaked, shaking her head fiercely. "I don't want to!" Her voice rose, panic detectable in her tone.

I gulped, confused as I rested my hands on her thighs, squeezing supportively to try to get her to snap out of it. "You don't want to what?"

Her eyes widened and latched onto mine as her features twisted with anguish. "Home. I don't want to go home."

I frowned, looking up at my nana for some help or some sort of explanation for this outburst, but she appeared just as clueless as me. "Why not?" I asked, cocking my head to the side and regarding my mom worriedly.

"It's too much, too many memories. Michael..." Her crying increased at the same rate as her desperation as she reached out and grasped my hands, squeezing tightly, her eyes pleading with me. "I can't. I can't go there. I don't want to! Ellison, please?"

Her reasoning hit me like a freight train; my heart squeezed in sympathy. She didn't want to return to the family home where all his stuff was, his clothes and belongings. The memories of him would be too strong for her to deal with in her fragile state. She might be healing physically, but emotionally she was still broken and wounded.

"It's okay, it's okay, Mom," I soothed, pushing myself up and hugging her, feeling her body tremble with sobs against mine. "No one's going to make you go home if you're not ready, it's okay," I whispered, stroking her hair like she used to do for me when I was sick.

"I don't want to go back there. How could I live there without him? I couldn't," she sobbed against my shoulder.

I looked desperately at Nana, wondering what we were going to do. She couldn't stay in the hospital if they wanted to discharge her; they probably needed her bed for someone else. But I couldn't make my mom go back to the family home if she wasn't ready to face it all and deal with it.

Nana had tears shining in her eyes as she stepped forward and set her hand on my mom's shoulder. "You don't have to," she said reassuringly. "You can come and stay with me for as long as you want. I have plenty of room for everyone. I rattle around that house on my own, it would be lovely to have some company."

My mom's eyes widened as she looked up at Nana, her lip trembling. "Really?"

Nana bent and planted a soft kiss on the top of my mom's head. "Of course. I would love to have you stay. You don't ever have to go back to your house if you don't want to."

Mom's body sagged in relief as she nodded, reaching up and patting Nana's hand, which still rested on her shoulder. The gratitude in her eyes was easy to see, and some of the life came back into them, too. Maybe the prospect of returning home was what was making her so worried and keeping her so low.

* * *

After Nana's suggestion, the air in the room shifted, became less stifling, and everyone seemed more relaxed, including my mom, who sat holding Kelsey's hand, listening to her talk about her science project at school.

Moving to the Poconos with my nana would cause a little issue with Jamie being an hour and a half away, but I was pretty sure we'd work something out. I wasn't losing him again now over something as silly as having to drive to see each other for a while; after all, it wasn't as if it was a full ocean away.

When visiting hours were over, we said our good-byes and I noted that Mom looked like she was in a much better place than she had been for the last couple of days. "Shall we go for lunch?" Nana offered as we climbed into my car.

I winced because I'd made lunch plans with Jamie. "Um, I can't. I said I would meet a friend," I replied, shooting Kelsey a look because a wide grin spread across her face when I said the word *friend*.

"Oh, maybe we could still go, Kels?" Nana suggested, turning in her seat to see Kelsey, who was buckling her seat belt in the back.

"Sure, that'd be great," she answered. "Maybe we could go to that noodle bar and then get ice cream after?"

"Sounds like a plan," Nana agreed.

My tummy rumbled at the thought of noodles, wondering what Jamie would suggest we eat for our late lunch. Then an idea struck me—I could suggest takeout to eat in his bed! A longing sigh left my lips at the mere thought as I started the engine and pulled out of the parking lot and onto the road. A few cars behind me, Ed pulled out too, looking bored as he followed.

I dropped off Nana and my sister outside the noodle bar and headed for home. Jamie hadn't called yet, so I wasn't sure what time we were meeting. I decided that when I got home, I would send him a message telling him I was hungry. Maybe I'd send him a naughty flash down my shirt and then pick out some killer heels to wear to lunch. I wondered if he still had a slight shoe fetish. My cheeks flooded with heat just thinking about it as I smiled to myself.

I stopped at a red light, turning on my radio and singing along with Sia about her elastic heart, bobbing my head in time with the beat as the light changed to green. I shifted into drive and rolled forward, signaling a left turn.

If I'd been looking properly, I would have seen the white van speeding toward the deserted intersection opposite me. I would have seen him run the light. I would have seen him twist his wheel ever so slightly so that he was lined up to smash into the side of my little bug. But I wasn't looking, I was too busy singing along with the radio, thinking about Jamie and food and my mom.

Everything happened so quickly, I barely even had time to react or fear for my life. The van struck the passenger side of my car with such force that it knocked all the breath out of my lungs and made my teeth rattle. Metal grated against metal, tires scraped against the road, gravel flew into the air. The windshield smashed from the force of the impact, spraying glass across my face and body. My head collided with the car door, and my vision blurred.

Pain gripped my body everywhere at once. The seat belt constricted, doing its job but forcing the air out of my lungs even further. My hands tightened on the steering wheel as the force of the collision shunted my car sideways several feet. My mind wasn't making sense.

There was a feeling of weightlessness; everything that had been on the floor of the car was suddenly on the roof, then the floor, then the roof again as the car rolled several times. The noise was the worst; the scraping, loud bangs, and crashes made my teeth grate and my ears ring.

When the car finally stopped moving, it was in a ditch at the side of the road and everything was upside down. My arms were dangling, touching the roof, which was now where the ground should have been.

I blinked a couple of times, turning my head and seeing the contents of my purse scattered over the roof of my car, mixed in with the glass and broken pieces of my beloved bug. I groaned, the pressure across my chest and waist immense. I could barely draw breath; my lungs felt like they were being crushed by the seat belt that pinned me upside down to my seat.

Blood ran down the side of my face, tickling where it touched, dripping with a *plop, plop, plop* onto the ceiling of my car underneath me.

I groaned, trying to lift my arms, but they were heavy and un-coordinated as I floundered awkwardly, attempting to reach the buckle of my seat belt so I could free myself. Maybe then I'd be able to breathe. But my fingers fumbled fruitlessly at the buckle.

I smelled gasoline, acrid and burning my throat as I panted, trying to fill my lungs. *I have to get out of here!*

"Help," I croaked, blinking as everything seemed to gray out and then come back into focus again. I tried my legs, notic-ing they worked although the dashboard seemed to be pressed against my knees, which would make freeing myself hard, even if I could get my belt off. "Help," I tried again, my voice barely above a whisper.

I turned my head, ignoring the sharp twinge in my neck, and could see a pair of feet heading toward the vehicle. They weren't rushing, just walking steadily toward me, the black boots worn and heavy looking. I blinked again, my eyelids getting heavier each time they closed. I could hear scraping on the driver's door, a crunching of something being pried open. I licked my lips, tasting blood there. I was blacking out, I could feel it coming. As the door finally cracked open, a man leaned in, dropping the crowbar he'd held and reaching behind him, pulling out a large silver knife. As he reached toward my seat belt with it, beginning to hack me free, I opened my mouth to thank him, but nothing came out. The last thing I saw just before I passed out was the large spider tattoo on the side of my savior's neck.

CHAPTER 26

JAMIE

AS THE DOOR to Ellie's house clicked closed behind me, I pumped the air with my fist in triumph. I had never expected she would take me back; I'd never felt I deserved the first chance, let alone the second one she was giving me, so hadn't expected to wake up next to her glorious body and beautiful smile this morning. I was walking on a cloud as I headed to the side of the sedan and bent down to lean in and talk to Ed.

"What's up, buddy?" I greeted him, grinning.

He raised one eyebrow quizzically. "Are you drunk?"

I laughed and ran a hand through my hair. "No, just woke up on the right side of the bed this morning." *Right bed, more like.* "I gotta go. I'll be back just after lunch to take over."

He nodded, his eyes flicking back to the house. "Yeah, I heard."

"I'll give you a call later," I said, already turning for my car, not waiting for an answer. I couldn't keep the smug grin off my face as I slid into my seat and started the engine. Before pulling away, I sent a quick message to Ray and Dodger, asking them both to meet me at the warehouse ASAP. I wasn't really looking forward to telling them the news that I was abandoning ship, but they were good friends; I hoped they'd understand.

When I pulled up at the warehouse, it was after ten and no one was around. After opening up and turning all the lights and the little space heater on because the place was like a freezer inside, I decided to spend some time working on my car. I was too wired to do anything else, and couldn't set the ball rolling on any legal business transfer papers until I'd spoken to the boys about it. I knew they'd be a while yet. Ray had replied to my message saying that he was at his eldest daughter's soccer practice, so he wouldn't be in until after eleven. Dodger would be in later than that; he hadn't replied, but he was a night owl and late sleeper. His day didn't begin until after lunch.

So that was how I spent the next two hours, elbow deep in my Subaru, giving her a fine tune-up. Not that it really mattered. I wouldn't be racing again. I'd promised Ellie I would leave this life, and that meant all elements of it. Now that she was back, I didn't need to risk my life racing when I would rather curl up around her and watch a movie. That trumped everything, even the adrenaline high I got from fast cars and boosting. Ellie was all I needed.

Ray came in first, gushing about his little girl and what a mean left foot she had and how she was a natural on the soccer field. Dodger arrived a few minutes after, still rubbing his eyes and yawning just after eleven thirty.

"Morning," I greeted him cheerfully.

Dodger just grunted his response and headed straight for the coffeepot, making a fresh batch and pouring himself a large black coffee. When he was done, he turned to me and his eyes narrowed. "I hope this is important. I just left a ballet dancer in my bed. Most flexible legs I've ever seen."

I smiled and wiped my hands on a rag as I nodded toward the stairs. "Let's go upstairs. I need to talk to you guys," I said.

Upstairs in my office, I sat on the black leather sofa and waited for them to sit, too. As I opened my mouth to speak, Dodger piped up first. "I know you're going to want updates, but there's not much to tell. Nothing's happened since last night. Lewiston says Alberto isn't getting out anytime soon."

Unfortunately for him, but fortunately for me, Alberto had been at the Salazars' cocaine laboratory on Thursday when Detective Lewiston and ten of his trusty officers had conducted simultaneous raids on the Salazars' businesses. They'd taken down most of their crew too and impounded all their shit. They had enough evidence to send them down for a very long time. The elder Salazar brother would spend most of his life in jail, from what I'd heard. But that still left the problem of the younger brother, the one whose heart I wanted on a plate.

"No word on Mateo?" We'd had the feelers out, people looking for him everywhere, but no one had seen or heard from him since Thursday after I'd spoken to him on the phone and told him to run.

Dodger shook his head, taking another sip of his coffee. "Nothing. He's gone."

I frowned angrily. "Keep looking. I need to know Ellie's safe."

Dodger leaned forward, setting his mug on the table, his eyes on me. "She *is* safe. Mateo wouldn't dare come back now. He's lost everything; his brother is in jail, and we all know Alberto was the brains behind their particular organization. Most of Mateo's crew are banged up, he's lost everything. What would he possibly gain from coming back? He knows you're after him, he's not going to be stupid enough to try anything with her again. He wouldn't dare."

I scowled down at the table, watching the steam rise from the mug in a swirl. Dodger thought he was right, and maybe he was, but in the back of my mind I couldn't shake the fear that Mateo was just biding his time. Men who had nothing to lose were the ones you needed to worry about because they were the most dangerous. I'd never be able to rest easy until I knew Ellie was 100 percent safe, and that meant I needed to find that fucker and kill him.

"Just keep looking," I instructed. "I know I might be being overprotective, but I want a tail on Ellie until he's found."

Ray nodded quickly, his eyes sympathetic. He knew more than anyone how much I loved this girl; he'd seen the lengths I went to after I was arrested, and it was his family member I sent on an all-expenses-paid trip to cheer my girl up. He'd also been the one who had found the private investigator to keep me informed about her while she was in England with Toby. He knew she was everything to me; maybe he was imagining himself in my position, how he would feel if it were his wife in danger. Dodger didn't quite get it because he'd never had a serious girlfriend before, just the occasional fling that he dropped when they lost his interest.

Dodger yawned loudly, putting his hand up to cover his mouth. "Is that what you woke me up for? I was awake half the night, only saw your message by chance when I got up to piss, otherwise I'd still be in bed with the ballerina right now," he grumbled.

I shook my head, leaning back in my chair, hoping they wouldn't be too pissed off with me. "No, that wasn't it. I wanted to tell you guys first... Ellie and I got back together last night." I grinned proudly, my heart squeezing as I said the words.

Ray's mouth popped open in shock and then stretched into a wide grin; Dodger fist-pumped the air and then held out his hand to slap me a high five. "That's great, bro! Does this mean you're gonna stop walking around with a face like a slapped ass?"

I laughed and shrugged one shoulder, returning his high five before shaking Ray's hand in a very grown-up gesture. His eyes shined with happiness as he grinned at me. "I'm so happy for you, Kid. You deserve good things, and I know how much you care about her and how much it tore you both up when you split."

A pang of regret sparked in my stomach. I should have been honest with her at the start; things would have been so different and we wouldn't have wasted the last couple of years trying to pretend we were happy.

"Thanks, guys, I couldn't be happier. But it does mean making a few changes." They were both looking at me expectantly. "I'll be leaving the organization."

Dodger burst out laughing, shaking his head in disbelief. "That was a good one," he chortled. But Ray's eyes tightened as he sat back in his chair, his posture now stiff. He understood. I sat quietly, waiting for Dodger to catch on to the fact that I was being serious. Slowly, his laughter died out and he looked from me to Ray and back again.

"Ah, shit. This isn't a joke?" he asked, his forehead creasing in a frown.

I shook my head. "No, sorry." I cleared my throat, looking at them both apologetically. "I want to make a life with her, and that means leaving all this behind." I waved a hand around the office in example.

"You going to quit boosting, too?" Ray asked.

"I'll be leaving everything. Ellie deserves me to be the guy she thinks I am, the guy I was when we were together the first time. I want that, too," I explained. "I'll have lawyers draw up the papers to have the haulage firm and the security contracts transferred into your names, split equally. I'm going to sell one of the downtown clubs so I can get some capital, and I'm going to keep Red's because, you know, I named it after her and stuff. Other than that, you guys can have the other clubs, too. You two can do what you want with the businesses: sell them, break them down, whatever." It was my parting gift, a multimillion-dollar enterprise that had been left to me and that I was now passing on to good hands.

Dodger held up a hand. "Wait, wait, wait. Why are you giving it to us? You could sell everything, buy a giant yacht, and sail your girl around the world or something. I don't understand."

I shrugged. I'd thought about it, but I just didn't need all of that, and I was pretty sure Ellie wouldn't be comfortable using that money knowing where it came from. I would sell one of the clubs for sure. Ellie's mother's medical bills would be piling up, and I wanted to be in a position to take care of those for her and relieve that stress on the family. I'd keep Red's because it had sentimental value to me—and of course I'd need some form of income. But I didn't need the lavish lifestyle I had now.

All I ever needed was Ellie.

We both deserved a fresh start and clean break. We'd never build a great future if we were always riding off the past.

"I just want to start again, on my own terms," I explained.

Dodger's lips pursed as he thought about what I'd said, but Ray got it. He nodded and sighed deeply. "So you're serious? What are you going to do with yourself?" he inquired.

I shrugged and felt the weight of responsibility lift off my shoulders. I could do anything I wanted. "Not sure. Maybe I'll start my own garage or something. Fix cars instead of stealing them, for a change. I always wanted to be a mechanic when I was younger." The possibilities were endless, and I had the rest of my life to figure it out with Ellie by my side. I'd never meant to slip into this life in the first place, but now here was my opportunity to get out of it all, and I was grabbing that opportunity with both hands and running with it.

"But won't you miss it? The thrill, the excitement?" Dodger asked, his voice skeptical.

I shook my head, grinning moronically. "I won't have time to miss it. I'll be too busy worshipping Ellie." *Starting this afternoon!*

Dodger's lip twitched with a smile. "You are so whipped."

I shrugged, unashamed. "When you meet the one for you, everything will make sense," I told him and smiled over at Ray, who nodded in agreement. He'd found his one a long time ago. "Ellie's my everything. It's all a new adventure and I can't wait," I added. "So now you two need to work out where you want to take the organization in the future. It's yours now." I sat back and interlaced my fingers behind my head, perfectly at ease as they looked at each other before the discussions started.

They were still deep in conversation two cups of coffee later, when Ellie's number flashed up on my phone. "Hey, little girl."

There was a muffled crackling on the line, then she spoke. "Jamie?" Her voice sounded off; the way she said my name, almost as a plea, made my spine straighten. A sharp yelp of pain from her made my whole body go cold. "Help me," she begged.

Those two words were like a knife to my heart. My stomach bottomed out.

"Ellie?" My voice was almost a whisper, and then another voice was on the phone, one I recognized, the Spanish twang to it making my teeth snap shut with an audible click as rage engulfed me.

"If you want her, come and get her. I'm at the docks next to where I *used* to own a thriving fucking business before you fucked everything up. You have exactly half an hour before I slit her throat and let her bleed out," Mateo Salazar instructed.

My body jerked; my hand gripped the phone so tightly I was surprised I hadn't crushed it. My mind was whirling. The docks. I knew the place he was talking about, and it was at least a forty-minute drive away. "It'll take me longer to get there!"

"Better drive fast then, hot shot," he snapped. "Come alone. If I see anyone but you, she dies. If you're even one minute late, she dies. If you tell anyone, she dies."

CHAPTER 27

I **PULLED UP** at the docks twenty-seven minutes later, my hands tightly gripping the wheel of my BMW. God knows how I'd made it on time. All I knew was that I'd do anything. I couldn't let Ellie get hurt.

Keeping my calm was a lot of work; inside me there was a war raging and I was struggling to retain my temper. I cut the engine, taking a couple of deep breaths, attempting to diffuse the fog of rage that had settled over me as soon as I heard her strangled yelp on the phone. I needed a clear head. I needed to think, not just be so angry that all I did was blaze in there, smash the fucking place up, and kill everything that moved.

When I was about as in control of myself as I was going to get, I leaned over and picked up my guns from the passenger seat, shoving one down the back of my jeans and hiding it under my sweater, keeping the other in my hand, one round in the chamber.

As I stepped out of the car, the silence struck me. This part of the dock was always deserted, but that obviously didn't mean they weren't there, hidden in the shadows, watching me. I raised my gun, stalking toward the gate, my goal clear: Get Ellie out, kill everyone else.

Gritting my teeth, I was conscious of the time ticking down and Mateo's imposed deadline looming. My feet moved of their own accord, driving me forward through the gate with the yellow police tape strewn across it and into the inner yard loaded with rusted containers and disused equipment. I kept my gun raised, my eyes straining to find people, any people, but there was no one.

I plowed on, skirting stealthily around containers, ears attuned to pick up any sounds of life. After a few minutes, I came to a clearing. Leaning my back against the side of a container, I peeked around the corner, expecting this to be it. He was probably in the center of the dock, away from any passersby that happened to walk past, away from any ears that might hear anything they shouldn't. If this were my meeting, this would be where I would conduct it. My eyes flicked around the open space, narrowing, zeroing in on all the shadowy places to see if there was someone hidden there. But nothing.

I gulped, pushing away from my hiding place, stepping into the open, and knowing I was exposing myself, but panic was beginning to rise in my chest. Had I come to the wrong place? What if there was some other dock I was supposed to be at and Ellie was there waiting for me to rescue her? Horrendous scenarios plagued my mind, visions of Mateo's knife cutting into Ellie's delicate throat that I had kissed a mere few hours ago. Visions of her blood flowing like a crimson river, covering her clothes as her eyes widened, then slowly the light dimmed from them as she bled out.

"Mateo!" I shouted at the top of my lungs. "Mateo! You fucking son of a bitch, where are you?!"

"Right here."

My whole body tensed as I brought my gun up, pointing in the direction of his voice. Relief flooded over me because I was in the correct location, but it was short-lived because he stepped out from behind a container opposite me with Ellie in front of him like a shield.

My heart sank as I looked at her. His hand gripped the back of her hair, holding her in place as she whimpered behind the duct tape that covered her mouth. Her hands were tied in front of her with blue cord, there was dried blood on the side of her face and matted in her hair, and one of her eyes was bloodshot, with her cheek showing signs of a bruise. Her arms were covered with dozens of tiny cuts; her jeans were torn and filthy.

Rage burned within me, and I shifted on my feet as murderous thoughts flashed through my mind. I was so angry I could almost taste it. "What the fuck have you done to her?" I growled, my voice low and full of menace. I was going to tear his fucking head off.

Mateo smiled, still using her as a shield as he walked forward a couple of steps. "She had a little car accident, didn't you, darlin'?" he said to her, leaning in and pressing his nose into her hair.

Ellie's nose wrinkled in disgust and my finger twitched on the trigger of my gun. A car accident. They'd forced her off the road, most likely, and then grabbed her. Had she been alone? Was her family in the car, too? Were they here somewhere as well, waiting to be rescued from this hopeless situation?

"I can see why you like this one, she's a feisty little thing. Had to tie the bitch up because she tried to escape twice. One time she even managed to knock out one of her guards." He chuckled almost proudly as he looked at her.

I raised my gun in threat. "Just let her go. You don't need her," I implored. Maybe reasoning with him would work; at this point I would try anything. "Ellie, you okay? You all right, little girl?"

Her eyes came up to meet mine, and the panic and fear I could see there made my anger double. A small nod was all she could manage with his hand in her hair like that.

I turned my attention back to Mateo. "Just let her go. Take your dirty, scumbag hands off her and I might let you live." My gun was pointed at his head; one quick shot and I could finish this, but he was just too close to Ellie and I didn't want to hit her. I was considering it, seriously considering taking the shot when movement caught my eye from either side of him. Four of his crew stepped out from the shadows, guns raised and pointed at me. They were probably the last of his men who hadn't been arrested in the drug raids or deserted the sinking ship when Alberto was busted.

Mateo laughed, a loud cackle that made the hair on the back of my neck stand up. "You're not the one holding all the cards here, Kid. I am." He pulled his ivory-handled knife from his waistband. As he moved it toward Ellie, her eyes squeezed shut and her hands clenched into fists.

When the knife pressed against her throat, I shook my head quickly, grinding my teeth, trying to remain focused and not lose my temper.

"Don't!" I ordered.

My mind was whirling, trying to think of a way out of this. Five against one and Ellie in the way of any stray bullets. This wasn't going according to plan. How long had I been here? Three minutes, four maybe? It felt like an eternity.

"If you hurt her, I swear to God I'm going to fucking pull your insides out while you're still alive," I promised.

Mateo smiled and jerked his chin in the direction of one of his men. My eyes flicked to the left, settling on the guy as he approached, gun raised, footsteps hesitant. He was the one from the club who had degraded Ellie, the one I'd already beaten the shit out of once. No wonder he appeared reluctant to approach me.

"Show me your hands," he ordered.

I smiled sarcastically, my other hand reaching quickly behind my back to pull out my second gun, aiming this one at the approaching guy as I held Mateo in my sights with the other. "My hands are right here," I answered sarcastically, my gaze going back to Mateo. "Just let her go free and we can sort this out. Man to man. Don't be a fucking pussy like this, Salazar. Is hiding behind a woman really how you operate?" I spat on the floor in disgust, trying anything to goad him into just taking that knife away from her throat.

Mateo's eyes narrowed at my disrespect, his hand yanking Ellie's head back by her hair, causing a muffled yelp to leave her lips. I flinched as the knife pressed harder at her throat. "Using any means to get what I want, that is how I operate!" Mateo barked.

I just needed to keep him talking until it was time. "Okay, okay, just take it easy."

A slow smile spread across Mateo's face, and he turned his head, looking behind him at something. "Come on out. Why don't we show him just how I operate?"

Almost immediately another figure materialized from behind a container. Ed. Now I knew why my frantic calls to him on the way over had gone unanswered. He stepped forward, walking to Mateo's side, a gun gripped tightly in his right hand. A short, sharp wave of understanding washed over me.

Double-crossing motherfucker!

A lazy smile stretched across Ed's lips as he raised the gun and used the barrel of it to scratch absentmindedly at his cheek. His eyes were like a shark's, watching me, assessing. "Surprised to see me?" he asked. "Assumed I was dead after fighting valiantly to protect your little girlfriend? News flash, Kid, you put your trust in the wrong person."

"Ed, what the hell have you done?" I couldn't believe this. "How much money did they offer you for this?" He'd been with me since I was released from prison; before that he'd worked for Brett. I'd known him since I was eleven years old. The betrayal hit me hard.

He snorted, his eyebrows knitting together. "It's not about the money. That's where you always go wrong, Kid. It's about the respect."

I gulped as everything clicked into place. Ed had never been happy working for me. I should have seen the signs, paid more attention to the looks of annoyance every time I left him out of the loop, not dismissed him so easily when he asked for more responsibility within the organization. I'd been cocky, too arrogant of my position to see this building within him. I'd missed it all, and it had been right under my nose.

"Doesn't matter now, though," he continued, turning to Mateo. "Mateo and I are starting a new venture. Just one problem to elimiate first...you." He arched one eyebrow, a smile twitching at the corners of his mouth. "As soon as I remembered that little redhead girl you were going to give up everything for, you were no longer untouchable. Wasn't sure it'd work at first; wasn't sure if you'd still be interested or if you'd moved on, but we decided to give it a try, anyway. It worked out better than I could have predicted. The plan was simple: Follow her parents, smash their car, and voilà, she's back, and you're seven shades of distracted and letting your guard down."

Realization hit me like a smack in the face. Ellie's father had died because of me. "You sick bastard!" I growled angrily.

My eyes flicked to Ellie, watching her face crumple as she understood this, too. She squirmed against Mateo's grip, fighting to get free, her leg kicking out toward Ed as her eyes blazed with fury.

Ed reached out, stroking the side of her face with the back of one finger, wiping her angry tears away. "Aww, honey, don't be mad," he teased. "We had to get you back here somehow." He let his hand drop as Ellie continued to struggle, screaming words that couldn't be understood because her mouth was taped.

Mateo grinned. "We weren't one hundred percent sure it'd work, though, not until that night in your club when you attacked Manny for touching her. That was when I really knew the plan was foolproof. Happy coincidence she was there and allowed us to really put the plan into action," he chimed in proudly. "Alberto didn't want any part of it, though—he never did—he said we were to leave you alone. You kind of did me a favor getting him banged up, we always had a difference of opinion on the direction of our business. He was happy to take the scraps you left for us, I wasn't."

Ellie continued to thrash in his arms, her tied hands coming up to rake at Ed's face. He grunted, pushing her hands off, and brought up his gun, pressing it against her forehead, his eyes flashing with anger. "Make one more fucking move and I'll decide you're no longer useful," he goaded her.

My temper was rising again; I was barely in control of it as I stepped forward, ignoring the four guns trained on me. "Get your fucking gun out of her face," I ordered. My hand was shaking, but not from fear or anything like that—it was the anger pulsing through my fingers. If he made one wrong move, I was putting a bullet in his brain. He'd be dead before he even knew what happened.

Ed's eye twitched, but he didn't look away from Ellie, who had stilled and gone rigid. "I wonder what her pretty face will look like after," he mused, pressing the gun harder against her head, causing her to whimper and shy away. I groaned in frustration. I didn't have the upper hand here, not yet. "Take one step closer, Kid, and we'll all find out," Ed reasoned.

I clenched my jaw, staying stock-still. "Ed, what happened to you? How did you become the person that would kill an innocent girl just to get what he wanted?" I'd never liked Ed; he'd always been a self-serving bastard, but I hadn't seen this coming. He was never this far gone; he'd gone power crazy. I could see it in his eyes; he would kill her in a heartbeat to get what he wanted. That look terrified me to the core.

"Get on your knees," he ordered me, his gun not leaving Ellie's face.

I swallowed awkwardly, a lump forming in my throat as my eyes met Ellie's. She made a muffled protest, and I could see the anguish and pain in her eyes as they silently begged me for reassurances I just couldn't give her. I mentally calculated the odds of being able to take down all of them before one of them tagged Ellie or me. Pretty slim. But then a bright glint from on top of the container off to my right caught my attention—it was there one second and gone the next—and my heart stuttered in my chest. That pretty slim chance had suddenly grown tenfold.

I smiled weakly at Ellie and then nodded in acknowledgment of Ed's order, holding my hands up as I slowly lowered myself to my knees on the dirt, trying to look defeated when in reality I was preparing myself to fight for both our lives.

CHAPTER 28

ED'S EXPRESSION WAS one of untamed glee as he looked down at me on my knees, his gun finally leaving Ellie's face. "Never thought I'd see Kid Cole on his knees begging for mercy. This is a sight I'll enjoy for the rest of my life."

However short it is, I thought, fighting a knowing smile.

Of course I hadn't come alone. I wasn't a freaking moron. Had they really thought I was stupid enough to believe that they would let Ellie go if I behaved like a good boy?

I just prayed that my plan worked how it was supposed to and that Ellie didn't get caught in the cross fire. At least this way she had a chance.

The light signal from moments ago meant Ray was exactly where he needed to be, and Dodger's distraction should be coming any second, just as we'd planned.

I glanced over at Ellie. Tears clung to her eyelashes; she looked so defeated, so devastated that it hurt my heart. All I could do was look back at her and silently will her to get ready for anything.

"Put your guns down on the ground. Slowly!" Ed ordered, his gun now coming around to point at me.

I lowered my weapons to the ground as slowly as humanly possible without making it obvious I was stalling. *Where is the fucking distraction? Come on, Dodge!*

Suddenly, behind me, an explosion boomed from just inside the compound. Everyone looked up, shocked, as bits of debris and dust blew toward us, knocking everyone off-balance for a second. I turned to see black smoke billow into the air, swirling up into the sky.

I fought a smile as Mateo cursed in Spanish and then sent two of his men off to see what had happened. Ed's gun was firmly pointed at my head, so I didn't dare move. I held my breath, willing Ray to intercede.

Ed's finger twitched on the trigger, and two things happened at once: an incredibly loud gunshot came from the top of the container on my right, and Ed's hand changed into a gory, pulpy mess as the rifle bullet tore through his wrist. Ed's scream was high-pitched and agonizing as his gun fell to the ground, and his gaze dropped down to the oozing, bloody mess where his hand used to be.

I didn't have time to sit around and watch. Diving forward, I picked up one of my guns and snapped my head up, seeing that Mateo had wrapped his arm around Ellie's throat as he yanked her toward him, using her body for cover. I squeezed one eye shut, aiming my gun, willing it to find its small target, the only exposed place on his body, as I squeezed the trigger.

The gun recoiled in my hand a little as the bullet shot out, flying through the air and ripping into Mateo's knee. He screamed out in pain, his grip on Ellie not loosening as he staggered back, bringing her with him.

Ellie's nose crinkled with determination, and she jabbed her elbow into Mateo's stomach while he was distracted, and my chest swelled with pride. Mateo groaned, half stepping to the left—and that was all I needed. I fired another time, this bullet ripping through his shoulder.

He fell backward, dragging Ellie with him, and they both smacked into the ground.

My breath caught, hoping she hadn't been hurt. But then she wriggled free of his grip and got to all fours, her eyes connecting with mine.

"Run!" I shouted. "Ellie, run, now!" She struggled to push herself up with her tied hands, finally getting to her feet only to stumble and fall again.

I caught a movement in my peripheral vision and snapped my head to find one of the Salazar crew standing ten feet from me, his gun aimed at my chest. I dived to the side, firing as I fell through the air. His bullets hit the ground where I had been milliseconds before. My shot smashed him square in the chest. His eyes widened and he looked down at the wound, blood gurgling from his mouth as he sank to his knees, then flopped face-first onto the dusty ground.

I blinked a couple of times, turned to see that Ellie was back on her feet now and running with a distinct limp toward the containers over on the left. I smiled in relief, but then saw Ed holding a shining silver blade in his good hand. His eyes were fe-rocious as he lunged at me. The blade slashed through the air, a breeze whipping past my face as I pulled my head back just in time.

As Ed lunged again, I kicked out, my toe connecting with his side. He grunted and doubled over just enough that I could throw my arm up and smash my gun directly into his face. The crunch was incredibly satisfying as his nose gushed with blood and his eyes became unfocused. The knife dropped from his hand as his body went slack, falling face-first into the ground, sending up a plume of dust around me. I fumbled in the dirt, picking up his knife in case he came to.

As I got to my feet, waving my hand to clear the dust, I could hear the sounds of a struggle around me. I looked up, seeing Dodger fighting hand to hand with one of the Salazar crew. In the distance, I could hear two people shouting in Spanish, probably the two who went to investigate the explosion now hurrying back to join the chaos. But then Ray was on the case, sending a rifle shot cracking through the air.

I looked around desperately for Ellie, not seeing her anywhere. I did see Mateo pushing himself up to a sitting position. Blood covered his chest and face, making him look like an extra from a horror movie.

His hand fumbled for something at his side and then closed around his gun, raising it, pointing it at Dodger, who was still wrestling with the other crew member.

I realized too late that my right hand held the knife instead of a gun. I didn't have time to think; I pulled back my arm and threw it as hard as I could, praying that my target throwing with the dartboard would pay off. The knife was big and heavy and unlike any that I had thrown before. I watched with wide eyes as it flew through the air and sheathed itself in the side of Mateo's neck.

His body jerked, his hand coming up to clutch at his throat as blood gushed out around the knife. His mouth moved like he was trying to say something, and his shoulders hunched before he fell back, eyes still open, bleeding out, just like he had threatened to make Ellie do.

Now that's ironic, I thought, pushing myself to my feet. I wasn't exactly pleased with the fact that I had killed him, but I didn't regret it for a single second.

I held up my hand, shielding my eyes from the low afternoon sun as I looked toward where Ray was camped on top of the container, sending up a quick thank-you wave. Dodger had just delivered a punch to a guy's throat that sent him to his knees, gasping for air. Dodger's face was still contorted with menace, determined, as he looked around at the scene, checking for more danger. My body relaxed. It was over, and we were all safe and relatively unharmed.

"Ellie?" I called, closing my eyes and taking a couple of deep breaths. Adrenaline made my hands shake as I opened my eyes and looked in the last direction I saw her. I stepped over Ed's body, pushing my gun back down the back of my jeans. "Ellie, where are you?"

She peeked around one of the containers, her eyes meeting mine. I smiled, relief washing over me as I took another step toward her. She drew in a big breath and then was staggering toward me, tears rolling down her cheeks. As she reached me, she crashed against my body, holding on to me awkwardly with her still-tied hands.

"Oh God, I'm so sorry I got you into this. Are you okay?" I asked, pulling away and holding her at arm's length, cupping her face in my hands softly. "Shit, your face." I winced, looking at her bloodshot eye, the bruises, the raw skin where she'd yanked the duct tape off her mouth, and dried blood coating the side of her head. "What hurts?" I asked.

She whimpered and pushed my hands away, closing the distance between us and crying against my chest. I folded my arms around her, pressing my cheek against the top of her head. "I'm okay," she mumbled against my shoulder. "I was so scared," she whispered.

"I know, little girl, I know. It's over now, though, it's all over," I cooed, stroking her back. I kissed her hair, noticing the gash on the side of her head and pulling back. "Are you sure you're okay? We'll get you checked out at a hospital." I looked into her watery eyes and hated that she looked so frightened and timid, like a little mouse.

"I'm all right. I just got banged up in the crash." She sniffed, reaching up to wipe at her face carefully.

I nodded, letting go of her long enough to step back and see Dodger sitting against one of the containers, wincing as he picked what looked like burned material from his side. "All right, Dodge?" I called worriedly.

He nodded and continued poking at his side. "Yeah, just got a bit too close to the car when it went up," he answered.

Car? That was his plan for a distraction, blowing up a car? Nice.

"I need to sit down," Ellie said, stepping away from me and leaning against the nearest container, sliding down until she sat on the ground. "Go see if he's okay, he looks like the macho guy who tells you he's fine even if his leg is falling off." She smiled weakly and pulled her knees up to her chest, reaching up to tentatively touch the side of her head.

I watched her for a few seconds, checking that she was really all right before crossing the clearing and heading toward Dodger.

Behind me, a gasp sounded and then Ellie cried, "Look out!" just as Ed slammed into my side, sending us both sprawling to the ground. I gasped, struggling to get air into my lungs as he landed on top of me, his hand instantly going for my throat as his knee came up and collided with my ribs. Gritting my teeth, I gripped his shirt, rolling so I was on top of him, pulling back my arm and throwing a punch toward his face. He whipped his head to the side at the last second so my fist slammed into the ground, a knuckle popping audibly. Pain jarred across my fingers and zapped up my arm.

I cried out, gritting my teeth against the pain, and threw a punch with my left hand instead, this one finding its target and sending Ed's head whipping to the side. I fumbled behind my back with my bad hand, trying to get my gun, but it wasn't there. It must have fallen out when Ed tackled me.

I punched Ed again, this time in his side, making him wheeze out a breath.

"Ellie, no!" Dodger shouted.

Distracted, I turned my head to the right and saw that Ellie had picked up my gun. Her hands trembling, she pointed the barrel toward Ed, who was on the ground struggling under me.

Ed's fist connected with the side of my face, sending me sprawling to the right...just as the gunshot rang out. Pain ripped through my bicep, stinging, searing-hot pain. I'd never been shot before; it hurt a lot more than I'd imagined. Ellie's cry of anguish behind me made my heart race, but I didn't have time to think about it as Ed gained the upper hand, using my distraction as he brought his fist down, punching the bullet wound on my arm, making me scream with pain as my vision swam.

His hand was around my throat, squeezing, as I reached up with my good arm and tried to push him off. Suddenly he stilled, his eyes widening as he looked down at me almost fearfully. His fingers released my throat and I gasped for air.

My eyes adjusted, and I looked up to see a gun pressed against the side of Ed's temple. I blinked, trying to make sense of it as I followed the gun up over the tied wrists, along the scratched-up arms, and over into the vengeful face of my girlfriend. Her chin trembled, but her eyes didn't leave his face for even a second.

I opened my mouth to tell her no, to tell her that she'd never be able to take it back, that it would haunt her, but there was no indecision on her face.

"This is for my dad." And then she pulled the trigger, shooting him in the head.

CHAPTER 29

I FLINCHED AS Ed's blood splattered across my face. He fell at my side, his eyes open and lifeless.

Ellie was standing stock-still, gun still outstretched, her lips parted, her eyes wide as she stared at Ed's unmoving body and the pool of blood that was rapidly forming around his head.

"Ellie, it's okay," I told her, using my elbows to push up to a sitting position.

My hand and arm throbbed, streaks of pain zapped down my forearm as I moved, and I could feel blood trickling slowly down my arm from where Ellie had accidentally shot me. She didn't move or register my words. I wasn't even sure she was breathing as she continued staring at Ed. Ignoring the pain, I got to my feet and stepped to her side, slowly reaching out and setting my good hand on top of hers, guiding her to lower the gun.

"Ellie, look at me," I begged, wrapping my fingers around the barrel. She still didn't react. "Ellie, please, can you look at me, little girl?" I coaxed, tugging on the gun gently.

Her eye twitched and she let the gun go, her head slowly turning toward me but her eyes still on the dead body. "He killed my dad. He was going to kill you, too," she mumbled, her words all jumbling into one.

I quickly shoved the gun down the back of my jeans. "He did, and he was. You saved me. You did the right thing."

I wished she hadn't done it. Not that I didn't want him dead—of course I did—but I would rather have done it myself to save her the remorse and guilt she was bound to feel over it. I wanted to protect her from everything, and if that meant I had to get my own hands dirty, then so be it.

With my good hand, I fumbled with the knots at her wrists, untying them and letting the cord drop to the ground. Ellie nodded, still not looking at me, so I cupped her face in my hands, being careful of her injuries and my own as I stepped directly in front of her, blocking her view of Ed's body. "Ellie?" I whispered, bending my knees so we were on the same level.

Her eyes finally met mine. "He killed my dad," she whispered back. "I don't regret it. I'd do it again."

"You won't ever have to do anything like that again. I'm out of this all now. It's just you and me from here on out, no more shady dealings, no more worry, no more bad guys after you. Just you and me. If you'll have me, that is..." I trailed off, looking into her eyes, hating the pain I could see on her features.

"Yes," she whispered. "I love you."

I pressed my lips to hers, feeling the rough, cracked skin of hers brush against mine. "I love you too, so much," I promised.

She sniffed, her shaking hands raised, touching my arm, and her fingers came away slick with blood as her face scrunched up in mortified apology. "Are you okay? I shot you!"

I smiled weakly, trying not to show her how much it hurt. "It's just a graze, I'm okay," I replied. It wasn't too bad now that the initial pain was gone; it was just a burning ache, and my hand hurt worse than that. "You're a terrible shot," I joked.

Ellie didn't answer, just reached up and gripped the zipper of my hoodie, undoing it and hastily trying to push it off my shoulder, her face etched with worry. "Take this off, and let me look," she insisted, trying to ease the material down over my arm but stopping when I hissed through my teeth at the pain. "Sorry, sorry," she muttered, wincing.

"Let me do it," I said, pushing her shaking hands away and tugging the sleeve off completely, being more careful of my broken, swollen fingers as I dropped the sweatshirt to the ground.

All eyes fell on my arm and the ragged three-inch tear across my bicep, just below my shoulder. I was right, it was mostly just a graze—the bullet had torn through my flesh but hadn't actually penetrated. I was lucky. It was still bleeding profusely, though.

Ellie whimpered as she looked at it, her eyes brimming with tears. "I'm so sorry. I was aiming for him, and then you moved and…"

Dodger stepped to my side, peering down at it and grinning. "Ah, come on, don't beat yourself up about that. It's barely a nick, he's just being a pussy," he teased, clearly trying to lighten the mood because Ellie was beginning to freak out and her whole body started to tremble. "Few stitches and he'll be right as rain." Dodger reached down and snagged my hoodie, pulling out a knife and roughly hacking off the sleeve before leaning in and attempting to tie it around my wound.

I gritted my teeth against the pain and reached out with my good hand to Ellie, touching her face, tracing the line of the bruise she had on her cheek.

"I'm so sorry. I'm so sorry," she said, turning her cheek and pressing a soft kiss against my palm.

"Ellie, I'm fine, I promise." I wrapped my arm around her, pulling her against my body, ignoring the pain it caused. She lost the battle against her tears, nestling her face against my shoulder and crying desperately, her body racking with sobs.

I held her tightly, looking over at Dodger and seeing his sympathetic expression as he watched Ellie. "You okay, Dodge?" I asked, my eyes dropping down to his side. Now that he was closer I could see scorched, raw skin on his side that looked to be blistering and must be painful.

He waved a dismissive hand. "It's all right. I'll get checked out later, rub some shit on it, it'll be good."

Ray was climbing down from the container, shoving his rifle in the duffel bag as he walked to my side.

"What are we going to do about this?" Dodger asked, looking at the six dead bodies that lay around the clearing.

Ray stepped forward. "I'll take care of it. You two go and take her to see a doctor. I'll call you once it's sorted out."

"Thanks, Ray." He really was a great friend. I was lucky to have him. I was lucky to have them both. I pulled back a little and peeked down at Ellie. "Can you walk?"

She sniffed and nodded, clinging to me as she continued to cry against my shoulder. As we made the slow walk back to the car, Ellie glanced back at the dead bodies, her face paling as her fingers dug into my side and her eyes widened in horror, as if she was only just realizing what she'd done.

"Don't look," I advised her, dragging her attention back to me. She nodded, allowing me to guide her along to where I'd parked, passing remnants of a burned-out car that Dodger had used as his distraction. Its shell was still alight; pillows of smoke filled the air, making it uncomfortable to breathe until we were past it and outside the dock gates, heading to my car.

I tossed Dodger my keys, and he opened the door, tipping the seat forward so both Ellie and I could get in the back. Ellie slid in first, her whole body shaking, her tears endless. I climbed in next to her, wrapping my arm around her protectively and pulling her close against my side. My mind was whirling, wondering how I was going to help her get over this. Shooting Ed would scar her; it was something that would never leave her. There would be a lot of ramifications from this day, but I would help her through.

"Which hospital?" Dodge asked from the front as he started the car. "There'll be a lot of questions. If they see you've been shot, they'll call the cops," he said, turning in his seat and nodding toward my arm.

I pursed my lips, thinking. "Go to Marlon's drop-in clinic," I instructed. Marlon was Brett's brother-in-law and was still on our payroll. We got special treatment for the crew if it was ever needed.

Dodger nodded, turning in his seat and pulling out of the docks. Ellie's tears had dried up now, but she still clung to me, her face pressed against the side of my neck. I pulled back slightly so I could look at her. "Ellie, we can't say anything about what happened here today. You understand?" I asked, watching her carefully.

She sniffed, her eyes meeting mine. "But we have to tell the cops, I mean... we killed people, we have to tell them."

I cupped her damaged face in my hands. "No," I said firmly. "They were drug dealers, really bad guys, and into a lot of bad shit. Whatever happened to them today was the result of their job. You understand me? We were never there. We were both in a car accident; that's how we got injured." My tone was firm, final. There was no telling the truth in this situation. Ellie blinked; I could see the confusion and indecision in her eyes. "You want to go to jail for the rest of your life for killing that scumbag?" I asked.

She shook her head weakly, her eyebrows pinching together. "No," she whispered.

"Then you do as I say. I'll take care of everything. I'll make all of this go away. I'll take care of you always, you just need to do what I say. Okay?" *Please be okay with it, please.* "Can you do that for me, little girl?"

She was quiet for a few seconds, and then she nodded and my heart rejoiced as I pressed my lips to hers, kissing her softly, incredibly grateful that we were both alive and that I got to take care of her for the rest of my life.

* * *

Two days later, everything seemed to have blown over very nicely. Ellie had told me where they had first grabbed her, so we had someone go pick up her car from the ditch. The police had been in touch about it, but we'd told them that Ellie and I were in the car when her tire had burst and she'd lost control, rolling into the ditch. We then made up a story about how we'd both gotten out and hitchhiked to a clinic for treatment. Medical records there supported our story that our injuries were sustained in the crash and not from anything else. We were home free. It had been Detective Lewiston who had taken our statements; he'd filled in some blanks and in return received a nice fat envelope of cash.

We hadn't even been questioned about the six bodies found at the docks on the same day as our crash. With the several kilos of cocaine and money found at the scene—thanks to Ray—and the Salazar reputation for dealing, police had chalked it up to some sort of drug deal gone wrong. News reports concurred, saying that there were no witnesses and no suspects, but added that the neighborhood was now safer with both Salazar brothers off the streets. I wholeheartedly agreed.

Ellie had done everything I told her to; she hadn't spoken to anyone about what had happened at the docks and had backed up my burst tire/car crash story. She struggled a little at first, asking me if we were doing the right thing by not coming forward, but I'd just reminded her of what type of people they were and that they had been willing to kill her and her parents just to get to me. That had soon set her mind straight and she hadn't asked again. She didn't regret killing Ed; she was adamant she didn't.

In the two days that had passed, a lot had happened. I'd met Ellie's grandmother, for one thing. I liked her a lot; she was a kindhearted woman with a great sense of humor. And she loved Ellie and Kelsey with all her heart, so that made me like her even more. Plus, she let me stay with Ellie at night so I could hold her while she slept and whimpered in her sleep, calling my name and her father's before she would jerk awake in a cold sweat. Each time I would kiss her softly and reassure her it was over and that I was there for her. Each time she would smile gratefully and snuggle up against my chest and go right back into a restless sleep.

One day Ellie would forget the horrors she saw and sleep peacefully again. I'd help her through it.

The other thing that happened was that I'd come face-to-face with Ellie's mother again after three years. I'd gone with Ellie yesterday to the hospital to visit. In truth, I'd forgotten how scary Ruth was. She was a little off with me at first, probably because I was standing in front of her with bruises on my face and my broken hand all strapped up. I'm sure I looked every inch the asshole who chased her daughter out of the country. But when Ellie had smiled at me, her eyes shining as she proudly held my hand, some of the tension had seemed to leave Ruth's shoulders. She'd made a real effort to speak to me during the visit, and I even gained a couple of smiles from her by the time we left.

Ellie and I knew it would take a while to win her over completely, but that she was accepting of our relationship and just wanted Ellie to be happy again. I'd win her over eventually; I had all the time in the world for that.

"Have we got everything?" Ellie asked absentmindedly, peering into the trunk of the car I'd arranged for her, seeing as hers was wrecked. The trunk was packed full of suitcases, boxes, and trash bags full of clothes.

Stacey snorted as she walked back toward the house to grab another bag. "You can't possibly have forgotten anything. Pretty sure I see a kitchen sink in there," she teased, pointing at my car, which was also crammed full of Pearce family belongings.

Ellie grinned and blew out a big breath before turning to me. "It would be easier if I knew how long we were packing for," she said, resting her hands on her hips.

I shrugged and wrapped my arm around her waist, pulling her to me. "Might be a permanent thing, you know. Your mom was pretty adamant that she didn't want to come back here." I watched her carefully.

She nodded, chewing on her lip. "Yeah, I know. Guess that means we'll have a bit of driving to see each other." She reached up, tracing her finger across the collar of my T-shirt, making my skin prickle.

"I'd drive to the ends of the earth every day to see you," I replied. True, there would be a fair bit of commuting each day to see her in the Poconos, but she was worth every second of it.

The corners of her mouth quirked up in a smile. "Corny."

"You love it." I bent my head and captured her lips in a soft kiss that quickly deepened and turned into something more. Everything always morphed into something more with her; it was like my body couldn't get enough of hers and was making up for the lost three years.

I groaned against her mouth as her hands gripped the back of my hair. Lust sparked inside me, and my hands slid down to her ass as I walked her back a step and crushed her against the side of the car, pressing my body against hers. A soft groan from her throat drove me wild, and I forgot where I was, forgot everything as our bodies rubbed together in ways that made me long to rip her clothes off and have her writhing underneath me.

My hand slid up her shirt, tracing the soft skin of her stomach, heading higher, my arousal spiking with every inch gained.

A loud throat-clearing made us both jump and I whipped my head around to see Ellie's grandmother standing there with one eyebrow raised and her arms folded. I smiled sheepishly and shifted on my feet, caught in the act. "Didn't you two get enough of each other last night, for goodness' sake?" she asked, pursing her lips playfully.

Ellie gasped and then laughed as I grinned and stepped away from her, being careful not to turn so her grandmother wouldn't see just how excited Ellie made me with a simple kiss.

Her nana winked playfully, laughing as she rolled her eyes. "Are we almost ready to go? I told Ruth we'd be there at three."

I nodded as Ellie straightened her shirt and tucked her hair behind her ears, her face full of embarrassment. "We're ready," she agreed. "Is Kels packed?"

"Yes!" Kelsey called, coming out of the house with a rucksack on her back. "Kels is packed and ready. Let's go get Mom."

While Kelsey stuffed her pack in the nonexistent space in the trunk and then struggled to close it, her nana climbed in the passenger side, setting her purse at her feet.

"Right, time for me to go," Stacey said, stepping forward, arms outstretched. Ellie smiled and the two girls hugged fiercely. "Call me when you get there, and I'll see you next weekend. Remember to snag me the biggest bedroom to sleep in and one on the other side of the house from you two raging nymphomaniacs so I can't hear you guys making up for lost time all night."

I laughed, kicking my toe into the grass, letting them say their good-byes. It wasn't really a good-bye, though, just a *see you soon*. Those two would never lose touch—they were way too close.

"Talk later. And thanks for helping me pack," Ellie said, hugging her again.

"Anytime. Say hi to your mom for me," Stacey replied, planting a deliberately noisy kiss on Ellie's cheek before bending and waving to Kelsey and Ellie's grandmother inside the car. Stacey smiled at me awkwardly, probably because she still disliked me for hurting her friend. I didn't mind; I was confident I'd win her over eventually, too. "Take care of them, Jamie."

"Will do," I promised, watching as she headed to her own car, shouting a final "See ya" before pulling away, waving enthusiastically out of her window.

Ellie sighed and then headed to the house, stepping inside the front door and checking that the lights were off before just stopping and standing there, her eyes taking in the empty living room.

I walked to her side, placing my hand on the small of her back. "All right?" I asked.

She nodded. "Yeah, it's just weird seeing the house with all the photos and stuff taken down," she replied.

I looked around too, seeing that they'd packed all the family photos, all the personality that made a house a home, into the backs of the two cars in the driveway. This was merely a shell left behind. "It's just a house, Ellie."

She sighed and turned to me, a smile lingering on her lips. "Home is where the heart is, right?"

I flashed her a smile. "Right." My home was her, because that was where my heart lay.

She took a deep breath and slipped her hand into my good one as we walked out of the house together. After she had locked the front door, we headed to the cars. I could tell it was hard for her, leaving the house she'd grown up in, the house filled with memories of her childhood and father. But that was the exact reason why her mother didn't want to come back, and everyone respected that.

I walked Ellie to the car that her nana and Kelsey were already seated in and kissed her softly outside the door. "I'm proud of you, you know," I whispered.

And I was. She took everything in stride, handled everything with grace, and came out the other side a stronger person. She smiled gratefully as I planted a kiss on her forehead and pulled away.

"I'll see you at the hospital," I called, walking back to my car.

As I walked, I noticed a hopeful spring in my step. This was a positive move for all of us; everyone—including me—could actually build a future together rather than just blowing through life on a breeze.

I watched Ellie start up the car and roll out of the driveway, heading to the hospital. After we picked up her mother, we'd be leaving the city behind us and heading to the Poconos. No one was sure if this was a permanent move or not—only time would tell—but even if it was I didn't mind one bit. I would follow Ellie anywhere.

EPILOGUE

ELLIE

I CLOSED MY eyes and sighed happily, listening to the Christmas songs playing quietly on the radio. This was definitely my happy place.

"Ellison, I made you a coffee," my mom called from the back room.

"Thanks, Mom," I acknowledged, opening my eyes and grinning when I saw the snow falling outside the window. The weatherman had predicted snow today, but my mom had been adamant the sky didn't look right for it. Seemed the weatherman was right, for a change.

I loved this time of year, I loved the snow, and I loved the cold. Winters in the Poconos were the best, and in a couple of weeks, we would spend our first proper Christmas here.

It had been almost nine months since we packed up the car and moved in with my nana, and we'd all mutually decided not to go back. Almost nine months of fresh mountain air and time to reflect and rebuild our family without my dad. It had been hard, but things were looking up for all of us: Kelsey loved her new school, my nana loved the company around the house, and my mom, well, she had found her calling late in life—fronting my store and doing the books.

My store, aptly called Jellie's Boutique—a name that Jamie had come up with and I had fallen in love with immediately—sold one-of-a-kind items of handmade clothing from a local designer...me! We also sold beautiful costume jewelry that I had commissioned from another local designer and jams that my nana made. The store had been open for six months now and was doing well. We weren't millionaires by any means, but we were holding our own and making a decent profit.

I worked long hours, often sketching or stitching late into the night when my creative brain wouldn't sleep, but it didn't feel like work. When you find something you love in life, doing it is never a chore. The pride of seeing someone wearing one of my designs was immense. Last week I had just finished an order of five bridesmaids' dresses for a lady who had driven all the way from Philadelphia to have them commissioned after she'd found me online—on a website my mother had set up all by herself! Who knew she was such a marketing whiz? Knowing that something I created was going to be included in someone's special day filled me with incredible pride and satisfaction. I was loving life at the moment and wasn't sure it could ever get better than this.

The store had all been Jamie's idea. He'd always loved my designs, and after we had moved here, my creative spark came back with a vengeance, but my newly crafted designs were just wasting away in a sketchbook. Jamie had been the one to convince me to make a few of them and sell them online. They had been a hit and sold like hotcakes. From there, he'd started talking about me opening my own store in town. It was just a pipe dream for me, a nice idea, but something I could never afford—until the day that Jamie handed over the keys to the newly purchased store to me. He'd sold his apartment, his cars, and one of his clubs to pay for it, giving up everything he had in favor of me achieving the dream I once had of owning my own clothing line. The store had taken a lot of work to get up and running, lots of late nights decorating, renovating, and outfitting, but we'd gotten there, and six months later it was thriving.

I never allowed myself to think of the bad things that happened before we left or the fact that I killed a man. I blocked it all out and just got on with my life. Ed and the Salazar people wouldn't steal any more of my life and happiness—I wouldn't let them. We moved on, all of us, and we were happier than we thought possible after losing my dad.

The bell above the door chimed and in stepped the genius who created the beautiful jewelry that I sold here. Simone was a thirtysomething single mom with pink and green in her hair, her style quirky and different. She lived just down the street from my nana's house and was a lovely woman. "Hi, Ellie."

"Hey, Simone." My eyes zeroed in on the box she was carrying and I squealed. "Is that the new line you were telling me about?" I asked, haphazardly hanging the last couple of dresses on the display rack before rushing to her side excitedly.

She nodded, lifting off the shoe box lid, exposing her beautiful creations. I gasped and my mother leaned in too, her eyes excited as we all reached into the box and pulled out pieces, setting them on the counter. "Oh, they're beautiful! I can already see these selling out," I gushed, picking up a silver bracelet with a bumblebee design intricately engraved on it.

My mom nodded in agreement, reaching into the drawer and pulling out her camera. "These are going straight on the website and social media pages. Great work, Simone."

Simone's face lit up; everybody liked compliments from my mother and took them to heart. "Thanks, ladies," she chirped before turning to me. "Hey, I just saw your man getting into his car and driving off. Where's he going in the middle of the day?"

"No idea," I answered, absentmindedly heading to the front window of the store and looking out across the street. When Jamie had sold his apartment, his club, and all of his cars so he could buy my store, he'd also purchased a little something for himself that just so happened to be across the street. A large brick warehouse that he'd opened up the front of and converted into his own workshop and garage. Jamie was living his dream too, fixing up cars instead of stealing them.

I loved that he was so close because it meant I got to eat lunch with him every day, and if I so desired, at any given point throughout the day, I could look out the window and marvel at the sight of him dressed in his greasy overalls, with his cap on his head, bent over a car with that delectable ass in full view. Every single time it made my heart thunder in my chest and my knees weak.

Jamie hadn't moved with us at the start, but after he drove to my nana's house practically every day for two months, my mom had finally suggested that he just move in too because he was already there so damn much anyway.

Until I lived with him and woke to him every single day, I hadn't realized I could love him even more than I had before, but I was wrong, oh so wrong.

Simone was right, though; he'd closed up shop and his car was gone. I frowned, hoping he drove safely in the snow. More than likely he'd gone to pick up a part for a car. There wasn't any other real place he would need to go to today, unless...

I gasped and turned to my mom. "Oh my God, do you think the sale has gone through? Maybe he's gone to pick up the keys or something?!" I jumped on the spot, my excitement bubbling up inside me like I was a little kid. I couldn't stand still. "The lawyer said it wouldn't happen until late in the afternoon, but it could have gotten done early, right?" I prattled.

Simone cocked her head to the side. "This for the house you two are buying? Is it going through today, sugar?"

I nodded, reaching up to cup my cheeks as my face flushed with heat and excitement. "Yes!"

"Calm down, Ellison. He's most likely gone to collect a part for a job he's on or something. If it's not due to go through until tonight, then it'll most likely be tonight, not lunchtime." My mom was always the voice of reason. That was my first thought, too.

My excitement slowly fizzled out. I'd been on tenterhooks all day, waiting for the phone to ring and tell me that Jamie and I were homeowners, but I could wait a few more hours for it. I sighed and nodded, resigned. "Yeah, I guess. Anyway, let's get these new beauties photographed and on display," I suggested, trying to keep my mind off our new home as I headed back over to the new array of jewelry we had to sell in the store.

* * *

Less than an hour later, Jamie was back. I heard the roar of his car engine as he pulled up outside. I resisted the urge to run to the window and just continued staring at the phone, waiting for the lawyer to call with good news.

When the bell above the door chimed again, I looked up in time to see the love of my life walk in carrying a bunch of pale pink roses. His smile stretched across his face and my heart skipped a beat. "Hey, little girl," he called.

I spun on the stool I was perched on and hopped off, heading around the counter to meet him. "Hey yourself." I went up on tiptoes, and his mouth came down and connected with mine.

His face was chilled from the wind, his hair messy where it had been hidden under a cap all morning, but he had never looked more appealing. Jamie could be covered in mud, and I would still want to jump his bones.

He pulled back, his eyes sparkling with excitement. I smiled and looked at the flowers. "Those for me?" I inquired, biting my lip.

He shook his head quickly, reaching in and plucking a single rose from the bunch. "This one is," he replied, holding it out to me. "But the rest are for..." He looked up and smiled at my mom before walking over and handing them to her. "...You," he finished.

My heart melted even more at the sweet gesture. My mom gasped, her eyes widening as she put them to her face and inhaled their sweet aroma. "Aww, Jamie, they're lovely. Thank you!"

My boyfriend had completely won my mother over with his charm and sweetness during the last nine months. She'd been hesitant about our relationship at first, but her new philosophy in life, after losing my dad, was that people needed to live life every day and grab happiness wherever they could get it. She just wanted me to be happy and recognized that he was the one who was going to make that happen. Now she treated him like the son she'd never had.

"What are these for, then?" she asked, inhaling the flowers again, her eyes shining with gratitude.

Jamie shrugged and turned back to me. "For having such a wonderful daughter and for letting me be part of her life." He reached into his pocket and brought out a bunch of keys, dangling them from one finger. "And as a going-away present, because we'll be moving out soon."

My mouth popped open. He *had* gone to get the keys earlier!

"What? Are you freaking kidding? Are they seriously the keys to the house?" I bounced on the spot, staring, transfixed, at the keys and our new beginning that was just around the corner.

"Not kidding. I just went to pick them up." Jamie grinned. "Want to go check out our new pad?"

I squealed and nodded, already running to the back to grab my jacket and scarf. When I was all bundled up, I headed back into the shop, seeing Jamie finishing off my hot cocoa that Mom had made ten minutes ago.

Mom grinned, coming to my side and reaching out to zip up my coat the last couple of inches and fiddle with my scarf. Her eyes were misted with tears as she smiled over at me. "I'm so happy for you two, and I just want you to know that your dad would be incredibly proud of the young lady you've grown into."

I smiled and reached out, pulling her into a tight hug. "Thank you. I love you."

"Love you, too," she replied. That was another thing she'd changed since the accident—she was now very forthcoming with her affection. It was a little weird to accept at first, but now I reveled in it. We had a superb relationship.

I pulled away and turned to Jamie, who was holding out a hand to me. "Ready?" he asked.

I nodded. "Hell yes!" I'd been ready to settle down with him since I was seventeen years old. This day hadn't come soon enough.

JAMIE

As we stepped out of the store and into the chilly wind, a young couple sitting on the wooden fence, kissing, caught my eye. I smiled but then cupped my hands around my mouth and shouted, "Kelsey Pearce, put that boy down!"

She jerked away, her face flushing pink, just like Ellie's did when she was embarrassed. "Shut up, Jamie," Kelsey called back, laughing and reaching up to wipe her mouth with the back of her mitten-covered hand.

Kelsey had turned fourteen last week, and as far as teenagers went, she was pretty cool and a good sister to Ellie. We actually got along great. She was around the same age my sister would have been now, so I liked to step in and do my big brother part.

"Just let me know if this gets serious so I know if I have to come kick his ass." I winked at her as the boy's body stiffened and his hand dropped from around her shoulders.

She grinned and waved me away with a flick of her hand. She'd really come into her own here; living in this beautiful place suited her. It suited us all.

Ellie smiled up at me, her eyes shining with excitement as I dipped my head and planted a deliberately noisy kiss on her lips before leading her to my car. On the fifteen-minute drive to our new home, she could barely sit still, fidgeting in her seat and babbling about all the things we still needed to buy. Luckily for us, the previous owners of the house were downsizing and had sold the house partly furnished—which meant we already had a sofa and some of the most important furniture. We'd make do for a while until we could afford our own stuff.

When we pulled up outside and looked at the building in front of us, Ellie let out a happy little sigh. The two-story house was a cozy three-bedroom set among the trees in a picturesque backdrop. The drive was curved and led up to the single garage. The house itself had wood siding that had been painted a slate gray. It was wonderful and was right at the top of our mortgage borrowing budget, so anything we wanted to do to the house would have to be done over time as we could afford it. Luckily, the house was essentially perfect for us as it was.

I dug into my pocket, pulling out the keys and jangling them, drawing Ellie's attention from our new home. "Want to go inside and look around?"

She squealed, the sound making my insides quiver with happiness as she reached out and took the keys from my hand. Seeing her so joyous made my heart ache and my skin tingle. "Yes! Come on!"

She climbed out of the car in a rush and almost slipped on a patch of ice before righting herself. I chuckled to myself and walked to the front of the car, waiting for her to reach my side.

The birds chirped from the snowy trees above our heads, singing loudly as we walked arm in arm toward the front door. As Ellie slipped the key into the door, she held her breath and my hand slid down her back. I was so overwhelmed with love for her that it almost knocked me sideways. We'd done this; we'd made it out and we'd just closed on our first home.

The door opened with a slight creak that I made a mental note to fix. Ellie exhaled in one big gust and turned to me, her eyes sparkling with tears. "I can't believe this is ours. I'm so happy."

I nodded, bending and capturing her lips with a soft kiss. "Me too."

Suddenly her excitement seemed to overcome her, and she grabbed my hand, pulling me inside, her eyes wide as she looked around the hallway. On the sideboard was a bottle of champagne and an envelope with our names on it. Ellie picked up the card eagerly, ripping it open and making an "aww" sound. "It's from the previous owners. It says: 'We hope you'll be as happy here as we were. We're so pleased that the house will feature in such a lovely couple's new memories.'"

I smiled at the thoughtfulness.

Picking up the bottle of champagne, I nodded toward the stairs. "We should open this on the balcony."

Ellie nodded eagerly, unable to contain her smile as her fingers interlaced through mine, and we walked up the wooden staircase. Ellie had fallen in love with the house immediately; the quirky upside-down layout really worked. Having the living area upstairs made wonderful use of the beautiful view. As soon as she'd seen the large picture window in the living room overlooking the lake, she'd turned to me and whispered that she wanted it, that this was the one. I'd made an offer to the sellers there and then, not wanting to go through the usual channels and have to wait for a reply from the agent. Seeing how in love with the house Ellie was, they'd accepted and the rest was history. That was eight weeks ago, and this was the first time we were back.

As we stepped into the living room, the huge picture window showed the trees lining our small yard, and in the distance, the lake and snow-capped mountains beyond. There were bifolding doors leading out to the large wooden balcony, the table and chairs all set up ready for people to soak in the spectacular view.

To the right, the seating area faced another large window that practically covered the whole wall. A solitary WELCOME HOME helium balloon was anchored to the coffee table.

"Aww, they bought us a balloon, too," Ellie cooed, heading over to it and catching the string.

"Actually," I said, "I bought that. I snuck in after I collected the keys and put it there." I grinned sheepishly, my heart beating erratically. A sudden rush of nerves made me shift on my feet as I set the bottle of champagne on the table.

Ellie turned and smiled lovingly at me. "You're so cute, Jamie Cole."

I took a deep breath, clenching and unclenching my hands, willing my nerves to subside as I stepped forward. "Did you notice the weight on it?" I asked, nodding at the balloon's string, which she had wrapped around one finger.

Her eyes traveled along the string until they got to the little red box tied at the bottom of it. Her eyes widened a fraction, but she didn't move. I smiled at her stunned expression and was grateful that her mom, grandmother, and sister had been able to keep this a secret; they'd all been bursting with excitement when I'd told them of my plan.

Ellie gasped as I got down on one knee, tugging the little box loose from the string and looking up into her face. She was now covering her mouth with both hands, her eyes swimming with tears as she looked back at me.

Come on, Jamie, don't screw this up! "Ellie, I know this isn't Paris, and we're not standing at the top of the Eiffel Tower, or in some amazing restaurant in Rome, or floating on the Dead Sea, or anything spectacular, but it just feels right to me to ask you the most important question right here in the middle of our new home," I began.

My hands were trembling as I lifted the lid of the ring box.

She squealed, her eyes widening as a lone teardrop fell down one cheek.

"I love you with all my heart, and I always will," I said, trying to keep my own tears in check. "I swear I'll keep making you smile for the rest of your life, just like I promised your dad I would." She whimpered as I said that, and I smiled. "Will you marry me, little girl?"

There was no hesitation in her answer, no indecision or thought needed. "Yes! Oh God, hell yes!"

I laughed as she bounced on the spot excitedly when I held the box out to her. The ring was the same one I'd bought for her all those years ago, the one I'd showed her dad. I'd never gotten rid of it. But it now had a subtle difference.

"I had it engraved inside," I told her as I stood, watching her squint to read the writing on the inside of the band.

"*Scars and all,*" she read. Her eyes flicked up to mine and the smile that stretched across her face stole my breath. "I love you," she whispered.

"Scars and all." I nodded in agreement before wrapping my arms around her and crushing her against my body as I kissed her, showing her with that one kiss how much I adored her and how grateful I was that she would give a guy like me a chance.

When I pulled back, we were both breathless. I took the ring and slid it onto her finger, where it would stay for at least the next eighty years.

It turned out happily-ever-afters could happen, even to people like me. All it took was something worth fighting for.

ABOUT THE AUTHOR

Kirsty Moseley has always been a passionate reader with stories brewing in her head. Once she discovered Wattpad, she finally posted a story. Seven million reads later, she self-published her debut novel, *The Boy Who Sneaks in My Bedroom Window*, which later became a finalist for the 2012 Goodreads Choice Awards. Kirsty lives in Norfolk, England, with her husband and son.

You can learn more at:
    KirstyMoseley.com
    Twitter @KirstyEMoseley
    Facebook.com/AuthorKirstyMoseley